Enter the Dreams

of Man

By Kitkoon Chan

Contact Information:
akfak8324zf@gmail.com

Cover Design by Kitkoon Chan

ISBN: 979-8-9904051-1-0

For my mother

And

In loving memory of my father

Part I

Bat And Dracula

1

Bat inches away from the crevice where he abides, then inches back. With each step he takes, his stomach churns. A matter of consequence is brewing. He is certain of it.

The dungeon has no windows and the cracks in the stones admit no light. A slab of solid oak bars the lone aperture. The pitch-blackness does not bother him, for he is intimate with every inch of the dungeon. He can trace, without looking, the pattern of the molds scarring the walls and crisscrossing the vaulted ceiling.

Like the knots in his innards, these disgusting fungi are resilient. The moment he thinks they have dried up and died, pristine green heads emerge from the dead mass, grow, and spread. He can smell their stench—if he allows himself, which he never does. Whenever he detects it, he instantly recalls the freedom he once had. The cleanliness of the open air, the scent of the conifers, and the fragrance of the blossoms return in full force. His spirits rise, veiling—if only fleetingly—the vileness of his predicament.

The jagged surfaces of the dungeon do not intimidate him. How many times has he flown close to the sharp edges—so close that they prick his skin and draw blood?

In his corner, Bat squeezes into a crevice that scarcely contains him, seeking seclusion. For the most part, he hangs upside down from the ceiling beam. Listening. Contemplating. No noise escapes him. A mother spider gurgles liquid silk from her glands. Diligent in preparation for her offspring, she drags her enormous abdomen along as she spins her web. He can hear her laborious movements. He has no intention of apprising her of her squandered toil. The jailers will haul in their prisoner. The shove of the door will tear apart the spider's new abode situated directly above it. He sneers.

Somewhere, water seeps through. It must be raining hard outside. *Drip!* A drop falls off. *Drip! Drip!* Then a loud roar thunders. The oak slab grinds open, letting in pelting rain and the flare of torchlight. The mother spider clings to a thread of her torn web, which the incoming gust of wind twirls ruthlessly. A weight topples down the stairs, and with a final shudder, the entrance seals itself back up. Darkness reigns again.

Bat trembles like a leaf. He must curb his emotions and compose himself. It is imperative that he present a confident self.

With effort, he subdues himself.

2

He was born thirty years earlier in Sibiu, Transylvania, on a moonless and starless night. The trees loomed as nebulous masses; so dark was the forest. The flights of the bats were audible; so quiet was the earth. A cry slashed the calm, followed by the wailing of a pup. The moon and the stars woke, and the forest came alive.

Insects and arachnids congregated, as a momentous birth had occurred. Their trills swelled to a crescendo. They were impatient to meet the newborn. Beetles, ants, earthworms, spiders, scorpions, and centipedes crawled, wriggled, and buzzed toward the bat cave.

The ones in the neighborhood had already gained access. Bat's mother, exhausted from labor, regarded the furry form on her chest with tenderness. To her surprise, Bat opened his eyes wide to gaze back at her and beamed.

"These damn bugs! Flaunting themselves in a bat cave. Don't they appreciate the danger they are in?" protested his father, shooing the bugs away.

"Our baby has opened his eyes and smiled at me!" exclaimed his mother.

His father's scrutiny switched from the bugs to the baby. "That's unusual. Behold the ebony fur," he said proudly (Bat's brothers and sisters were born naked). An idea struck him. "We will call him Bat." He enunciated the name as though the infant was being crowned. Bat nearly expected the colony to hail his birth. He cherished his name from the start.

A portly beetle deposited herself next to his mother. "Madam, please accept our congratulations! We're here to pay homage to the young master," she said, crooking her hind legs in a curtsy. His mother's orbs gleamed with wonder and hilarity, driving the beetle into thorough solemnity.

"We have augured this blessed event. With the buildup of the menacing clouds and the drop of atmospheric pressure, a storm was imminent. However, it did not materialize. We suspected that something else was up. It turned out to be the birth of your cherub."

The long-legged spider, the fruit fly, and the spiny caterpillar concurred, as did the rest of the congregated creatures.

"What makes you so sure?" inquired Bat's father, whose curiosity was piqued. He had banished the idea of getting rid of the bugs.

A tiger moth who had elbowed his way to the fore of the swarm barged in. "A vision struck us—simultaneously, mind you!" He paused for effect, then hurried on to ensure that he was the narrator of the story. "Picture a predawn, without fog. A bat glides along, ever so stealthily, so majestically. Engrossed in his flight, he is unaware that the ridges below have acquired snowcaps. In solitude, he flies. Over oceans and lands."

"Then he can't be our Bat. He will always have our company and protection," Bat's mother said, sweeping her wing to include the whole clan.

The portly beetle flung the tiger moth an impatient glance and regained control. "Madam, I assure you, there is no cause for concern. The young master will hold his own if he finds himself alone, crossing mountains, oceans, and continents. As to how we can be so sure, sir, that your infant son is special," she directed this to Bat's father, "we all shared the same vision the tiger moth described, at the precise moment the young master was born." His parents gasped. The colony clapped. Applause shook the cave.

When he was young, his wings were toys of a sort to him. He folded them into various shapes, forever amazed at how flexible they were. Suspended upside down, he paraded them to the moon. With limbs spread and golden rays illuminating his silhouette, he fancied himself a bright, bright star. Other times, he danced *Wings* with his friends Gravity, Snotty, and Orange.

Arms folded, the juvenile bats hung wingspans between them. *Tweet* … the robins sang. *Tromp* … they thumped and flapped their wings, flushing the twilight sky orange, brown, and black. *Tweet* … they swapped positions. He switched next to Orange—orange against black. *Tweet, tweet, tweet. Tromp, tromp, tromp, tromp!* On they fluttered.

The four friends foraged together from five weeks of age. Their smaller-than-normal size banded them together throughout childhood and adolescence. Since the day her father went out to hunt and went missing, Gravity wore a perpetual scowl. She tired herself out caring for her baby brothers and sisters. In spite of her solemnity, she was flippant with Bat. Orange and Snotty imitated her, treating Bat as the baby of the group even though he was not the youngest. He was coddled and teased. When he found them with their heads together, they at once relaxed their seriousness and chattered merrily. Eventually, Snotty elected to enlighten him. Gravity firmly resisted addressing grave issues with Bat. She judged that his naïveté precluded him from empathy.

They enjoyed delightful diversions together.

"Let's play *King*," Orange suggested. He had finished grooming himself. His fur glinted. Orange was proud of his appearance. He groomed himself constantly. Snotty measured Orange with disdain. *Orange is too vain*, censured he. Truth be told, he would have given anything to be as beautiful! At the thought, he puckered his face to hide the pasty markings under his snout.

"One, two, three," they counted.

Speedily, they expelled sound waves from their mouths. Based on the intensity and pitches of the echoes, they speculated on the species of the nearest insect. Whoever guessed with accuracy and speed was the winner. The winner got to be king, and the vassals would pamper him, proffering all their captures of the night.

The echoes yielded a ladybug on a fern among the flora. Bat was about to declare himself the winner. An element in an echo halted him. He fixed his sight upon a birch beyond the fern. Inside the hollow of the birch, an adult bat was resting. If he had not focused, he would have missed the bat. But here it was, shielded from the world, in repose.

"I won!" The usually somber Gravity shrilled in exaltation. Seldom a winner, she was ecstatic. Snotty and Orange conceded their defeat.

"Let's pledge allegiance to the king, Bat," they said in unison. Bat did not respond. The three of them, copying Bat, peered at the tree hollow.

"Isn't that your father?" Snotty asked.

Bat nodded. Their stares had alerted his father, who stared back at them. Shyness hit Bat. Instead of calling out his greeting, he blushed. What transpired next was remarkable. His father flushed crimson too, wavering on what to do, and in a wink, flew away.

3

Dracula pushes himself up. He rubs the aches in his gangly limbs. Rolling down the stairs bruised him in several places. He fumes and curses. He curses the jailers for kicking him, Mehmed for confining him, and Radu for instigating the imprisonment.

He has never been fond of Radu. At present, he hates him! Radu has installed himself as the centerpiece of all events for as long as Dracula can remember. The fools have never been able to bypass the curly locks. His solitary dimple on one cheek is especially endearing, they say. It carries the charm of two. They call him their little angel. Their darling has schemed to jail his own brother in a dungeon!

Father has lectured him to be less reticent. "You are the older son; you must command. The ability to communicate is crucial for an effective ruler. You don't need your subordinates to love you, but you must garner their respect. Assert yourself. Cow them," he said. The advice is undeniably sensible but difficult to act on. The consciousness of his shortcomings impels him to be doubly introverted. It is unfair that some people are naturally uninhibited. This injustice steers him back to Radu, and his anger boils over.

Drip.

The trickle checks his rumination, recalling him to his environs. He can hardly discern his surroundings. His wrath recedes. Apprehension takes over.

A stir drifts over from the far nook.

He tenses up.

Take courage, he urges himself.

No further rustle ensues.

Did he imagine it?

Drip!

He jumps.

The drip dominates the enclosed space and perturbs him. His heart is in his mouth. What could be out there behind the gloom? A leak? Something more sinister? He hopes his sight will swiftly adapt. He will be fine once he can see. His fingers grip his thighs, spine taut.

There is nothing he can do but wait.

A while later, he can distinguish the adjacent areas. He is relatively safe: no threat exists in his vicinity, and the far end is quiet. The stir must have been imaginary.

Drip!

There! To his left. The drop does not sound half as threatening as before. He listens, but the dribbles have ceased. Bracing himself, he gets up and steals toward where the trickles may have originated. It is safer to be stealthy: he may be spied on.

A proper examination reveals a labyrinth of spiderwebs. They must be spun in the obscurity above as well. As if to validate his conviction, a spider descends on a strand to graze his forehead.

Remnants of insects are snared within the labyrinth. There is no leak here. A drip will provide clues on its whereabouts.

Silence.

Dead silence.

He counts inaudibly, fearing that the counting will be amplified into a scary boom. He gives up at one hundred. Even though he wants to locate the leak, he does not relish having to search for it.

His hands work on a moderately clean section, ripping the webs. With the soles of his shoes, he scrapes away the dirt. The dust balls dance up just to reclaim their territories afresh. He keeps at it until a patch is swept. This achievement fails to boost his morale.

He slumps down.

Anger recommences. Its targets now include his father, who is partly responsible for his woe. He chokes back his tears. He has been told that he favors his father. Not yet fourteen, he is as tall as most adult males and will soon assume his father's imposing height. They both have narrow, straight-edged noses. The thought of being likened to his father furnishes little consolation.

Where is Father? Has he forsaken them?

Winter, spring, and most of the summer have passed. Father has not shown up. Is he injured? Is that why he has broken his promise of collecting them? Has a catastrophe trapped him? Or worse? Panic seizes Dracula, but he pushes it away. No, Father is alive. He has to be. Why would the Sultan want his father dead? They ought to have been notified if Father were killed. Mehmed would have apprised Radu, and despite their animosity, Radu would have reported it to him.

As a hostage, he has been treated well enough till now. But this deterioration is the work of Radu, not the Ottoman Turks.

4

They reached Gallipoli Castle. The heavy snow that had fallen during their ride through the peninsula had dwindled to a flurry. Fluffy flakes twirled in the air.

The tall edifice funneled the blast from the strait toward them, freezing their flesh. Cold, exhausted, and ravenous, they were anxious to get inside. Sharing their sentiments, their horses fretted and whinnied.

"Unbar the gate and bid us welcome! Voivode Dracul of Wallachia has arrived," Dănuţ, his father's squire, hollered up at the battlements from his fidgeting horse.

Two watches conferred. One gestured to the ground within the fortress, and the massive latticed grille was raised. They filed in; their horses' hooves punched trails of holes in the snow.

The garrison in the courtyard disconcerted them. Soldiers confronted them, shoulder to shoulder. A multitude flanked them and barricaded their rear.

Voivode Dracul dismounted, and his troop followed suit. They were immediately grabbed and disarmed.

"What is the meaning of this? At the Sultan's request, I am here with my sons, Prince Dracula and Prince Radu. Is this how Sultan Murad receives his guests?" demanded Voivode Dracul, trying to wrench himself from the soldiers' grip. The soldiers tightened their hold. One bound him with a chain.

Dănuţ broke free. He hurled himself at the soldier who had bound Dracul, knocking him sideways. Dănuţ dropped on top of the man, trapping him between his knees. He pinned the soldier down with a hand and aimed at his jaws with a fist. Soldiers surrounded Dănuţ, pulling him off their comrade and beating him down onto the slush. Dănuţ curled up, arms warding off the kicks to his skull, and clenched his teeth so as not to scream or groan.

"Stop!" Voivode Dracul boomed at the assailants. "This instant!"

Soldiers yanked hard on the chain restraining the voivode.

Dracula shivered with rage over the treatment of his father. Action had to be taken—to halt the stomping on Dănuţ and to unbind his father. But the harder he wriggled, the tighter his captor's clutch became.

The stomping continued.

Aaggg! burst out. Radu had sunk his teeth into a soldier's forearm.

In the midst of this, a grizzle-haired warrior parted the throng. He wore a burgundy cloak. Despite stooping, he was as tall as Voivode Dracul.

The stomping ceased.

Dănuţ remained lying on the ground, his lip split and bleeding.

"This is an outrage, Field Marshal Demir. The Sultan invited us here. Release us and apologize!" said Dracul, recognizing the grizzle-haired warrior.

Demir apologized, but he did not free them.

"Sultan Murad is currently in court, and he requests your attendance. He is furious with Hunyadi. Damn Hungarian bastard! Launching a Christian crusade against us," he tutted. "It's understood that you have aligned yourself with the bastard. You see, we must be cautious." His gaze fell on the chain. "Fret not, Voivode Dracul. Sultan Murad intends to express his goodwill toward you and your entourage. It must have been a difficult ride from Târgovişte in this weather. Let's seek shelter and have a meal, shall we?"

The soldiers drove Dracul and Dănuţ, who was back on his feet, onward. Dracul resisted.

"My sons and their page will come with us," he said.

Demir countered this assumption.

"You and your squire will journey to Adrianople—as the Sultan has decreed. Your sons will stay here and be our honored guests. They can retain their page if they wish."

Dracul took a stride toward Dracula and Radu. The soldiers held him back. He drew himself up to his towering height and glowered. Demir signaled the soldiers to let him be.

"Sons, I'll go to Adrianople tomorrow. I promise to be back here as soon as I can. Attend to your princes." The last sentence he spoke to Ilie, the page. He then glared at the soldiers detaining Radu and Dracula. Without uttering a word, he conveyed to them that they would have to pay if any harm befell his sons.

5

Life plodded along for Bat and his father. They did not mention the accidental encounter between them. Being a child, he thought no more of it. It resurfaced from the depths of his memory years later. Out of nowhere, it flashed into his reverie, and he grasped its import. By then, he and his father had become close. The bond between them was robust.

Had the incident tied him to his father? All without his realizing it? Why would a father act shy running into his child? Orange's father would have said, "Don't stay out too late, children," whereas Snotty's would have teased them and poked fun at their games. His father fled in bashfulness.

He was glad his father responded the way he did. The unusual reaction revealed to him a characteristic of his father that he had never conceived. What he saw, he liked. An awful lot, indeed.

Father didn't teach them how to hunt. Mother did. He didn't romp with them either. To them, he was their father, an authority to be respected and to be in awe of. He wasn't indifferent, for sure. He brought bugs, such as crickets and spot beetles, home for them to partake. They might consume the gifts straightaway. They might let the insects go, only to be recaptured. The sport continued until it bored them.

The family huddled together deep in the cave. Father and Mother whispered about their day. Mother reported on whether the children had been clever or mischievous. They discussed activities in the community. The siblings listened far into their slumber.

One night, Father invited Bat to join him. Lacking an excuse not to, he acquiesced. He felt anxious, he must say, as thus far Father had not taken him anywhere.

They hastened out of their native territory to an immense structure. Bat had never beheld such grandeur. "It's a fortified manor for the nobility," Father explained.

Bastions flanked the tangerine gatehouse. The guard tower stood at a corner of the curtain wall. Far behind, the keep monopolized the upper bailey. Turrets projected from its summit. In the distance, mountain ranges provided a splendid backdrop. Nearby, autumn foliage dabbed the landscape purple, red, orange, and yellow.

Light spilled from the slits on the keep.

The activities within enthralled Bat. There must have been a hundred candles—in a brass chandelier affixed to the ceiling, in candelabras on the mantelpiece and on pedestals—illuminating a ring of dancers. Hand in hand, noble ladies and their superbly attired lords and princes swayed to and fro. The gilt buttons on the men's garments glittered with spurts of gold as they swayed. The dancers hopped; satin and silk gowns of fern-green, lavender, rusty coral lifted to the ballads of the lute and then fell. A prince broke into a song, which spread like a wildfire among the dancers. As the song intensified, so did the hops. The maidens' cheeks reddened; they giggled, flirted, and pirouetted.

Thus, commenced Bat's fascination with the human.

He could not rid himself of the images of the cornflower blue and cream costumes, the braids (raven, brown, auburn, and blond) festooned with ribbons and jewels, and the sheer veils. In comparison to such an array of fineness and colors, along with the ambiance, skipping, and music, their cave seemed dull.

Must I live in a cave? Why not in a castle—a castle of my choice, no less? thought Bat.

"Humans are the most powerful creatures on earth," Father said.

"Mightier than the hawks, owls, and lions?"

"Yes, in many respects."

Quit being an imbecile, he scolded himself. Of course, human beings are mightier. They build shelters, create candles for light, and craft clothing for warmth and refinement. They probably possess countless qualities that he venerates.

Father must have read his admiration.

"But they can inflict abundant harm. They kill us and the animals of the forest for profit. They are a menace. Slyer than the snakes. That is why Mother and I urge you and your brothers and sisters to shun them. They also murder their own kind—in the thousands."

Then he narrated the wars between the Hungarians and the Ottomans, tales communicated through generations of bats. How kings and sultans fought over power, territory, and religion. How mankind posed a grave threat to nature. How they slew animals and birds and axed the trees. How fathers battled sons and brothers contested brothers. Women, too, were embroiled in the struggles.

He drank up Father's words, utterly captivated.

6

Dracula observed his father, Dănuţ, Demir, and a retinue of soldiers cantering up the motte. Voivode Dracul was to be detained in a secluded area.

In the bailey, toylike abodes huddled around a mosque. The irregularity of the layout produced a charm a uniform counterpart could not have. The setting sun tinted the dwellings scarlet. Carved arches adorned these ancient homes, their curves warped by the weather. Soot streaked the slanted roofs.

Soldiers shepherded them to a dwelling with a frozen garden out front. A guard was left behind to stand watch. Warmth pervaded the parlor. Amidst the commotion in the courtyard, Dracula had forgotten about the cold. Now he felt it prickling his face and fingertips.

A woman was tending a stew over a low fire, her fleshy back obstructing the cooking vessel and the flames. Smoke curled upward and escaped through vents in the grimy ceiling. The woman abandoned her cooking to welcome them with a colossal smile.

Her name was Zehra. She said in Turkish, "Come sit by the fire, children," while gesturing the words.

Nobody responded; they were gawking at the grotesque wart planted on the ridge of her nose.

She did not appear to be offended; maybe she was used to being stared at. She jovially waved them to sit down. Food bubbled in the pot, causing Dracula to swallow. Zehra grinned. To conceal his embarrassment, he quickly took a seat and pulled Radu onto the chair next to him. Ilie unloaded their saddlebags and Radu's lute from his shoulders. The soldier maintained his position by the door.

Zehra sang as she cooked. Dracula caught enough lyrics to deduce that it was about a joyful family reunion.

A hall spanned the interior, with the firepit and a pillar at its center. A laundry line was strung between the pillar and the wall. The gaps in the laundry disclosed a bed.

Ilie was inspecting the contents of the jars on a shelf. To prevent mischief, Dracula bade him to check on their horses. Ilie was eager to comply.

Dracula beckoned to the soldier.

Dracula spoke in his native language. Father had decreed that, to govern a foreign underling, one's own language was to be employed. Dracula had asked, "What if the underling doesn't understand?" Father reproved, "Make him!"

A soldier was a subordinate. He hoped it would be a simple task and would not require him to explain.

"I would like my page to attend to our horses. Could you—"

The soldier interrupted him and said, "It isn't necessary. They've been taken care of."

Dracula flushed at the refusal. The soldier's Romanian was flawless. This might be why he was assigned to chaperone them. The situation soured more quickly than he had anticipated.

Zehra was about to speak but changed her mind.

He must be firm. Straightening his back, he insisted on sending Ilie out to the stables. He loathed his boyish treble. Nevertheless, the soldier acknowledged his request, saying, "Very well, if that pleases you."

"You will find your horses in the farthest stalls," he added as an afterthought.

Ilie darted out the door, and the soldier returned to his post.

With this drama concluded, Dracula felt relieved. He resolved to be firm with his subordinates from now on; he would demand that they address him properly. In the midst of his reflections, he realized that Radu had been silent. Radu was not his usual self. Instead of flitting about and tweeting away like a bird, he had sunk into a despondent mood. This suited Dracula well.

Zehra ladled stew from the cauldron onto plates. Dracula dove into his, savoring the rye and lentils. Without tasting his meal, Radu shoved it across the table. A stack of empty wooden dishes intercepted the skittering plate and toppled off the edge upon impact.

Stew slopped across the tabletop.

He gave Radu the evil eye, which turned out to be a mistake. It was like pouring water onto hot oil. Nostrils flaring, Radu lunged at him. Dracula choked on his stew. He thrust back, jostling Radu onto the floor. Radu bawled.

Zehra hauled Radu back onto his chair and buried his face in her ample bosom. Radu pelted Zehra with his fists. Perhaps he was repulsed by the wart, or perhaps he sought to unleash his tantrum. Zehra cradled his small frame. Radu submitted to her coos.

They lay down on blankets at eventide. Radu curled up next to Dracula, his chest undulating gently. Dracula, too, succumbed to his weariness. The last image he retained was Ilie and the soldier chewing their dinner at the table.

He shuddered awake. The unfamiliar surroundings disoriented him. *Where am I? Why am I here?* He almost shouted for his mother but aborted his impulse. From infancy, they were encouraged not to cry for their mother. As princes, they could be future voivodes. They must be tenacious.

Recollections cropped up. Father had been chained up and hustled away, and they were held hostage.

Radu was snoring softly. For a change, Dracula was glad of Radu's proximity. A familiar soul. A kin. He placed his hand on his brother's arm and left it there.

The hall was frigid and dreary. The smoke permeating it had dispersed.

The wind whistled through the cracks.

Fatigue besieged him. He dreamed that he was seated, though it was unclear on what he sat. Opaque water encircled him, bobbing him up and down. He had this conviction that he could tread on the water. But his body had locked itself in position, with the least inclination to act.

The scene shifted. The contents of a sapling basket mesmerized him. A fish, deprived of water, was struggling for its life, thrashing about.

He jerked up. Ilie, who had leaned down to wake him, backed away. Radu, slouching, rubbed his sleep away with his knuckles.

"They intend to transfer us to Kütahya and want an early start," Ilie announced.

"Kütahya?" Dracula asked.

"It's in the Turkish mainland," Ilie said, obviously proud to possess this knowledge. Dracula suspected Ilie had acquired it from whoever had been discussing their departure from the peninsula.

Ilie, from another noble family, entered their household at the age of seven. His father arranged for him to be nurtured into a knight. He had been serving as a page and was taught, along with the princes, equestrian skills, combat, the Latin language, and playing the lute. Being below average in intelligence, Ilie lagged behind in reading, writing, and grammar. These shortcomings led him to congratulate himself on any accomplishments, real or imagined.

"We'll be traveling to Eğrigöz in western Kütahya," he declared proudly.

"Father is coming with us," Radu said, rather to himself than to them.

"No," Ilie corrected, ecstatic about his command of the circumstances. "He isn't. He will head for Adrianople. Don't you remember?"

Radu scowled belligerently at Ilie. Dracula knew that his brother remembered. Like him, Radu yearned not to be separated from their father.

"The sultan's son, Mehmed, will be in charge."

Who was in command was immaterial to Dracula.

Radu sulked.

Zehra, a wart on her nose, ambled around the firepit. From the crook of her arm dangled a bundle. She deposited it by the pit and then detached the steaming kettle from its hook above the cinders. She brought the kettle to the table to pour hot water into a pot. Throughout, she behaved distractedly. Ilie, who rose early, had already eaten. The tea was for the princes.

Zehra angled the slats of the louver to let in the grayness outside. The princes ate buns and drank tea. The bitter taste caused Dracula to grimace, but thirst impelled him to take another swig. Radu dunked a bun inside his mug and quenched his thirst with the soaked bun. The bun tempered the harshness of the tea. Radu could be creative.

The sentinel, who had guarded them, came around to the table. Their voyage began. Zehra retrieved the bundle and handed it to the soldier. She said, "Be safe, son," embracing him.

"She's his mother!" Ilie exclaimed. "She, fat as a cauldron, and he, a twig. Who would have guessed it?!"

The soldier crimsoned to his ears.

Dracula refrained from kicking Ilie in the shin, which would have drawn even greater attention to themselves. It was a consolation that the mother was unschooled in the Romanian language. She did not react to Ilie's exclamation.

Surely, resemblance between mother and son was nonexistent. She was fleshy; he was all bones. Her hair was flat; his was tightly curled. She dwarfed him. Their facial features were different too.

The soldier freed himself and departed without bidding farewell to his mother.

They grabbed their saddlebags and followed him.

Zehra accompanied them to the door. With a stiff back, the son strode on. Dracula was amused: he himself would have reacted the same.

Their horses were in the forecourt. A stable boy tended to them. Cavalrymen in mustard tunics and burgundy trousers loitered about: several were munching on buns; a group of three were bantering; a man was letting out incessant yawns. They glanced at the newcomers.

The stable boy hovered nearby after the horses were claimed. Ilie ignored him. Dracula pulled out a silver coin and flipped it to him. Coin in hand, the grinning lad swiftly disappeared.

Horses' hooves clattered from the barbican. Dracula pleaded with God for his father to ride out. His plea was crushed. An adolescent and a man with snow-white hair and beard cantered toward them. The adolescent's size and physiognomy indicated that he was Dracula's junior.

The tunic, the sword—in an ornate scabbard, tied to the leather belt at his waist—and the deportment proclaimed that the adolescent was Mehmed. His tunic was an appliqué of tan squares. The sepia cloak over it looked black. It was when the first light cast upon the folds that the true color showed. He wore a turban cut from the same fabric as the cloak.

The venerable gentleman turned out to be Mehmed's tutor, Aksoy. Mehmed did not approach anyone. The cavalrymen mounted their horses. So did Dracula's party. They cleared out of the gate. Three soldiers led the way, succeeded by Mehmed and Aksoy, and then Dracula's group. In the rear rode another three soldiers, including the Twig, Zehra's son.

The party hurtled on.

Radu gradually pulled himself out of his brooding. He rode alongside Mehmed. Here was a playmate, a powerful individual, coming to that. Dracula was unable to catch what he had spoken to Mehmed, owing to the clops of the horses' galloping hooves. Mehmed responded with a nod and rode on. This lack of enthusiasm did not discourage Radu, who kept pace with Mehmed.

7

By midday, the squad had traversed woodlands, heaths, villages, and hamlets and was out of the peninsula.

They entered a grove. The temperature plummeted. Aksoy suggested pausing for food; the party was inclined to oblige. They tied their horses to the beech trees and sat on dead vegetation. Those who preferred to stretch their legs stood about.

Radu sat across from Mehmed. Dracula was some distance away, on Mehmed's side. Both Radu and Dracula reclined on gentle slopes. Ilie, who idolized Dracula, settled himself at Dracula's feet.

Dracula was puzzled by Radu's reservation. Between sips from his flask, Radu nibbled at his bread, seemingly contented. Periodically, he stole glimpses of Mehmed jesting with a cavalryman.

Aksoy gulped down ale from his flagon and rubbed his knees to ease the soreness from the ride. Using the trunk of an ash tree as a backrest, he immediately dozed off.

Radu stored the uneaten chunk of bread and the flask back in his satchel, brushed the crumbs off his hose, and stood up. He fetched his lute from his horse and struck up a tune upon his return.

Everyone listened. Radu had played the instrument since the age of three and was now a master. He plucked the strings, his eyelids cast down dreamily. The gelid air seemed to warm by several degrees.

The notes swirled upward, lingering among the foliage before the updraft spirited them away.

Mehmed drew near Radu to sing along. The cavalrymen followed his lead. Aksoy woke to the song and music. Even the Twig, who had been stern and distant, joined in. He was completely transformed, swaying his body and humming to the tune.

Dracula's stomach sank. A forlornness gnawed at him. Though Radu had always monopolized the admiration, it had never tormented him to the present extent.

In this desolate spot, with the tip of his nose frosting and Father gone, these strangers—potentially hostile—displaying such zest was unbearable.

He did not particularly want to belong to these men who had abducted them and were surely using them to pressure Father into unwanted compromises.

Yet he ached to belong.

His desperation must have been palpable, for Ilie hesitated before taking a bite of the cake he had saved. Ilie, who had a fondness for sweets and for saving treats for later enjoyment, offered the cake to Dracula.

Dracula swatted away Ilie's hand; the cake arced away, landing in a tuft of dry grass. Ilie darted over to retrieve his pastry. Dracula fled.

He needed to be alone.

Shame, distress, self-pity, anger, and even greater shame overwhelmed him.

Why do I have to belong? Am I so weak? Am I beneath Radu? Beneath our enemies? Where is my pride?

He attacked a stump with the heel of his boot, splinters flying. What he longed for was to succumb to his emotions and weep, but he could not. Since he had not strayed far, his enemies would hear him if he did. That was the last thing he desired.

Instead, he relieved himself and watched the hot stream carve into the frozen mud. The thawing spread steadily, the yellow stain widening. This crude creation assuaged his turmoil.

He had behaved disgracefully in front of the foreigners. It would never happen again. He would not be defeated! Not by anyone, least of all by Radu!

With determination, he headed back to the others.

8

Bat was an adolescent. After visiting strongholds within a range that he and his father could comfortably achieve, his competency in fortifications had improved. A monastery perched along the cliffside touched him most. Its chalky-gray edifice, integrated into the rock, was stunning. Simple and at once powerful, the structure loomed as an extension of the precipice. The red clay roofs, a brilliant touch, accented the structure's splendor. The rooms, which faced south, radiated with light from morning till evening. At night, the moon cast elongated silhouettes across the floors.

On the flat summit stood a church with a square tower. Ledges graced the ridge and midpoint of each of the tower's walls, interplaying horizontal and vertical lines in the most exquisite fashion. Embedded between the ledges were three perpendicular bell-shaped slits.

A staircase spiraled down from the summit to a lower elevation. Where the stairs ended, a narrow path began. To its left, a vegetable and herb garden flourished. To its right, against a fence, roses flaunted their maroon and pink petals. Their fragrance and the mild scent of the herbs mingled.

Bat and his father flew on.

The path wound to the edifice, ensconced in the escarpment, and ended at an arbor attached to the east wing. Grapes crammed the lattice. Underneath the clusters stood a bench with arms and a back. Bat visualized a monk drowsing on it. With a slant ray of sun on his body and the drone of a bee among the vines, the monk vowed that he was in heaven.

The east wing housed the library, rich with parchments, tablets, scrolls, and religious texts and manuscripts. A ladder leaned against the shelves. Owing to its height, reaching the top shelf was akin to reaching the sky. An aura of divinity abounded—the demigods being the wisdom and history amassed within the volumes. An alcove opened onto the annexed infirmary, whose front entrance also provided access.

The infirmary, half the width of the library, was redolent of medicine. Here, divinity espoused a different mode—it was nursing and healing incarnate. No invalids were currently tended on the straw beds, but folded woolen blankets were at the ready. On a sturdy table lay a mortar and pestle, along with saucers of pounded herbs and spices. Thyme to remedy digestive issues, coughs, and bites. Dandelion to support liver and kidney. Basil, chickweed, chamomile, parsley, and barks were also available.

At an angle to the herb and vegetable garden stood a dormitory. The refectory and kitchen dominated the ground level, above which were the monks' cells.

The cells were empty because the church bell had pealed. The monks had assembled for a night vigil. On the altar, candles burned. Attired in black cowls, long-bearded monks chanted, their chant melodiously expressing the poetry of the Psalm.

Father had also guided Bat through a community of peasants; he must have wanted to introduce Bat to the bottom ranks of humanity. The village was terraced on a knoll. In the flat acres, peas, cabbages, turnips, onions, and beans were cultivated. The homes were wattle-and-daub huts, with a sizzling orange color blended into a few exteriors. Insects crushed and mixed into the mud produced the orange hue.

They alighted on an open shutter. Father had detected motion within.

A girl, her back turned toward them, was in the midst of dressing. Around her straightened elbows coiled a thin frock, ready to cascade down her bare back. Her waist tapered and then broadened to accommodate her round hips. She squatted on her calves, her buttocks against her heels. The gown skimmed over her flesh, like waves caressing the warm sand.

She lit the rushlight on a low stand. The hens, in a cage, clucked. She pursed her lips to shush them. *She must be about my age in human terms,* Bat surmised. The girl observed the forms on the goatskin rug. Her sister and brother had curled up next to her father. Her mother yawned but did not rouse from sleep. She admired her mother's will. She craved to lie back down too. But that couldn't be helped, for she had duties awaiting her. As quietly as she could, she poured water into a basin to clean and tidy herself. Her grogginess remained uncured.

She crept over to the dining table to wash down a slab of barley bread with ale. Having eaten, she stoked the fire in the pit to heat a pot of water for her mother. Her mother's daily routine consisted of feeding the hens and, while the hens ate, pilfering their eggs from the nests. It also included boiling gruel (peas, beets, or turnips) for the family and then toiling in the field or making cheese and butter at home to be bartered for grains, sugar, and such. Once a week, her mother brewed ale for sale and for their consumption. Her sister, Catrina, who was nine, took care of the chores in the hut. Catrina would soon be employed by Lord Cantacuzino; their father had given his word. She had wanted Catrina to be a milkmaid like herself, but Lady Cantacuzino insisted on training Catrina as a lady's attendant.

The girl tiptoed over the threshold of the front door with the basin. Along the house ran an irrigation ditch. Owing to the recent rain, the ditch gurgled gaily. The wench emptied the water into the ditch and reentered the hut. She put straw shoes on her feet, a wrap around her body, and a coif over her plait.

The nip in the air outdoors galvanized her. After the stale stench inside, the brisk air smelled wonderful. She breathed deeply. The neighborhood was dormant.

She descended the slope to the pathway that led the villagers to town.

The mist had dampened the path, and dew clung to the blades of grass along it. The fields in the valley were still slumbering.

Farmers would soon change that. She trod along, tightening her wrap to ward off the chill. The inadequate length of her outgrown frock exposed her ankles. Somehow the thought of her dimpled ankles evoked the handkerchief, a gift from Lord Cantacuzino's son, in her sleeve. She pulled the memento out and brought it to her nostrils. She inhaled the young lord's scent on the fabric as her heels kissed the wet road.

At Lord Cantacuzino's estate, the sky above was dim, with a pink strip traversing the horizon. Here, the dirt road curved through lush meadows. At the bend of the road stood a barn.

The girl pulled open its doors. The smell of manure gushed out. A hen, chased by a rooster, squawked.

Bat and his father, who had been trailing behind the girl, hid among the rafters.

The cows in the stalls lowed at the girl. Chickens pecked at the dirt.

The girl adored the cows, each of which she identified less by appearance than by how they reacted to her. Their enormous udders proclaimed the painful pressure within. They had to wait their turn to be relieved.

A cow with doleful brown eyes bellowed. "You want to be first?" she said, scratching behind the cow's ears. "Fine, you got your wish." Seated on a low stool, she prodded the udder with her fist to relax the muscle. Her wrap slid off her shoulder, exposing its shapely contour.

She cleaned a teat and squeezed it. The opaque liquid streamed into a bucket, from which a sweet aroma emanated. She fell into a rhythm.

This was when it unfolded: a likeness of the girl detached from her physical self. It consisted of her head tilted backward and her back straightened. With her coif removed, her braid hung freely. A hand lifted her chin. The milkmaid and the hand's owner had locked their lips.

Bat doubted what he was seeing.

A sensation on his skin disrupted the spell—Father had sent him a signal. His father nodded toward the outside and then departed the barn. Bat ought to follow but vacillated.

The mirage faded. The girl labored assiduously.

Did Father witness the mirage too and wish to give the girl privacy? Too shy to expound on what he had beheld, Bat hesitated to inquire. As a compromise, he asked Father if he had noticed anything unusual in the barn.

"No," was the reply.

To obtain a proper response, Bat realized that he needed to be more explicit.

"The girl left her body while she was at work," he declared.

"What? What exactly did you see?"

"I saw the girl kissing. The powdered wig and the bejeweled fingers marked her seducer as a fop. I didn't imagine it. The scene did transpire."

There, he did it. He had turned scarlet in the interim.

Father did not seem to notice or pretended not to and then became pensive.

"The handkerchief," Father said.

Bat tried to puzzle out his father's meaning.

"That must be from her beau. She was fantasizing about him, and you caught glimpses of her daydream."

9

Beyond Dracula's chamber window, barren slabs stretched for miles. Directly ahead, the declivity was sheer as the fortress of Eğrigöz sat on a cliff. The land leveled off, only to dip and ascend repeatedly before giving way to precipitous mountains in the far distance. If greenery sprouted on these mountains, it was too far for him to discern.

Blizzards raged and subsided. The snow that had coated the expanse thickened. Ilie swung a pan of hot coals above Dracula's bed to drive away the chill. Ilie babbled on with any silly bits of gossip he had hoarded. The prattle brushed over Dracula. Irrelevant as it was, it lent a sort of comfort. The mildly warm bed served its purpose until drafts invaded and frigidity set in. Even so, he was resolved not to mingle with the populace at the fireside in the great hall.

He wondered about his father often. *What is he doing? Is he well? Where is he? Is he going to fetch us? Will we ever return to Wallachia?*

He missed his father's presence, even his sternness. Not until now did he realize that his father's severity represented so much love and security. Though strict, his father was capable of mirth. He missed his thunderous laughter and generous, trusting nature. But was his father too trusting? Shouldn't he have foreseen the possibility of being captured at Gallipoli? Should his father have declined the Sultan's invitation altogether? They shouldn't have faith in the Turks!

To rescue them, Voivode Dracul would ride up the boulders at the front. The back of the crag, where Dracula's latticed window overlooked, was too formidable for anyone to scale. His father would not sneak around, anyway. The battlements offered a panorama of the region. As hostages, they were prohibited from accessing the parapet, and thus his father's advent would not be revealed to them.

He sorely missed him.

Now that the freeze had dissipated and they were well into spring, he had adapted to his daily routines and began to take an interest in them. This did not imply that his father had ceased to be a preoccupation.

His leisure was spent at the casement—his sole connection to the outside world.

The forest to the west would have enhanced the vista. But it refused to participate in the landscape, no matter how he peered through the lattice.

Not every day was dull.

On a luminous day, the azure firmament provided a sense of joy, and his mood elevated. On days following a warm spell, the mist, perhaps from an adjacent lake, settled in, forming a glorious silvery ocean with the crowns of the rock formations as its islands. Tiny droplets of water entered through the window, moistening his skin. The sun pierced through the clouds, shafting its gilded rays amidst the sea of mist below. The landscape totally entranced him. He forgot his troubles and appreciated being where he was.

Since their arrival, stark scenes had been common.

Worry not, though, for he had devised a diversion to combat the bleakness and monotony.

He started with the smoke. *See, there it is, puff after puff!* With chimneys, there must be dwellings. He envisioned it as a prosperous, leading community where chimneys were used to expel smoke instead of venting through roof holes.

Next, he conjured the marble dome of a mosque, prominent above the glen. An august mosque, it was. Under the dome, a circular prayer hall rose above a square, terraced platform. The masonry was splendid. Minarets adorned the four corners. From their balconies, the muezzin called the faithful to prayer. Quranic verses inscribed on the minarets invoked divine protection and blessings.

He created and perfected the mosque in his mind, as magnificent as any that truly existed.

In dreary weather, he fashioned pieces of a settlement. A hamlet in the belly of a valley blossomed, with domiciles and a mosque, complemented by the blacksmith's shop, the bakery, and the carpet weaver's gallery. The inhabitants bustled about, each immersed in their tasks.

Ting, ting. Hear that? The blacksmith is forging a horseshoe.

A whiff of the baker's delights drifted over. It's no fantasy, Dracula swore.

On the narrow winding streets, children jostled, nudged, skipped, and clamored. They were filled with glee.

Suddenly, an inspiration struck Dracula.

A girl, aged six, materialized. The girl squatted on a crate. In a scarlet dress. Under her charcoal bangs, hazel eyes fixed on her peers, capturing their every move. She didn't attempt to join them, and they didn't invite her.

The villagers wore clothing of muted tones and shades. The scarlet set her apart.

Did her dress hinder her from belonging to the group?

Soon, a woman badgered the girl, who refused to surrender her dress. She locked her arms across her chest, pinning her attention on the ongoing games, and did not budge.

Her mother headed toward the laundry tubs. The launderers were glad the blowing breeze allowed them to hang their laundry to dry. They wore aprons tied at their waists and kerchiefs over their hair. On occasion, they straightened up to alleviate the aches in their lower backs, massaging them with their soapy palms.

Dracula had stowed the hamlet within himself. It was his sanctuary, a haven where he was intimately acquainted with the inhabitants' lives.

He could compel the girl to surrender her dress and join in the revelry. But he would not. He had decreed this as soon as he created her. The girl was destined to be alone. Alone. Without friends. Solace soothed his heart, and he rejoiced in his own power.

A loud knock disrupted his reverie.

He had instructed Ilie not to pound. The foolish page was prone to forgetting. Dracula swung the door wide open.

Here he was—Ilie. Dracula's manifest annoyance reminded Ilie of his mistake. He grinned sheepishly, holding a parchment in his hand.

Time for their lesson with Aksoy.

The morning comprised gaining proficiency in the Ottoman Turkish language and literature. The afternoon was dedicated to arithmetic, geometry, and theology. They also practiced archery and lancing under the tutelage of the cavalry commander.

Ilie and Dracula made their way to the room at the far end, which Aksoy used for their lectures. The great hall, with its tumult, was unsuitable for such a purpose.

The sounds of merriment wafted toward them. The giggles belonged to Radu, and the snickers to Mehmed. They were bantering in Turkish. Radu's attempt to win Mehmed's favor had been transparent. His Highness—in manners befitting the son of a sultan—had been courteous and distant in response. But the informality that Dracula now overheard between them was unmistakable.

Mehmed was proficient in Ottoman Turkish. He had private lessons on it and participated in group schooling only in the afternoon. So why was he present at their morning lesson?

Mehmed and Radu, sitting side by side at the table, had stopped fooling around and adopted a serious demeanor. Nevertheless, their torsos quivered with barely stifled laughter.

Dracula and Ilie took the seats across from them.

Footfall boomed and ceased. Aksoy entered, a leather satchel attached to his shoulder and a wand in the opposite armpit. He bowed lightly to Mehmed. It struck Dracula that he should have greeted Mehmed. He had forgotten his manners.

The four of them stood to acknowledge Aksoy's entrance.

"How fare you, my princes?" Aksoy said, gesturing for them to sit down. "A cavalry officer, en route to Adrianople, has arrived. He carries these precious scrolls to be submitted to the Sultan. I am most grateful that we have been granted with the opportunity to appreciate them."

Standing at the end of the table, he untied the satchel. From a compartment, he extracted a cylindrical container, and from the container, a scroll.

Aksoy unfurled the scroll. A depiction of a swordsman, aged about twelve or thirteen, galloping on a stallion, came into view. The adolescent cavalier—attired in a purple turban, a cream doublet, and pale orange trousers—was enchanting. In his raised fist, he held a glinting sword.

The drawing was rich and velvety.

"It's in pastel," Aksoy said. "A medium that is still quite unknown. But mark my words, it will gain popularity. It may not happen in my lifetime, but someday, this medium will be widely embraced and accepted. Note the natural hues—" He waved the wand at the swordsman. "Subtle, with radiant luminosity, and deeply pleasing. You smudge the pastels to achieve smooth transitions between colors and values."

"Radu, what is your assessment of the portrait?"

Taken aback, Radu hesitated. Indifferent to the visual arts, he preferred to dedicate himself to playing stringed instruments and singing. His attention had drifted during the interval.

Quickly recovering, he said, "The boy reminds me of myself. He fearlessly rides the mighty horse. And the colors—what do you call them?—are creamy."

"And what do you have to say?"

It was Dracula's turn. He held the same opinion as Radu but was reluctant to give an identical response.

On the other hand, why shouldn't he?

"The cavalier reminds me of myself," he said. At this, Radu pouted. "Spiritually rather than physically." Radu elongated his pout. "He charges with vigor and purpose. I, too, am charging—being in an unfamiliar environment and acquiring new knowledge."

"Well said," approved Aksoy, nodding at no one in particular.

Radu rolled his eyes.

"The papyrus is ancient, as reflected in its yellowing and brittle material. Its excellent condition is a marvel," Mehmed said. "What makes the drawing precious is that it captures the mood of the swordsman and eloquently depicts his spirit."

"The papyrus has been part of Boyar Avci's heirlooms. A special case in the Boyar's vault protected it from moisture and sunlight," Aksoy said. "This explains why it is so well-preserved."

From the satchel, Aksoy produced a smaller scroll—a sketch of a funeral procession. Men and women in mourning apparel walked in pairs. The folds of their black robes and gowns overlapped and unfolded as the cortège crossed the parchment.

The individuals had vivid and distinct countenances. One lady looked so forlorn that she might collapse any minute.

Dracula devoured today's lesson. He ambled to his chamber, his mind alive with the images. At his desk, he recalled the scrolls.

The soft click of a latch interrupted his reminiscence. Radu never handled his door this gently. He got up to investigate. Radu's door opposite was shut.

Has Radu entered or exited his chamber?

He hastened past Radu's room. Radu, treading across the lower landing, was in disguise, with a cap hiding his hair and wearing one of Ilie's outfits.

Dracula stole behind.

Mehmed had been tarrying outdoors for Radu.

The mates traversed the courtyard together. There was tension in their gait.

Dracula hid behind a stable stall. He deduced that they were in the midst of sneaking away. His Highness could come and go with a page or knight in attendance. Therefore, to be precise, Mehmed was smuggling Radu out—as a page.

A wrinkled warden and his pubescent subordinate were at the gatehouse. They could be two generations apart. His Highness dictated to the warden, who bowed and sent the minor to operate the hoisting gears. The portcullis rumbled up. Mehmed and Radu filed into the recess. Next, the outer portcullis cranked and squeaked as it was raised and lowered. Radu and Mehmed had cleared the gateway and were outside the rampart.

What are they up to? Where are they heading?

Curiosity filled Dracula.

Without the means to bypass the keepers, Dracula was limited to speculating from the stables.

10

A lifetime has passed since the milkmaid. His parents, siblings, and colony have long been deceased. For a decade, he has made the northern corner of the dungeon his home. An intuition came to him the instant he set eyes on the fortress of Eğrigöz. He felt that its dungeon would bestow upon him an heir to sustain and heighten his power. Through this successor, he would experience life's grandeur and indulge in his fascination with heavenly human females. Most importantly, he would be free. Free of constraints and burdens.

He has been patient.

None of the prisoners chained up there are whom he seeks: no bearer of promises. They lacked dignity, ingenuity, and the power to dominate. He had no desire to speak to them. But he trusted his intuition, which had guided him throughout his life. The dungeon would present his heir to him.

About six months ago, an omen manifested itself.

He had been nervous and anxious. Whether his restlessness conjured the apparition, he did not know. A giant shackled to a tree emerged. Bat was not dreaming. The apparition was real. Gore caked the giant's temple. A bluish swelling blinded an eye.

The giant had been severely beaten and fainted. Bat inspected the wounds. Crimson beads oozed out of cuts on the giant's bald head. Bat salivated at the beads. However, they were not what had captivated him. What was it, then?

Ah, a presence and a scent, not the giant's own, had fueled the urgency.

Bat must establish their origin.

He must access the giant's memories.

The giant was breathing evenly and drooling. Despite the bruises and cuts, he seemed at peace. Bat cooed into his ear, "Wake up ..." The giant twitched. His uninjured eye opened and then drooped back down. Bat cooed again. It reopened, looking at Bat without seeing him.

Hovering in midair, Bat peered into the iris—an amber marble with an inky center. The center was of unfathomable depth, a chute into the giant's soul. It contracted an infinitesimal amount, so small that it was almost imperceptible. Then it enlarged by an equally minuscule amount.

Contracting, expanding, contracting, expanding went the iris. Bat allowed himself to be hypnotized and gradually dissolved into nothingness. In this nonexistent state, he entered the giant's pupil, swam through the vitreous humor and along the optic nerve, and journeyed deeper into the brain, eventually reaching the temporal lobes.

Immense networks of neurons spread over the lobes. A mass glittered. Convinced that its networks harbored the anticipated memory, Bat coalesced into it.

***

The giant exhales chilly breaths, a ritual he adores. Since he cannot partake in this delight during mild weather, the puffs enrapture him. Outside, the snow, which fell on and off during the night, has blanketed the scenery white. He has been doing well this winter, hauling stones from the quarry for the mason. He has three copper coins set aside but should be frugal. The church renovation, owing to a shortage of funding, has stalled.

He kindles a fire. The fire serves to cook the barley porridge and bake the biscuits that supplement his income. The villagers ridicule him because he is simple-minded. Even so, everyone relishes his biscuits. He is able to sell dozens in town, in addition to the vegetables he grows. He uses his stock to barter with fellow peddlers for eggs and grains or vegetables absent in his garden.

As he crouches to ignite the logs, Misty rubs herself against his breeches. "Ah, be patient, Mist," he pacifies her. Sparks fly up;

the logs burn. He rises. A suspending plank stows milk, eggs, a hunk of cheese, and a block of butter—inventory he does not want Misty to reach. Misty trails alongside him and mews. He grabs the jug and pours the contents into a dish. He can ill afford to feed Misty milk. But her zest for this luxury merits it. The cat laps up the creamy liquid.

The giant rescued Misty from a ditch. The kitten was badly injured; her flank was mangled, and a hindlimb was fractured. Perhaps she was mauled by the neighboring dogs. Slowly, the wounds healed, and Misty was able to reclaim the deftness of her limb. The giant was especially proud she had rehabilitated into such a sleek cat. He had to earn Misty's trust. She used to flinch from his touch. He surmised she was abused. Gradually, his affection conquered the cat's misgivings.

They are inseparable now.

He always carries Misty along to town. He walks the three miles. Misty, in the pannier on his back, mews along with his hums. At the market, she roams the booths while he transacts his trade. She is partial to the fishmonger, who never fails to chuck her a scrap of fish.

Now she lazes at his feet, purring. He flakes flour onto her, giggling. He called her Paws and Fluff, in honor of her white paws and her downy hair. She would not respond to either name. Various other nicknames also suffered rejection. But she straightaway embraced Misty and mewed to it. The giant believes he couldn't be more blessed: the hut is warm, Misty is by his side, and he's doing what he does best. He massages the dough, adds water, and continues massaging. He rolls out the dough and starts a fresh batter. Sugar, a pinch of salt, a whipped egg, and butter are blended into the flour. He kneads with adequate pressure so that the biscuits will be flaky. He will cut the dough into small triangles and garnish them with morsels of crabapples. The biscuits will be delicious!

The flame expires. He places the biscuits into a lidded earthenware pot, which he carries to the hearth to be buried in the embers. The aroma of the butter and baking drifting out stimulates his hunger. As usual, the gruel doesn't sate his appetite. And as usual, he must wait for a proper meal until after the market outing. The biscuits will sell fast. The proceeds, along with the copper coins in his pocket, may fetch him a piece of salted mutton. He salivates at the image of the feast.

Loud hammering at the door startles him. A biscuit slides from his hand. The biscuits are ready. He is laying them out on a flat stone on the table to cool. Who can it be in these early hours? He doesn't have callers. Maybe a neighbor in need?

The arrival is a diminutive stranger. Behind him, four riders hover on horseback. "I'm Dănuţ, squire to Lord Dracul. We braved the storm during our journey. Luscious whiffs have attracted us here. We wish to share your food with you. My lord will pay you, of course."

"You may have the biscuits, but I've got no ale."

"No worries," says the squire, patting the flask strapped to his waist, "We have our own supplies."

The squire motions to the party on horseback to dismount. He then joins a boy in tying the horses to the black locust trees. The giant assumes that the squire's assistant is a page. A stocky man and two lads approach the hut. They shed their capes to shake off the snow, but their boots drag in clumps of ice.

The personage is attired in quality wool. The stateliness of his olive tabard and tall leather boots proclaims him an aristocrat. The emblem of the Order of the Dragon embroidered on the tabard seals this fact. Indisputably, he is Lord Dracul. His sons are in silk shirts and doublets—maroon and teal, respectively. With their refined noses, marmoreal complexion, and cultured bearing, they personify elegance and grace. The prince in red, a child of six or seven, is a beauty. With dazzling curls, lush lashes, and lips ruddier than his garment, he knows his worth.

The giant has not met any nobility up close. He bows to Lord Dracul, hoping that he has rendered the appropriate etiquette. He sweeps flour off the seats with his sleeve to allow his lordship and the princes to sit down. Short of chairs, the squire and page stand about. The fuss has enlivened Misty, who jumps onto the table, sniffing the tabletop, the rolling pin, the butter, and the biscuits. A shadow falls over her. A hand reaches for her. Misty flees from the table to dodge the pat. She darts across the floor and hides under the stool. From this refuge, she peeks at her admirer. The gorgeous prince chortles, parading perfect teeth, and then scrutinizes his nails. Deeming it safe, Misty crawls out to groom herself. She is too slow in detecting the grasp on her belly. Her captor thwarts her attempt to wrench free. "Now, who'd you say is cleverer?" taunts the prince as he strokes the cat merrily. Misty struggles and mews.

"I implore you to let her be, my prince," begs the giant, explaining, "She isn't used to visitors. She is terrified."

"Radu, leave her be," says Lord Dracul. The older prince frowns at his brother.

Radu releases the cat but spies on her surreptitiously.

The five interlopers devour biscuits and drink ale from their flagons. Within moments, the biscuits are consumed. Lord Dracul stands up. Dănuț tosses coins on the table. Their departure relieves the giant. Any delay, and he will suffocate. As they file out, Misty meanders between their shanks, contemplating catching a lark in the field and hunting mice. With swiftness, Radu bends down and scoops up Misty. He pulls his purse off his belt and flings it at the giant.

"I'm taking her with me," he declares, marching out.

"No, my prince, she's not for sale!" booms the giant.

The child glares at the giant, annoyed.

"Count the coins inside. They will feed you for at least a year!" says Dănuț in defense of his prince.

The giant thrusts the purse back to Radu without examining the contents.

He entreats, to no avail. Radu struts away, a squirming and mewing cat in his clasp. Radu mounts his horse, which the page has untied. The giant pulls him off. Landing sharply on his elbow, Radu yelps in pain.

Misty breaks loose but does not get far because the snow impedes her progress and the page seizes her by the scruff. She wrestles and wails. Maddened, the giant grabs for the page, but the boy slips away. On the second try, the giant collars him. The tip of Lord Dracul's sword is immediately at the giant's throat. "Release my servant," he orders. The giant, whose animosity peaks, hesitates.

Knowing that defiance would seal the giant's fate, the older prince snatches Misty from the page and presses his dagger to her throat.

"Try anything, and I'll slash her throat," he threatens. The giant lets go of the page. Dănuț chains the giant to a tree trunk.

"This is for you to remember me by," says Dănuț, bashing the giant with a mace he has unfastened from his horse. The page and Radu whoop in support. "That's enough," Lord Dracul commands his squire. The mace lacerates the giant's crown and fractures his ribs. As he faints, Misty's yowls echo in his ears. Lord Dracul directs his retinue to depart.

***

Bat approved of the older prince, whose decision to force the giant to free the page had saved the giant's life. It was better for the giant to lose the cat than his life. The decisiveness of someone so young—seizing control in a crisis—was impressive.

Bat was ecstatic. The older prince, thirteen or fourteen, enraptured him. The stripling walked erect. His emerald eyes exhibited a kaleidoscope of sentiments, fluctuating from savagery to gentleness, secrecy to naked frankness, loneliness to aloneness, sadness to childish exaltation. These turbulent currents whisked you away. You refrained from shouting for rescue. Instead, you let yourself bob in the cold and hot waves. Nobody could resist those eyes. Not a soul. Surely, there was insecurity he tried to conceal. At thirteen, who would be free of doubts? Within him, forces thrived, destined for omnipotence. With time, his presence would throw your senses into unbridled imagination. People were going to be bewitched. The successor, whom he had been pining for, had arrived!

11

Routines went on as usual. Aside from attending lessons, Dracula tended to and exercised his horse. At Târgovişte, he delegated the grooming to the stablemen.

Here he had cottoned to the responsibility. Alexandru's affectionate nudges were enough incentive to prompt him to the stall. His relaxed jaw and soft snorts announced his pleasure at the scrubs. Dracula congratulated himself on the splendor of his horse. Since Ilie's inclination to tattle—with just about anyone—could result in leaking confided secrets, Alexandru was his confidant.

Mehmed and Radu—again in Ilie's outfit—crossed the courtyard. He fixed his gaze on them. Alexandru tossed his head and whinnied. Although he was reluctant to leave Alexandru, Dracula waved to the stableman to finish the task.

Dracula was keen not to be excluded. He gave chase.

Once Radu and Mehmed vanished into the passageway of the gatehouse, he offered the warden a handful of coins. The warden squinted at the money and at Dracula's costly raiment. With a smirk, he blocked Dracula. Dracula could hear the outer portcullis rising, hauled by the young keeper working the winch inside the gatehouse. He had to make haste lest it be lowered.

He threw his purse skyward. While the warden tried to catch it, Dracula dashed into the arched passage. The warden did not pursue him: his guffaw, ricocheting from surface to surface of the hollow enclosure, served as his proxy.

Outside, Radu and Mehmed trekked along, Radu behind Mehmed. Dracula was thankful that the rough terrain had slowed his quarries down. Delayed by the warden, he could have lost them. The duo hugged the wall, wary of the sentinels posted at the lookouts. Dracula too edged forward. They had to be careful not to tumble down the serrated slopes. Radu clutched Mehmed's doublet.

Near the back of the fortification, Radu and Mehmed disappeared among the boulders along the descent. From a distance, Dracula could hear the crunching of pebbles and dried sand as they slid and skidded down the steep hillside. Muffled shrieks also echoed.

He trudged to where the two had vanished. No man could have continued further, even if he had tried, for a cliff stood yonder. Dracula forked left. Anyone with a broader build would be unable to squeeze through the gap between the rocks. They might get stuck.

Dead twigs crushed under his soles. The snap might reveal his proximity. But it was impossible to stifle the sound. Fortunately, Radu and Mehmed were also focused on moving forward, not the distant commotion. In addition to watching his footing, he had to avoid the thorns of the blackberries growing between the boulders. His flesh had already suffered several cuts.

The slope suddenly flattened. Pink stonecrops thrived. Vegetation bloomed.

There was no sign of Radu and Mehmed. A squirrel stuck its furry head out from behind a trunk and fled up it. Radu and he used to torment them with their slingshots. He could spot them from afar and dispatch an accurate shot. But it wasn't the time for sporting with squirrels. He had to locate Radu and Mehmed.

Where could they have gone?

Not to the hamlet which he had created solely for himself. Anyway, the journey there and back was so vast that their absence would be noticed at the fortress. Heading toward the hamlet would be unwise.

Dracula opted for the wood, an uninhabited and unfrequented area. Birds flew off from the bushes as he passed by. He searched for signs of footprints but only discovered animal tracks. The shrubs had concealed any traces of Radu and Mehmed. Since

Radu was fond of water, they must have headed for the stream. He pressed on, confident he was on the right course.

After a while of chasing, the shrubs and ferns thinned out. Footprints imprinted in the mud lifted Dracula's spirits.

A breeze blew, drying the moisture on his temples. He found the sensation remarkable, realizing only then that he had been perspiring. The breeze carried the scent of the creek, and he could hear the gurgling of water and catch glimpses of its shimmering surface.

Oaks lined the stream, their massive roots exposed along the bank. Dracula had the option to go up or downstream. A yellow leaf, flipped over by the water, made the choice for him. It was caught in the vegetation. Dracula witnessed it freeing and righting itself.

Dracula followed the leaf downstream.

His choice proved shrewd, as he soon spotted Mehmed and Radu nearby. He took cover behind a tree.

They had chosen an ideal spot. The water had formed a pool, with an oak tree spreading its branches over it. The tree was not particularly tall. Its limbs dipped close to the pool. Mehmed had installed himself in the crook of one of the branches. He swung his legs, unclad up to the knees, back and forth while watching Radu, who was in the water. Radu had also removed his hose, with water covering his ankles. He was shirtless. He had draped his shirt and hose on a branch and hooked his ruby cap on a twig.

Mehmed poked Radu with his big toe, jabbing his shoulder and ribs and laughing. Radu dodged the jabs. The mottled pattern on Radu's skin rippled along with the flutter of the leaves above. Dracula was certain that Radu, with his back turned, had pouted his lips in feigned annoyance.

So, their intimacy went deeper than they had let on. Dracula felt a sharp pang of envy. Perhaps he should have suspected something. The sweetmeats Radu flaunted should have been a clue. Who else could they have come from but His Highness? He detested the jealousy biting at him. Part of him wanted to rush out and taunt them, letting them know they had been caught. However, his feet sensibly remained rooted in place. It was prudent to stay hidden.

"Aren't you coming in the water with me?" Radu said, evading Mehmed's pokes. "Come on, you promised!"

"In a bit," Mehmed replied.

"Then I'll bathe without you."

Radu turned to look at the water, hesitating. His fondness for water did not overcome his apprehension of it. After all, as an infant, he had almost drowned in a washtub. The incident had left him wary. The center of the pool glistened black, indicating its depth, and there could be snakes lurking. Radu prolonged his indecision.

Whoosh! Radu toppled into the water. The aim was precise. Mehmed had kicked Radu and doubled up in laughter.

Radu steadied himself and wobbled toward Mehmed. He grabbed Mehmed by his ankles and yanked hard. *Splash*, bodies smashed into the water. A shearwater dove down, grazed the pool, and then glided upward and away. The bird's exit was as abrupt as its entrance. You glimpsed its snowy belly and, the next moment, its smoky back. Then it was gone. Balletic, graceful.

Suddenly, Dracula sensed a pair of eyes on him. He was no longer screened by the tree trunk. The shearwater had drawn him into the open, and Radu was gaping at him in disbelief. Mehmed was searching overhead and was oblivious to Dracula's presence.

Dracula ducked back behind the trunk.

Was Radu going to betray him?

Immobile and distressed, he stood.

Then he heard successive plunges. The friends had submerged into the basin. It was safe to steal away.

12

The hounds, a pack of twelve, bayed. The horses whinnied and pawed their hooves against the earth. Dracula was as anxious as they were. Three months had elapsed since he ventured out. He had ignored Radu's and Mehmed's pursuits and did not know if they had further escapades. Radu and Mehmed were insignificant to him; he tried to persuade himself. Radu, for his part, had not mentioned noticing him during the clandestine outing and had, by and large, snubbed him. This suited Dracula well.

This was no covert excursion; they had convened for an expedition. Dawn enshrouded them. They constituted a band of twenty: He, Radu, and Ilie; Mehmed and his page; the hound-master and Mehmed's cavalrymen.

Once out of the barbican, they eased down the slope; the dogs skipped from rock to rock. On a level plane, the party rode into the labyrinth of cedars and firs. Birdsongs permeated the environs. The hounds howled at the birds in the foliage, sending mice and rabbits scampering through the underbrush. The hound-master whistled to the dogs to prime them for the hunt.

With another whistle, the sport commenced.

Into the wilderness, the canines sped. Prey was at hand.

The riders pranced over a ditch and went into a gallop.

A boar trampled the low-lying vegetation, his dusty fur dimly visible. The hounds had scented him from a distance. Delayed by his nocturnal enterprises, he was now repairing to his nest.

Mehmed discharged an arrow at the boar but missed.

Speculating a thicket to be the swine's destination, Dracula trotted toward it, away from the gang. Thus situated, he loaded an arrow onto his bow and shot.

With the arrow stuck in his neck, the animal squealed. The hounds converged upon him. Cornered, he rallied the last of his energy. The canines positioned themselves, crouching low, tails stiff. Their prolonged, guttural growls amplified the tension in the atmosphere.

The quarry lunged at the lead hound, his tusks akin to honed sickles. The dogs assailed him, piercing his flesh with their teeth. He staggered and collapsed onto his flank, a lump of lacerated flesh, the shaft of the arrow protruding upward. Life sapped from him.

At the hound-master's signal, the dogs backed away. Dracula rode Alexandru, his mahogany bay, at a lope toward his prize. The rest of the hunting party circled in. The hound-master had dismounted and was examining the carcass. His countenance stiffened. He turned toward Dracula, antagonistic. Dracula dismounted his horse, bewildered by the man's hostility.

The hound-master pulled out the arrow.

"How does this come about?" He shoved the arrow shaft at Dracula's face.

Dracula whitened. Just below the fletching, a cursive "M" was engraved on the shaft in a deft and unique hand.

How could Mehmed's arrow have mixed up with mine?

"My prince, this is your arrow," said the hound-master, presenting the arrow to Mehmed, who had been observing from horseback. Murmurs of disbelief erupted among the assembly.

Dracula unstrapped the quiver of arrows from his back and swung it around.

Inside the container, a cursive "M" was carved on each of a dozen arrows! He was doomed—it was a grievous offense to steal from royalty.

Censure supplanted the murmurs of disbelief. A cavalry officer kicked the backs of his knees, sending him into a kneeling position, and then restrained him.

A theory forming in his mind directed his gaze to Radu, who was smirking down at him from his gelding alongside Mehmed's. *This is Radu's doing. Is Mehmed in on it?*

The scorn on Mehmed's face answered him. They were punishing him for probing into their business.

"What do you say about this, Dracula?" Mehmed said to him.

"I'm innocent, Your Highness."

"Innocent?"

The cavalry officer pushed hard on his shoulders, forcing him to bow. His peers sneered.

"Someone has swapped my arrows with yours."

"Who would have done such a thing?"

It was fruitless to answer this question, and he did not want to deepen his trouble with an accusation against Radu. He had no evidence.

He focused his strength on straightening his back and succeeded. "I am innocent," he reiterated firmly.

Mehmed roared. Radu joined in. They treated it as a raucous jest! The cavalrymen howled. Hilarity and yips of dogs shook the greenery overhead.

13

Dracula falls asleep on the patch he has cleaned in the dungeon and begins to dream.

***

He stands in the middle of a vast room, a room that parallels his parents' bedchamber in size. He pictures his parents' canopied bed with the curtains tied to the posts.

This chamber is bare.

A crack zigzags from the ceiling like a lightning bolt, dividing the wall into two halves. It penetrates an inch into the bricks and reaches as deep as four inches in places. To produce such a gash, the sword or chisel used must have been whetted and made of quality steel. It also could have been the work of lightning.

He stretches out his arms to bracket the crack in the distance. Easing sideways, he has sidled too far to the right. He adjusts to the left. Inch by inch, he positions half of himself to the left of the crack and half to the right. Focusing his thoughts, he wills the bolt to plummet into him—first cleaving his skull, sending fissures outward, and then splintering his spine and sweeping downward to his heel.

He has wanted the jolt to fragment him into a thousand tiny pieces and still further into a thousand tinier pieces, so forth and so on until he disintegrates into nothingness. But it is not meant to be: something has infiltrated his consciousness and sabotaged his concentration. This organism crowds behind him, not actually touching him. It is nonhuman. Goosebumps prickle his skin.

What could it be? Its carcass-like mass hovers above him. He holds his breath, for if he backs up a fraction, he will collide with it. What's to be done? His back senses its existence. The thing must be suspended in midair. Or missing the section below the waist.

It is as transfixed as he is.

And as frightened!

This insight heartens him. He twirls to challenge it.

Emptiness greets him. There is not even a shadow or a shade.

He presses forward to the next room. A cell. Its possession is a bulging piece of metal, wedged between bricks.

The bulge is the product of two nails, one twisted, shortening it by a quarter-inch. It has transformed into its partner's hump. In their original forms, the nails would have been of similar length.

The warped fellow latches onto its partner, which bends under the burden. Rust corrodes the hump and is most severe where the pair touches. The rusting is destined to escalate.

Dracula aches to rescue the encumbered half.

Pulling the dagger from his belt, he squats down. The mates are so entwined that it leaves only a minuscule aperture between them—an oval gap, large enough for him to insert the tip of the blade. Thus braced, he applies pressure on the dagger to separate them. The nails hold fast as a unit. He repeats the effort to no avail.

A different angle may do. He pries. *Plonk!* The unit flies in an arc and lands a few feet away, tightly entwined.

Sweat moistens his forehead. As frustration and defeat overcome him, the Thing announces its presence—by breathing down his neck!

He spins around and bellows into the vacancy.

"Get away from me!"

He gets the impression that it backs away, up toward the ceiling.

"You will never disjoin them, for they are one and the same."

Did the specter speak to him? No, nobody has spoken. The assertion sparked in his brain—but he hadn't formed it.

"They are one and the same." An odd dictum. But deep inside, he appreciates its truth.

He switches to a wardrobe. There are no cracks, no nails. A smudge, the size of a thumbprint, mars the otherwise blank enclosure. The markings on it are intermittent. The moldy center swells outward into a filthy brown. It manifests decay. As he inspects the smudge, a molar on his lower jaw assaults his nerves ferociously. He sucks on the molar to assuage the pain.

For reasons unfathomable to him, he obsesses over the filthy smear, etching into his soul its intricate lines—fragmented or intact, curvy or circular—and hues of degeneration. He is reluctant to look away: there is no telling what will befall him if he does. This petrifies him to a greater extent than the Thing lurking and spying on him.

He has no appetite for the Thing, which mercifully shows keen perception by keeping away.

The vigilance, the molar ache, and the terror prove taxing. He collapses but struggles up.

He is yet in another empty space. It does not even have any enclosures. Despite this, he feels squeezed in and unable to breathe. He cries out. All that accosts him is the ponderous void. Even the Thing is missing.

***

Dracula rouses. He has slept badly; fatigue and strain still lurk. The inkiness of the dungeon has deepened, if that is possible. The drip has not recurred recently: the rain must have stopped. He blows into and rubs his palms to alleviate the numbness. His stomach rumbles. He has not eaten since breakfast.

A dim shuffle filters into his ears.

Something high up has shifted.

Then stillness recommences.

An aura of familiarity envelops him. He has the distinct feeling that whatever is aloft, he has had a brush with earlier and is averse to reviving the confrontation. Fragments of a retained dream veer, collide, and thread together into vivid clarity.

The Thing!

He shudders.

14

The tension has been excessive for Bat. From his lair, he has monitored Dracula.

The boy reined in his nerves, explored, cleaned a patch for himself, and rested. The child's repose brought a rare moment of peace. Bat slipped into his dream. How could he have resisted?

Since Dracula entered the dungeon, Bat has stayed rigid so as not to disturb and alarm him. It has been hard on Bat, this immobility. He has badly wanted to swoop down, introduce himself, and initiate the process. The restraint makes him edgy and restless. He has to force himself back to immobility.

The dream he stole into has deepened their bond and cast new light on Dracula's inner world.

Their pact shall begin!

He wants the child to approach him of his own accord. In his estimation, Dracula will.

He shifts. To announce himself.

So, the Thing is real? And has it rustled? Could it, after all, have been a mouse? No, not for an instant does Dracula believe this. The entity is there, at the far end. And it was in his dream. Why? How did it gain access? He did not voluntarily dream about it. Why did the Thing intrude on him? Does the dream symbolize anything—it is so extraordinary and real? What does any of this represent?

What should he do?

He has to confront the entity. This is obvious.

He shudders at the conflict that is to transpire. Sadly, it *must*. Only then will his apprehension be purged.

To maintain his distance, he stays where he is and yells, "You, over there. Muster your courage. Show yourself. Now!"

His command ricochets—he has forgotten how sound magnifies in the hollow. When it dies down, nothing but a hush responds. The silence irks Dracula. "All right," he tells himself. "I'll demonstrate what pluck is." He steers toward the peril and seeks his dagger at the belt, just to recall that it has been confiscated by the jailers.

Midway, he almost trips on a loose stone. He ought to be careful. The dungeon floor is uneven and pitted. The chains from the ceiling are also hazardous, hanging so low that he might collide with them. He regains his balance and lets the sting in his toes subside. More than ever, he is determined to brave the apparition.

As Bat has predicted, the child is drawing close. It takes grit. He will introduce himself and actualize his vision. Dracula is beyond what he has hoped for. Dracula, at this stage of his life, may not comprehend his emotions, but he is receptive to them. The way he expressed them in his dream—in a spectacular fashion—was exceptional. Dracula's intensity, originality, self-doubt, and self-absorption perfectly suit the role he is destined to espouse. Together, the two of them will govern the realm of dreams. Forever.

In the far corner, Dracula scans the ceiling. He cannot distinguish much. Joists traverse the gloom hither and thither. That is all he can establish. He must summon the entity.

"You, up there, listen. Don't think for a minute that you can hide from me. I dare you to reveal yourself!"

Scarcely has he issued his challenge when a whiff of air caresses his hair. An entity plummets from the ceiling, careens forward and, in an instant, lands on a chain.

Dracula gawps at the negligible mass inches away. A bat. It dangles on the chain, its folded wings cloaking its miniature body. It must be, at most, two and a half inches in length from snout to tail tip. *Could it be the Thing, this cipher?* In his dream, the Thing was substantial, ominous, scary, and a specimen of power. The bat has twisted upward. What does it want? How preposterous!

Bat clutches a low-hanging chain with his talons. His alighting has been so smooth that the chain quivered ever so slightly. No clanks—not even a ding—rang out. He is in top form, the turmoil and fervor tormenting him notwithstanding. He is at eye level with Dracula. His yearning has arrived at a juncture.

They meet.

All of a sudden, shyness entangles Bat, and he cannot find words.

It is amazing that he still has it in him. He had thought himself rid of his shyness. In his early childhood, he was not averse to peers' timidity but mistrusted his own, which signified a sort of weakness to him. As a teenager, the bashfulness turned beneficial, equipping him with an appeal to the female bats. Slowly, he resigned himself to it, whether affliction or asset, and allowed it to transition into a sort of reclusiveness. His solitude has hardened the reclusiveness, and thus he holes himself up.

Dracula has rekindled the bashfulness. The incredulity, disappointment, and disgust coursing through the lad's face in succession exacerbate it.

Bat collects himself and reclaims his equilibrium. He elects to brush off Dracula's superficial judgments and affront. Nowadays his form is nothing to brag about—longevity has dulled his once gorgeous fur to a mousy gray and the inward mayhem has reduced him to a bag of bones. The lad simply has to recognize the deception of physical appearance.

He twists his head upward.

"Hail, Dracula," he says. "Our previous encounters didn't occasion a formal introduction. Pray allow me the pleasure of introducing myself—I am Bat."

Yes, that same voice, thinks Dracula, which does not travel through his ears though he *hears* it. It is tantamount to the internal murmur that admonishes or eggs him on. Such was the case when he was about to pilfer his mother's comb. He must have been five. He had sneaked into his mother's boudoir where he was explicitly forbidden to go. Being forbidden only tempted him and urged him on.

It was a lucky break, for both Mother and Nurse had been called away. Mother's boudoir was nothing special. Why she banned entry to it puzzled Dracula. Even his father was barred from it. Her maid was allowed in to tidy up. The upholstery and fittings were ordinary. Dracula browsed the books strewn about— all uninviting. He climbed onto the stool to examine the items on the dresser. Among the trinkets was a bone comb inlaid with pearls. He lifted it up to his nose and inhaled. It was as if Mother were at hand. As he debated whether to proceed with the theft, a voice in his cranium goaded, "Go on! Purloin it." He wavered— Mother would be beside herself. "She has many that surpass this comb in craft. Take it. It'll serve to keep her close." He pocketed it.

Dracula goggles at the bat.

"Is this always your mode of speaking?" he asks.

"Eh, pardon?"

"You don't exercise your lips, and the words don't resonate in my ears as any normal vocalizations do. How do you produce them?"

"I send out sound waves. I presume you receive them through the normal channels—that is to say—your ears, your auditory nerves, and your brain. Surely you are far more versed in your hearing system than I."

Is the bat taunting him or being serious? The aged creature could be feigning and stronger than what its constitution suggests. Dracula must be heedful. Bizarre events are about to befall him; he is convinced of it. He should accustom himself to the impossible.

"If you prefer me to use my mouth, it can be arranged. Either my nose or mouth can be engaged to enunciate," says the bat. Sturdy, sharp teeth line its jaws. *It's sagacious of me to be wary,* reflects Dracula. It is irrelevant which organ Bat employs to articulate. The perception that the remarks originate within Dracula persists.

Suddenly, recognition dawns on Dracula.

The critter has said, "Our previous encounters didn't occasion a formal introduction," which is a telling clue. He has never run into this bat or any bats, for that matter, anywhere in real life. His recent dream is where they could have met. The bat must be the Thing. But is it possible? How did this mite create the aura of omnipotence?

The boy is skeptical of me, mulls Bat. His harping on not hearing me through his ears is a distraction. He ought to value how special it is that he can hear me. It affirms a unique bond between us, which I don't forge with other human beings. Disruptions must be curbed. The sooner he concedes to our tie, the better.

"Do you remember me from your dream?"

"So, it was you!"

Now he has the boy.

"How did you do it?" demands the lad.

"'Do it?' You mean how I accessed your dream?"

"No—Yes. Well, how did you become so omnipotent? You impressed me as robust and formidable. In reality, you are a measly creature and have to be a hundred ... And yes, I also want you to disclose the tricks that enable you to penetrate my dream."

Bat breathes and says, "No trick whatsoever is used, dear. Entering dreams requires extraordinary ability. To master and perfect the craft, talent alone will not suffice. Resolution is essential.

"I'm not quite a hundred," Bat cracks a toothy smile. "I have spent most of my life pursuing this aspiration. Along the way, sacrifices were made."

Bat commences to relate about himself.

"I left Sibiu years ago. I had no idea that I was about to embark on a life journey of this magnitude. My father, mother, and siblings were there to see me off. Since birth, I had always been with them. Departing from where I was born and raised perturbed me not a single bit. I was about your age, naïve and not into pondering. I envisioned life continuing as it always had been.

"My parents conducted themselves as they always had, but I discerned a disguise about them. I was too inexperienced to define what it was. Now I comprehend the masquerade. Having always been surrounded by affection and security, I was blind to aches and losses. But there they were, masked by my parents' placid façade.

"I've flown back to Transylvania twice."

The boy is all ears. There is an incident Bat has not allowed himself to recall. The incident has been engraved in his heart. He must let it out.

"In my second homecoming, my brothers and sisters had families of their own and migrated to a warmer climate with an abundant food supply. My parents had clung to the cave—waiting for me.

"Dotage and illness had reduced my father to an invalid. He didn't seem to recognize me. He looked at me before slowly drifting away, back to the cocoon in which he had enveloped himself.

"The evening before I was scheduled to leave, my mother let me spend time alone with my father. My father and I lounged shoulder to shoulder. By then, I was accustomed to the absence of communication between us. An hour or so into our lethargy, he suddenly shook off his detachment. 'Mother and I won't be with you. Take good care of yourself, you hear?' The voice was frail, but he resembled the father I used to be close to. The love in these sentences was boundless. He'd wrestled out of his phantom cell. For me. I nodded and averted my gaze. If I hadn't, I would have lost control of myself. When I faced him, tenderness and concern had regressed to where they were trapped. He was again detached.

"Those were our last words together, for he was mute and remote the remainder of my visit and died several years later."

Dracula transfers his weight from leg to leg. So, he and the scrawny bat share similar experiences: the bat was also separated from his folks in boyhood. At least he has Radu. Albeit an unfavorable fact, Radu is blood. They will reunite with Father. He will not postpone it until Father is sick and aged.

"Why didn't you go home earlier?"

Bat delays his response. "A worthy question. Why, indeed?" he says.

Noticing Bat's exhaustion, Dracula is willing to forgive Bat for sneaking into his dream and scaring him.

"I'm afraid life got in the way," the bat adds. "You see, I was on a constant tour—throughout Transylvania, Wallachia, and the Ottoman Empire. I was bent on absorbing as much as I could. Acquiring skills was foremost; nothing else mattered. Also, by force of habit, we adhere to routines. Our familiarity with them deludes us into thinking we are in control. Anything beyond that demands effort. I am no different. Returning to Sibiu would have been an undertaking that I couldn't handle—at least, that's what I deemed then."

Dracula disapproves of Bat's explanations. The bat is hiding behind excuses, but Dracula is too tired and hungry to unmask him. The grumbling of his stomach is embarrassing.

"The turnkeys will bring food tomorrow morning. They always do. I'm sorry you have to wait. Try to sleep it off. We'll resume our conversation tomorrow."

With that, Bat releases his talons from the chain.

15

Dracula stirs. He has heard the jangle of keys and the squeaking of hinges. He squints at the blinding light flooding in. Crockery is being pushed through.

He races toward the glare. Too late. The door shuts with a boom. He remains imprisoned. The smell of food tickles his nostrils. He sprints up the stairs and finds a jug and a plate of food up top. Settling on a step, he gorges. The lamb melts in his mouth. He chews on the bones. Even they taste delicious. His stomach is about to rupture. He licks his fingers and then drinks from the jug. The plate is essentially empty. It was a generous amount of food. All of a sudden, he grasps that he has eaten his ration for the day. Before the next feed, he is left with a wedge of bread, morsels of loose meat in greasy puddles, and a half jug of goat milk as provisions.

He broods over the hunt. They have made sport of him— Mehmed the loudest, and Radu the most insulting. They exulted over their ruse. The rats! He will avenge the humiliation if it entails a year or ten. He will conquer the Turks. Radu will not be spared either.

His mood improves. He burps. There are plenty he wants to find out. Speak with the bat, he shall.

Bat feels it is a bother to feed. He consumes the scantiest amount of food. At times, he eats nothing. The limited selections are part of the problem. The resident spiders are about as unappetizing as crunchy dead ants. He subsists on insects that have unwittingly blundered into the dungeon. They are not anything to rejoice in either.

He hibernates to conserve vitality. But what with the giant and the anticipation, his vigor has been ebbing away. The proximity of

Dracula has accelerated the ebbing. At this pace, how long can he last? Survive, he must, in order to bestow the magic upon Dracula. The duration Dracula will be imprisoned is an issue. A week? Two? He must rely on the lad to be a quick student.

Bat lapses into a slumber. He dreams of the oceans that he traversed. Their sheer size and the power prowling beneath the waves enliven him. It is so uplifting to be with raw nature and in rapport with the oceans. Then he hears the barking of his name.

"Bat, Bat, come out. I'm ready."

He sleeps on. He is a child again—he and his siblings cuddling up to their mother. How cozy and safe they are. They cuddle on, bound in happiness. A whack explodes. His mother says farewell to him.

A fresh blow deprives him of a reply. An object has struck his roost, waking him completely. A bone, having smacked the rim of the crevice, careens downward. How maddening! He must quash the intrusion.

Bat pokes his nose out.

"You, stupid boy, don't you understand that bats snooze during the day? Cut this old bat a break. Go away. Retire to your patch. We'll talk tonight."

The boy has to learn to be nocturnal. Bat wants to reclaim his dreams: such jolly imagery seldom bechances him. But the rhythm is wrecked. It is Dracula's fault.

The silly child is destitute of company. Bat can't remedy that. Nights are for enterprise; days are for preservation. He curls up.

Dracula surveys the dungeon. After acclimating to the darkness, he can see pretty well. Bat's sanctuary is a hole in the masonry. He wants Bat to prove that Bat is the Thing, but the selfish brute refuses to comply.

Around him, chains hang from the joists while shackles and torch sconces line the walls. The reek of excretion and sweat is not oppressive. The place is apparently rarely used. The reason must be that it's located beneath an isolated stronghold. Mehmed is here to be trained as a şehzade, and he and Radu are his hostages.

The smears on some of the manacles resemble dried blood. Prisoners must have been chained up and beaten. The captives had to be savages since they were fettered. At least he himself is free to wander.

***

Night arrives. The tranquil dungeon intimates that its effervescent occupant is dormant. For a while, he was a ball of energy, fidgeting about.

Bat's mind is in chaos—placid one moment, tense the next. The coming days are critical. He is anxious for progress. There is no room for failure in this final stage of his life. He must accomplish his goals. Ever since setting foot in the dungeon, he has intended to liberate himself. The dungeon *has* delivered: Dracula is with him, and he will roam free. His life will never be as it was prior to the dungeon. He and Dracula shall be inseparable.

Ting, ting.

Searching for a bell, Dracula catches Bat striking a claw against a chain. He is not annoyed. Boredom has steered him into dreamland. He might as well get up and talk to Bat.

After gulping down the leftover goat milk, he wipes his mouth with the back of his hand and proceeds to honor Bat's invitation. The critter sways on the ring where he introduced himself the previous night.

"Did you have a nice rest?" Bat says.

Dracula nods.

"It's past midnight."

How does Bat ascertain this? The piercing stare, aimed at Dracula, deters him from inquiring. The creature is strange.

"Want to flee from here with me?"

Dracula is dumbfounded: is the bat insane?

Bat trills.

The *hehehe* twirls and encircles Dracula. *Hehehe ... hehehe.* The cyclone of laughter plunges him into an expanse that dims and brightens. Clouds blow by. Among them, he floats on his back. The white puffs lend their caresses. A cerulean sky envelops him. He spreads his limbs as he would in a pond. He does not have to expend energy to be buoyant. His muscles relax. Is this what being in heaven is like? No, he is not in heaven. A weight has crept inside him. The realization of this frightens him.

He stumbles. Regaining his balance, he finds himself out of the dungeon! Fog engulfs him. The ground he is standing on is unstable. *Where am I?* In his confusion, he shouts, "Bat, where are you? Where have you taken me?"

"*Shhh!* You will alarm the girl."

What girl? It is unnecessary to scout for Bat, who is wedged within himself. The rogue's heart pumps within his chest. The rogue's bony limbs and flesh meld with his own.

Shocked and disgusted, he retches but heaves not a drop of vomit. Dracula shakes himself violently to be rid of the scoundrel, cursing and raging.

A blackout ensues.

The convulsion and swoon subside. He is back in the dungeon. Bat chortles on the chain.

Dracula wonders if he has gone mad.

No, he *hasn't*. The pest was inside him. He doesn't care how the pest did it and why. He doesn't want to repeat the experience— ever! He glowers at Bat and is blinded by tears. To stamp out his inner jitters, he snaps, "You creep, *don't* do that again!" and then hurtles away.

16

Dracula's outburst does not faze Bat, nor is he surprised by it. Events have been unfolding as anticipated—better than anticipated, even. He coalesces with the kid with ease. They are the nut and bolt that fit. *Thump!* Their hearts beat in unison, and their blood flows in harmony. The glory of it is that despite being conjoint, he remains a distinct entity, with Dracula as his continuity.

He cheers.

The boy will adapt to their union and should be ecstatic to have a mentor and a partner rolled into one. He had to struggle alone. When defeat smothered him, he fled from it all. This cowardice exacerbated his depression. He agonized until his misery escalated to a crisis. Then, an internal spark ignited, spurring him out of the abyss. Victories and defeats cycled round and round.

He ultimately conquered. Which was electrifying!

Into Man's dreams, he drilled.

***

The aqua, fuzzy boundaries vie with the azure interior. Surrounded by the aqua and azure lies the gray navel through which I, a speck, tunnel.

Under closed lids, Mari's eyes twitch. The frothy waves of her flaxen hair glisten and undulate.

I propel on.

Mari rows a boat not far from shore.

She leans over the edge of the boat and peers into the water. Exhilaration bubbles out of her as the water gleams. A fish leaps from the ocean, dewing Mari's flesh and chemise.

Fur wet and body heated, I pant.

My soul and I hurl faster and faster.

Mari giggles and giggles.

I whistle air out of my lungs.

I am inside Mari's dream.

I exult not solely in having conquered but in beauty and passion.

***

Will Dracula be as affected? With his guidance, Dracula will have it easier. Will having it easier diminish the ultimate success?

"I thought you were eager to learn how I penetrate dreams," Bat hollers at the retreating Dracula.

Dracula freezes. Should he dismiss the revulsion of coalescing with Bat and rejoin the critter? Or should he shun the disgusting vermin?

Curiosity wins out; he accosts Bat.

Bat guffaws.

"Why don't you instruct me, and I'll do it on my own?"

"That will be impractical, if not downright impossible. Child, I don't have time to wait for you to fumble."

"Can we do it without you lodging in my bowels?"

"What are you scared of?"

"I'm not scared!"

"Beg your pardon. Any offense is accidental. May I ask why you are distraught, then?"

Dracula compresses his lips, piqued. Their fusion has repulsed him. The odious creature is retaliating with these belittling queries. He is not going to gratify him.

"To be remarkable, you have to renounce your comfort zone," stresses Bat. "You and I are suited like membranes to bones. It's extraordinary. My supervision will smooth the process. In due course, you'll develop your personal style and treat my presence with apathy."

Dracula is quiet, but eventually he says, "Fine. I'll give it another attempt."

"Glad to hear it. Here we go. Savor the ride."

Bat lets out a laugh. The eerie *hehehe* spirals.

Dizziness develops; Dracula floats upward. He is aloft, whereas his intellect maintains that his feet are moored to the ground. There are two of him.

Steadily, the airborne self dominates while the dungeon recedes.

He and Bat are fused together. Bat is driving them onward.

He tries not to concentrate on that to avoid being appalled. Mist has blurred the atmosphere. Amidst the murkiness, a fragrance drifts. *That of burning wood.* Are they nearing their destination?

Suddenly, he sees a girl weeping. Well, he does not actually see her. She is but a semblance in his imagination—vivid and real, nevertheless. The girl is in distress. As he is about to explore the source of her anguish, she evaporates.

Bat has abolished flapping his wings, and in concert with the dynamics of their thrust, Dracula keeps his arms by his flanks and his legs together. The mist has dispersed; they are being sucked down a vacuum. The pressure pinches his flesh, his skin tightens, and his hair shoots straight back.

As the suction intensifies, so do the wafts of odor. Something roasting. He cannot place what is being burned.

He squeezes shut his eyes to protect them from the escalating pressure.

The universe stops.

All is well again.

Dracula has landed on a marsh.

Grass culms sway in the breeze—an ocean of them. In a clearing, a log pile flames. The smoke assaults his nostrils. He sneezes. The caretaker of the fire, a girl, looks up as if she hears the sneezes. Without delay, she immerses herself once more with her activity.

Dracula's breathing quickens: she is the distraught girl. *Am I inside her dream?*

"Introduce yourself to her," advises Bat.

Dracula has forgotten about Bat, who has detached himself. Dracula is free to act on his own.

"Go on," urges Bat.

As Dracula hovers over the girl, objects align and sharpen. Soot smudges the tip of the girl's nose. She must be ten or eleven. She has neglected to comb her hair. Strands have loosened from her plait, and it is frizzy all over. Her threadbare, patched smock and battered sandals attest to her peasant status; she is a specimen of the destitute. She snivels and is oblivious to Dracula's proximity. Should he introduce himself? He is averse to the idea.

The girl pokes at the pyre; a charred elbow sticks out from underneath the mound. This is a funeral rite. She is incinerating a relative. And he is intruding. He recoils. The prospect flickers. The grass goes in and out of focus.

"Steady on. You must proceed with caution. Abrupt movements aggravate her," Bat whispers. The susurration is entirely superfluous as only Dracula can hear it. Bat's comments are encased in Dracula's head. The old bat is trying to be dramatic.

Dracula wants to offer the poor mourner a little money to lessen her misfortune. If this involves revealing himself, so be it. He tiptoes up to her and clears his throat. The girl straightens up.

"Don't be afraid. No harm will befall you," he says.

The girl resumes her task.

"Hold on," beseeches Dracula, rummaging his tunic pockets. "I would like to contribute to the expense of the burial."

He freezes: his pockets are empty. The contents have been confiscated along with his dagger by the jailers.

His awkwardness kindles the girl's humor. She draws back her lips in a smile.

He unbuttons his tunic and bestows it upon the girl, who hugs it and rubs her cheek against the downy fabric. It has not formerly impressed upon Dracula how beautifully coral his tunic is. It also occurs to him that the tint of parchment, or subtle variants of it, is everywhere. It has been so since he trespassed into the girl's dream.

Yet the soot on the girl, the dirt underneath her nails, her rumpled clothing, and the charred elbow are pronounced. Colors are not essential in dreams, then—items emerge as animated without them.

As he marvels at this, the surroundings fracture, commencing with the girl and expanding outward. In a twinkling, the marsh dissolves.

The girl has roused.

Dracula is back in the dungeon.

17

The boy radiates. Entering my maiden dream, I must have been as incandescent, Bat muses. But nobody was present to envy my glory. The child is a natural. He gave away his tunic with a gentleness beyond compare. The dreamers are going to be won over.

Bat's spirits buoy up. His selection is superb. Dracula will not only preserve Bat's talent but also enhance it with his own excellence. In Dracula, Bat and his genius will thrive.

The boy grows pensive.

"The dream lacked hues. Recalling mine, they are the same. Of course, the coral was conspicuous."

"It was magical, wasn't it? You may not realize it, but you saw the coral because you chose to."

Dracula is astounded: did he choose to do that?

"The dreamers also apply colors. To allure you and stimulate themselves."

"They will tempt me into their dreams? That seems incredible. I would dissuade anyone from penetrating mine. Won't they be frightened? Outraged? Repelled, even?"

"It depends on how you handle yourself. The young girl wasn't frightened, outraged, or repelled by your manifestation, was she?"

"The girl was ignorant of my invasion; she must have judged me a component of her fancy."

"Listen: you didn't *invade* her dream; you paid a visit, and she *let* you. If she hadn't wanted you there, she would have banished you and woken up. That would have sent you packing, and there was little you could have done. Her allowing you there is a compliment to you. Conquer and be conquered. You are destined for a good bit of fun!"

Bat can hear the mother spider exchanging signals with her babies. She has tucked herself and her brood far from the door.

Dracula's faculties crank, switching between visualizing and reasoning. There is a mountain of information to absorb.

He poses his inquiries.

"What if my choices of colors clash with those of the dreamer? Who conquers under such circumstances?"

"Excellent questions. Be aware that you can assign colors to items connected to yourself and nothing connected to the dreamer. The corresponding principle applies to the dreamer. She has the advantage of also assigning them to the setting. Don't forget, it is her dream. What you've picked for yourself may indeed clash with hers. Obey your instinct. At this juncture, try to complement. You did well with the tunic. Its magnificence has imprinted itself on your memory, hasn't it? I dare say the girl felt a similar impact."

Bat carries on, "Induce a clash if doing so provides an edge to you. On the whole, embellish if it yields an advantage. The important thing is to experiment and assimilate, my boy."

Bat lets Dracula imbibe the wisdom imparted.

Then he announces, "The same color produces different effects under different situations. The effects are equally compelling. In one instance, red accentuates pearly skin. It brings the skin's radiance to the fore. Picture a damsel's chemise fluttering in the breeze, dew on a petal, a kiss blown, a whisper that melts the bones. What can be more desirable? In a separate instance, red thunders along, coursing up the veins. *Boom. Bang.* The hearts of those involved can't help but race. Along the way, green lightning bursts. Magnetizing and urgent. The red quivers in blissful trepidation while the hearts and heads spin round and round. Till every bit is spent."

Overcome by the eloquence of his own speech, Bat pauses before summarizing with fervor. "You know, for all the power of colors, what wields the most power is the absence of them." He fixes his gaze on Dracula, who is gaping. Bat crows.

Dracula is stunned. How can such a negligible entity talk such wonders? He has never conceived of red and green in these terms, which conjure up sensations and notions that he has harbored of late—sensations and notions that he savors and is embarrassed about.

Has he misinterpreted Bat and projected his partiality into the mix?

He is fascinated and predicts that these chats will have a profound influence on his future involvement with the dreamers.

"Like water, colorlessness is fluid, fleeting, unfathomable. Like air, it can be smelled but not beheld. Inhale: lose yourself in the ever-so-tiny trace of tang, the ever-so-tiny trace of musk," Bat says and inhales. His bearing flaunts his inebriation. "There's more. Colorlessness is the zenith of the red, yellow, and blue of the world and their blended products. Rapture, frenzy, and zeal combine into a unit. At the same time, it is coolness and serenity. At this single point, adverse and complementary dynamics tug, splinter, and assemble. Sight, sound, and touch are superfluous."

The intoxicated bat is not through. "Sorry, I'm ahead of myself. In my earnestness, I might have touched on subjects you aren't ready for. If what I've said is unintelligible, I apologize. It's altogether my fault. My advice to you is not to ponder anything. By and by, all will make sense. Now, go. We'll reconnect tomorrow."

18

With the guidance of Bat, Dracula has stolen into several dreams. He is ashamed of these unsolicited visitations. Dreams are private, and he has breached that privacy like a peeper.

As the dreamers take no offense, his guilt and his awe of them slowly wane. Sensing that the dreamers feel less threatened if he restricts himself to the periphery, he allays his guilt by obliging them.

Attending as a silent bystander doesn't lessen his influence. Any of his actions will alter the dream.

He prefers not to interrupt yet.

He enjoys being the spectator. A dreamer is an individual, and a dream is an entity that conveys the dreamer's sensibilities, longings, agonies, and fantasies. Irrespective of how mundane a dream is, there is an aura about it that captivates him.

Dreams may be hazy or as crisp as reality. Dreams could switch from theme to theme. They could be tidy. Do these qualities owe more to the dream or the dreamer?

Though the dreamer, as the owner of the dream, ought to be the shaper, his conviction is that the dream rules much of its pulses. Has he not lacked control over his own? For this reason, the dream bewitches him to a greater degree than the dreamer.

There is always an exception—someone whose allure overpowers the dream's pull.

The dreamers he has met so far are his age, except for this lass. She was beating her wash in a basin with a maple rod, her back turned to Dracula, as he moved into her dream. The stringy hair escaping from her hood and the broad and muscular back hinted she was not a notable beauty. The subtle halt of her arm indicated that she was cognizant of Dracula on the periphery.

Moment after moment, the lass transformed under his gaze. At first, her hair acquired a brown tint that glinted. Whether the sudden gloss of the hood had initiated this sheen in her hair, Dracula was not sure. Meanwhile, a gentle glow, bit by bit, relaxed the lass's shoulders and back. Even the harshness of the muscles had faded. What remained accentuated the softness of the lass's waist and hips.

Have her features undergone a parallel transformation? What do they look like? Dracula was avid for a disclosure. He lingered. The seconds ticked by. Finally, she turned! Dracula's mood leaped but plummeted next, for the lass veered toward him slightly and then desisted. He did not even catch her profile. This very tease persuaded Dracula of her awareness of his proximity. She had intuited what he wanted.

The lass battered her wash so that stars of suds dispersed. Each pound whetted Dracula's appetite. In the end, his agitation overcame him.

If she refused to oblige, he would impose an encounter.

He sprinted forward.

Without warning, a beating rod rolled into his path. The inevitable occurred: he tumbled headlong. The object of his infatuation spun to witness his mishap. Despite being devastated by humiliation, he strove for a hint of her visage. As he did so, his world shattered into fragments.

Dracula riveted toward a shard of the wreckage. Though no larger than a thumbnail and seen only briefly, he had no doubt it bore a sliver of cherry lips. Within the pouting bloom, pearly teeth lured. These were lips suited for beckoning. This enchantment, coupled with the lass's deep voice, convinced him that she must have been three or four years his senior. She laughed— wholeheartedly—and her laughter hung in the air in her absence. It contrasted with the infantile titters he had heard from girls; hers was smoky and entrancing.

He could kick himself; his impatience had instigated the nymph's decision to wake herself. What impelled her to torment him? He bemoaned not having fulfilled his yearning.

Bat creased up with merriment. The madder at himself Dracula became, the louder the bat's hysterics grew. Soon, the critter was convulsing with laughter. How revolting! Dracula failed to comprehend what was so comical. He was dead earnest. He had begun to feel comfortable with the scoundrel, who had to go and ruin the rapport.

Dracula curbed his temper and beseeched Bat to access another of the nymph's dreams. Bat refused. Dracula pleaded and cited his motive—he must see her face. Bat stifled his hilarity (it would serve him right if he choked on it) to say, "There is a profusion of flies in the web. Why obsess over an individual bug, eh? You'll link up with besotted dreamers in the future. At this stage, it behooves you to procure as many contacts as feasible. Chew over the experiences. Profit from your mistakes—and triumphs."

Dracula stormed away, sulking.

Bat exults over Dracula's progress. The child is capable of operating on his own. Amazing! He executes his undertakings with finesse. His inquisitiveness about the dreamers has not diminished his sensitivity to their feelings. He has also demonstrated passion and fortitude. Needless to say, the boy has plenty to assimilate and experiment with, but he can labor over them unaided.

Dracula will surpass Bat in the craft. Bat's service is to propel Dracula into dreams. This is Bat's trump card—Dracula will never be free of him. Bat will persist within Dracula even after Bat's physical self has expired.

The boy shakes off the sulks and is as fervent as ever. Wooing a cunning girl is never a smart strategy. The nymphet is a sly specimen. Perceiving that the sudden coloration of her dream places her in the best of light, she goes ahead and paints. She teases the boy's patience, a most effective tactic in this cat-and-mouse game. Letting the boy peek at the snippet of crimson lips is ingenious. Bat resists discussing all this; Dracula should appreciate the machinations by himself.

Nothing has higher staying power than a win procured on a person's own merits. It is especially satisfying if the win derives from overcoming a setback.

Industry and endurance were vital in polishing Bat's skills. They are required of Dracula as well. Ah, how the ordeal has changed Bat! He left his clan in a haze, with minimal memory of the occasion. His kin were there to send him off; it could not be otherwise. Snotty and the gang could have been there too. Such a rare and important event—his parting from his family—and he retains not a single detail!

The haze did not arise from anticipations or misgivings. He suffered none. Back then, living in blithe haziness was the norm. Naturally, he had concerns, a large chunk of which was not to disappoint his parents. He had fretted about being bigger and stronger, or at least of normal size. On and off, he had dreamed of being more handsome. These dissatisfactions had never dominated him. They were merely irritants, a fact of life. He abided within his bubble, not apt to analyze himself or what was happening around him.

Was the haze a product of a loving, protected upbringing? Or was it his innate personality? Or both? Whatever the basis was, it had insulated him from apprehensions. Nowadays, steps that trigger major adjustments cow him.

He was callow and a real baby. Didn't Gravity stress this to their circle of friends? She refrained from discussing with him topics she deemed solemn. This resulted in his not learning about her woe until a generation had cycled past. Orange and Snotty divulged then that, in the absence of her father, Gravity was strained by her mother's ineptness to cope with the situation.

He does not regret his naïveté but laments that the haze has dissipated, as it contributed enormously to his achievements. Free from burden, he used to approach life with total optimism.

Optimism breeds success. Conversely, his achievements have not been as kind. Striving for them comes at the cost of dispelling the haze, exposing him to self-scrutiny, perturbation, and torment.

Will he ever delight in his bliss again? Will it cycle back to him? To secure a chance, the perpetuation of his being within Dracula is of the utmost importance. The bliss is liable to manifest itself in an altered form. Say, as a mature, sophisticated euphoria, if such elation exists.

19

How did he evolve from a faraway youngster to the currently tense, exhausted, self-conscious, worry-plagued self?

Quitting Sibiu, he flew from dusk to dawn. He was in the clouds both physically and figuratively, focused on reaching his destination. Barring the initial route, which he and his father had taken, he found himself in unaccustomed territory. It was incredible that he had not gotten lost. His father's training must have produced this miracle.

The arrangement was for him to fly to the Bucegi Mountains. A local would receive him. There he was: the local bat, somewhat older than himself. This bat has been inexplicably etched in his brain ever since. Apart from the bulbous stomach, fitting for a stout adult rather than a pubescent mammal, everything about him was average: brown fur, small dark eyes, and sharp teeth. Even today, he can conjure up these common features. As for the bat's name, Bat can't say; it has never registered. *The Greeter* he will eternally be.

The Greeter shepherded Bat to the cave that would be his home. Bat's parents had omitted to specify the duration of his absence, and not accustomed to forethought, Bat had not inquired.

"All the transients dwell here," said The Greeter. "Don't be shy. Grab a spot—if it's vacant, nobody will complain."

Families snoozed together. Several occupants scowled at Bat, who had anchored at the mouth of the cave. When feasible, he would search for a safer berth. Once he was settled, The Greeter hurried away.

Bat slept until bodies fidgeted and chatter erupted. Outside, an orange and cerulean sky hovered. Bats groomed themselves. A few brawled.

When the dying twilight dispersed, the cauldrons set off. Babies clung to their mothers' bellies. Bat debated whether he should blend into one of the swarms. He wished The Greeter were on hand to advise him.

The cave emptied. He fluttered his wings and was off.

Shortly afterward, a bat caught up with him.

"Did you just arrive?" asked the bat.

Bat nodded.

"Where are your people?"

"I'm alone."

The bat whistled.

"Want to join us?" Another bat had joined in and extended the invitation.

Both of them wore tawny fur. Black wings, large eyes, and elongated snouts characterized them. Their wingspan was at least twice his own. The one extending the invitation was called Nectar.

"He's wild about nectar of any kind," volunteered the other tawny bat. "I'm Twilight. The name doesn't denote my love for twilight. In the afterglow of the sunset, my mother gave birth to me. She favors the name."

"It's a beautiful name," commented Bat.

"That's precisely the problem!" trilled Twilight. "It's excessively feminine. I'm a masculine male. *Night* is proper, but Mother won't have that."

"Why aren't your parents with you?" asked Nectar.

"They want me to be independent," said Bat. He kept secret the belief that he was destined to be eminent. His new acquaintances might scoff at it. To have the prophecy bear fruit, his parents believed he must not be cooped up in Sibiu. From birth, a plan to send him off at a tender age brewed. He was to nurture his potential. What the potential was, not a single bat had ever voiced. They were clueless.

"You are lucky," said Twilight. "I wish mine would let me be on my own."

"No, you don't," said Nectar. "Who would feed you if you lack nourishment? Which is often—a glutton like you." He pivoted his head backward. "His mother frequently replenishes his food."

Twilight shrugged the remark away.

Bat copied Nectar and found about thirty bats trailing behind. The families of Nectar and Twilight must be among them.

The band had journeyed from Egypt for the plum season. Bat had no inkling where Egypt was but was unwilling to ask about its location, lest it betray his ignorance. He promised himself to tour this foreign country in the future.

"We have an assortment of fruits. Dates, pomegranates, grapes, figs—you name it. But the plums in this area are delicious. There are twenty-seven of us. Back at home, we belong to a cloud of a thousand."

Fruits did not impress Bat. "What about insects?" he asked.

"What about them?" countered Twilight.

"He meant what kind of insects he could have in Egypt, silly."

"Ugh," said Twilight.

Bat reddened. "Insects are tasty," he said in the sternest manner he could muster. And he added, "I bet you have never snagged one. It demands skills."

To demonstrate, he snapped up and gobbled the gypsy moth hiding beneath a chestnut leaf. The motion was so adroit that Nectar and Twilight chirruped.

They flew on. With no stars and moon, the heavens had adopted the inkiness of a cave. The branches of the firs below resembled eagle wings, poised to pounce. To evade these perilous shapes, the bats sped up.

They slowed down after a mile. Plum trees replaced the ashes, elms, and spruces.

The birds had ceased twittering. Even the nightingales were reposing. The chorus of crickets arose, accompanied by the sweep of the fruit bats.

Red plums beckoned.

In unison, the colony glided downward to the boughs. Crunches bombarded the air as the bats gobbled the fruits. The ritual engrossed Bat.

"Perch next to me, Bat," invited Twilight. He slurped the juice with his tongue. "They're scrumptious. Sort of tart—the piquant taste I relish."

Bat was doubtful.

"Have you eaten a plum before?"

Bat had not.

"Try one. It's succulent," said Twilight. "Watch me. It's easy: sink your teeth into the flesh and suck out the juice. Use your tongue if you prefer." Twilight backed up his words with a fruit and fell into a state of bliss. He reined himself in to cajole Bat into indulging with him.

Bat jammed his teeth into a fleshy plum and choked. He coughed and spat out the juice. But the tangy taste adhered to his palate. Then and there, he resolved to be done with fruits.

20

The clan of Nectar and Twilight had adopted Bat. While his adoptive family ate plums, berries, and mangoes, he scavenged fruit flies, moths, caterpillars, and crawling insects. The supply of food was endless. He was full of glee and adored his companions.

Nectar, the shrewd roamer and exceedingly adaptive, navigated the Bucegi Mountains as though they had always been his playground. The three of them ventured into the idyllic summer night. When sporadic rain cascaded from the heavens, they sought shelter in the cradle of an alder or ash, marveling at its relentless momentum.

"We had a near brush with a thunderbolt in Anatolia," said Nectar. He and Twilight had huddled together. They suffered from the slightest decrease in temperature. Bat was not the least affected. "Does lightning rattle you?" Nectar asked Bat.

"No," said Bat, emphasizing, "Never." He hated boasting but had been doing it a lot lately.

"They can be dangerous," said Nectar. "We were foraging. The wind speed had escalated but not to a threatening degree. There was no sign of a thunderstorm. Suddenly, that changed: the clouds reshaped and amassed, molding into mounds and then towers. The bolts that ensued ignited a raging wildfire. The conflagration destroyed a third of the forest. Trees, shrubs, and bushes were reduced to char or ashes. Beasts, birds, and insects were killed by the scalding heat. We were lucky. The cloud-towers—differing from what we had formerly encountered—warned us off. We fled early enough to avoid being struck."

It was this sophistication that awed Bat. To him, even the absentmindedness with which Twilight comported himself bespoke sophistication. These bats had traveled extensively. They had wandered as far north as Poland and as far east as France, not to mention their native Africa. Bat had not heard or dreamed of these regions.

If only they had bragged, he would have been able to count them his equals. But they had not. Their narratives were unvarnished and never condescending. Nevertheless, they intimidated Bat, a sentiment he deplored.

In a unique aspect, he excelled beyond his friend. He discovered this several months into their companionship.

They were dozing on a sprawling elm. An elbow nudged the napping Bat. It was Twilight. "Hey," he whispered. There was mirth in his voice. "You are wanted," he urged.

Groggy and befuddled, Bat yawned at the playful Twilight.

"You have an admirer."

Bat followed Twilight's gaze to a tiny bat on a branch at an angle to them. She repaid his attention with melodious chittering. The bashful Bat glanced away.

"She's been eyeing you," chirped Twilight. "She is probably smitten. You ought to go over and introduce yourself."

The commotion had woken Nectar, who asked what the matter was.

"Bat has got an admirer."

"No, I haven't."

Twilight indicated the angled branch. The tiny bat had released her talons to fly away but not before sending a chirrup their way.

"Chase after her," goaded Twilight. "She's pretty."

"Why don't you chase after her yourself if you're so enticed?" countered Bat.

"Who says I am enticed? I'm enthralled for your sake. She was gawking at you, not me. Besides, she isn't a fruit bat."

"You've lost me: I am not a fruit bat either, but you've befriended me."

"Well, there's a difference, isn't there? You are male, and she is female. She might steer me to a situation I'd rather avoid. With you, I'm safe."

"I still don't follow."

"What Twi is saying is that he will consort with any bats, whether fruit-eaters or not, but as for coupling, he prefers sticking to his breed."

"I get that. The point is, why limit yourself?"

"To begin with, excuse me for answering on your behalf, Twi."

Twilight swayed to and fro to indicate his acceptance. Nectar dispatched his gratitude and began to express his thoughts: "I'll explain why sticking to one's own kind has its advantages. Primarily, it's simpler. You have common habits, enjoy the same food, and frequent the same haunts. A shared upbringing and mutual understanding foster immediate rapport. And when it comes to offspring, mixed stocks exhibit exotic traits. Straying from the norm could be risky—they might face teasing or, worse, become easy targets for predators. I trust Twi agrees with my assessment."

Twilight nodded his assent, drifting sideways and back with an absent air. His movement was unhurried, his expression dreamy. "If I were charmed by a bat of a different lineage, I'd essay to make it work. Love conquers all, they say. With that said, I absolutely will strive to prevent it from transpiring. Ease is my motto. Having to surmount barriers is enough to dissuade me. Are you saying you don't have such reservations, little brother?"

All attention was on Bat.

"I've never given it a minute of consideration. Marriage. Progeny. They are never in my musings."

"Doesn't the opposite sex appeal to you?" asked Nectar.

"Yes, they do. Their prettiness feeds my senses and discomposes me. I fantasize about cuddling up to and adoring them. Beyond that, I've not contemplated."

"You don't have a predilection for a particular breed, then?" wondered Nectar.

"I don't suppose I do. A species does beguile me. It is outside our lot. The humans." This declaration elicited sharp whistles from both Twilight and Nectar. Bat shocked himself. He had not reflected on the appeal of mankind to him and had not planned to justify it. Now his fervor spilled out. "In power, they may not rival the lions or elephants; in knowledge, they may not rival the oceans, heavens, or primal cypresses; in intelligence, they may not rival the bees or dolphins. In looks, they are no match for the stallions or us," Bat grinned. "However, when you aggregate power, knowledge, ingenuity, and appearance, humans have no competitors."

"So, you aspire to court your superiors?" said Nectar. He coiled his tongue far back into his throat, skimming Bat and Twilight and debating if he should proceed. His audience kept mum. He continued, "From what I understand, those of us who fall for someone we judge superior belong to one of these categories: one, we envy and hate the objects of our longing and are totally obsessed with them; two, we idolize, worship, and hanker to be with them; three, we delude ourselves into believing we are them. An inferiority complex is at the core of all three. They are lost souls. The first group tortures themselves to no purpose. The second group is idiotic minions. As for group three, we won't deign to contemplate it. Please enlighten me about the fourth group to which you belong."

Bat had never dealt with such probing. He revered humans, and they profoundly attracted him. Did these emotions stem from an inferiority complex? Was he a minion? He refused to credit that. On what basis, then, was his attraction to human beings, and what was his aim?

An interval lapsed. He said, "There may or may not be a fourth group. It isn't important, is it? What you've stated—the three categories—are opinions of yours. Excellent, though, they are. What I'm about to remark on are feelings—specifically mine. Foreign entities have always entranced me. They represent the unknowns. Unknowns could be frightening—but also invigorating. They engender elation and thrills. Humans provide the ultimate dissimilarity to bats. I hold their intellect, innovation, dexterity, and fortitude in high regard. They are blessed with agile and sturdy limbs and a strong torso. Their physical and mental capacities promote infinite possibilities. The shelters they've built and the devices they've invented to plow their fields, to weave their clothes, and to defend their territory combine to corroborate this.

"I happen to think that they are beautiful. Their brows, their locks, their skin, even their freckles serve to captivate me. The masculine muscles and the feminine curves—"

"You are idolizing them," interjected Nectar in excitement. Nectar was in his element, playing the devil's advocate and loving it. "You do know they are not perfect?"

"Humans have flaws. I'm cognizant of that. They could be selfish—" Bat summoned his father's skepticism. "Cunning, vengeful, cruel. They could be violent and malevolent. They could display the worst characters ... But I choose to ignore their faults and emphasize the positives."

"The idealist! The born optimist," piped Twilight. For once, he did not pace, riveted by the discourse. "Undeniably, it's fun to court the sunny aspect of things. Since we are naïve and foolish, I don't see why not."

"I commend your attitude, Bat," said Nectar, smiling. "Speaking as a pragmatist, if I were you, I would interrogate myself."

"On what?" put in Twilight.

"Such as, what will I do with the allure? Or, specifically, what could I do with it? Will I be able to overcome the disparities between humans and bats? Do I want the challenge?"

Bat was unused to dissecting his aspirations. He had let them be and never fussed about the whys and the what-thens. Brows knitted, he said, "Currently, I have no answers to give. I have always been reluctant to analyze myself—or others. You've truly edified me. I realize questioning myself can be beneficial and may even be essential.

"The pull the humans have on me far exceeds that of the bats. It enlivens me. I perceive a connection between mankind and me. I don't want to transmute into them. I don't intend to couple with them. We are conjoined in a special manner. Don't ask me what it is. I have no idea."

21

Routine reinstated. The three bats reverted to casual chats and jesting. They hunted and dozed. The exchange had, in fact, impacted each of them. A stage had concluded. He was still a child but not childish. For the first time in his life, Bat pondered his future, wondering how long he should remain in the Bucegi Mountains. With the plum season almost over, the fruit bats' transit back to Egypt was inevitable. They could be gone any day now. He could attach himself to Purr's clan. Yes, he had befriended the tiny bat who was supposed to fancy him. It unfolded spontaneously.

He had been on his own, which he occasionally desired. Leaving his friends to their fruits, he jaunted to a freshwater swamp in the lowland. Mosquitoes, which he craved, were plentiful. He competed with the dragonflies, whose expertise in snatching mosquitoes equaled his own. But he had the advantage—he could prey on them. If he fed on a dragonfly that had fed on a mosquito, would he be feasting on two insects in a single stroke? Could it function that way? What an amusing notion.

Bat targeted the dragonflies by the water's edge. Among them was a hunter—a gorgeous chaser—who, in a trice, had devoured abundant prey. Should he test out his theory of killing several insects in a stroke? He vacillated. It would be a shame to kill the chaser whose sky-blue thorax was attached to a head the deep blue of the sea. His wings displayed an intricate pattern of cream and white, which transitioned to the blue of the thorax.

"Debating if you are hungry?"

It was Purr, the tiny bat—startling him. Flustered, he was at a loss for words. Composing himself, he said, "I am admiring the coloration of the chaser."

"You don't say! You see color!"

Bat answered in the affirmative.

"We're blind to them," the tiny bat said. Bat was silent. "No? It is unusual for us to discern them. How lucky you are. What are they like?"

Bat's parents and siblings distinguished colors. He had assumed the same for other bats. *What are colors like?*

"Well," he began but faltered. Don't panic; breathe, he coached himself inwardly. They were ubiquitous: red, white, green, yellow, pink, blue, and an endless combination of these. Into the spectrum, he said, "Has your heart ever felt a yearning—like a burn? That is red. Red's heat and the bloom on your cheeks." The tiny bat blushed. "You chew a pot ant with a belly of bitter juice. You grimace, and your teeth go weak. That is green, a prickly green, if you will. Green can be affable. The meadow, grasshopper, and seedling. Gentle and peaceful is blue, such as the limpid firmament. Turbulence is also blue, the soul of the sea. Yellow ... yellow is the sunshine and, analogous to the sunshine, can run to excess. With conceit, it stands out among its brethren, oblivious to their existence.

"A spectrum exists. You can go on and on. At one end is white. Elusive as a butterfly. It's the snow, thin air, pride. Opposite it is black. The night, the cave, and my fur." He studied Purr. "This is my interpretation of the many colors. There are various ways to depict them."

"Why can't I see them too!"

"You can," he said sweetly. "Look about you. Burrow into yourself and let your mind float. I dare say the splendor you see surpasses what I've described."

"Oh, you are wonderful," chirped the tiny bat, inclining her head. Bat coveted the comely top against his chest, but it remained angled as it had been.

He and Purr had been together since. As the parting of Nectar and Twilight was at hand, he divided his pursuits between them and Purr.

Twilight and Nectar had also changed. Twilight evinced less buoyancy, and agitation sprouted from the stoic Nectar. Bat attributed these changes to their impending exit, but the actual cause was more pragmatic.

"Fancy this, little brother: we will be adults come our reunion," said Twilight.

Twilight was correct. Adulthood was nearing. Would they ever reunite? The apprehension saddened him.

"We will each have broods of our own. I want to have wee copies of myself. So does Neco," said Twilight, nodding toward Nectar, who was feasting on mulberries.

"Nectar seems less composed lately. Is there a problem?"

"Oh yes. A bit restless, he is. Plans have been made for him to mate once we alight on our homeland. He didn't tell you? Well, his father wants to propagate his clan. One's compelled to harbor such ambition, I suppose. Neco's mother already has candidates lined up."

"Nectar isn't happy about this?"

"No, he is. But he is also uneasy. He's not even an adult. He'll prevail, though, being so sensible."

Bat nodded. "What about you?" he asked.

"Me? My getting to mate?" Another nod from Bat. "No arrangement has been concocted, and no proposal has been forwarded to me. Folks say that I have some maturing to do. Father is always at me: 'Banish your languor. Galvanize yourself, Twi.'" With these tidbits disclosed, Twilight's features disintegrated into hilarity.

The fruit bats departed in early autumn. Anon, the weather churned. The wind blasted, and a freeze gripped the great forests. The subsequent day, the freeze and wind vanished. Peace did not last. The fierce weather revived, more savage than it had been. In a few months, the high elevations would be snowbound. Winter would invade the universe. Bat's second adoptive family was on the verge of migrating south. He had not yet committed to being a member.

Bat debated if he should quit the Bucegi Mountains, where he had been for two seasons and where his parents had arranged for him to observe and participate. This wilderness was supposed to procure for him the fulfillment of the prophecy that his clan had presaged but was uninformed about its details.

At dusk, the rain ceased. Gnats, moths, and various bugs surfaced, which benefited Bat and Purr. After feeding, they lolled about on a bough. The woods murmured.

Neither of them spoke until Purr said, "To figure out what it is that connects you to the humans, oughtn't you interact with them? The prospect of you and the human race making contact in this remote region is slim. You may stumble on a huntsman, a rover, or an individual who has lost his way. Will that be enough interaction?"

The comment came without warning. He was fond of Purr's company: she could be quiet or voluble, in accordance with the mood of the moment. She had tan fur, sublimely structured wings, and delicate nostrils. Except for her fiery russet pupils, an inheritance from her mother, every feature of Purr was delicate.

Days earlier, he recounted the strongholds and villages he had explored. Purr did not interrupt with opinions or questions. Throughout the account, her animated visage showed how extraordinary he was. This feedback did not lessen his misgivings. How would she receive his confession of the spell human beings had on him and his belief in the link between him and man?

Gathering courage, he made a full revelation. His worry turned out to be unfounded. She did not judge him, shrink away, or lecture. She was not even astounded.

"This doesn't surprise me. Your tones and gestures have betrayed you—I could tell that you're infatuated with the humans.

You are a funny sort—in an endearing way, of course—so unique."

He clicked at her in such a way that she crimsoned. Oh, so proud was he of himself and her. And how sweet it was not to have to explain oneself.

No further conversation had been initiated on the subject.

Now, this questioning! It was astute of Purr, though. He must establish contact with the humans. But where to go?

Purr coaxed, "Travel south with us. We mean to have a recess in Târgovişte."

He gave no reply.

Purr summarized, "Father, Mother, and I will roost in a church. Father was born there. On the route of a migration, Grandmother went into labor. A number of bats were pregnant. The births weren't expected until the exodus was over. Father arrived early. Grandfather sped onward after entrusting two companions to Grandmother's safety.

"Grandmother delivered Father without complication. The membrane of his baby wings contained a fragile network of tissue fibers. Grandmother named him Vines. Father wouldn't miss this rare opportunity to visit his birthplace.

"We can stay behind in Târgovişte—say, for a week. Father will consent to it. We can join them later. You can study the locals and get to know the humans."

Bat fared well with Purr's parents, Dot and Vines. Dot was a fatter and faded version of Purr. Bat adored this portrait of a weathered Purr. Vines had patted him with his wing. The senior bats treated him as their own. Purr was born to parents past their prime. Dot had only Purr. Vines, on the contrary, had numerous offspring.

Dot was smitten with Vines, and vice versa. Time had not diminished their affinity. When Vines was away, Dot's spirits dulled. Conversely, his return lit up her face. Wrinkled and cheerful, it resembled a bright moon reflected in the rippled pond.

This kind pair moved Bat.
He was honored to be in their company.

95

22

In mid-autumn, they removed themselves to Târgovişte. Bat had persuaded himself that his parents would have approved of his plan. His father's choice of the Bucegi Mountains was brilliant: he had interacted with transients of diverse backgrounds and learned from them and about himself. To obtain broader experience, he must press on.

Once the decision was reached, Bat was jubilant. He awaited the adventures in store with zest. Purr was equally ecstatic: she had secured Bat by her side.

Their flight was serene, with the celestial bodies steering their way. They traversed lofty ranges with snow-bedecked tips; dense groves wedged in vales; and plateaus overlooking steep canyons. Through the ravines gurgled a river, where they quaffed water. They also sped over gelid lakes. At the outskirts of town, the four of them forged ahead while the flock nestled in the leafage below.

Purr and Bat sang along the way. In contrast, Vines had descended into muteness. His energy was devoted to his navigation. Dot struggled to catch up. Vines slowed down, but Dot signaled him to accelerate. Purr lagged behind as her mother's consort. Bat flew abreast of Vines.

A moat and a bulwark unfolded in the distance. They were above a fortified village. Vines slowed down, contemplating a church among cottages. He was trembling.

Vines glided downward toward the belfry. He hooked onto the tower, shaking fiercely. To give Vines space—and because Purr and Dot had not yet caught up—Bat scouted the church alone.

It was a humble construction, taller than it was broad. A semicircular apse adjoined a square chapel.

When Bat checked on Vines, Purr and Dot had alighted. Vines had calmed down and was talking to his wife and daughter. The three of them were examining a hole on the bell tower. Shaded by a projection, the aperture would remain in shadow even during the day and be difficult to spot. And night had obscured it. Vines beckoned Bat to perch next to him.

"You're back in time. I've been reminiscing about my birthplace. Mark the crevice there. Concealed in it, Mother and her attendants took turns grooming and nursing me. Mother was keen to recite the anecdote of my birth."

He added, "I apologize for my prior nervousness. I've been yearning to be here for ages. I'm gratified."

Dot ran her thumb down his back.

"Why haven't you journeyed here before, Father?" asked Purr.

"As you know, darling, the colony favors hibernation. I don't blame them as it's an extensive migration. Previously, the opportunity has not presented itself."

The senior bats shrank into Vines' special cranny. Bat and Purr rummaged through the village. Its layout was chaotic, and the dirt tracks, instead of being constructed, were the product of repeated trudging. The cottages differed in size. The materials varied as well, ranging from stone and timber to mud. The disarray directs your sight from section to section through the neighborhood.

"Humans generally herd together," said Bat. "There are solitary individuals who live alone and interact with the community when necessary. Humans are analogous to us to a greater extent than you'd think. See that pocket—" His wing pointed toward the cluster in the center. He then swiveled half a circle. "And the lone cabin at the boundary?"

"The bulwark is a pile of stones," remarked Purr. "Not buttressed like the others we've come across."

"True, it is of a modest height but serves as a deterrent nonetheless. Its rough composition accords with the haphazard mode of the village. Anyway, it's the inhabitants that appeal to me. Should we spy on them? Let's pick a target."

They chose the cabin, which stood out in its isolation. The seclusion lent safety to them. It would be easier to tackle a few dwellers than many if they were exposed.

Bat clutched a vent in the cabin wall. Purr followed.

The toss and turn of a body echoed upward. They shrank back.

Bat murmured, "I detect a person. Do you?"

Purr nodded.

"A woman, deducing from the contours. She's on a straw mattress—it's her roost. The wealthier humans place their mattresses in an arrangement called a bed. Beds provide greater comfort—that's what they believe."

"What should we do?"

"We'll hang here. She won't bestir herself before cockcrow. I can explain the pieces of her possessions to you in the interim."

It was a typical peasant's shelter: scantily furnished. This home was sparser. Stools served as substitutes for tables. Cookware, bowls, and plates—cracked and chipped—were gathering dust on a shelf. A stack was in danger of tipping over. No items ever seemed to get thrown out.

A plank supported by bricks constituted the tidiest area. A tub of apples and a hamper monopolized its ends. In between were arranged three clay pots, sealed with oilcloths. Nearby, pine needles strewed the floor. The caps had been removed, and the needles were usable. The base of a basket lay among them.

"She must be a basket weaver," said Bat. He peeked at Purr and discovered her dozing. He had been too occupied with his mission. Purr must be bone-weary, and he was detaining her. He prodded her gently with his nose and said, "Let's head back to the church."

"No," she insisted, in defiance of the apparent fatigue. "I'm fine. We could tarry here."

He caressed her with his snout and snuggled up to her. "The first blush will be upon us. She will be up. You'll see."

A loud snore sounded. She twitched—it had come from herself. *Who else could it have been from?* She endeavored to salvage her sleep. It was hopeless. She could not do it. Her eyeballs roved, and then the lids fluttered and lifted. She lay on her back, staring at the ceiling. She had been waking up earlier and earlier. Retiring at a later hour had not improved matters. She had come to accept it. Reminiscences relieved the inaction. She recalled her beloved leather pouch. Her father had caught and skinned a snake and stitched the pouch for her. She was the envy of the girls around. She used it until the leather tore. Another wave of nostalgia surged in. Her husband ducked in the entranceway, his tall silhouette delineated by the glow behind him. How arresting he was!

Lately, memories had difficulty surfacing. Her brain had deteriorated as much as her limbs. It fogged up or was vacant.

"She's awake. Why doesn't she get up?" wondered Purr.

"Humans don't cherish the dark. They panic in it and, at the very least, find it inconvenient. They work in daylight. She'll rise soon enough, you'll see."

Eventually, the woman stuck her feet out of the mattress. Buttocks at its edge, knees bent, she primed herself. In no event should she trust the stool by the pallet. It had toppled—along with the candle—when she pushed on it. It was lucky that she did not stumble and the candle was not lit. A lit candle upending onto the straw spelled disaster. She had better rely solely on herself.

She pressed first with her fists against the mattress and then her soles against the floor. Fortune was with her—she stood up with a single attempt. Pain seized her knees and hips. *How much longer would she be able to endure this?* She sighed and was upset with herself. Self-pity served no purpose. She would prevail somehow.

Slowly, the stooped frame shuffled toward the pit. She was so used to this routine that she could walk to the pit blindfolded. She had the essentials there: tea in the teapot, food, logs. Her toes struck a stool leg, scraping it across the floor. She had made it.

With the aid of a cane kept there, she lowered herself onto the stool to spark the tinder. A twig ignited, its light glinting off a strand of her silver hair. She added kindling and a log. A small flame would do the job. Water was already in the kettle hooked to the framework. The fire burned and licked the bottom of the vessel with its orange flicker. She tried to conjure up her husband to banter with him. Alas, he was absent this morning. She had to acquiesce to her solitude.

The tea brewed. She breathed in the aroma. The beverage was invigorating. The plate of buns on a stool beside her fell short of stimulating her appetite. Tea was sufficient for now. She could cook onion and parsnip soup later.

A ray sneaked into the interior to erase the obscurity of her surroundings. The apron was not on the peg where it should be. It was nowhere to be seen. Where could she have stowed it? She raised herself with the cane, accomplishing the task with relative ease. It must be in the hamper. She maneuvered through the clutter toward the plank. The receptacle did not yield the article. An idea struck. With unusual agility, she hustled toward the trunk. Bending down with her palm flat on the trunk for support, she groped the gap between it and the wall with her free hand. She found what she was seeking. For good measure, she shook the apron. Dust motes danced frantically. She tied the apron at her waist, tucked its hem into its strap, and then half emptied the tub of apples into the fold.

Dense clouds threatened. She was glad she had come outdoors wearing her mantle and cowhide boots. She hoped the clouds were not the forecast of a storm. The vegetables in the garden were far from ready for consumption. A storm might damage them. She hobbled to the well. Thank God they had the prudence to dig a well in the yard. Without it, she would have to resort to the village fountain. To have to haul the water the distance back was inconceivable. She cranked the lever. The pulley squeaked as the bucket lowered into the well. The bucket hit the water with a splash and was rapidly filled. She cranked the lever the reverse way. Twice the vigor was called for to reel the bucket up. She poured water into a pail that she had left on the wall of the well. The scoop within bounced merrily.

She staggered toward the garden and plopped the pail down next to the beets and onions. Relief swept over her. She panted and was tempted by the raggedy chair in which she refreshed herself now and then. Today she was disinclined to indulge herself. A mountain of chores was waiting to be done. Her obligations were not limited to garden work. Baskets had to be woven. A wash was due for her tunic and apron. Meals had to be prepared. But before all else, she had a visit to make.

She went around the vegetables to the burial site in the backyard.

Apple remnants scattered on the soil.

"You ate your apples," she said gaily.

She flung the scraps into the grove behind her abode, wiped her hands on her apron, and replenished the plate by the tombstone with fresh apples.

"Old dear, you didn't drop in the cabin. Are you having a lie-in?" She smiled at the tombstone. "It's time to be up. You used to wake me. It's my turn to repay the favor. You must be overjoyed that our tree is laden with apples. Remember, it bore so few fruits? It's compensating. The apples are crisp and sweet, aren't they? Eat as many as you want; there's a bountiful supply of them ... I'm doing well in general. My body aches, but that's aging for you. I can't complain. My fortitude hasn't slackened—I'm able to look after myself. Did you shadow me just now? I lugged a heavy barrel of water for a distance. You're smart to have dug the well. I can't manage without it. Well, I must be off. Duties are calling me. Till tomorrow, then, love."

Bat and Purr had been observing among the foliage.

23

They ventured north. The sky had refused to darken; its violet hue was caught on the terrain below, purpling the grass. The flat country extended for miles, with the tributaries of the River Ialomița serving as the water sources.

Low walls bordered isolated cabins with barns for animals, grains, and sundry other riches. Men and beasts had reposed. Crickets supplied staccato notes to the songs of the horned beetles. Near town, the farms ceded to denser communities. Coppices or cultivated fields divided them into pockets.

Bat and Purr reached the square. No sign of life showed.

"There's no activity," said Purr with dejection.

"We can nap a bit," said Bat with exaggerated jollity to lighten Purr's humor. Purr essayed a trill.

Here, the calling of the insects was inconspicuous, for their habitats had been encroached upon and their numbers had dwindled. The inn and shops stood crammed together. Grass plots were scarce.

Bat and Purr balanced on the chimney ledge. From this vantage point of the inn, they monitored the rutted lane, scrutinizing anyone questing for lodging. Bat swung on his claws while Purr pretended to be napping. A fly darted near her. She ignored it. It whizzed away and whirred back. *Buzz. Buzz. Buzz.*

The buzz suddenly died off. Bat had swooped into flight and, in a flash, snatched the pest.

Purr beamed at Bat.

A thin adolescent emerged from a shed, alerting Bat and Purr. *How could he have not considered the backyard?* Bat reproved himself. The bored Purr had obviously distracted him. They hurried to the back of the inn.

A girl of about fourteen or fifteen, candle in hand, was treading toward the inn. Her footsteps had roused the dog by the well. Identifying a familiar figure, he swallowed his growls, wagged his tail lazily, and settled back to his rest. The girl slipped into the building.

Purr and Bat wondered why she was up in the middle of the night. They flew to a glimmer in the lower story. The girl had placed the candlestick by a plate of gourds and parsnips on a table. Gloom hovered over a section of the kitchen. In the lit area, the girl was bending over a basket of linens. She heaved it up and propped it against her hip. The temperature indoors must be as raw as that of outdoors, for her breath misted up as she blew it out with the effort.

She plodded to the candle. With the load at her side and the candlestick in her hand, she trudged to the hall. Her strength amazed Bat. The linens must weigh as much as her bones and flesh combined.

The candlelight spilled on her kin by the grate. Her mother grumbled, her father scratched his chin but snored on, and her brother, next to him, did not react. "Afina, is that you?" her mother inquired, but the girl skulked away as if she did not hear.

In an upstairs vacant unit, she unloaded her burden and set down the candle. She then folded back the shutter to ventilate the mustiness. Bat and Purr, who were outside, puzzling over how they could watch the girl, were aghast. They backed away but not swiftly enough to evade being discerned. To their amazement, neither yells nor thrown articles assailed them.

The girl, ignoring them, inhaled hard and deep. The purple cast had dissipated. A slate tone loitered. The steeple of the church across the narrow street was visible. By day, crows dallied and bickered on the cross until the tolls of the bronze bells dispersed them. The bells chimed at dawn. This reminded her to make haste and wrap up her tasks. The idea of bumping into the guests sickened her.

She was plunged into this terror of strangers when a toddler. Patrons, lured by the recent brew, crammed the inn. The smell of ale, salted pork, smoked fish, perspiration, and sour breaths swelled into a stench. Afina, who was playing on the floor, wheezed.

All of a sudden, the confined cacophony gripped her. It was deafening, menacing, and of all sorts. Dins, yawps, crude jokes, the clacking of pewter tankards, farts, belches—all infused with dissonant, drunken songs. Sweat poured out of her. She was surrounded by wild beasts. Her stumpy legs sprang into action. She was up and dashing away.

The next moment, hands seized her by the armpits, lifting her into midair. Bloated flesh confronted her. An acrid stink invaded her nostrils. A kiss wetted her cheek. She squalled so loudly that the drinkers fell into a hush. Forthwith, bedlam recommenced, aiming at her and her tormentor. Her mother rescued her from the drunk. Afina yowled on until her father knocked her unconscious with a slap.

Her phobia toward strangers intensified along with the years. The approach of them, even from afar, tensed her up. Flee, she must. Any delay presaged disaster. The nearer the intimidators advanced, the faster her vitality drained away. Escape became impossible. There and then, akin to a lamb being led into a slaughterhouse, she surrendered to her fate.

She trembled and had difficulty breathing. A choking sensation strangled her. She moaned. No sound flowed out. All that remained was to endure the impending annihilation.

The strangers, for their part, were mostly oblivious to her suffering. They passed by without heeding her. This did not pacify her. Teeth clattering, she pursued them with her eyes. When the oppressors perished from view, stability slowly settled back in. Those who noticed her were merciless: they fussed over her as if she were a wounded animal. Swooning would have spared her the agony, but she never did. She shrank to a puny frame to limit the pats and caresses that came. The torturers had the least idea of the anguishes she bore.

She must keep these menaces at bay at all costs.

A broom and a bucket of water (a rag draping from the rim) were in position. Her brother had fulfilled his commitment, though Valeriu tended to forget what he had promised to do. She was thankful not to have to sneak back for the implements.

The occupant had been tidy, which allowed swift cleaning.

When the room was dusted, she listened to the noises in the corridor. All seemed to be tranquil. Bracing herself, she stepped into it. The candle she carried flickered in the draft. Eeriness lurked. She resisted the impulse to bolt. The clomping of her shoes would disturb the occupants. It would be terrible if they sprang out of their rooms. It was crucial to remain quiet, which was not easy while juggling the bucket of water, the broom, and the candlestick. She had left the hamper behind and tucked clean linens in the fold of her apron.

Tread after tread, her footfalls echoed ominously with the creaks of the boards. Her peripheral vision flicked to the passing doors on either side; someone might stick their head out to accost her. Despite her dread of confronting him, if a lodger appeared, she must—without delay—locate him. Conflicting forces besieged her. What else did she have to tolerate?

A loud pop exploded. Her heartbeat halted. She sucked in her breath. She faced where the pop initiated and immediately backed away. The crooked shape she beheld was a fiend. It retreated too! She almost screamed. Thanks to ample practice, she was able to stifle the shriek. Inwardly, she grasped that it was her own shadow. The joints and boards must have settled and popped. She moved on.

Bat and Purr had lost sight of Afina. They listened for her bustle. Window hinges whined. They glided toward the whine. The girl within was about to strip the sheets from the bed.

"I think she feels oppressed," said Bat.

Purr fixed her mystified gaze on Bat.

"Didn't you pick up on her fear?" Bat was incredulous. Afina's disquietude was so palpable to him that he inferred Purr must have perceived it too.

"I didn't—how could I? Our view was interrupted. She was hidden from us. Now I see that she is pale and tense. What has frightened her?"

"I have no idea. Her trepidation was present before the corridor, but it escalated afterward. My heart pounded along. She calmed down a little subsequently. Perhaps the crisis, whatever it was, had subsided. I wanted so much to comprehend what was happening. Something made her timid; that was clear. I'm eager to uncover what it is."

"Ask her if you are so deeply impressed. I'm dumbfounded, though, that you could divine her emotional state."

The grate was lit to chase away the chill. Afina exhaled her tenseness—the day's ordeal was over. Her parents were engaged in inn activities somewhere else. Valeriu was wiping the tables. He regarded her drowsily, without greeting. Valeriu understood her ways and left her be. This insight of his brother relaxed her. In the right mood, they even managed a conversation of sorts.

With her parents, there were all monologues—delivered by her parents, obviously. *Peel the gourds, Afina. Beat the mats, Afina. Wash the linens. Feed the dog. Don't mumble, girl. Liven up, girl. Ungur, down the street, has died of tuberculosis. His daughter, who has married miles away to a thatcher, will attend the funeral. She'll bring her babies, all seven of them. Fancy that! The patrons crave my ale. In his day, your grandfather was the best brewer in town. I've bested him.* Her parents persisted with what they said. Her lack of rejoinder never deterred them. They used to reason with and cajole her. Ultimately, frustration and resignation drove her parents to acquiesce that they could not rescue her from herself. Now, she served no customers directly and was allowed to inhabit the storage shed. She cloistered herself there whenever she could. But her duties were endless. Periodically, she did her darning in there, in lieu of the main building. Because it entailed the use of a candle, its occurrence hinged on the indulgence of her mother. The lack of illumination in her cocoon did not daunt her. She kept to herself. With the inn asleep, she sat at the doorway to soak in the moon rays. The stars soothed her, as did the murmurs of the nocturnal animals. Once a horse summoned her with his nickers. Her suppressed spirits flared up. Renouncing the usual prudence, she slunk toward the stable. Luck was with her: she encountered not a soul and was able to pet the horse without incident.

Her stomach rumbled—cleaning and scrubbing had triggered her hunger. Trotting toward the kitchen, she almost smacked into her father, who was backing out, arms loaded with logs. She jumped to the side. Despite the heavy load, he paused to speak. But she slipped away and regretted it once more. She had told herself over and over to be civil. After all, she was fond of her father and loathed offending him. Yet somehow, she was always in the wrong. The demon in her always spurred silence.

"Want me to fetch you a mug of my latest brew, Afina?" boomed her father at her back. "It's definitely my best! I've outdone myself."

"Don't trouble yourself, Father. She won't drink it. She never does," remarked Valeriu. It was so: no one could impel her to drink ale, which perpetually evoked the nauseating reek from the past. The bloated drunk she recalled was ever disgusting.

"Tea is in the kettle, brewed for a while," said her mother from the worktable. The kitchen smelled of leek. "The leek soup has begun to bubble. You can have it with your tea and cheese. Then make the cabbage rolls with me."

Having deposited the broom in the closet and splashed the dirty bucket of water into the yard, she poured herself some tea. A lump of sugar would have perfected the tea, but she used it as a bribe for Valeriu. To get the bucket and broom arranged for cleaning, she had to go without the sugar. Any action to lessen the risk of bumping into a guest was worth it.

"Take a lump," said her mother. Noting her hesitation, her mother added, "You can take an extra one for Vali."

Happy with her mother's offer, she savored a chunk of cheese with satisfaction.

"Should I really speak to her?" Bat confirmed with Purr.

"Yes. She is heading to the shed with her food. Be quick. Intercept her. Don't let her slip in there."

Bat called. The girl did not hear him.

He reiterated his call to no avail.

"Try ag—*Ow!*" Purr shrieked and accelerated upward. A pellet had whizzed past Bat, missing him, and struck Purr. He shot upward as well.

They ascended to a safe altitude. The mongrel by the well joined the commotion below with its sharp yapping. It must have gone away; else the yaps would have been discharged earlier. The rumpus had induced its return. It bounded about while a juvenile hurled pebbles at them.

"That's enough!" Afina was livid at her brother for shattering the placidity that enveloped her. "Stop it. They are harmless. Look what you've done to my potage."

Valeriu scratched the back of his neck and tittered shamefacedly at the inverted bowl. To attack the bats, he had set the bowl of soup meant for Afina on the ground and tipped it over. Mimicking his pubescent master, the mongrel relinquished his ruckus and busied himself with the spilled soup. Finding it not to his taste, he resumed bombarding the sky, even though the bats had absconded.

24

Bat and Purr retreated to the crevice Vines and Dot had vacated to migrate onward. Valeriu's aggression had agitated Purr, and the sore in her lower abdomen vexed her. She was in a foul temper.

The ensuing evening, Bat proposed they haunt the inn. Purr declined his invitation. "A migration is transiting through here. My cousin is in the group. I plan to meet with him and tour the woods," she explained.

Bat compensated for his disappointment with a touch of relief. Mixing with the humans was not for every bat. If Purr were with him, his concern about whether she was entertained would distract him. There was also her safety to reckon with. It might be for the best that he stalked the inn by himself.

That was what he did the next several days.

The lass adhered to a uniform schedule: she got up in the wee hours to ready the guest accommodations and afterward laundered the linens in the backyard. The only variation was where she took her breakfast. In the shed, she ate and unwound. In the kitchen, she tackled chores amid sips of tea and bites of bread.

Bat had established a great deal about the girl. She was most at ease sequestered in her den. Bat sensed her relax, the strain in her body dissolving. She hummed a tune. With her folks, she acted taciturn and impatient. Bat surmised that her thirst for solitude brought about these behaviors. Her moods in the guest quarters were wholly different. There, worry was the norm. She was pure nerves. The corridor outright overwhelmed her. The root of her anxious moods had to be the travelers staying at the inn. There must have been conflicts between her and the travelers. Bat was determined to prove his belief. So far, getting her to acknowledge it had been futile. She was deaf to his clicks, try as he might.

He refused to despair. There had to be a conduit to connect them. He would unearth it. Purr might want to participate in the endeavor.

He arrived at the church. Purr was already there. She had been with her cousin again. She chirped happily, "This is a splendid region—the vegetation verdant. There is not a sign that we are in the depths of autumn. And there is no shortage of sustenance for us. Let's roam the thickets after resting."

Bat countered, "I was about to request your company at the inn." He related what he had assimilated. Purr said, "Since you have plans, I won't persuade you to wander with me. But we should consider leaving. Father and Mother are expecting us. My cousin and his cauldron have volunteered to be our guides."

They parted: Bat to the inn and Purr to her cousin. By midnight, Bat was at the inn. People had bedded down.

Inside the outbuilding, Afina, the subject of his interest, was pacing and gibbering to herself. An oddness nagged Bat. He recognized what it was—Afina's eyes were glassy. The oddest of all was his ability to see her. The walls had become transparent. He blinked to rid himself of the phantasm, but it was real: the interior of the shed was visible.

What has enabled this miracle?

A scheme hatched.

He chittered at her, "Miss, do you hear me?"

The girl stopped pacing and mumbling. She gazed at the spot where the chitter had come from.

She can hear me!

"Am I visible to you?" asked Bat.

No response came.

"You are as plain to me as if you were out here with me."

"Through the wall?" said a bewildered voice.

"Yes, incredible, isn't it? I'm the bat who has been shadowing you. You've had glimpses of me before; don't know if you recall. My name is Bat. What is yours?"

"Afina."

"Afina, could you come outside? It's easier to talk face to face."

Her expression clearly said, "No."

"Fine. Why don't you let me in?"

With uncertainty, Afina moved toward Bat. A slit opened up for him to enter. The slit drew itself closed. They were in obscurity. Bat explained, "I have striven to attract your attention without success. You didn't hear me. Now, we can chat. I'm jubilant. What has caused this outcome?"

Afina sagged.

"Are you well?" The slouched person was inert. "Afina, am I losing you? Do stay with me. We must capitalize on this opportunity."

The girl unfolded herself. Her conduct was so singular that Bat was at a loss as to what to do. She murmured to herself, "Sleepwalking ... Mother says I walk in my sleep."

Sleepwalk? Ah, while being up and about, she's actually asleep.

This is what did it! This low-conscious state has altered the dynamic between us: she hears me now, and despite the obstructions, I can see her. Exploit this, I must, and learn what ails her.

He hazarded: "You're scared of something, am I correct?"

Afina angled toward Bat.

"Your distress is pronounced, especially upstairs. Do the guests terrify you?"

No reply.

As Bat pondered how he could attract her attention, she said, "I don't want to be terrified."

"Sure. You don't. I wouldn't either. What's the reason behind it?"

"They're beasts."

"You mean the sojourners? But they are human beings."

"Beasts." She insisted.

A trauma must have befallen her, and the customers of the inn were the culprits.

"You are not afraid of me, are you?"

"No, I'm not."

"Why not?"

"You are quiet. Quiet is welcome ... Beasts are loud. Grotesque. Loathsome."

Bat conjured up the taverns he and his father had observed. The patrons could be boisterous, crude, and abhorrent. Poor Afina must have had an unpleasant experience. He pitied the girl and wanted to heal her wound.

"The owls used to frighten me. Their ability to rotate their heads almost in a circle, without repositioning their bodies, certifies them as one of our biggest threats. Remaining stationary, they lie in wait for their prey. Their hoots pierce the wilderness and used to petrify me.

"My mother believes a composed self can better handle such a forbidding predator. In the proximity of an owl, she hid us in the hollow of a tree trunk. I shuddered uncontrollably. As the eerie cries reiterated, the trembles slowly ebbed. Practice transformed my trepidation into acute vigilance.

"You could do the same. Confront your fear. That's how you overcome it. Would you give it a try?"

The dull countenance shifted into unease.

"This is our best chance. Your sleepwalking has affected us positively. You might very well find yourself calmer. The travelers are harmless. They merely journey through—" Afina's wince cut Bat off in mid-sentence. However, he doggedly plowed on.

"As I was saying, your condition makes unfeasible proceedings viable. The upper story may be less daunting under the current circumstances. Why don't you visualize yourself there and assess how that feels? No harm will come of it."

Afina closed her eyes. A flicker of nervousness seized her, then faded. Peace ensued. Bat judged that she had honored his guidance and the result was favorable.

"How did it go? Did your visualization finish without incident?"

Afina offered no reaction. Her lethargy bolstered Bat's belief.

"Terrific! The real test is to be there physically. The guest quarters might frighten you, just as the owl once frightened me. Face it. Your affliction will abate. Ultimately, you won't suffer from being there."

Afina stared blankly.

"Shall we verify how easily it can be done? I predict success. I'll provide my support if you permit me."

His invitation was accepted. Bat almost screeched with joy.

Afina crossed the yard and slumped against the back door of the inn. Alarmed, Bat dove to prevent her from sinking into a complete sleep but realized that she was keeping it open for him. He explained, "Oh no, I shan't fly inside. It'll be foolish to trap myself in an enclosure. The consequence will be dire if an inhabitant discovers me. I'll be outdoors, which shouldn't be a problem. I can capture your movements despite barriers. If you need me, holler."

Afina traversed the kitchen and the hall. A bat had emboldened her to take this trip. It was about facing fear. What fear?

She climbed the flight of stairs. Of course, her dread of strangers. Why was she so muddled?

"Marvelous effort. Be bold, amble to the far side, and then back. Prove to yourself how easily it can be achieved. There's no reason to be disconcerted."

The bat encouraged her through the walls. Yes, she was here to cure her phobia. The denizens must have retired, as the gaps beneath the doors were dark.

Her pulse thudded, yet no perturbation stirred within her. She felt detached. Her intellect warned her not to be complacent. She had a mission—which was to traverse the corridor. The mission spurred her into motion. Shortly, she reached the far end.

"Excellent. It has been easy, hasn't it? You aren't scared, are you? Now, turn around to this side to conclude the experiment."

She did as bidden. Suddenly, a door groaned. A chink opened, and a vertical shaft of radiance fell onto Afina, who had spun toward the source. The chink widened. A tall male, candle in hand, took shape. His broad chest strained against the nightshirt, and his bushy brows rivaled the thick black of his hair and beard. These traits, together with the stiff demeanor, bespoke severity.

The man intended to inquire about the tramping but held back as blood drained from the girl's complexion. She quaked so violently he supposed she was having a seizure. Lastly, a wail gushed out.

Afina fled at top speed, alarming the entire inn. Confusion spread. Afina's parents had risen. Valeriu muttered in annoyance.

"Her malady must have struck," said her mother. "I'll attend to her. You go and pacify the patrons."

Bat spoke to Afina, but she had woken up and could not hear him. Her mother's entrance into the backyard prompted Bat to retreat.

The outing had been a success. He had stumbled upon a method to communicate with the mortals and looked forward to telling Purr. Afina had done well. He had wanted her to loosen up

before tackling the guests. Unfortunately, the bearded man ruined
the plan.

25

Bat left the flat district in search of Purr. He accelerated north and veered eastward at a dale, which gave way to an oak grove. Then he sped north again into the mountains, following the brook described in Purr's directions. Water eddied gently along the streambed. Bat revived himself with cool sips.

He located the roost of bats in the woods. An elderly male shot him an indifferent glance. Bat addressed him.

"I'm in search of Purr. I'm her partner."

Hearing the name Purr, the elder warmed up. "We haven't had the opportunity to be acquainted. Are you of Purr's colony?" Bat denied the linkage. "Ah, I didn't think so. I used to belong to it. I watched Purr grow up. Any associates of hers are mine too. She and her cousin have gone to the swamp. Fly downstream. Aim for the spruces. Situated among them is the swamp."

Bat thanked the bat and pressed on.

Tall evergreens with scaly bark shot skyward. Above the waterline, crabs crawled along the trunks. Their grayish-brown shells blended with the bark, rendering them imperceptible. Hiding from Bat's detection was another matter. He sized them up as he dove downward. Perceiving danger, toads with bumpy skin swiftly plopped into the swamp.

An echo prompted Bat to swerve and catch a glimpse of Purr. She was partially screened by the spruce needles. Happiness surged up in Bat. As he was poised to call out, the branches crackled. A waft of pheromone stung his nostrils. A bat of powerful build flew out. It soared upward and, midair, reversed direction—then reversed again in an instant. Purr darted after the male into a pocket of dense foliage. The usually wary Purr was evidently mesmerized, for she missed detecting Bat, who was nearby. At the rustle of the needles, Bat flitted away.

Males had always been attracted to Purr, and she toyed with them. Bat was amused. But the cousins were not merely trifling; they were mating. How was he going to treat Purr? What should he do? He raged at Purr's disloyalty.

He flew back to Vines' birth cranny. Far off, a line of orange diffused the horizon. The orange mellowed upward into amber. Next followed a series of blues—subtle to vivid to profound.

Exhaustion overcame Bat. Without realizing it, he fell asleep.

When he woke, the anger from the betrayal had waned. A touch of sadness and regret took over. Fixated on educating himself about mankind, he had neglected Purr. Outgoing and fun-loving as she was, it was inevitable that she sought affection elsewhere. He was smitten with her. It was a pity that the displeasing episode had transpired. He pondered on what to do. Should he pretend nothing had happened? This he could not do. Should he remonstrate, then? Foremost, should he escort Purr to the south? If he pulled out now, their relationship would be severed. Was it what he wanted?

A tingle disrupted his thoughts. Purr had alighted, chipper and radiant. "How have you been? Ready to go? We'll hook up with my cousin and his gang near your beloved inn." She sent him a mischievous grin.

She's lovely, reflected Bat, and it's delightful to be with her. Nonetheless, he responded, "Forgive me, Purr, I will forgo migrating." Astonishment crushed Purr's gaiety. "I hope I'm not causing any inconvenience," added Bat. "I traced you to the swamp."

Purr jittered. She said, "Why didn't you announce yourself?"

"You were busy with your cousin." Purr blushed crimson. Bat was gratified but at once felt like a brute.

"Is that ... is that why you changed your mind? You know that you, not my cousin, are important to me. If you'd rather not voyage with a group, we can fly south by ourselves."

"To be honest, what you did with your cousin infuriated me. However, it isn't the basis of my decision. The occurrences at the inn are. You and your cousin merely precipitated the verdict. My endeavors have progressed to the point that I can converse with Afina." Purr's russet pupils doubled in size. "She was walking around in her sleep. In this peculiar state, she could hear me. It was a miraculous discovery. Barriers between us did not impede my vision of her. I became part of her world. I want to delve into this. And hence my decision."

A brief interval elapsed.

"Is there anything I could do to dissuade you?"

Bat asserted there was none.

Purr comprehended the finality of it.

"I'm sad about your decision." The corners of Purr's mouth inverted, but her dignity flattened them out. "I respect it, though, and won't try to persuade you to revoke it. It will be useless. Forgive me if I have enraged and hurt you. It wasn't done on purpose ... Our intimacy was fantastic, wasn't it? I treasure every bit of it."

"Me, too."

Both meditated.

"I guess I should say goodbye," Purr said with a hint of reluctance. She feigned a cheerful chirrup and departed.

A short distance onward, the mist swallowed all traces of her.

Bat frequented the inn. Afina had three sleepwalks. He spurred her toward the dreaded quarters, and with each episode, her aversion lessened. Overcoming her challenges soothed her. Her attitude improved. She handled herself with a degree of assurance and fidgeted less. To Valeriu's chagrin, she stopped bribing him. The extra trip to pick up the broom and bucket aggrieved her less and less. The definitive reward would be her ability to endure the sojourners. Bat chose to leave Afina to her own devices. There had to be a more favorable avenue than somnambulism to contact the human species. To establish this efficient way, he must expand his domain.

26

Bat has promised to hurl Dracula into the dream of an older girl as a sort of recompense for mocking him and refusing to revisit the cherry-lip nymph. So far, Bat has not fulfilled his promise.

They have infiltrated a dream since Bat's pledge. It was compact. The owner of the dream was an elfin girl of eight or nine. The elf bounced a ball against the path as she skipped. That was the extent of it.

Dracula doubts whether the elf noticed him. Even if she did, it would have been immaterial, as she was absorbed in her play. There was *no color*—not even the pallidity of parchment—in the dream. A tranquil incandescence prevailed. The scene, like those of the previous dreams, was lucid. The elf's hair was cut to the hairline and fringed her oval face. She wore a sash-tied jacket and open-toed shoes, an ensemble for boys. The jacket, characteristic of a stripling, was hip-length.

He is amazed he has maintained this much detail. As he mulls, details sprout. The dream grows engrossing. The elf's maneuvers were as sinuous as an eel's. She was fixated on the ball as she slithered. Half an inch of a seam on the orb had split. The peeled-back leather granted a peep of the stuffing beneath.

Unbeknownst to Dracula, this dream will be pivotal in his next venture.

With considerable delay, Bat delivers on his promise.

The dream belongs to a seventeen-year-old who broods on a balcony. She must be tall, as her bosom is above the balusters. Her elbows rest on the rail, tapering fingers fidgeting with a handkerchief. She shows off a houppelande of wool; its sleeves drape along her lanky body. Her forearms and the V-neckline of the houppelande disclose a chemise of linen. The damsel's chest quivers, as if in yearning.

She looks striking in the teal garment, the sun glossing the ridges of its folds. A raspberry belt fastened under her bust accentuates her shapeliness. The chemise is pale yellow. A tress of honey-gold hair clings to her breast.

The weather is crisp, as is she. The damsel has not bordered her dream with haze. Perhaps she plans to gaze into the distance. Her balcony looks down onto a bed of shrubs. Copying their mistress, the shrubs flutter in expectancy. They switch from lime to orange, lavender to violet, and back to lime.

To modulate the shrubs' nervous vivacity, hefty stones loll among them.

A shower suddenly trickles down, wetting the dog-roses creeping along the wall. The damsel collects the raindrops with her palm. As she does so, she catches sight of Dracula loitering below. Annoyance gathers her brows. Brusquely, she averts her eyes. Is she, like the cherry-lip minx, pretending to snub him?

Patience is the key. He resigns himself to it. The damsel—being the owner of the dream—holds the authority to make the initial move. Since she is copiously painted, what crafts could she resort to? *Patient! Patient!* He cautions himself.

Minutes pass with no development. Dracula devotes himself to the pensive beauty. Is she tarrying for a swain? Or is she dreaming of a life beyond her balcony, beyond the garden—running free? Are all maidens so dreamy?

They are intriguing, undeniably so.

The inactivity prolongs and galls Dracula. He scrapes the lawn with his shoe. The damsel remains aloof. He must act. He whistles a ballad that sails along the soft breeze. Meanwhile, he fends off the glare of the sun with his hand. Manly knuckles have already emerged on his slender, youthful fingers. The hands and the person will flourish into masculine entities.

The damsel glances his way. A trifling acknowledgment from her would appease Dracula. Instead, she quickly loses interest and is on the brink of forsaking him. Dracula panics. At this instant, the image of the elfin girl bouncing the ball billows up in his memory and gushes into the open space. Casually, yet forcefully, the elf skips in the expanse between the young pair. Dracula is as astounded by the turn of events as the damsel. They gasp.

Against the vibrant backdrop, the colorlessness of the mirage rules supreme. They have never envisioned such stunning beauty. Color teases and excites. Colorlessness transcends and pacifies. It exudes a silkiness that invokes one's desire to touch. Except that one hesitates, lest the contact sever the fragile link that ties beauty to man. The elf flows with grace and ease. At the same time, her actions are spirited. As is the lively ball. Each twirl uncloaks the frayed seam and the pink stuffing underneath. The pink stands out in this achromatic splendor.

Dracula drags his gaze away to check on the damsel. Tears of rapture roll down her cheeks while the petals of her lips tremble. Dracula cannot say whether she or the mirage is more seductive. He exults over this. But felicity is not for him to keep. The gate clangs. The damsel pivots toward it. Upon the entrance of her beau, her heart blossoms. The rest of the world vanishes.

Dracula howls   and breaks up the damsel's dream.

Thwarted, again! Back in the cave, Dracula sighs. He has been acquiescent. It was not to be. He promises himself, though, that he—not any other man—will melt the hearts of women. The promise shall be fulfilled.

Suddenly, Dracula awakes to Bat's scrutiny. The bat has been studying him. He stares back. If Bat belittles him, he shall revolt.

Bat does not scoff but watches.

What does he want?

Their association has not facilitated Dracula's ability to read Bat. What he can see is the creature's decline. Since Dracula came under his tutelage, the critter's decay has worsened. Lately, his fur has been brutally shedding, exposing blotches of raw skin. Bat looks piteous and absurd. Is he dying?

To be independent of Bat, Dracula must be able to propel himself into dreams. Bat has resisted imparting the technique. Whenever Dracula broaches this topic, Bat preaches patience. Every transaction has its time and place, the creature says. Since it is abominable to beg, Dracula tolerates the rejections. He will devise a method on his own.

Despite being well-versed in Dracula's wishes, Bat is reluctant to oblige him. As it is, he is jealous of the child who, within two weeks, has achieved what consumed him for an era. The child has the advantage of dealing with his own kind—a categorical advantage. Hurdles Bat has to overcome don't exist for Dracula. Yet the child remains dissatisfied. The arrogance of youth!

Jealous of a child! He ought to be ashamed of himself, but he is not. Being close to his deathbed, he feels entitled to indulge himself.

Whether Dracula values it or not, they will always be inseparable. Their ability to communicate outside of dreams is proof of their connection. Bat has been unable to establish this link with anyone else. The snugness they share as a unit is another testament. These pieces of evidence soften Bat's attitude toward the child.

Lacking the innate capabilities of a bat, Dracula has no chance of ever calling up and thrusting himself into a dream. So what harm is there in divulging the technique? It will show Dracula what Bat has endured—and how clever he truly is.

27

Bat settled in the center of town, several miles from Afina's inn. The tavern sold drinks and food but provided no lodging. Accommodations could be had at the local inn, similar to Afina's establishment. A hole in one of the tavern's exterior pillars served as an ideal spying berth for Bat.

At the crack of dawn, the rumbling of cartwheels and the clopping of hooves erupted. The unloading of wares, the laying out of merchandise, a whistle, and a guttural song trumpeted the start of the market. As the animals were herded into the fair, the moos of cows and the bleats of goats augmented the clamor. There were also the clucks of hens in crowded crates. The stalls displayed a variety of goods: vegetables and fruits, fish, grains, spices, pots and pans, apparel and shoes, and livestock.

Haggling permeated the public square. Adults sniffed out bargains and squabbled about the price. Children capered about and whooped. Not until dusk did the place calm. Even then, a wagon heading for the inn or the voivode's palace rumbled past.

The squabbles revealed to Bat the essence of humanity: a relentless quest for the upper hand. Even over a pittance, buyers haggled incessantly. The victors marched off with an inflated ego. In such a match, the hawkers, as a rule, proved to be the true winners. Society loved gossip. Many frequented the stalls for that purpose. A joke at somebody else's expense relieved monotony. A juicy tale alleviated the tedium of life.

The interplay between people was bewitching. Bat observed, assimilated, and relished the goings-on. He combated fatigue to follow the actions. He wore himself out, which was a blessing in disguise, for it imposed a respite. Eventually, Bat got tired of it all.

It became an obsession for him to interact. The city center was devoid of bats, which was understandable, as a populated community posed substantial risks for them. The dearth of somnambulists tormented him. He searched for potential subjects and struck none. He spied on the commoners as well as the voivode and his court. His vigil was futile. He had not formulated an effective tactic to communicate with the humans either.

It was critical to push on.

He relocated to Bucharest.

Weeks had expired. There was no noctambulist nor bat. Rain had moistened down the dust in the lanes and accumulated into puddles. Lacking motivation for activity, he shrank into the depths of his crevice. The locals shared his lassitude: they had deserted the neighborhood. He reminisced about a fierce deluge. A cat sprang onto a windowsill to scratch with her paw, begging to be let in. In a separate downpour, a dog yapped at the torrent from the shelter of an awning. Now, in this rain, no dog or cat loitered. The incessant pelting had driven them away. Even the tavern sign that swayed and whimpered in the feeblest breeze hung lifeless, conceding to defeat and letting itself be soaked without complaints.

No birds, no cats, no dogs, nor a living soul were to be seen.

Dreary raindrops confronted Bat.

Footsteps advanced. The patter rippled from the preceding block and skittered below him. Bat investigated. A lady was scampering across the alley, her back to him. Her hands were cupped over her brows to shield her face from the rain. Wet fabric adhered to her shoulders. Beads on her brimless hat converged and slid down her nape. With the absence of shelter, she scuttled on. The hem of her gown was smeared with mud and grimy puddled water. The lady rounded the bend into another alley.

The arrival and departure of this solitary woman reminded Bat of his own isolation. Sorrow overwhelmed him. He missed gamboling with Nectar and Twilight. Should he have accompanied Purr to a temperate climate? As he moped, a gilt thread spun out in the sky. He resolved to head toward the glimmer.

The decision turned out to be excellent. Bat perched close to a cluster of bats, counting on being invited into the group. A few bats appraised him. Their demeanor seemed to say, "Why is he on his own—a fledgling like us?" and "What is he doing by himself?" They were brimming with suspense and respect.

A middle-aged male with coarse, gray fur queried Bat. "Are you alone, son?" At the nod from Bat, he said, "Have you lost your way?"

Bat said he had not and explained that he had been without his colony for four seasons.

"This is extraordinary—a pup by his lonesome. You appear fit and healthy. I presume no misfortune has struck you. What has befallen your people? Where are they?"

Inquisitive bats had encircled them.

"My parents reside in Sibiu. They sent me out into the world. I have dwelt, in solitude and with colonies, in the Bucegi ranges, Târgoviște, and Bucharest."

"I say, it's quite an experience for a pup. Your folks must have abundant faith in you to have let you do this."

Bat shrugged. He had never contemplated his situation in this vein. The gray male's comments made him proud of himself and appreciative of his parents.

"Where are you off to now?"

"I don't have a fixed plan."

"Then, migrate with us." This was from a lively pup. Having chirped his invitation, he let out an *Oops!* at the gray male for not consulting him first.

The gray male ignored the underling and said to Bat, "We're migrating to the Rhodope Mountains. Do you know where they are situated?" Bat shook his head. "Almost three hundred miles from here in Bulgaria. The chains are ravishing. In addition, if you haven't had a chance to admire the oceans, the Aegean Sea lies to the south, and the Sea of Marmara is farther southeast. You are welcome to participate in our expedition. It's an excellent opportunity for you to build up knowledge."

28

Romping in the Rhodopes with fifty or sixty bats swept away Bat's loneliness and gloom. The easygoing gray male inspired them to live to the fullest. Their activities—whether scavenging, rollicking, mating, nursing, or lounging—were carried out in joy. The buoyancy bolstered Bat's optimism.

The Western Rhodopes, with their ravines and network of springs and rivers, were as enchanting as the gray male had claimed. The gorges served as glorious playgrounds for the bats. In the twilight, they could be seen meandering between the sheer walls of a chasm. Suddenly, a bat plunged downward. One by one, the band followed. The darts dove nine hundred feet down moss- and fern-draped cliffs to the cooing river below—to drink, or to skim the water. The droplets they kicked up were most refreshing.

The day waned. The bats thrilled at the vista before them. The fading sun had bestowed mellowness upon the austere clefts. Its radiance abated by degrees. As the surroundings adopted a smoky tone, the bats vacated the conifers to embark on their hunt. Jackals filled the wilderness with their yips.

Sculpted by water, the caves were as breathtaking as the canyons. The ceiling draped down in the shape of icicles. Alternate formations mimicked pendulous sleeves—one could easily visualize them ruffling in the breeze. The caves were the products of carbonic acid. Rainwater or melted snow absorbed the carbon dioxide in the ground to form the acid, which dissolved the underlying soluble rocks. Decades passed. The caves evolved.

Their galleries harbored hundreds of bats. In one section, a community hid in the folds of the pendulous sleeves. Farther into the cave, a different species nestled in peace on the ceiling. A member proclaimed himself as an exception. He shrilled at a peer twice his size. The diminutive mammal was agitated. He protruded his chest to gesture an attack. His adversary answered the threat with a scowl. A cluster cheered them on. The angry bat shrieked and jabbed his thumb. Being vastly smaller, his thumb scarcely achieved the midriff of his enemy, who glanced at where he was poked, frowned, and withdrew. His mien indicated that he had had enough of the nonsense. The tiny aggressor lurched toward his foe but thought better of it. With a screech, he terminated the fight.

In the deepest recesses, yet a separate breed reposed. They incited no disorder or outcries. At dusk, they would be ready for their forage.

Bat reveled with the motley groups and basked in his popularity. They teased him. Bat indulged them. He embraced the power he had over the females and adored them in return.

He cherished Squirt, the juvenile bat who had invited him. Squirt's ability to rotate 360 degrees in flight, sometimes twice in a row, captivated Bat. It was a novelty to regard a fellow bat as a little brother. So far, he had always been the junior, irrespective of his age. The misconception stemmed from his stunted size, infantile physiognomy and, to some extent, disposition. Had he graduated from the junior status?

With the autumnal gold, orange, and red suffusing the region, the gang aimed for a milder climate. They flitted over rivers that reflected the kaleidoscopic forests and, many summits later, reached the southeast Rhodopes. Here, the peaks were substantially lower than their western counterparts. The gathering of vultures and eagles rattled the bats. These were birds to be revered from afar. Whether separated or in a kettle, they presented a spectacle.

"A testimony of power and grandeur," Bat's father had said to him. He and his father had ensconced themselves in the cavities of a tree trunk. They detected a mighty bird dominating the vault of heaven. "That is what their flight is. If you entangle yourself in their trajectory, you must outmaneuver them. Take advantage of our ability to turn sharply—they're no match for us in that." Now, venerating an eagle from afar, he recalled his father's words.

A fog swirled in. The vapor revived some of the melancholy Bat had previously suffered. He mused about home. His noticing the goat with a tuft of beard aggravated matters. It was late. The stars sparkled. Bat was out with Squirt. All the animals had retreated to their dens, so they were intrigued to hear tapping. A woolly goat scaled a cliff as though it was there solely for his use. The only sign he might be tense was his bustle. The palatable shrubs did not entice him. The steep incline was equally ineffective in slowing him down. Was he severed from his flock? Had he recovered his track and was racing to unite with them? It struck Bat that he himself had gotten lost too and should double back to Sibu.

The gray male opposed his plan. "Winter is at hand. Long journeys aren't advisable, especially not for solitary wanderers," he said. "What's the urgency? Suitable weather will soon be here. Explore the ocean before you return to Sibu—that's my advice. You have the options of the Aegean Sea or the Sea of Marmara. Even the Black Sea is not much out of your way. They are all majestic."

When spring arrived, Bat opted for the Aegean Sea. Squirt wanted to tour with him but was forbidden by the gray male as their camp was expected back in Hungary. Bat grappled with sadness and exhilaration simultaneously. Instinct instructed him to regroup within himself—to sharpen his focus before engaging with humans again. To do so, he ought to be unattached. An extended period of companionship also boosted the appeal of solitude. He felt ungrateful, particularly since Squirt had ceremoniously somersaulted twice as a farewell gift. Bat was touched by this loving gesture.

The Aegean Sea at eventide was a silver sheet, undulating with waves. The sheet blended into the horizon. By the coast, froth rang the protruded rocks and nibbled at the dusky sand. Where the water caught the remnants of the sun, the sea shimmered gold.

A distant rasp diverted Bat away from the enrapturing panorama. He traced the sound to a fisherman in a honey-yellow doublet and rust breeches, dragging a trap along the beach. On his back hung a creel of his catch. He tramped toward the cottages on the hills.

Off the shore moored a boat, on which a woman was folding a net. She wore a turquoise headscarf and a sepia smock, covered by an apron of coarse material. The waves bobbed the boat. Task over, the woman uncoiled her body and tittered at the man's rushed strides.

The husband and wife rekindled Bat's curiosity about humans. This passion of his had never deserted him, and the couple roused it from dormancy. He was anxious to reignite his fervor. But he must call on his clan first. Would his colony find him improved?

At Bucharest, Bat inhabited the cranny that he had formerly occupied. The location called to mind his demoralizing prior stay, where he had searched diligently but found no somnambulists. Should he apply himself again? He was tempted, eager to renew contact with humanity. On the other hand, he was not mentally fortified to confront defeat. What if the frustration recurred? Should he delay the pain that was to come?

A rustle emanated nearby. An urchin—whom Bat, lost in rumination, had missed—sat up across the street. The child must have nodded off. The glazed eyes on this five- or six-year-old betrayed him as a noctambulist.

What luck! Without exerting himself, what Bat wanted had materialized beneath him. He dove.

"Hey," he chirped.

The sluggish eyes rested on him.

"You hear me, don't you?" he said.

The irises enlarged, and the ragamuffin squealed.

"Hush. Sorry to have frightened you—may we talk?"

The scream swelled to an ear-piercing level.

A hag stuck her head out from the dormer above them. The curses she inflicted on the waif intensified the child's distress. The hag withdrew to the interior. A minute later, she dumped the contents of an ewer straight down onto the street.

The ragamuffin gagged. Urine dripped from his greasy hair onto his brows and nape. He flicked it off with his fingers.

Bat pitied the poor sufferer and regretted that he had caused him misery. He failed to foresee the terrifying effect of his greeting. It was impossible to reverse what had been done. Leaving the urchin seemed to be the best option. He should have practiced caution. The general public was not as accepting as Afina.

29

"I revised my tactics," says Bat. Dracula, on the brink of speaking, is interrupted by Bat, who asserts, "No, I didn't realize then that dreams were the channel to my success. The idea sowed its seed during my sojourn home. I spent a lifetime nurturing it and bringing it to fruition."

"I could have told you dreams were the natural next conduit," volunteers Dracula.

"Could you now?" Bat says mockingly. The child is unenlightened as to the toil required to slip into the dreams of others. His conceit irritates Bat. Bat must rectify Dracula's misconceptions. "Is it really so natural to transition from somnambulism to dream-entering?"

"Dreams also transpire in the course of sleep. Since sleepwalking serves as a channel for you to contact us, it stands to reason that our dreams can promote comparable results. Few of us sleepwalk, whereas we all dream—often multiple times a night—yielding abundant opportunities for you. It also eliminates the drudgery of searching for somnambulists. You can easily deduce that dream-entering is your next act."

"Is it so apparent? Educate me on how to manage the transition."

Dracula squirms. He says, "Saying it's a logical progression, I refer to the 'what,' not the 'how'."

"To locate a willing somnambulist is laborious and exhausting. It is viable, though. Interacting with her in her dream is a challenge. How does one steal into a dream, which is not a physical entity? Transitioning into dreams is far from intuitive, contrary to what you believe."

"I maintain that it is—in concept, at least. You are right—to actualize the concept involves deliberation." Dracula concludes with a grin, a sign of his concession. His deportment proclaims his ardor in the topic.

"Besides deliberation, industry is an essential component. I have to thank my father for his guidance, which enabled me to fulfill my ambition."

The enthusiasm generated by Bat's visit waned after he had called on relatives and friends and dealt with curious members.

He met with Snotty and Gravity once and Orange twice. Snotty had become a father. During their adolescence, Snotty was plagued by his appearance, but having pups seemed to have shifted his perspective. He donned an air of sophistication. Gravity had also become a parent, with pups of her own. She scrutinized Bat up and down. Bat swallowed and waited for the appraisal to end, which took a while. Finally, Gravity chirruped, "My, you look so foreign. You resemble the transients who stay in our habitat. Your size is constant, though. I've anticipated a lengthier and sturdier build, a globe explorer as you are. But you haven't grown—not even a wee bit."

Bat rarely looked at his reflection, so he had no idea whether he'd changed. As for seeming foreign, no one had ever mentioned it before. What was she insinuating? Since Gravity was pleased with her remarks, Bat let them slide. She chattered on about her pups. When he asked after her mother, she said her mother was well. Then, she resumed babbling about her offspring.

Orange lacked a mate. A sentiment Orange emphatically disputed: "Who says I've no mate? I have had my share. None steady, that's all. Who would want to be tied down, eh? Not me." He was as attentive to his preening as ever and relished the adoration thus induced. "Unlike you, I am not the exploratory sort," he said to Bat. "Novelties could be exciting. But they aren't for me. This forest meets my needs."

Ample cordiality had survived between Bat and his childhood playmates, but they were not reacquainted well enough to warrant sharing his secrets. He fared no better with his relatives.

One night, the stars livened the firmament with their twinkles. He and his father tarried on a branch of a leafy poplar. Bat fixed his interest on a beetle.

Camouflaged in the green hue of lichens, the beetle crawled along the mossed limb, his slender legs industriously engaged. Approaching Bat, he discerned danger. He pulled his legs and antennae under his hardened forewings.

The balled-up insect was frantic. Bat had not intended him as a meal. He had already eaten. He was disinclined to harm the minuscule bug.

To placate the bug, he backed away—but the gesture only worsened matters. Certain that a predator was near, the beetle unfurled its hindwings. Buzzes of frenzy punctuated his mad escape.

"Haven't dropped your habit of toying with your captives, eh?"

Bat dismissed his father's banter. "I backed away to avoid startling him. He was ambling along. I ruined his tranquility."

"My son has matured," jested his father.

Bat rejoined solemnly, "Father, I beg for your guidance."

Since his return, in stages, he had related stories of his new mates. Depicting Nectar and Twilight to his family resurrected the affection he had felt for them. He had not missed them. Nor had he missed Purr. Was he heartless? Did he lack sentiment? No, both assessments were false. He was positively sentimental. He was even attached to the hollows in which he cuddled. But he had not missed his friends. They popped up in his reveries, and that satisfied him enough. This characteristic of himself rather puzzled him.

His siblings, who had adhered to the same locality throughout their lives, squeaked at the physical attributes, habits, and food of the bats he recounted. Foreign groups had ventured into their territory, but these were brief and limited events. Indifferent toward the humans, his siblings eschewed the excursions he and his father took together.

His parents were joyful. Having him near, any tales he narrated were worth hearing.

Bat concealed his courtship with Purr. He also kept secret his contacts with the somnambulists and the debate he had with Nectar and Twilight on bonding with the humans. It wasn't that he didn't want to share them. The words got trapped in his throat. Why was it so difficult to divulge these special experiences? Could it be because he never had to express himself? Growing up, his worries had been adolescent frets. His innermost feelings were latent. Being raw and abstracted, it never occurred to him to dig them out, let alone disclose them to his peers.

His family were introverts. Their private nature inhibited them. He finally broke with tradition and blurted out what he had to say. It was only logical that he entrusted his father with his confidences—their intimacy made it so. Once initiated, the narration flowed out more easily. He detailed his adventures, especially those with Afina. His father listened with evident approbation.

"All this is fascinating," his father said. "You have wandered far and endeavored much. I had noticed the draw of the humans on you, but never suspected that you would dare to contact them. And with such success."

"But I am stuck. Somnambulism isn't the solution. So far, a productive method has eluded me."

"Don't let being stuck frustrate you. This is a well-deserved break. Difficult tasks demand time and energy. It is normal to come across an impediment along the way. It's wise to unwind.

You will feel refreshed. You understand these. That's why you're here."

His father patted his back with his wing.

"Father, what would you advise? I don't want to be restricted. My goal is to communicate with any human I want."

His father mulled.

"Well, examine the skills we possess. They very well may serve to overcome your obstacles."

30

Bat assessed the skills he was born with: flying, adeptly capturing insects, hanging inverted, and using the rebounds of sound he sent out to navigate and hunt in the dark. All were noteworthy talents, but what did they have to do with achieving his goal?

He had faith in his father's advice and reasoned that his skills were the key to unlocking his problems. The remarkable calls of his species circled back to his meditation. However, he had sent them out to the humans, and nobody except the somnambulists heard him. So, what could the calls do for him?

After leaving Sibu, Bat navigated eastward along the Transylvanian Alps and then northward up the Eastern Carpathians. He roosted in mountains where settlements were established. The massifs, with their depressions and plateaus, suited his purpose. Hamlets sprouted in the depressions and on the plateaus halfway to the peaks.

He must confirm that humans were incapable of hearing his calls. To do so, he launched a series of experiments. He lurked high up in the territory of a goatherd. The herder and his animals tramped up the slope. The goats grazed from plant to plant along the way. They must have been recently shorn, for they were without their wool.

Pines bordered the pasture up top in an undulating line. They spanned the volcanic ranges that sheltered the valley. At the crest, the groves yielded to harsh rocks.

The goats were guided to a tract of sorrel and grass. The herder operated with dexterity; his charges fell in line with waves of his staff. Sweat covered his forehead from the climb; he mopped it with his sleeve.

Bat conducted his test, chittering at the herder. No response came. Altering his tone only heightened the discouragement.

He tested the city denizens: a physician, a cooper, a carpenter, and an urchin. None of them heard him either. Humans were unable to hear him—at least, not in their waking hours.

Bedtime was his last resort, which worked to his advantage. It was far safer for him to operate at that time. He haunted the settlers, studying them by the lancet arches of the windows and sending them clicks. The goal was to master the residents' habits and attain a breakthrough.

The breakthrough came one night.

Bat had been watching a woman sleep. The woman's breathing and eye movements slowed down. Her muscles relaxed with random twitches. Gradually, the eye movement ceased and muscle activity greatly diminished. The woman was in a deep sleep. After a while, her breathing sped up. Her eyeballs moved back and forth rapidly under closed lids. Her arms and legs, on the other hand, seemed to have become paralyzed.

Bat was riveted. He almost forgot his mission. He clicked his tongue to elicit a response from the sleeper. A likeness of her popped up instead. A daisy in her hand, she was smiling at the giver of the flower. Despite the pockmarks that marred her features, the joy on her face made her fetching.

The portrait evaporated. It allowed him no chance to react.

Had he seen her dream? If he had promptly reacted and spoken to her, would she have heard him?

"See, I am correct!" exclaims Dracula. "Dreams were your obvious choice, the best communication channel. If we were acquainted then, I could have saved you a lot of trouble."

"Precious boy, you don't get it, do you?" says Bat, vexed. "The 'trouble,' as you call it, is worth it. Major pursuits involve a process. The knowledge accumulated can be cultivated into power. Even those we believe useless could end up valuable."

"If you had deduced, without delay, that dreams were your objective, it would have spared you the tedium of monitoring people fidget in bed," retorts Dracula. "What use is the observation?"

"Here you are wrong. *Dead wrong.* I've garnered crucial information from it. Vivid dreams occur in a phase during which the muscles are inert. The exceptions are those controlling the eyes, which make random rapid movements. These tidings perfect my timing when entering into man's dreams."

Dracula utters no rejoinder. He yields to Bat's blunt contempt with a hurt mien.

Bat hiccups.

"Stop being a fart, Bat," he says to himself. "It's normal for a fourteen-year-old to jump to conclusions. Wasn't I the same? I, too, was impatient for outcomes and thirsted for success straight away. Life taught me that it was ineffectual to be rash. Dracula will learn the workings eventually."

To make amends for being harsh, he says, "There's merit in what you said, son. The interminable vigils did get dull. The snores and grinding of teeth grated on my nerves. The worst was the constant defeat. Let me acquaint you with the process and its hardship. Strained by my abortive undertakings, I hid from humanity. To cool off and heal my bruised spirit. There, in my refuge, the songs of the insects and the rustles of the animals mollified me. Even the *who-o-o* of the owls evoked conviviality, reaffirming familiarity and dependability. Optimism germinated. Travails appeared endurable. The solace resuscitated my resolve to meet the obligations at hand.

"But often the stress lingered in my seclusion. Guilt for ducking responsibility weighed me down. Reengaging myself in the villages entailed a mighty will."

For four years, Bat had witnessed numerous dreams. He was restricted to being a viewer. He ached to penetrate the dreams, be a component, and communicate with the dreamers. None of these was achieved. He consoled himself that time and determination would remedy the situation.

Seeing the images of the dreams was an accomplishment. Buoyed by the leap forward with the woman with the daisy, he redoubled his efforts. In the early stages, failures far exceeded successes. He caught a meager number of dreams. Usually, he drew blanks.

Trying to shake off his melancholy, he summoned thoughts of the insects he relished and busied his mind with mundane concerns. All these were unproductive. Despondency persisted, destroying the feasibility of a real escape. Insomnia reduced him to bones.

He never gave up. Not because he was brave. He dared not bring himself to quit, plain and simple. If he gave up, what would life be? He mentally blocked off the option, forbidding his mind to wander down that path.

Forging onward, he must.

Optimism reasserted itself. Courage was revitalized. He bounced back. Labor plodded on till the next letdown.

He was spun through these down-and-up cycles like yarn on a wheel.

Worries and qualms plagued him.

What is behind a call versus several to summon up the visuals of a dream? Why is he met with a void, irrespective of how he strives? What constitutes the successes—and the failures?

All amounts to how his calls interacted with the dreams; he was sure of it. Only if he were well-versed in what transpired inside a human's skull.

Through trial and error, he limped along.

He could hear the dreams he had captured. However, anomalies had struck.

Bat encountered this abnormal defect after an unsuccessful experiment. The muttering coming from the person was a sign that they were experiencing an eventful dream. Bat's inability to seize the dream exacerbated his resolve to score one.

The glare of a window caught his attention. He found a baby peacefully dreaming in the bosom of its mother. Bat cooed to the baby, and a beautiful picture emerged: the baby suckling at its mother's breast.

Something was amiss. The loud and wet suckling was delayed by a fraction of a second. The sound lagged behind the visuals.

Why? What triggered it?

Bat reasoned. The dreamer's brain was interacting with the pitches of his calls. If the synchrony between the brain and the pitches was off, either the picture of the dream refused to surface or the sound foundered.

Through experimentation, his success rate in coaxing forth dreams increased. The key was to emit a pair of clicks close in pitch and tight in sequence. He was unable to dissect the reason behind this with any accuracy. The depth of the night helped; the deeper into the night it was, the longer the individual lingered in the dream stage.

The echoes of his calls carried back the activities of the dreamer's body and eyes. From these activities, he learned that the dream state coincided with rapid eye movements while muscles were paralyzed.

He honed his auditory system, stimulating the receptor cells in his ears. Listening intently, he registered each and every movement of the sleeper. Practice taught him their behaviors. Over time, he forecast the advent of the sleeper's dreams with precision.

Diligence and tenacity earned him the ability to embrace any dream. A skylark's song, the surge of a tide, or a casual dialogue within it was crisp. So was silence.

"Silence? Are you referring to the buzz you hear when nothing stirs?"

"No, not that," said Bat. "What you describe is external. I'm speaking of an internal essence tied to the dreamer.

"Envisage a vista of cypresses, with two rows across from each other. Rain is falling. A gallant, in black—a hooded onyx cape (slightly lifted in the act), an onyx shirt (slightly puffed up in the breeze), and onyx stockings and boots—bounds along. A navy sheen glorifies his shoulders and muscular thighs. He is not in haste. Maybe he adores the sensation fostered by the rain. Maybe he relishes hurrying on without actually hurrying. His feet lift off and then alight on the wet gravel. The gallant dances on, dream-like, as it ought to be. For we are in a dream.

"Neither his footfalls nor the splashing of the rain issues forth. Silence shrouds the spectacle."

Dracula gaped.

Bat continued, "Most melodic it is, the silence. The dreamer adjusts its cadence and rhythm to prolong and arrest the moments. The gallant soars and descends weightlessly; he is in bliss.

"Listen, the silence is not a sound, though it is melodious. It shields the event. It shields the emotions of the dreamer."

Dracula radiates keen interest. "The dreams we have infiltrated so far were devoid of this marvel. Can we enter one that allows me to experience it?" he hazards.

"I doubt it. The probability of hitting upon such a dream is low. Imagine how difficult it must be to capture the moments and modify their cadence at will. An unfeasible feat, I'd say. With the hundreds of dreams that I have engaged in, I encountered it once. If I were you, I wouldn't harass myself. Nature dictates that, as a novice, the visuals and content are your priority. As it is, they are electrifying. Why rush? Why not savor the present? The future will come. It always does. If by luck you stumble across the rare dreamer, she may or may not allow you into her silence. Your adeptness will enhance your odds. This is a case in which later rather than sooner works to your advantage."

"What if I keep calm? Will that boost my chance?"

"Keep calm! Do you seriously think you can? Consider your nerves tingling, your heart quickening. Have you forgotten the sensations and exhilaration of being in the dreams of your brethren?"

Dracula is in earnest.

"I've exceeded expectations and made significant strides," he stresses. "I am convinced that she will indulge me."

Bat weighs this. The child is peerless. But to fulfill his ambition, intuition and sagacity are insufficient. Chasing down the pertinent dreamer is an issue. "I've no idea where she will be," Bat says. "If hearing the silence is so important to you, I recommend you seek out your own."

"Seek out my own? How do I do that?"

"You need to figure it out yourself. I have not essayed to pursue mine. The tumults gnawing at me would've undermined my attempts. Silence within us is difficult to attain. Serenity isn't the sole prerequisite but a key ingredient. Your sense of urgency already exposes you to a disadvantage. Don't force it. Be honest with yourself—down to every bit of how you feel. Progress inward to gain equilibrium. Then, you will hear the euphony."

31

Even though Bat's clicks brought up people's dreams at will, there was plenty to assimilate. His role as a spectator persisted. There was no interaction between him and the dreamers.

A summer evening rectified this.

Bat was in the Sighişoara Citadel, lazing on an archway. A separate arch stood at an angle further away. Having taken on the dying sun's rays, it exuded a comforting warmth.

Footsteps, intertwining with a sort of rasp, issued from the angled opening.

A man, handsomely attired, shambled into view. He wore a long-sleeved, apple-green robe with a violet hem at his ankles. His flat-topped cap was grayer than his mustache. His arm cradled a thick volume.

He bore a peculiar gait, dragging his left foot along the cobblestones. This piqued Bat's inquisitiveness. The character slowly lumbered to where Bat perched. Under the archway, the scraping deafened the ears. The scholar's clubfoot, supported by a worn wooden brace, resembled a crescent moon; the upper surface of the brace grated harshly against the gravel, the toes bent upward beyond it. Each advancement of the right foot was painstakingly trailed by the scraping of the left. His back and healthy leg must be tremendously taxed. The hardship did not distress the man, who displayed no sign of grievance but rather poise.

Bat was mesmerized. With great effort, he refrained from mimicking the scholar's gait. He always had an urge to imitate mannerisms that were out of the ordinary and excited his imagination. He was deeply fascinated by the scholar.

Bat chased behind the man into the square. They passed the monastery and town hall to an ascending stairway. If the scholar was aware of Bat's presence, his deportment conveyed indifference. At no point did he acknowledge Bat.

The clubfoot battled the incline, flanked by laurels and a railing. The railing, knee-high, was too low to furnish support. Why had the invalid omitted to carry a cane? Bat was glad that, at the platform, the scholar aborted the clamber. The ensuing segment was steeper and easily doubled the length of what had been mounted.

The scholar caught his breath and produced from his sleeve pocket a piece of fabric to sponge his sweaty temples. He carried out his action coolly. A few minutes later, the sage—still drying his brow—entered a building consisting of a main wing and an annex, both with whitewashed façades and orange-tiled roofs.

The architect had juxtaposed the windows—two per wall—so that they acted as art objects, with the walls serving as canvases. This design was reflected on the western façade where windows placed in an L-shape adorned a lower corner.

The walls lured the eyes. So did their composition as a unit. They cut into each other and the space to bring out the grace of the structure as a whole.

The sage was not in the front section of the house. Bat scoured the rear.

Bat located the man among a sea of books in the study. Texts bound in calfskin overflowed the shelves. One was placed on his seat, squeezed between his thigh and the arm of the chair. He seemed oblivious to the disorder. Nor was he responsive to the fragrance of the myrtle flowers, which had floated indoors. He was engrossed in a manuscript on the desk.

Except for the intermittent buttock shift, the sage was inert. Bat, to break the doldrums, slipped away to the roof. The height afforded him a panorama of the square and the residences lining the narrow cobbled streets. Far beyond the citadel, the river coursed. Its outline faded as the sky darkened, then eventually disappeared.

The wind blew. The myrtle and the climbing ivies whispered: *sha, sha, sha—sha, sha, sha.* Bat dove back down. To his frustration, a candle had been lit, and the man, instead of having retired, concentrated on the pages.

Bat waited.

The gloom redoubled. The candlelight magnified the intelligence of the sage's countenance and the bulk of the volume. The wind had died down. The periodic flipping of a page was audible.

The monotony fatigued Bat.

He sprang awake from nodding off. The sage had fallen asleep. His eyes darted underneath shut eyelids!

Bat readied himself and clicked. He had assumed the echoes would carry back the sage's dream. Instead, they pricked his flesh and jolted him. He clasped the window ledge with all his might. If he fell, he was certain he would plummet into the abyss.

His skull was stuffed up to the stage of explosion.

The tremor in his body lasted for a few seconds, leaving him dizzy. An acute sensation of floating enveloped him.

Suspended within an invisible enclosure was a bar, the ends of which dissolved into fuzzy zones. The sage had hooked onto it with his clubfoot. He swung gently upside down, completely at ease.

The sage oscillated upward 180 degrees to face Bat. From that height, he gestured warmly to Bat. "Welcome to my sanctum," he said.

"Are you addressing me, sir? Am I in your sanctum?" asked Bat, astounded. "How did I get here?"

The sage unhooked his clubfoot, somersaulted into the air, and let himself sink downward. A magnificently crafted hardwood chair, materializing out of nowhere, enthroned him. Amid the blanched ambiance, its burgundy attracted notice—like a magnet.

Bat cried, "I'm in your dream!"

"Indeed, you are," said the sage on the throne.

Bat was ecstatic. "It's happening! I've gained entry into man's dream!" He wanted to flit around to celebrate, but not knowing where the hidden boundaries lay, he held back. If there had been something to cling to, he would have swung excitedly back and forth. Nothing of the sort offered itself. Even the bar had evaporated.

"You have—by my permission."

"By my permission?" This appendage curtailed Bat's exuberance.

"Well," the sage scanned the surroundings. "Sorry that there is no available seat. Why don't you relax by hanging from the ceiling?"

"But there's no ceiling."

"Don't be so sure. Don't hover about."

Bat contemplated the emptiness above.

"Pull out your claws."

Hesitantly, he pulled out a thumb to snatch at the void above him. A surface pressed down to meet him. It was tender to the touch. He hooked onto the tissues. The sage winced. Then he pulled out the fingers of his other hand and clutched. The sage winced anew. Bat had latched onto an invisible ceiling.

In and out. In and out. The unseen boundary pulsated.

"Contented, eh?"

Bat, brushing aside the queer pulsation, nodded. "You said you permitted me into your dream. So, without your consent, I would not be communicating with you?"

"Ah, that. Correct: without my consent, you wouldn't be able to. You would have been an external spectator. This limitation should be temporary. Your steadfastness ensures an ultimate victory."

"I'm perplexed. What have I done to earn your permission? Could you enlighten me?"

"It's because we are family," came the reply. At this, Bat gaped. The image of the sage hooking upside down on the bar struck Bat.

"Oh, no," amended the erudite master, "not that. I'm not suggesting that we are of the same order. I don't fly. I don't produce high-frequency waves. I don't feed on insects.

"You see, my deformity has impaired my mobility but not destroyed it. Nor has it inhibited my faculties. On the contrary, it has spurred my creativity. You've witnessed my athletic abilities—in life and in this dream. To reach where you are, you too must be resourceful, inventive, and resolute. Now, do you agree that we're simply kin?"

"If that's your reason for admitting me into your dream, it's disheartening. Most humans wouldn't see me as kin. I'm fated to remain an outcast."

"Now, now. Think; don't fret."

The ghost enclosure beats.

"You see, it took me forever to bring up man's dreams with ease. The technique had been faulty. Either the dream kept out of sight, or there was a time lag. I—"

"Can you identify the sources of the mishaps and, likewise, the successes?"

Bat cannot.

"Our brain is active during the dream state when our eyes jerk in bursts. Its cells vibrate and generate electric waves. Your clicks enter our ears and are converted into electrical signals that are sent to our auditory cortex. If the signals are in lockstep with the dream waves, you see the dream. Otherwise, you behold none. What you have accomplished is phenomenal."

"I strained my resources and suffered for four years."

"Mm. With your shorter life span—" The sage mused aloud. "Four of your years, I estimate, are equivalent to twelve of humans'. A sizable stretch. But to conquer a challenge like this, the duration isn't excessive."

"I struggled constantly in the beginning. Sending a pair of clicks close in pitch improved my success rates. For them to work, the second click had to follow the first with just the right timing.

In the end, the echoes of my clicks transport the dreams forward seamlessly."

"Ah," exclaimed the sage, the invisible enclosure throbbing riotously. "Most impressive! As for the working behind this." He organized his logic and said, "You send the dreamer a pair of consecutive sound waves that are close in pitch and 180 degrees out of phase with each other. They overlay, and their amplitudes cancel out. A wave of much lower frequency results. This lower frequency harmonizes with the brainwaves in the dream state. That is, once our auditory system converts the resulting sound into electrical impulses and sends them to our brain, the impulses coalesce into the dream circuitry. *Poof*, the visuals of the dream spring up—by way of the echoes of the sound you produce. Sublime! Simply sublime! Not all frequencies blend with the dream waves. You must apply pitches that will derive the appropriate frequency. Which you have managed to do. Totally astonishing!"

Bat grinned.

The sage clapped.

"There was this curious defect—the sound faltered behind the visuals for an instant. This cropped up in a couple of initial dreams I had brought up. At that period, my successes were sporadic. What could have gone wrong?"

There was a brief pause.

"Was the humidity low when the defects unfolded?"

"I can't say—they occurred in the distant past. The air could have been dry."

"Dry air can slow the travel of sound compared to humid air. Temperature also affects its speed. Ignorant of the conditions under which you encountered the delay, it would be difficult to determine what caused it. The disruption likely stemmed from atmospheric factors rather than any action of yours—but wait. Did the lag disappear once you started discerning the dreams smoothly?" Bat affirmed with a nod. "I stand corrected, then. The delay might have originated from you—a temporary shortfall in your sensory function, perhaps.”

Unable to fathom what was said, Bat made no comments.

“It is possible that on those two occasions—you did mention two occasions—your temporal lobe was slow in synchronizing with your occipital lobe, resulting in the delay. Why did this deficit occur, you may ask? If I were to hazard a guess, I’d say your nerves largely provoked it. As you acclimated to the process, the delay ceased. It could also have been a trick of your mind. You were so focused that you weren’t heedful of what you heard. With the host of variances, we may never get to the bottom of it.”

“We should disregard that for now,” Bat said. “I don’t foresee a recurrence of the defect. As mystifying as it is, we had better not dwell on it. In my opinion, being able to enter dreams consistently is more pressing. Will you counsel me?”

“Sure, I’ll advise you. Your job is to connect with the dreamers as you have with me.”

“But I’ve no clue how I connected with you.”

“You do. You absolutely do. As soon as I trudged into the archway, you intuited our connection. That was why you shadowed me.”

“So, you were conscious of my tailing you?” inquired Bat. Receiving no answer, he moved on. “Something drew me to you.”

“Something?” remarked the sage humorously. “My maimed foot, you mean?”

Embarrassment burned Bat.

“Not just that—I couldn’t put my finger on it. Still can’t. As I flew behind you, the itch intensified, and I was determined to explore your dreams.”

“See, you do comprehend how you connected with me—by intuition. It drove you to tail me. A powerful tool it is, intuition. Utilize it. You must also incorporate industry. So far, you have accessed our mind; next is to access our heart.”

“How do I do that?”

"By means of toil, ingenuity, and resiliency—the ingredients that have gotten you where you are. Study our dreams, which will divulge manifold hints about us, even our innermost secrets. You've mastered our dream state and the art of extracting our dreams. Bold innovation will steer you into our dreamland. Channel into our emotions, you must. If you channel into our emotions, you channel into our hearts. The mutual bond that binds you and me is rare. You must be prepared for hard work. I'm not saying you have to be accepted by every human, but enough of us must be at peace with you for you to belong.

"Once you are inside a dream, what the dreamer can do is limited. They may dispel the dream to get rid of you. They may resist you. It will be a slow evolution—conceivably slower than what you have experienced so far."

"You're scaring me. Are you saying the fight will be at least as long?"

The sage concurred. "Unfortunately, the answer is yes ... Don't be dejected. We are talking about the heart. The intangibles are what concern you. You appreciate the difficulty, don't you? Setbacks will be plentiful. It is important not to be discouraged; no doubt you're alive to all this. Be comfortable with yourself. If you aren't, how are we supposed to be comfortable with you? Achieving ease is challenging. Understanding yourself is an effective start."

32

"The recommendation of the sage is judicious," says Bat. "Understanding oneself boosts one's confidence and consequently one's comfort level, both of which I lacked. Not being of your species had amplified my difficulties. The public, in general, distrusted me. A number of them still do."

***

Once entering the dream, Bat was apprehensive. The usual resolve was absent. Should he risk it?

He gambled and advanced. Sensing his intention, the mistress of the house stood up, her demeanor glacial. The legs of the chair she had occupied scraped angrily against the floor. Bat froze. He appealed to the daughter, who was gawking at him from her seat. The mistress yanked her daughter up and away. The girl twisted around to prolong her gaze but was jerked into an alcove. All along, the mistress had refused to glance at Bat. It would have been beneath her.

"Why do you have to infiltrate my dream and outrage my wife?" said the master at the table. His intonation was icy, and he glowered with hatred.

Bat apologized, "I regret it if I have intruded. I don't mean to offend. Merely wish to be a friend." The tremor in his utterance was alarmingly conspicuous.

"Friend? Be real. A lowly, hideous anomaly, and you want to consort with us!"

The disdain cut Bat.

"If I am so intolerable to you, why did you allow me in your dream?"

"I didn't. You sneaked in. Be off! We don't want your kind here."

The aristocrat grabbed an apple from a plate on the table. Bat flinched, ready to duck. But instead of hurling it at him, the man sank his teeth into the glossy fruit and stared him down.

***

"This was how humans viewed me. They strove to bar me from their dreams as well as their environs. The passage of time has mellowed a few hearts. These individuals have learned to be less threatened by my presence and reconcile themselves to it. However, a mass remains steeped in their insecurity. They loathe me and things foreign to them.

"Steadfastness has trained me to deal with the dreamers. I have a good handle on their perception of me when I'm at the threshold of their dreams. For those who choose to converse, I'm happy to indulge. For those who ignore me, their dreams march on as if I am not there."

"How do you cope with those who openly reject you?"

"There's not much they can do, is there? I am already inside their dreams. They seethe. They resent me. A few try to be clever by dissolving their dreams, which results in frustrating themselves because their dreams are now truly disrupted.

"Human beings applaud people with confidence. Perhaps because that is what they lack. Perhaps it's harder to knock down someone secure. They tend to approve of such characters. I exhibit my poise. That I stand on ground as solid as theirs. That I am composed before them. Sensing this, some drop their guard. By dint of hard work and practice, I have succeeded in haunting any dream. Permissions from the dreamers are superfluous."

"Why do you inflict yourself on people who don't want you in their dreams?" Dracula asks and then blinks. "Ah, I know—you want to win!"

Bat pauses to think.

155

"I refuse to back down. Is that what you mean by my wanting to win? I've earned my right. Gaining access to dreams has been a daunting task. I've grappled with sorrow, joy, fear, shame, anguish, anxiety, guilt, and more. I have become excessively aware of my feelings. I brood over every behavior of mine and am oversensitive. However, comprehending my feelings has its rewards; it enables me to empathize with others. The dreamers exude shafts of emotions. Into these shafts, I navigate. Into the dreams, I journey."

"Even so, it is jollier to be welcomed. We humans aren't all cruel. There's a broad spectrum of us. Some would offer you cordial receptions. This is the group you should seek."

"A minority does appreciate us. Bats are essential in the cultivation of crops—by dispersing seeds and pollen. We curb the population of unwanted insects, such as mosquitoes, crop-eating beetles, and worms."

"Did you consult with your mentor further?"

"No," replies Bat. "He wanted me to be on my own and barred me from his dreams. After my ultimate triumph, I confined myself here. As I've met you, I'll bestow my insight on you and thrust you into dreams. To attain your goal may take a lifetime. Don't let that harry you. Significant goals often require a lifetime to consummate. We progress bit by bit. On and on we go. Slowly— very slowly—a framework is constructed for us to hold onto. It is far from perfect. To polish and beautify it, we toil on. Such is life."

"All this sounds bleak," says Dracula.

"Bleak? No. Far from it. Life is poetic."

Bat marvels at his own assessment. A little while ago, the adversity of life gnawed at him. The confinement in the dungeon was unbearable. The trepidation that what he yearned for might never materialize was equally poignant. Often, he was petrified of having to meet the future.

The drive to accomplish has stopped him from simply letting things—and himself—be. Enjoyments have deteriorated into duties. Duties into burdens. How can he pronounce life as poetic? And yet it is his sentiment, and poetic is the precise word he wants to use.

"Yes, life is poetic. It is a collage of our moments. Your collage is in its inception. Affix as many pieces as you can. As for myself, I'm exhausted, and rest beckons."

33

Dracula listens intently. The empty space hisses. The hiss is neither beautiful nor special: definitely not the melodic silence Bat has praised.

Go inward. Obtain equilibrium. What strange terms! Bat believes they are a means of achieving inner silence. The best interpretation Dracula can formulate is to concentrate. Even that proves to be difficult. The harder he exerts himself, the surer his thoughts drift. Frustration winds him up. Maybe the old bat is right: he is too greedy.

He persists, centering his faculties. The surrounding buzz escalates. Focus. Don't stray. Drill inward. Drill inward. But it leads to no accomplishment. He lies down and dreams.

***

In a field, two saplings grow, their branches devoid of foliage. Behind them, their siblings, also naked, line up in a row. None of the tree limbs touch.

The gray brightness of winter permeates the landscape—more gray than bright. The snow around lacks shimmer. Its uniform whiteness deepens the desolation. Patches of ice clamp on the brittle boughs. They are frigid and unrelenting, these patches. No birds sail along. No beasts parade themselves. The field is forsaken.

Dried spiked rampions pierce above the snow. How has he wound up in the field? The quiescence hits him. Not a single whirr or hum. Has he struck the silence of the dream?

***

He wakes in exhilaration. Almost simultaneously, thunder explodes, shattering his gaiety. The boom is not that of thunder but of the dungeon door roaring. This enrages him. He longs to sample the silence in his dream, wondering if it is indeed the silence Bat claims. Having been interrupted, he would never find out. A sudden conviction quells his wrath. In the midst of the glare at the entryway looms a silhouette. A torch in hand, the silhouette sashays down the steps into the dungeon. The keys fastened to his belt jingle. Directly behind is a similar outline. The jailers have come to release him!

Dracula leaps to his feet.

"Here he is," says a coarse voice. The torch illuminates Dracula. "Looking well, aside from being soiled and dusty."

Dracula becomes sensitive to his foul condition. His armpits stink. Why has Bat not expressed repulsion?

"Don't worry, prince. A wash will remove the grime," cackles the jailer. He signals his associate to marshal Dracula toward the exit.

"Hold on a minute," Dracula says and speeds off.

Dracula fades into a dim area from which rings out, "Hey, hey, are you up?"

"Who's he jabbering to?" says the leading jailer.

His partner says, "Nobody else is locked up here—as far as I know."

A crack resounds, followed by a clack.

The jailers dart toward the commotion. Dracula flings a broken piece of floor stone at the wall. *Smack!* It strikes a protrusion and ricochets off. To dodge the ricochet, Dracula twirls aside.

The jailer elevates the torch. From a fissure in the masonry below a rafter, dried claws stick out.

"God almighty, a dead bat!" squawks the jailer. His associate mumbles a series of curses. Both recoil from the ominous sight.

"Dead?" says Dracula. He asks for the torch. The jailer hesitates but complies.

The jailer's assertion is accurate. Bat is dead. The claws are stiff. His shriveled carcass is rigid and lifeless. Sadness weighs down Dracula. The image of the forlorn, recent dream wells up in his mind. Is the dream a premonition of sorts?

Bat's death does not come as a shock. The old creature had deteriorated to fur and bones, shedding mercilessly, and had appeared to be on the brink of exhaustion.

What is surprising is the depth of grief Dracula feels in his chest. It is more profound than what he would ever have contemplated. He has harbored disgust toward the relic. Bat's weirdness fomented a mixture of awe and scorn in him.

His mentor is dead; henceforth, he has to fight his battles unaided.

Oaths shoot out behind him. The proximity of a dead bat warrants such vehemence. The jailers jostle him along.

At the threshold, he pays his respects to the dungeon and suddenly shivers. A bat with sleek fur flies from the interior to the outdoors. His mental faculty must have gone wild. His gut insists it was no phantasm. What he caught a glimpse of was as real as the jailers nearby. The snout, the button orbs, and the baby fangs were distinctive. Triangular, conspicuous ears sealed its impishness. It wiggled an ear at him. It was Bat, a child version of him.

Part II

Dracula

34

Desert sand gold.
The bodice which clings to
Her bosom and waist.
Buttercup yellow.
The lace crisscrossing
Her bust.
Naked:
Her pliant neck,
Her earlobes,
From where dangle delicate chains.
Attached to each—
A black pearl.

The flute hums,
Merry and rich.
Dracula makes his entrance.
A musk of masculinity
Tinges the air.
The cleft that rises
From between the dimples of her buttocks
To her nape deepens.
Her neck slants
To elongate the eager jugular.
She weeps
As passion penetrates
Every inch of her.

The flute pipes on.
Pulses accelerate.

Green,

Purple,
Blue,
Orange
Bubble in the mind,
Whirling the senses.

A gasp.
A rush of
Metallic odor.
The fangs
Sink in the flesh.
Music desists—
Silence.
Colors convert into a glow.

35

He dabs lavender-water on his brows with the tip of his little finger. The scent titillates him. His emerald orbs sit in symmetry above his nose. They have hypnotized thousands of mortals. People succumb to their power. It will always be so. A grin plays on his lips. Ah, as to his fangs, Countess Movilă, Princess Mihalovici, Madam Drăgoi, Baroness Velica, Aurelia, Margareta, Violeta—to list a few of his conquests—are giddy with bliss as the points dig into their flesh. Need he say more?

He is Count Dracula, king of the undead, ruler of the night. Why then is he wretched? He puts the bottle of perfume down. What accounts for his dull heart? His hearth is chilly. Can a crypt be any other way? It's a crypt suited for a king. Here is his canopy bed with its muslin curtains, his embroidered pillows, and silk sheets. The sconces, above the night tables on each side of the bed, shed two spheres of velvety light. With a rug over his knees and *The War against the Ottoman Empire* on his lap, he lolls on a sofa, away from the luminosity. He revels in reading about his valor on the battlefield. He has always been as powerful as the sun. With knitted brows, he sighs, for the sun—which he once worshiped— has long become a hazard. Darkness is his consort.

He sought to vanquish the Ottoman Empire. A wandering healer advised him to drink human blood—to gain superhuman power, even immortality. He took her advice and started his reliance on human blood. In the end, he abandoned the living and embraced the undead.

Three centuries ago, Bat propelled him into dreams. He envies himself the euphoria he once felt. He even envies himself the discontent and rage that had boiled within him. Anything is a relief to the numbness he is experiencing.

He has surpassed Bat in astuteness and attainments, and now rules the dreams of man. Sadly, the sense of sovereignty no longer exhilarates him. When was he last in a dream? He has lost all interest in fanging princesses and countesses.

As a young child, he rejoiced in the morning rays, dancing through the lace curtains. He snatched at the shafts. How smashing it was that he could see them yet not capture them. There, in bed, he lay until Luminiţa breezed in with a bouquet of lilies.

Luminiţa, vigorous and loving, bent to kiss his forehead. He dimpled at her as she bent to kiss him again. He smiled afresh and earned an additional kiss. Only upon Luminiţa's entreaty of "Up you go, pet," did he bounce out of bed.

Sweet ballads enchanted Luminiţa. Whether she was perfuming the bathwater with rosemary, bathing Dracula, or putting laundered clothes on him, she sang, her song weaving around him.

He skipped to the table and ate in the company of Purgy, his doll. He preferred Luminiţa eating with him, but she was constantly busy with chores. In her stead hovered old Teodor. As Teodor poured him tea, his arthritic hand spasmed. It was a miracle he had never spilled the tea. Not a drop. Teodor was proud of this. His blurry eyes proclaimed, "See."

Ştefan Madoşcu tutored him daily. Luminiţa always showed herself then, sometimes even twice. She fluffed the cushions for Madoşcu and set down the tea tray. Madoşcu nodded slightly when he felt inclined; otherwise, he was aloof. Once he thanked Luminiţa, enrapturing the girl. Luminiţa was smitten and avowed that Madoşcu was the finest of men. In spite of being a child, Dracula had a dim apprehension of the futility of Luminiţa's infatuation.

Ştefan Madoşcu wore a garnet tunic in the winter and a stylish blue substitute of thin material in the summer. It being summer, he had his thin tunic on. He compensated for his medium height by holding himself erect, whether standing or sitting. A trimmed beard masked his chin, and a high collar concealed his neck; nothing but his face and very white hands were on display. At this moment, he had lowered his head to organize Dracula's exercise book—the back of his neck taut above the collar. Dracula swallowed hard at the veins underneath the translucent skin. Madoșcu concentrated on the exercises to feign unawareness of the child's attention.

Madoșcu straightened up to address the child. The collar concealed the flesh once more. Ștefan Madoșcu reverted to the austere master. Dracula, sensing he had behaved naughtily, simpered. He wished Madoșcu were more malleable and would continue their game.

Dracula's intrigue with the neck surfaced as a vague impulse—one that developed into a hidden thrill. Not till he was king of the undead, ruler of dreams, did he thrust his fascination into the open. Thenceforth, he nurtured it into an emblem of his myth, as famed as his lore. Now that fervor is gone. How could a passion he has cultivated steadily evaporate so mercilessly?

He is quite isolated, both physically and emotionally. This has been his mode of life. Surely, it can't have led to the loss of his passion.

Death has erased shrewd, wizened Bat. In his stead lives a child. Dracula had tried to converse with the child and eventually conceded that such an act was fruitless. He was fourteen then, and child Bat acted no older than five.

At five, Bat remains. He is engrossed in himself. A flight in the air or into a dream is magical to him, bubbling him up to no end. Anything else is beyond his concern. His former self has made it clear a life without burden is what he covets. Dracula has honored that and refrained from interfering with child Bat.

All these years, Bat has resided in Dracula's bones and soul. Bat has been an integral part of him, like an arm or a leg. Dracula seldom takes notice of Bat.

Dracula's dependency on Bat has been eliminated. Dreams are at his disposal. He penetrates them at will. He summons and dismisses the dreamers, as he chooses.

Despite his prestige, he assumes a solitary existence.

His solace is Purgy, the doll, even though it is heavily stitched and patched.

Rum, rum, rum. The lid of the coffin grumbles. Neculai, bulgy eyeballs and all, descends the stairs into the tomb. Dracula shoves Purgy under his gown.

"What do you want?" growls Dracula, clasping a limb of the doll. "Acting as my steward doesn't grant you the right to intrude on me!"

This is unfair. It is Neculai's duty to minister to Dracula. Tending to Dracula's wardrobe is part of it.

Dracula has been acting dispirited, cooping himself up in his tomb. He may allow Neculai to dress him; he may resist and mope around in his nightshirt. Neculai can endure Dracula's temper and caprice, but what he cannot bear is Dracula failing to be Dracula. To Neculai, there is no greater danger than Dracula persisting in this seclusion and its dire consequences.

"Pardon me, Count," says Neculai. "It's midnight. Might Your Excellency take advantage of the invigorating weather and go for a stroll?"

"A stroll! What rubbish you say!" Dracula retorts.

"It's just a figure of speech, Your Grace."

"Get me the reserves. I intend to stick around; I'm not flying anywhere."

"But it's heavenly outside—ideal for roving."

Neculai rolls his tongue. Dracula has not observed anything as abominable. His steward's mouth, which elongates from ear to ear, repulses him to no end. The buffoon probes into alchemy and sorcery relentlessly; it's absurd that he clings to a frog's peculiarities, unable to improve his appearance.

"Didn't you hear me!" explodes the Count. "Get out of here and bring me the reserves!"

Neculai bows and backs away. Dracula is vexed at himself; he should not have let an officious fool irritate him so.

36

Neculai met Count Dracula in the Carpathians. A silky moon idled in the sky. Stars swayed to the love songs of the mockingbird. Neculai croaked throatily by the pond. Hundreds of frogs colonized the mire. He had no trouble attracting a mate.

All of a sudden, fog developed. A moan emerged: the moan of a woman. *Why would a woman be in the marsh at this hour?* The search for an answer diverted Neculai; copulating shifted from his focus. He investigated.

The gaps between the tall grass revealed a man stooping so that his cape draped along his side. As suspected, a woman was in the gallant's arms. Her unfastened chemise exposed her shoulders and a round breast. Neculai gasped.

The beau removed himself from the neck of the fair lady. Crimson fluid dripped down his fangs. The lady attempted to reengage him. "Don't stop, Count," she implored.

Dracula released his conquest. She thudded onto the matted ground. Hanging onto the Count's calves, her posture evinced her lust.

Dracula licked the dribbles off his fangs. Bending to lift her chin, he said, "No, Sonia, darling, enough for the moment. You'd better be off." He exhaled a breath onto her face. She shivered as the iciness ran down her spine. In a trance, she staggered up, pulled her garment together, and melted into the cattails. The mist dissipated.

"I'm honored to be in your company, Count," said Neculai, who was enthralled by what he had witnessed. "I've heard about your legend. Never would I have presumed to meet you. And in a tract like this!"

"Who are you?" Dracula demanded. The orange and green frog on a sedge was half the size of his palm. The pupils of the amphibian glistened with reverence.

"Like you, Count, I am a prince," said the frog. "I'm Prince of—"

"*Ribbit,*" croaked the Count.

Perturbed, the frog scrunched his eyeballs inward with a faint squelch. Dracula roared.

Neculai was mortified but exercised restraint not to retort. When the Count's jollity subsided, Neculai elongated to full stature and averred, "I am Neculai Costin Anghel, Prince of Moldavia. A pleasure to make your acquaintance, Count Dracula."

The frog doffed an imaginary hat and bowed to the Count.

"What's the cause of your present predicament, my dear prince?" Dracula enwrapped the frog's diminutive hand in his own.

"Haven't you heard the tale of the wicked witch who was jealous of the fair Camelia? She cursed Camelia's sweetheart into a frog. The sweetheart was I. That was the long and short of the story. Popular belief has it that I was allowed to hop riotously in my parents' home. What hogwash! The blow was harsh: I was exiled far from civilization." Neculai sniveled. "You haven't had news of her, have you? No, I don't suppose you would. She's the sweetest of girls. We were to be married. But the witch interfered." Neculai sighed. "I won't spare any effort to establish what has become of her. I dare not imagine her staying bound to me in marriage."

Neculai sobbed without constraint. A puddle pooled at his feet.

Dracula tendered the frog his handkerchief.

"Thank you," said Neculai with a nod.

The handkerchief cascaded alongside him. He blew his nose. A perfume permeated his nostrils. *Could it be Sonia's—her fragrance steeped in the handkerchief?* He evoked the voluptuous breast and the ravishing nipple. Having swallowed his saliva, he declared, "You've rescued me, Count Dracula. I have inhabited this mire for too long, basking in the life of a frog. I sing all day, snap flies on whims, and enjoy an infinite supply of female frogs.

Thank heaven, you and Sonia reminded me of the superior human life!"

"We aren't exactly humans, you know?" Dracula winked at the frog.

"I'd give a great deal to emulate you. Will you undo the curse for me?"

"I don't see what I can do."

"You can restore me to my original form. As a frog, my options are limited, and it's unlikely I can fix my situation."

"My power is that of a sovereign, not an alchemist," pronounced Dracula. But on account of the comical amphibian tickling him, he relented, "I have a potion you may try. I don't guarantee any result; it depends on the individual."

Neculai bowed to the Count.

Neculai might be of service to him, reckoned Dracula. Unfazed by the sun, Neculai was free to run errands and could manage Dracula's property.

"You can live in my castle on the condition that you obey my rules and respect my privacy. If you ever defy my commands, I'll crush you with my thumb," warned Dracula.

37

Squatting, Neculai meditated on the towering beaker clamped onto the tabletop. *How can I empty the potion into it?* It would have been so easy for Dracula to pour it in for him, but the Count had flatly refused to assist. "It's your mission. You grind it out yourself," was his excuse.

What to do? Neculai must exercise his ingenuity to meet the midnight deadline. At the gong, he had to sink into the medicine. If missed, a protracted period might elapse before a full moon fell on the fourteenth again. Only if there were a miniature ladder at his disposal! Lacking one, he must improvise.

His pupils rounded at the two books stacked up on the table.

Like a shot, he was by the stack. Hands against the lower volume and legs splaying, he pushed—*hard*. The tomes, each as thick as the combined length of his body and outstretched legs, did not budge. He pushed with all his might. It was futile. In defiance of his shoves, the boulders moved not a fraction.

He changed his tactics. He tackled the one on top. With an individual book, his labor bore fruit. It yielded—sliding forward and leaving a gap for him. He hopped onto the gap and, puffing, pushed it along its lower counterpart. He persevered until it slid free and smacked onto the table. Gasping for breath, he permitted himself a respite. He must transport it to the beaker.

This he accomplished—taxed to the extreme.

He hopped onto the volume. The beaker remained lofty. He was unable to empty the potion into it. Despair overwhelmed him. Dracula had plotted the challenges. Such a tall beaker was evidence of it. The bulky tomes were stacked up on purpose. These contrivances fit Dracula's warped sense of humor. Neculai could not decide whether to laugh or be angry. He was firm about one thing: the task at hand was to haul the remaining book and devise a ladder.

With difficulty, the texts were lined up in succession. It was easier the second time around. He could have improved his pushing skills, or—having overcome the initial sluggishness—his physical strength had reasserted itself. The source of the energy was irrelevant. He was grateful for the result. Trials still loomed ahead: he had to stack them up.

It was an ordeal to wedge himself underneath the second book. When it was heaved up enough for him to sidle underneath, its weight shifted. He had to dart like lightning in order not to be squashed.

Now with it on his back, he pushed upright with full force and managed to shove an end onto its companion. His goal was to erect a stair. He achieved this by sliding the book along the surface of its stationary partner, forming a step.

He bounded up his creation to reach an adequate height. Then he returned to drag the bottle of potion to the top, poured it into the beaker, and flung the bottle away, not caring that it smashed into pieces.

He clapped.

Howls of wolves eclipsed his applause.

Neculai shuddered. He had never heard such hair-raising yowls, not even in the Carpathian wilds. The moon, disconcerted, went into hiding; Dracula's castle and its vicinity plunged into obscurity.

The fourteenth of the month had arrived.

Neculai held his breath and dove into the liquid. The foulness choked him, but he must bear it. He had to absorb the potion and cast his skin.

The concoction infused his veins and dazed him. Camelia, rosy with health, floated in space. Her hair eddied. Together, they spiraled downward. In the next instant, Camelia melted away. He was a naked baby, gurgling with delight. The witch burst forth and chanted a curse. The baby transformed into a frog and plummeted into the abyss.

Flop! The frog lay spread-eagled.

Neculai pushed on his limbs to stand up. Dizziness caused him to wobble and fall back down. "Damn!" he grunted. He battled to straighten up. His proportions were off. His toes were miles away! He examined his arms. They elongated into hands with flexible fingers! He leaped up rapturously. Upon alighting, he found a thin web spread between his toes. "Well," he said, with a wry smile.

He inspected himself in a mirror. The mop of orange hair on his scalp caught the rays of the moon and blazed. The moon was luminous. There were no traces that it had been rattled into hiding.

His hair was his best feature. His bulging eyes and wide mouth both conformed to a frog's. He lashed out his tongue and found it too short to touch his nose. Definitely the end of insect-snapping.

"What rotten luck," he muttered, knitting his brows. "The attribute I'd have gladly preserved is erased." A pat on his shoulder interrupted his brooding. He whirled around.

Dracula had materialized without warning. The tales of the Count raced through his mind. A glimpse at the glass confirmed that Dracula's reflection was not visible. Neculai was thrilled.

Dracula frowned at Neculai. "Is this the best you can do?"

"Yes, Count. For now, sadly," replied Neculai. In a happier tone, he added, "I can again engage in pursuits. I'll repair my appearance to your satisfaction, I assure you."

"Let's hope that will be the case," said Dracula. "You ought to adopt an identity. Be my steward."

38

Neculai counts the reserves on the shelves. Given the current situation, twenty bottles will serve for less than a month. Dracula's recent behavior nettles him. Acting high-strung is disgraceful enough. The Count's exasperation doesn't become him and is most offensive!

He must tolerate all of this.

Neculai has no illusion of Dracula counting him as a peer. To Dracula, he is a pair of willing ears to be claimed or banished on a whim. The snub hardly bothers Neculai. He is a prince, born to a boyar with noble blood. He will reclaim his status. Dracula often speaks in monologue. It is not that Dracula admires his own voice. He is too cocooned in his private world to be concerned with such conceit. He desires a listener, perhaps even needs one. Neculai is proud to be chosen.

Though no words of fondness or allegiance have ever been exchanged between them, Neculai has faith in their mutual loyalty. Dracula would dispute the existence of such sentiments and, of course, is entitled to do so. But fact is fact. Else, how has Neculai's collection of alchemy and medicine texts been mysteriously augmented? With the Count's nocturnal limitation, acquiring the volumes is a chore.

Neculai bathes in Dracula's glory. The Count rules the night and the dream domain. Hasn't Neculai himself been a beholder of the man's gifts? The power of the man is unmistakable.

Everything is nearing a crisis. The Count's erratic conduct has spiraled from bad to worse. His temper is vile, and his assignations with his mistresses have stalled. Their recent conversation is most troubling.

Dracula had breathed into Neculai's ear.

"Don't squander the night away, Nicu," murmured Dracula.

Neculai started. Grogginess notwithstanding, he was ecstatic that Dracula had left his tomb. The clock chimed half past four. The August clamminess was oppressive. Neculai reclined in bed. Dracula retreated into himself and paced back and forth, mumbling.

"It's about the size of a baby's nail," Dracula described the mole on Countess Andricu's earlobe. "The teensy hairs on it have me riveted. They are the source of the mole's velvety touch." Suddenly, he regarded Neculai feverishly. "Have I ever mentioned how delicate my mother's fingers were? They were slender, with pinkish tips. My nose lingered on them until she drew her hand away and chided me for being a silly boy."

Dracula lowered himself onto the sofa. There he fretted. His eyes, intensely green, snared your soul. *No wonder his captives are enamored*, thought Neculai, imagining the sensation of having the Count's fangs digging into his flesh.

"Are you happy?" asked Dracula in earnest.

Neculai processed the question. "I suppose I am," answered he. Having yawned and scratched his brow, he expanded on his reply: "My countenance isn't in its proper form. It shall improve. My stacks include lauded books of alchemy—partly thanks to your efforts and generosity. I'll develop a cure. For now, what I have suffices."

Dracula sneered. Envy tinged his expression. Sensing this debased emotion perturbed Neculai. Could the Count be envious of him whom the Count treated as an inferior? This was very sad, indeed. A tête-à-tête might let slip hints of how Neculai could remedy the abysmal state of affairs. But Dracula sank back into his sulks and altogether ignored Neculai.

Neculai offers Dracula a bottle of reserve. Dracula is fully donned.

"You're going out, Your Excellency!"

Dracula waves Neculai away and flies out of the mausoleum as a bat. The heavens, as Neculai has proclaimed, are divine. A multitude of stars sprinkles the inky expanse; the temperature is balmy, and the universe is tranquil.

The bat flies on.

In town, he alights on a bough. A red squirrel steals away, rippling the foliage. Earth beckons. Smoke from the chimney stacks disperses the scent of crackling logs into the atmosphere.

Not far away, Countess Andricu whispers Dracula's name. She sounds feverish. Dracula rushes into her dream and brushes her ringlets away with his fingers. He bends toward her neck. Countess Andricu's chest heaves violently. As the Count's fangs dig into her flesh, she pants. Her muscles tighten. She lets out sighs of ecstasy. On the verge of her climax, Dracula pulls out his fangs and dissolves from sight.

Countess Andricu staggers to the window. Dracula is nowhere to be found.

Dracula flies aimlessly above the town, his stomach nauseated. He feels unhinged. He wants to be rid of the taste of Countess Andricu, which has fouled his tongue. "I should have stayed in the crypt," he fumes. "It's Neculai's fault, the fool. Neculai despises my inertness, addressing me as *Your Excellency, Your Grace*—the lower the bow, the greater the derision. The worm, what's it to him anyway?"

An inn draws Dracula to it. A face pokes out of the entrance and beams. The person to whom the face belongs lets Dracula in. Her crown barely reaches Dracula's mid-chest. Her frame swims in her nightgown.

She reminds Dracula of a rat that he has once ruffled. Hanging from a twig, he spied movements at a clump of soil. A rat sniffed. Her head rotated from left to right and then from right to left. She sneaked out of her nest and scuttled through the shrubs toward the stream. Dracula swooped toward her. The clever rodent ducked into a tangle of roots and reversed direction. An interval expired. Her nose protruded above her burrow, whiskers jiggling as she chortled.

"I've been on alert for you, Count Dracula," the tiny woman remarks and chortles like the rat.

Dracula scowls at her.

"You visited my dream—" the woman pauses to giggle at Dracula's glare. "No, don't misconstrue me, no fangs in my neck! No, no." More giggles ensued. "I'm Madam Chan. I dreamed about you; that was all. You said you had two accounts to present. I was to choose between your disappearing act or you and the children."

Dracula is dumbfounded.

"Come, sit down," coaxes the Chinese woman.

Dracula hesitates. He has an irrational belief that madam possesses deep insight into him. What she has to say repulses and lures him at the same time. The lure wins out. He follows Madam Chan to an oak table. She pirouettes to the sideboard to ladle liquid from a pot into a mug.

She hands Dracula the mug.

The pixie is an enigma. Her youthful agility defies her flabby jowls and liver spots. He can picture her unleashing the euphoria of a child. Simultaneously, he divines in her a weight amassed from years of living.

"Drink this. It will wash away the revolting taste in your mouth."

His instinct proves true: Madam Chan has him in her clutches. She is conversant with his problems.

"Drink up; there's nothing repulsive about it. It'll lift your mood."

The turbid tonic is devoid of smell. As he detests the disgusting tang on his palate and is a little afraid of the impish woman, he gulps down a mouthful. Contrary to being hot, as the steam suggests, the mouthful is as cool as spring water. His palate tingles. Another swig clears it. The tankard empties. The tension in his neck and shoulders subsides.

"Do you dream about me often?"

"By no means. Merely last night. Naturally, I've heard about you and your talents. I must say your delivery was stunning. See, I selected your vanishing act. *Puff!* You evaporated without a trace. Then you knocked, but I found no caller at the door. You did that twice. Despite your physical absence, I was alive to your proximity. And something besides—"

Dracula winces.

"Your loneliness," asserts Madam Chan.

Dracula stiffens. He gets up, fists clenched.

Madam Chan grabs his wrist.

"Won't you hear me out, Count?" she implores.

A brief debate in Dracula's mind settles him back into his seat.

"There's no shame in feeling lonely," says Madam Chan. "All of us, mortal or not, are susceptible to it. The affliction crops up sporadically. We can't mend it by encircling ourselves with people. The fact is we suffer our loneliest in a crowd."

Dracula ponders.

"Loneliness is no stranger to me," he says. "You don't think, having lived for centuries, I've been able to elude its grasp? Up till recently, it has always ebbed away without damaging consequences. I scarcely brooded over the woes. Solitude fortified me. It granted me power—power over myself. Even as a child, I was fond of being a recluse. Becoming the voivode of Wallachia, I lost that luxury to the constant demands of my subjects.

"Being ruler of the undead has inverted the circumstances. I indulged in my isolation and planned my myth. These preoccupations contented me. This attitude persisted throughout my exploits. I even believed loneliness romantic. Such fantasy hatched precisely because I was not lonely and thus at ease with being alone. It's difficult to pin down at what point the positivity began to crumble, but crumbled it has—until it perished. I have hit a dead end."

"A dead end? You mean nothing entices you anymore?"

A nod from Dracula.

"Not even love?"

"Love?" Dracula sniggers. "I laughed, not because of anything facetious. Love, to me, is dead serious. I loved my father, who was a formidable warrior, even if not an astute leader. Because of his wavering allegiances, Radu and I were taken as hostages by the Ottomans. While we were in captivity, he was assassinated. His death, and my inability to prevent it, ravaged me. I swore to avenge him. My wars against the Ottomans were, in part, born of that vow, though they were not the ones who struck him down. My affection for my mother blossomed in my forties. She was in her sixties. I esteemed her stamina and intelligence.

"As for amours, I've wrestled with a handful. They were mostly brief and disastrous. Brief and disastrous because they were all-consuming. I surrendered my entire self to each affair, to be drowned in its glory and pain. In renouncing mortality, I've forsaken these passions."

"Are you saying you aren't attached to any of your mistresses?"

"We have performed reciprocal services for each other. Our affairs were delectable. They affirmed my potency, and I delivered what they wanted. My attitude has changed. I no longer lust after them. Our liaisons have become distasteful to me. The worst is that the solitude—which I used to treasure—has begun to engender pain. I feel lonely, not alone."

"I concur, Count. Being alone can be fulfilling. It's essential in our lives, equipping us with opportunities to ruminate, to dig inside ourselves, or simply to relax. Conversely, loneliness breeds emptiness and despondency."

"I am at a loss as to what to do."

"I beg to disagree. You are not at a loss. You visited my dream on purpose. Your repeated knocks and concealments intensified my perception. They were premeditated maneuvers. You laid bare your desolation. You wanted me to be aware of it."

"What can I do? Be succinct, madam."

"Proceed with the children."

"Proceed with the children?"

"Don't act so baffled! It's the narrative you have omitted to relate. I'm eager to follow its development," Madam Chan says and winks.

39

Neculai stands outside the orphanage. He is heartened by the undertaking, which shall steer Dracula back on track. He has heard that the blood of the young is most effective in restoring vitality. It is a shame minors will be involved. Dracula cannot be weak and sick; he must equal his legend. Even if it means sacrificing children, so be it.

He has driven out at daybreak. The sun is at its pinnacle. Neculai pulls up to a two-story timber building. The reek of manure is strong, but no cows graze on the pasture. They must be in the byre. How the schoolroom, dormitories, refectory, and remaining facilities squeeze into such a middling structure puzzles Neculai. Nevertheless, he acknowledges that this orphanage will suffice as well as any institution.

The door opens before he can knock. A child, fresh as a daisy, has apparently been waiting and heard him approaching. The sight of Neculai fills her with mirth. To hide her amusement, she whirls and speeds up the stairs in the vestibule. The plaits by her ears fly sideways.

If tidying has been attempted, it is buried: boots have deposited muddy prints on the treads. The small footmarks indicate that they belong to the foundlings, who must have completed numerous farm duties before their lectures.

On the benches in the lesson hall sit the scholars in shabby raiment. Their ages range from five to fifteen. The girl who greeted Neculai has claimed a back-row seat and is chattering animatedly to her playmates. Her gesticulation leaves no suspense as to whom the object of her chatter is.

All gawk at the caller. Uproar explodes: laughter, jeers, and riotous claps.

The teacher, bloodless as a corpse, abandons the writing board. *Is she a conquest of Dracula's?* muses Neculai. *What an absurd speculation! She's far from Dracula's type.*

The woman gapes at the carrot-colored hair and frog-like features until Neculai's grand attire breaks the spell, informing her that Count Dracula's steward has arrived. She has received word from the Count and selected the scholars in accordance with the arrangement. She mends her manners and reins in the class. The mistress is as despicable to Neculai as her pupils.

"Neculai Costin Anghel, steward to Count Dracula," Neculai introduces himself and bows. "At your service, madam."

"Mistress Hossu and her students are honored by your presence, sir," replies the schoolmistress and bobs. She then orders a lass and two lads to the front: "Come greet Master Neculai."

"It's *Prince* Neculai," corrects Neculai. "Prince Neculai of Moldavia."

Mistress Hossu registers incredulity, which she rapidly suppresses. "Come welcome Prince Neculai," she says to the three children.

The trio is scrubbed clean and smells of soap; nonetheless, their clothing is as worn as that of their peers. The girl's frock is patched at the elbows and is blotted with a sizable stain below the waist. From underneath her dress protrude worn boots. In less than a season, the rips in the leather will expose her toes. She curtsies. The boys bow to Neculai. The older boy endeavors to stifle the titters bubbling up his throat. He is shorter than the girl but stouter. The sleeves of his jacket ride up above his wrists, and the breeches bare his knees. The younger child busies himself with a mosquito circling his head.

"Both Crina and Anton will turn twelve in a few months, and Petrica is nearly seven years old. Anton and Crina have been with us almost from birth, and Petrica since he was a toddler. They are our finest and most intelligent scholars. Crina has excellent culinary skills; Anton is skilled with woodwork. Both of them can read and write. Even Petrica knows many words, and each of them has a marvelous command of our language. They are our elite."

Neculai tips Petrica's chin. The child grins from ear to ear. Capitalizing on his distraction, the mosquito alights on his ear. Petrica smacks it hard, flattening the pest. He flicks its dead body off his palm. Mollified, he restores his attention to Neculai and says, "I once netted a frog the size of my fist. An orange splotch adorned his crown. You'd have been smitten with it!"

Buffoonery erupts. Mistress Hossu quashes the commotion and hustles Crina and Petrica away. Neculai and Anton bring up the rear. The class follows but is forbidden by Hossu, who promises harsh punishments to those who disobey.

Once outdoors, Neculai gives the schoolmistress a pouch. Untying the bag, joy overcomes her. The coins inside signify bread, meat, and boots for her pupils.

Neculai seats Crina and Petrica on a bench and Anton opposite them. The valise, he deposits next to Anton. Thus arranged, he climbs up to the driver's box.

The vehicle jerks away. At the orphanage windows, foundlings jostle for a peek.

Anton leaves his seat and plunks down by Crina. The three of them cuddle. On the vacant bench, the luggage bounces as the wheels bump over the uneven lane, prompting them to half-expect the catches to release from the hooks and the lid to spring open. Crina has packed their washcloths and undergarments. She has placed a comb and a baby tooth of Petrica's among the clothing. Petrica sleeps with the tooth underneath his pillow.

"How will it be to have parents?" speculates Crina out loud.

"Are we going to have parents?" asks Petrica.

"A father."

"The frog-man," Anton jests.

"Oh, don't be silly," says Crina, giggling. She adds, "Mistress Hossu said Count Dracula would be our father. I have no memories of my father or mother. Chances are our new father will be kind to us."

The children observe the passing view. Crina and Anton are familiar with the city square. Cook has taken them there. The lasses in the orphanage perform the domestic tasks, while the lads tend the animals and the fields under the supervision of Cook's son. They purchase their provisions at the village. A spin to the square is infrequent. The rarity, compounded by the renown of the square's hubbub, entices the orphans. Those appointed to accompany Cook are the objects of envy.

It is not a market day; few people are around. A gypsy and a gnome-like man vend their wares. The gypsy sells cuts of fish: salted sturgeons, flathead mullets, breams, and live lampreys. She hawks at the carriage, whereas the gnome watches it nonchalantly from his cart. It is unnecessary for the gnome to advertise: the clucking and quacking from the cages around him manage that for him. Not far from the peddlers, the shoe-mender, a local fixture, is repairing the heel of a shoe in his booth. His customer waits patiently.

Once out of the municipality, they barrel past miles of sparsely inhabited fields. The tedium knocks the trio out until the jarring final leg. Petrica whimpers. Crina and Anton rouse as well. They are buried in a shady forest, rumbling up an incline that nearly causes them to slide off the seat.

The oil lamp on a pole beside Neculai whines. *Creak ... creak.* Transmuted by the gloom into grotesque demons, the trees lunge with their boughs. The ghostly limbs are ripe to reach in and snatch them away.

The halting of the rig breaks their fearful thoughts. Anton detaches himself from his mates to gaze out. Blocking their passage is a soaring wall, snaking its way into the shadows. He calls out, "Come! The frogman has gotten off."

Indeed, he has and is dragging open a gate of wrought iron. The lamp shines on his person. Neculai hops back onto the vehicle and steers it into the compound. They are disrupted again for Neculai to padlock the gate.

Within the compound, the road remains rough and steep, though it is broader. Brambles thrive on both sides. Among the tangled briars, hovels recoil. In fright? Or shame? The lamp reveals creeper-sealed fronts and roofs with abominable holes.

Their journey terminates at a box of bricks. The voyagers alight. They are at the foot of a crag. A fortress monopolizes the summit.

Neculai vanishes into the brick box. A flame wavers within. Out he brings a lit lantern.

"Quit loafing about, you lot. Hike to the top," instructs the frogman. "I'll be right behind. Discard that," he says to Crina, who has removed the valise from the carriage. "I'll carry it up. Carry this instead." He thrusts forward the lantern.

The little group starts their ascent, the lantern guiding their way. The crude stone treads compel them to negotiate gingerly. A third of the way up, Anton pants and puffs. He wonders what Neculai is up to. The scary sight of the vertical drop below sends him on his buttocks and wrenches an expletive from him. He pulls himself together and is able to locate the brick structure. Lamplight spills from it. Neculai and the rig have withdrawn from view; their valise lies by the roadside. Neculai must have stowed the vehicle and stabled the horse—a sign that he will mount the crag promptly.

Crina and Petrica climb in concert. "Thirty. Thirty-one," counts Petrica.

There are a hundred steps in total.

The air at the crest is thin and biting for late summer. The ground has hardened, and their breaths are visible. The castle looms above them. Massive and ominous. From its apexes, project turrets of various sizes. Count Dracula must have retired; no glow radiates from any of the castle's edifices. Where they have gathered is far from dim, though. The confined gleam of the lantern is not the source of the brilliance.

An incandescent blotch has burst from behind the clouds to hound them. Its sheen is at odds with the inky environs. The hairs on their skin stand on end. The keens of a wolf would be appropriate. But there is only the weeping of the icy wind.

Anton shudders. He blows out a condensed breath and mutters, "There is no moon nor star. Where does the blotch come from?"

"It must be from the moon, hidden somewhere," Crina says, uncertain, for she too is unnerved.

"I didn't see the glare at the base of the crag. Nor did it exist during our climb, or else I would have noted it. It materialized a moment ago. And it targets us!"

Crina's response is to shiver.

Little Petrica is undaunted. He has run up a flight of stairs and is on tiptoe, clasping the ring of a gargoyle knocker. His whacks resonate. There is no sign of anyone inside.

Crina jogs up to Petrica. Anton dislodges himself from the pull of the sinister glare and joins his friends. Masonry shields them. The macabre luster succumbs to the primeval stonework and expires. The three, inadequately garbed, squeeze together. Exhaustion paralyzes them.

The wobbling light of a lantern signals Neculai's approach. The youngsters are chilled to the bone. In no small measure, they welcome the frogman. Their enthusiasm is not reciprocated, for Neculai grants them not a hint of cordiality. However, he marshals them indoors and says, "Food and the fire will do you good."

40

Crina is allotted a boudoir of her own. A stomach satiated with quail pie, a fire in the grate, and the comfort of the furnishings have altogether dispelled her unease. She sprawls upon the thick quilt, head buried in the fluffy pillows. At the orphanage, the foundlings huddle to keep warm. She rolls off the coverlet to caper to the vanity table. She strikes various poses in front of the oval mirror and curtsies as if to a dignitary. The reflection of the nightdress placed on the footboard of the bed captures her interest.

She hastens over, slips into the sleepwear, and whisks back to appraise her image. Yes, a pretty princess she is, in a dancing costume and garlanded with honeysuckle! Once her fancy flits by, she sticks her tongue out at herself.

On the table lies an assortment of brushes and combs, the paddles and handles of which are inlaid with gems. She runs her finger over the ornaments. Never in her life has she stroked anything so beautiful. She loosens her braid and grooms her hair with the set. Lined up next to the implements is a receptacle, also exquisitely adorned. She pulls off its lid. Perfume emanates from the scented powder inside the container. Charmed, she dabs the powder puff on her nose.

The embers have burnt out, and the candle is low. In a trice, she is out of her chamber, scurrying down the passage to seek the boys. Anton is snoring. She nestles up to Petrica, who crawls into her embrace.

Fingers pinch her cheek, and a voice entreats. Planted inches from her is a frog face.

"Get up, missy," the frogman bids her.

Her grogginess lingers. Anton, garments rumpled, looks aggrieved. Next to her, Petrica fights to reclaim the eiderdown quilt that has been yanked off him.

Neculai orders them out of bed.

He furnishes them with elegant vestments. Fatigue and annoyance dull their zest. They don the garments perfunctorily. Petrica struggles with the buttons. Neculai kneels down to fasten them for him. The frogman is not devoid of kindness, concludes Petrica.

Crina's cotton dress has lace sleeves. A ribbon encircles her waist. Anton wears a linen vest and breeches. Petrica is in a cream ensemble. The jacket comprises a folded-down collar and twin columns of brass buttons.

Neculai marches them down the corridor and then two flights of stairs to the great hall. Above the wainscoting, tapestries bedeck the walls. Arched ribs enhance the ceiling. Despite the raging grate, its vastness allows frigidity and murk to imbue the place. The fire is lit in their honor, Neculai has mentioned, as the Count prefers a glacial temperature.

At the upper end of a dining table, dimness enshrouds a man. He is thin and tall, his shoulders inches above the back of the chair. His hair is swept back and tied at the nape. The regal deportment he adopts stamps the man as Count Dracula.

Dracula's eyes glitter like those of a cat. Crina and the boys are brought forward to be introduced. Crina would have prolonged her gaze if not for her friends, who tug at her sleeves to divert her attention to the food occupying the length of the table.

In the middle of the platters is a candelabrum, supporting five wax candles. Around its branches and cups weave leafage and blooms: roses, edelweiss, peonies, and rhododendrons. Vines drip from the floral arrangement. The lit candles accentuate the flowers and the palatable dishes. There are sausages, roasted pheasant with baked carrots, onions, and parsley, as well as cheese, apples, pears, and an assortment of cakes and bread.

The Count invites the children to sit down.

Anton and Petrica hurry to the middle of the table to be next to the feast. Crina joins them. Neculai steps in, shuffling them to seats by the Count. Petrica and Anton face Crina.

Neculai waits on them. They pile up their plates. Anton and Petrica gorge themselves. Crina admires the utensils. The aroma of the pile of food on her plate is heavenly. What should she start with? No contest there: the pheasant meat. Evidently, Anton concurs. Drumstick in hand, Anton rips a chunk off with his teeth. She is appalled: the dolt has thrown decorum to the wind. Short of yelling at him, there is little she can do. If Anton were not so captivated, she would have mimed her reproof.

She checks if the Count is offended and discovers that he is observing her. She blushes and pretends to be occupied with her meal.

Crina summons enough nerve to peep at the Count. The Count is studying the boys. Petrica, having eaten enough, plays with a carrot cube with his fork. Anton attacks a piece of cake. Food always absorbs Anton. There is jocularity in Dracula's countenance. He finds them droll.

Dracula is not as young as Cook's son, who is twenty. He may be old like Mr. Hagi. Cook has said the warden of the orphanage is on the wrong side of forty. It is difficult to determine the age of an adult.

The twitch on the Count's temple suggests that Dracula is cognizant of being spied on. Instead of rebuking her impertinence, he feigns ignorance.

A mischievous notion percolates: what if she altogether skips eating to concentrate on the peep? Will the Count keep up his pretense? Without delay, she executes the idea. The Count appears to comply. Crina grins. Her jubilance dies in its embryo. For Dracula swivels around. The abruptness stuns Crina. When she composes herself, Dracula has remolded his expression, dismissing its severity. He appears as gleeful and smug as a monkey who has gotten a banana.

41

Dracula is no ordinary father. He inflames the trio's zeal. The children are unused to being up in the dead of the night. This preference of the Count puzzles them. To Crina's inquiry of why they don't carry out their activity in the daytime, Dracula replies, "Must we mimic the crowd? Plebeian habits shouldn't have a bearing on us. Don't you adore the night? The magic of it?"

They frolic in the courtyard, hemmed in by a curtain wall and the turreted structures. The towering assemblage makes the yard look smaller than it is. With the lamps never lit, you get the impression of being trapped at the bottom of a well. When the moonbeam tunnels downward, the impression evaporates. The enclosure transforms into a stage, with the revelers as its performers.

Dracula has detached his cape and is snapping it. He drapes it over a dwarf juniper with bald limbs. The three friends concentrate on the cloak. *Ting, ting,* chimes a set of bells. Dracula sweeps the cape away as Petrica races to uncover the secret beneath. Rich foliage now covers the juniper. *Ting-a-ling. Ting-a-ling.* The leaves jingle. In the zenith above, a skein of bats darts into the plump moon.

The youngsters bask in their new life. Hunger is behind them. The coarse food they tasted at the orphanage is history. Here, food is plentiful and delicious. Fire blazes in the hearths. There are no lessons to burden them. They are free to roam the keep. They even get to wander in the dark. Candle in hand, Anton leads the explorations. Petrica grips Crina's pinafore as they march behind. The candlelight produces an atmosphere that is unmatched by natural light. Dimness promises unpredictable fun. Shadows jump out for them to scream at and giggle to their hearts' content.

Neculai's chamber is situated across from the boys' bedroom. The trio is banned from it. Neculai is a prince and demands to be thus respected.

Each chamber contains a four-poster bed with a feather mattress, a potty underneath, a bureau, a settee, and a low table. Round or oval mirrors perch on the bureaus. If the dresser lacks a looking glass, a floor mirror compensates for its absence. Anton and Petrica have such a piece. Crina's is oval. The floor features a garderobe. Awakened from repose, they opt for the potty, which is handier. The fireplaces are rustic, reinforcing the hominess of the decor.

In the kitchen, the redolence of food soaks into the cupboards. Pheasant pie or roasted meat is available. The pantry stores bread, pastries, cheese, and eggs. Petrica relishes cracking an egg and eating it uncooked.

Below the pantry is the cold larder, where haunches of raw meat on hooks, pea pods, lettuce, and other vegetables are stored.

The keep is trapezoidal. On the broader backside, the kitchen and library occupy corners at either end. In the library, sofas invite readers to indulge in a volume from the shelves. A mahogany desk and chair set sits under the window. Artworks decorate the walls.

Succulent pears spill from a basket onto a tablecloth in a painting. The tablecloth glistens silver along an edge. The adjacent canvas is a still life of an overturned pewter vase. Purple carnations lie on a lime cloth. Water dribbles off the rim of the vase. In the painting, the corners of the tabletop are exposed, and its veneer harmonizes with the ebony background.

The piece on the opposite wall portrays Count Dracula's castle. The circular turrets have cone-shaped roofs. Apertures dot the battlements and the buildings within. The depiction includes no eerie anomaly or devilish gloss. The stronghold is impregnable.

They have been in every nook in the keep. Where are the Count's apartments?

"Must be in a different building," says Anton.

They tear from the library into the hall, race its length, and burst into the courtyard. The surrounding edifices are locked.

"We should ask the Count," says Petrica.

"To unlock every structure or to disclose where he sleeps?" says Anton.

"It is fruitless to ask," says Crina, brows knitted. "He never offers a straight answer."

Anton concurs, "Like when we asked his age, he said age was relative and he was ancient to us but a babe to eternity. What kind of reply is that? Why not simply tell us how old he is?"

Crina nods and says, "But what he said sounds reasonable."

"Does it now?" counters Anton sarcastically. Then his tone warms: "All right. Should we obtain the information from the frogman?"

Petrica glances at Crina.

"We may try. We won't get anywhere with him either. He's as uncommunicative as the Count, though in a different sort of way," says she.

"So, you notice it too. The frogman maintains his distance from us. Without cause, I must say. He may be a prince, but he's in service. He—"

"He's not unkind," interjects Petrica. "He manages our daily needs and has never scolded us."

"He's not above us," contends Anton. "That's what I meant. Crina has volunteered to cook. Even though he could use her help, he rejected her. He lets us do the dishes because he doesn't have to be present. It is obvious he shuns us."

"Correct. He speaks to us out of necessity. He's far from taciturn. I have heard him drivel on and on to the Count—it has to do with reserves depleting, whatever that means. He is anxious about the Count's health. I sympathize with him. The Count's too thin. He doesn't eat. Not the delicious cakes, sweetbreads, or any delicacies. A spoonful of mush with brandy is enough to fill his lordship."

"He has boundless energy, though, you must admit."

"Yes. Maybe my worry is pointless. Back to Neculai: he mumbles to himself a lot and is reticent only with us. He is seldom around. In order to engage in clandestine dealings, I bet."

"You have him there. But enough of the frogman. We're onto the Count's nest, aren't we? With the locked buildings, how can we ferret it out?"

"I'll ask him," says Petrica with such firmness that his mates goggle at him.

42

Having adjusted to the gloom in the courtyard, the children can distinguish the outlines of the objects in the vicinity.

"Let's play hide-and-seek," proposes Dracula.

Anton collects four twigs shed by the sapling near the arcade. Dracula, who has drawn the shortest twig, is to hide. With backs to Dracula and eyes closed, the seekers count to a hundred and then start their search.

Anton prowls among the boxwood hedges while Crina scrambles into the fountain bowl. The water being off, the bowl is littered with yard debris. She circles the marble statue in the center. There is no Count Dracula.

Then Petrica shouts, "I've found him!"

Crina and Anton join Petrica, who points at a bat cocooned in its wings on a branch.

"That's not the Count," protests Anton.

"*It is!*" retorts Petrica. "Look at those eyes!"

The bat's eyes flash emerald.

"Come down, Count," chant exuberant young voices.

The bat releases the branch and unfurls its wings. A fog develops. In the haze, the bat elongates into the dapper Dracula. Applause thunders.

"How do you do it?" asks Anton.

Suspense hangs heavy in the atmosphere.

"By the employment of an illusion that levitates our minds."

"Levitates our minds? You mean playing with our minds?" says Anton. "Teach us, Count."

"Please," chime in both Crina and Petrica.

The exhibited naïveté charms Dracula.

"Perhaps someday," Dracula says and then excuses himself.

"We want to find your living quarters," cries Petrica after the Count.

Dracula turns around.

"Is that so?"

"Yes, we have gone through the keep."

"But we found nothing," adds Anton.

Crina and Petrica nod in unison.

After a short delay, Dracula says, "Have you considered secret ramps and hidden rooms?"

He winks at the astonished faces.

The possibility of secret passageways sends the friends into a frenzy. They scrutinize the pieces of furniture and the items in the keep. They probe inside drawers and under chairs and beds. They pull on knobs and handles, hoping for the sudden pop of a concealed barrier. Nothing pops. Their quests end in naught.

Do the hidden areas exist? Is the Count's insinuation merely a tease? The Count has a penchant for confounding them and hurling them into a whirlwind of uncertainty.

"We should just stop," asserts Anton, "and act like we don't care at all. We need to stay calm. If his purpose is to provoke us, let's not give him the satisfaction."

Crina has a faraway look.

"Are you listening?" complains Anton.

Crina springs from her seat, obviously onto something.

"Come," she gestures to Anton and clutches Petrica's hand.

Next, they are in the library, studying the painting of the castle.

"You see the keep? See the rows of windows on it—to be precise?"

She pauses.

"The top row belongs to our accommodations. Below them is a solitary window. The next row belongs to the hall. The single window—"

"The single window belongs to the hidden space!" cuts in Anton. "Our climbs up and down the stairs haven't led us to a level in between. The mystery's solved."

"We've found Count Dracula's hideaway," chimes in Petrica, dancing about merrily.

"Not quite. We have to find the entrance to it first," says Crina.

"We should reinspect Neculai's suite," says Anton to both Crina and Petrica. "I wager we'll unearth what we want there."

"What do you base your wager on?" asks Crina.

"It's a hunch. Because he serves the Count, it's likely he has easy access to his master."

"But the single window isn't under his suite," says Crina. She pushes a chair over, scrambles onto it, and points at the window above the single window on the canvas. "Considering the layout of the keep, this belongs to the spare room opposite mine."

"Then, we'll examine the spare room also," declares Petrica.

"Excellent idea, Trica." After jumping down, Crina gives Petrica a hug. Then, to Anton, she says, "Neculai will probably oppose the inspection of his chamber. He made such a fuss during our previous search. If the Count didn't intercede, we wouldn't have been able to rummage through it."

"We won't ask for his permission," says Anton. "He'll insist on being there. I don't want him observing us."

"Should we really ignore his consent?"

Petrica, with brows creased, concurs with Crina.

"We'll do it while he's at the market. On a Thursday."

"How can you be so certain of the day?" asks Crina with incredulity. "We're abed. Never have I been aware of his comings and goings. Have you actually witnessed him quit the premises on a Thursday?"

"No. I don't need to. The stock in the pantry shows that he has. Fresh eggs, fruits, and loaves of bread appear on the counters many Thursday evenings. That implies he restocks our provisions on Thursdays," Anton replies knowingly. "Whether he purchases our food from the city or the local village doesn't matter. To travel the property alone consumes a portion of the day, creating an opportunity for us to investigate."

"If you are right, you and I shall be guards glued to our posts on Thursdays."

"Of course, I'm right."

"Let's take turns watching the frogman—you and I, that is."

"I want to be on patrol too," pleads Petrica.

"Let Anton and me handle it, sweetie. We'll probably end up dawdling since we can't guess the frogman's schedule. It's bound to be tedious. Wouldn't you rather wait for something merry?"

It is thus settled that Anton and Crina will monitor Neculai.

43

Anton begins his spying on Thursday. The frogman's quarters are across the corridor. Should Neculai set out, Anton will hear him leaving.

A little into his vigil, Anton drowses. He ought not to have eaten the mutton and cheese nor drunk the mead earlier. He listens. All is dormant. He has not missed anything.

He trudges to the window and pulls the curtains aside to peep at the exterior. A dark void greets him. It will be an hour or two before daybreak. The courtyard below must be buried in shadows. Should he light a candle? Petrica twitches under the sheets. Anton takes it as a sign of admonition and decides it would be silly to let a glow leak into the corridor. He paces about. Ennui and fatigue eventually induce him to lie down.

The lethargic clock on the mantelpiece plagues him. Its ticks multiply his torment. He moans.

Finally, the clock's hands join. He is to relinquish his post at noon. The frogman never starts out past noon. If he does, he will not be able to finish errands and be back at five.

Invariably, Neculai prepares their dinner at five. His sausages, pies (pheasant, hare, or partridge), and stuffed cabbage are among their favorites. Sturgeons and carps are rare treats. Count Dracula forgoes the regular meals. Before he meets with them in the early hours of the morning, they are on their own.

Half-past the following midnight, Dracula and the trio gather in the parlor.

Since the Count is haggard, games will be skipped. They will enjoy music instead.

Dracula is at the piano, shoulders loose. His fingers prance along the keys. The melody spirals. His left hand crosses over his right for the higher notes. He leans toward the keys momentarily, then rotates away.

Petrica stands by the piano, mesmerized. Anton and Crina spirit themselves away to their private universes. Hymn singing is the extent of their accomplishment. Without hesitation, they all exult in the sorcery of the tune.

Abruptly, the music stops. Then comes a clash, a thud, and Petrica's wail.

Anton and Crina leap to their feet.

The piano bench lies on its side, and Dracula sprawls next to it. Crina and Anton dash over and kneel by the Count. Petrica mimics them.

Dracula has fainted.

"Get Neculai, quickly!" screams Crina.

Anton rushes off.

Crina and Petrica shake Dracula and cry out his title.

Panting, Anton places his sweaty palm on the doorknob of Neculai's chamber. As the knob turns, he remembers the frogman's firm instructions to knock. Well, the recollection has arrived too late.

The moon illuminates the interior; Neculai is not there. Anton crosses the main room to the adjoining den, which is also vacant.

He should leave. However, he is nailed to the spot. Neculai came upstairs earlier and hasn't gone back down. Where is he?

Intuition insists that Neculai is in the hidden area, possibly accessible from Neculai's chamber. Curiosity diverts Anton's attention away from the indisposed Count.

At the muffled noise, Anton pricks up his ears. Here it is— coming from behind the panels. Footfall, that's what it is. Someone is approaching from behind the wall! He scampers behind the settee. Heavy treads reverberate. From the gap underneath the settee, he gapes at the pendulum clock pivoting outward as the panel to which it is attached opens up. A shoe edges out. Then, its twin. Neculai has squeezed out sideways. The panel seals up.

The shoes head his way!

Anton sucks in his breath.

A weight slumps onto the seat, succeeded by a loud sigh.

Anton pictures Neculai slouching with a drooped head. What has aggrieved the frogman? Has he come from the Count's living quarters? Has an incident there upset him? Is he worn down by his duties? If that is the case, he has himself to blame for rejecting Crina's offer.

Suddenly, the chamber door rattles. Petrica squeals, "Anton! Anton!"

Anton nearly jerks upright out of alarm and is relieved he didn't. *Oh God, don't let Petrica march forward.* Skulking into the den, without consent, is bad enough. To have spied on Neculai— in his sanctum—is treason. The frogman's rage—should he catch Anton—will be horrendous.

To Anton's horror, the patter of feet grows louder and louder. Petrica's holler booms out as he charges into the den.

"How dare you trespass?" rebukes Neculai, who has stood up in indignation. "Why do you seek Anton here?"

This stalls Petrica. From his hiding place, Anton watches small feet fidgeting.

"But why, Prince Neculai? It's *you* I want! Hurry! The Count has fainted."

Anton relaxes. It's fortunate that Petrica has his wits about him. It might have been a reflex. Anyhow, it triggers the coveted development.

Neculai lunges and is off, with Petrica at his heels. Anton is safe.

He crawls out of his refuge. The panel with the pendulum clock draws him like a magnet. He breaks the spell midway. It's stupid to scout the place now, he reasons. The frogman may return. But the lure proves too strong. He tiptoes to the panel and pushes on it, hoping it will swing outward. The panel stays as it is. Additional maneuvers are equally unproductive. In any event, it behooves him to wait for his companions, who would otherwise never forgive him.

As he walks away, it strikes him that if Petrica had not shown up, he would be unable to decamp. Crina's impatience has spared him from detection and punishment, for Petrica must have been sent by her.

Dracula hunches on the piano bench, his pallor wan. Crina, Petrica, and Neculai have circled around him. Neculai shoves the children back. "Stand back and give the Count space."

"I've predicted this," grouses Neculai. "To subsist, nutrition is essential."

Dracula waves his hand contemptuously.

"Here you are!" exclaims Petrica at Anton, who is striding toward the group. "Where have you been? You're flushed." Crina and Neculai scrutinize the latecomer.

"Well, I've been running."

"You were gone for an age," says Crina.

"I searched for Prince Neculai upstairs. But here you are."

Neculai assesses Anton but lets his suspicion go. There are exigent matters to devote himself to.

"Leave off the fussing—I'm fine. Take me to my bed."

Neculai helps Dracula up. Crina assists in supporting the Count, but Neculai motions her away.

Dracula says, "It's right for you not to follow us. You are to locate my apartments on your own. There shan't be any cheating." He laughs, but his laughter ripples out so weakly it resembles hiccups.

44

Neculai contemplates the recumbent figure of the Count. The slumbering posture does not deter him; he will have his say.

They have exhausted the reserves. Dracula has not replenished with his mistresses, nor has he recharged with his wards. It is deplorable that they have to resort to this extreme measure, but extreme measures are required.

Although the trio must have derided him along with their fellow orphans, they have respected him thenceforth. Their ability to entertain themselves is impressive. Being caged in a building and a modest courtyard would have driven him crazy. No sign indicates that they are dejected. It would have been a disaster if they had clamored for constant supervision.

Crina has volunteered to chop up the food and do other preparation work. He has declined. There shall be no ties between himself and them lest his resolve be weakened. Dracula will draw sustenance from them. Neculai is resolute in that.

The luscious food and a leisurely life have led to Anton's pudginess. Crina and Petrica, too, have flourished. Dracula has gone against the goal established by Neculai. Instead of feeding on them, he has bonded with them. Maybe he has never intended to suck their blood, which is fine if he procures it from his mistresses.

Neculai wants to howl, so frustrated he is at Dracula's degeneration. He has put aside his scorn, handling Dracula with the tenderness due a senile grandfather. He wishes Dracula would look at himself and admit to the sorry plight he is in. His hair has lost its sheen. He has acquired a stoop. His pasty complexion further attests to the deterioration.

The hypnotism in his eyes endures. They sparkle with an intensity that is unprecedented. Is it the hollow luster preceding death? Neculai discards this notion. Dracula has been around. He doesn't die. But he can turn decrepit, which is indubitably worse.

"Count, it's incomprehensible to me why you've renounced your trysts. Pray heed your health. Your body demands nutrition. The youngsters are ripe for your choosing."

Dracula abruptly props himself up against the pillows.

"You don't understand a thing, Neculai, do you?" Dracula enunciates his words as if to an obtuse lackey. "You want me to drain the children. Don't you grasp the diversion they have granted me? I haven't had this sort of fun since I was a little lad. Radu was a big baby, too conceited for my liking, and our older half-brother did not consort with us. Circumstances rendered me a precocious adolescent; I judged recreations I now revel in as silly. Petrica, Crina, and Anton are artless. I readily fool them. I'm brilliant at disguises. I am a lizard with stripes—the most glorious creature on earth. I hiss and slash out my tongue. The three back away. *Heh, heh, heh* … Illusion, a potent, electrifying tool."

The situation is dire. They can't afford to idle. Should he propose himself to the Count?

Dracula has apparently read Neculai's thoughts, for he raises a brow at his protégé and smirks. "Don't be ridiculous, Neculai. I consented to your stewardship here without any design of jabbing you. Why would I do it now? Can't you accept that I don't want my mistresses? They bore and sicken me. I don't want their blood or anybody else's. It's as simple as that. Frail though I am, I am cheerful with the children. They rejuvenate me."

Neculai isn't about to be fooled by this speech. The Count won't survive if he prolongs this absurdity. Dracula is seriously ill and will be bedridden without proper nutrition. Since the Count refuses to redress the wrongs, Neculai will do it in his stead.

After Neculai retreats, Dracula dozes. Dreams bubble up. A plant wilts in the desert. The temperature climbs. As the heat sucks up every ounce of moisture from the plant, Dracula writhes as if he were the dying plant. His skin resembles the cracked sand. His heartbeats weaken. The dream collapses. A gleeful visage pops up. Does it belong to Anton? Petrica? Or Radu? As Dracula stoops toward it, the delight vanishes and is replaced by horror. A scream resounds.

Dracula jerks alert. Did he or the visage shriek? Terror fills his being. The melancholy that he believes has been alleviated by the amity between him and his wards weighs him down. Is he dying? Is his end imminent? Is expiring what disconcerts him? Or has he mistaken the situation completely? He sighs, long and heavy.

He had fainted earlier and woken to a pair of eyes looking down on him. Mama's eyes. No, they weren't Mama's. They exhibited more warmth than intellect. They resembled Mama's but belonged to Crina.

He has taught his charges the fundamentals of piano technique, demonstrating the notes—including flats and sharps—and explaining the patterns of the keys. He also allowed them to strike the keys and create melodies. The young people were ebullient, as they always are.

They want badly to assume the shape of a bat or a lizard. He denies their pleas to shield them from defeats. They are incapable of such artistry. No mortal is capable, particularly not junior mortals. Only he himself, the august Dracula, is adept at these metamorphoses. Even then, it is in the world of the undead that he secures such prodigies.

His dependency on Bat, thrusting him into dreams, was a nuisance to him. Child Bat succeeded wise Bat. His desire for autonomy was ignored by child Bat, who was self-absorbed and reticent. Ultimately, he ceased his struggles and refrained from initiating conversation with Bat. They resorted to a silent coexistence.

But he *must* rid himself of his dependency.

In a starlit flight, years into their silent coexistence, he resurrected his request to be self-reliant. Bat dipped and rose without issuing any rejoinder.

Dracula's attempts to converse were all slighted. His patience ran out. "Listen!" he demanded. "Don't pretend not to hear me. I have respected your preference to be aloof. The least you can do is to indulge me this once. Answer me!"

Bat forwent his stunts and adopted a steady velocity. Bat said, "Don't bother to dispose of me—it will be futile. You are stuck with me. Nothing will change that."

Hearing it after such a significant lapse of time, the voice jarred Dracula. The recognition was immediate. It belonged to the remote past. The dungeon and the astute creature surged up in his mind. He labored to subdue the tumult of his emotions and said, "No need to be vexed, old chum. An eon has elapsed since we spoke. I've matured into a man—a powerful voivode at that. That's how long it has been. I must say I'm gratified you responded. Rest assured, I have no intention of getting rid of you. You can continue to live within me. My goal is to enter dreams without you steering us. How can I achieve it?"

"If you can fly."

"No human can fly."

"Are you certain of that?"

Dracula hesitated.

"It'll be the case if you think like a human," cautioned Bat. "The mind has many planes. Transporting yourself to a level you aren't accustomed to will do you wonders."

"A different plane? Do clarify what you are alluding to."

"You must decipher it yourself. Failing to do so, you are doomed to rely on me."

Then Bat regressed to a mute partner.

Conveying himself to a different plane had, for a period, obsessed Dracula. As difficult as it was, he stole a snippet of each day from his obligations as a voivode to ponder this fantastic proposition.

Did Bat intend him to conjure an illusion? While Bat propelled him into dreams, he thrust along—as a bat. He was also conscious of being grounded. He was aloft and yet tethered. He was a bat as well as a human being.

His mind was as stuck as his body. The bat was never him but Bat in flight.

The claims of life and the inability to formulate a solution combined to weaken his fixation. He stowed the riddle away, letting it resurface in his mind periodically—much like the way he treated a cherished lover he had dismissed.

The moment he crossed into the domain of the undead, he puzzled out what Bat had said to him. His soul and intellect had transcended their usual plane! He had elevated them.

On the elevated plane, all concepts are fluid. Illusion and truth are interchangeable. Being undead is real. It is also an illusion.

An illusion he has crafted for the common folks. They deem him rich and powerful, a conqueror of female hearts. The public thirsts for these attributes. Its zeal to embellish and inflate abets the illusion. He sucks blood, they say, and is sinister. Ah, a jot of perversity always spices things up. The harder he frightens them, the deeper they sink into a state of inebriation over him.

A perfect illusion.

And a perfect truth.

Only when humans lift their minds will they perceive the alternative world as real as the moon in the sky.

The alternative world relieves him of his need for Bat. He is in control. He beckons and banishes dreams at will. He looks into the dream puffs and chooses.

He does not abandon his physical self when soaring. He is a bat—in every respect. He and Bat penetrate dreams as one.

Oh, the wonder of the mind.

He can transform into a lizard. A lizard with rhomboid scales. A lizard with coral specks. A lizard with taupe spines.

Lizards are iridescent, sublime, and ubiquitous creatures. Many are loners, except during mating. What animal is more apropos?

He can't metamorphose into just any animal. He is not a sorcerer but rather a believer in truth, a worshiper of the imagined. He doesn't metamorphose into a lion or a tiger, for instance, because he is neither. He is a lizard. He is a bat.

Illusion materializes when it is the truth.

45

"You have what?" Petrica can hardly contain himself, hearing the smashing news.

"Exactly as I said—I've discovered the secret passageway!"

"How did it happen?" asks Crina. "Was this why you disappeared for so long?"

"The frogman emerged from it. I was holed up behind the settee in his den!"

Petrica whistles.

"*Shhh!* Are you trying to send the frogman upon us?" Crina grouses and then urges Anton, "Do spill out what has transpired."

"I was in the frogman's den. Pattering sounded behind the paneled wall. I hid myself. The panel on which the pendulum clock was attached swung outward—"

"What? A wall panel opened up!" Crina is awed.

"Yes! Quit interrupting if you want to hear the story. The panel swung open and out sidled the frogman. I caught his shoes and stockinged ankles from the narrow gap. They were his buckled pumps. Then Petrica waltzed in, yelling for me. I well-nigh wetted my breeches." Petrica's lips round into an "o." "Instead of exposing me, he rushed Neculai away. Clever boy! I relinquished my nook. The panel summoned me. On account of you two, I fought the temptation to investigate."

"Marvelous!" says Crina. "Come Thursday. We'll explore."

"How far off is that?" asks Petrica.

"A week, silly," says Anton. "My sleep-deprived vigil was less than twenty-four hours ago."

"I wish it were today," says a disappointed Petrica.

"So do I," agrees Anton sourly.

"Is it that bad—to keep watch?"

"You try it and see."

"I will. It's my turn next."

The friends chat on until exhaustion claims them. Petrica curls up beside Crina. Snores erupt from Anton.

Crina occupies herself with rumination. The Count must be convalescing. She is thankful that, with the support of Neculai, he was able to stand up. The stare the revived Dracula fixed on her was fervent. It expressed not the customary mesmeric intensity but joy—and also affinity. Did he discern a quality in her he valued? What could it be? She held his stare. An intimacy between them was born.

Will the Count be able to attend the games later? Anton has chanced upon the movable panel. The discovery unfolded in the most fantastical way. However, there has to be a more fitting avenue to the Count's chamber. It is absurd to suppose that Neculai's den is a conduit to it. The Count has exited the keep with Neculai. Might the chamber's true entrance lie in the courtyard? They praise themselves for carrying out a thorough search; apparently, their efforts aren't without faults.

Her mood darkens: what if Neculai stays in? The stock in the larder can sustain them for a long stretch. An extended delay will be insufferable.

Creaks of hinges issue from across the corridor. She livens up. Boots squeak. Neculai's footsteps diminish steadily and then fade away. Has he descended from the story? Is he heading out? What is the purpose of his outing? Perhaps to acquire medicine for the Count?

She prods Anton, who brushes her off with his back. She straddles him and pulls off his blanket. Anton grumbles and curls up into a ball.

Crina decides to stalk Neculai on her own. She pops her feet into her slippers and scuttles into the corridor. The obscurity does not hinder her. She scurries along and, halfway down, dives onto the curving stairs. The slits high up let in the pale dawn to guide her.

Neculai likely has negotiated the length of the hall. A slam affirms her suspicion. As a precaution, she peeks into the hall. It is empty. She lopes to the door and plants her ear on it. Not a noise is transmitted through. The thick panel deadens all sound. She surveys the tall stained-glass windows. They are useless for peeping out. Neculai must be crossing the courtyard to the round tower. The tower is the portal to the exterior lands. They passed through it on their arrival. On parade were the shields and swords and the suits of armor. She and her companions had wanted to marvel at these displays, but Neculai hurried them on.

Neculai's prolonged absence confirms that he has left the castle and she can safely proceed into the courtyard.

The courtyard she enters is dreary. Frost has coated the forecourt and the short flight leading down to it. She traces the footprints. Her breaths vaporize into misty droplets. Her thin nightgown hardly wards off the cold.

She tries to enter the tower but fails. Neculai must have locked the place from within. She has enough evidence that the frogman has gone out and should alert Anton and Petrica. She spins toward the keep and, in her haste, slips. The slip triggers a shock but causes no serious harm.

She races back to her playmates. The task at hand is to wake them. With the weapons she possesses—her icy hands—she shall prevail. She hops on top of Anton, dispersing the smarting cold she has gathered. She cups Anton's cheeks in her palms. A furious Anton jolts up and creases his brows.

"Curse you, witchy wench!" he shouts.

"The frogman has decamped."

Anton glares at Crina but abruptly dispels the animosity. "You don't say!" he exclaims.

"I heard him shuffling away and dashed after him. His tracks led me to the round tower. He's left the place. Let's wake Trica."

Anton blocks Crina. "Don't use your icicles. I don't want him startled like I was. We can manage without being cruel. Go and part the curtains."

Crina sticks her tongue out at Anton.

Waking Petrica is an arduous undertaking. The morning light licking his body produces no effect on him. After much tickling and coaxing, the child frowns at his tormentors. When it sinks into his skull that Neculai has withdrawn from the estate and exploits are forthcoming, his dullness evaporates. He shoots up, animated.

The trio tiptoes into Neculai's apartments. Crina has discarded her half-frozen slippers and is wearing a pair of Anton's wool socks. The quilt from Petrica's bed adds warmth to her nightdress.

They press on to the inner sanctum.

Anton tugs back the curtains to let in the light. The clock is as tall as Anton and Crina and occupies the width of the panel. The glass front exhibits the dial and pendulum.

Crina pushes the timepiece.

"It moves outward. We should pull it out, not push it in. I don't see a way of doing it."

Chimes peal. The children, alarmed, back away. Crina and Anton say in chorus, "Perhaps there is a sort of crank inside."

Petrica twists the oval knob to open the glass front. With the interior exposed, the tick-tocks resonate loudly. The workings include no crank.

Casting off the quilt to gain mobility, Crina nudges Petrica aside and crouches down. On the walnut base is a carved flower that she rotates.

A mechanism drones. The panel pivots outward.

The chums cheer.

Petrica prances into the aperture.

"Hold on," says Anton. "I'll fetch a candle." He hustles over to the mantelpiece and returns with a lit candle.

Petrica eases aside for Anton. Below them is a stairway.

Anton halts Crina at the threshold. "We should file down. I'll descend first. Trica, you tail me, and Crina follows at the rear."

The staircase plunges downward, its steepness daunting. The ceiling arches over them. There is no railing. They plow on.

"The Count won't expect us at his hideaway so soon," Crina says.

"He'll be proud of us," adds Petrica.

Anton whispers, "We'd better hush if we want to surprise him."

The trio entertains their private reveries. Crina muses about the progress of the Count's convalescence. His fainting spell is so recent. Will they be interrupting his rest? Should they abort their mission? Not really. They're near their target. Anton and Petrica would elect to proceed. So would she. She is eager to witness the Count's reaction. He inspires awe in them. Now it's his turn to be awed. Anton is proud of himself for unearthing the passage. The Count will declare him a genius, and rightly so. Petrica pictures the Count's hospitable reception. The Count has never hugged them, which is soon to change. Flinging into the Count's embrace becomes so real that he accelerates and bumps into Anton's back. The collision nearly causes them to tumble down the stairs.

"What are you up to? Want us both hurt?" snaps Anton.

"I couldn't help it. You stopped so suddenly!" counters Petrica, also fuming.

"*Shh!* Be quiet," says Crina. Then she sees the sharp bend that has detained Anton. The triangular tread his feet are on hardly supports them. After the bend, four successive steps terminate on level ground. They creep forward. A door is nearby. The victors suppress their elation. Anton simulates raps with his fist. Upon Crina's consent, he performs the same mime on the door, but it produces no response.

"Should we enter?" murmurs Anton.

Petrica and Crina nod.

"We're here, Count," says Anton, working the handle.

A peppery, piney tang pours out at them. All three sneeze. They wiggle their noses at a host of scents they cannot identify. In the center of the spacious laboratory, a mammoth table stands.

The friends draw close to the table.

Fixed onto the tabletop is a display rack. Bottles and vials, some partially filled and others entirely, cram the shelves.

They parade cinnamon, marsh-green, violet, lavender, and copper-red liquid. The lower shelves, stuffed with dried herbs and roots, present a complementary band of hues. On the table are a weighing scale with brass pans and a granite mortar and pestle.

Sheets of paper, beakers, and flasks strew the remaining tabletop. Measurements mark the sides of the beakers. Tubes, sprouting from their lids, connect the flasks.

Books pile up on and under the table.

"This is not the Count's chamber," moans Petrica.

"Definitely not," grunts Anton. "What's this about? Such an array of flasks and beakers?"

"Let's skim the papers," says Crina. "They may furnish us with clues."

The papers depict the anterior and lateral views of the skull. They illustrate its sections and annotate the innumerable bones. Terminology is printed next to the bones and sutures. They are terms the trio has never heard of and is unable to pronounce.

A volume is opened to page eighty-nine. Crina reads out loud, "Given that you have taken your celestial journey, with nature and self as guides, you are endowed with the means to concoct your unique remedies—herbal or spiritual. Within you is the ability to transmute a mundane form into a substance of great merit." Crina shrugs at these silly, unintelligible sentences and closes the book. On the leather cover is the word *Alchemy*. The lettering winks at her. Crina knits her brows. It must have been a flight of fancy, for her subsequent inspection yields a title as static as the cover itself.

Anton, clowning near her, grimaces and bares his teeth at a piece of paper. On the paper, a skull boasts even teeth.

Crina moves on to examine the next volume, titled *Anatomy and Physiology*. The pages inside illustrate the physique of both sexes and detail the internal organs. She studies a diagram of the female anatomy and then flips the pages. The caption "Cells: The Building Blocks of a Living Organism" baffles and intrigues her. She is about to read about cells when Petrica whoops, "Come see this!"

Crina and Anton bounce over.

Petrica is holding a stack of papers bound together.

An ink sketch greets the three of them. Underneath the three-dimensional face on the page, a date is recorded. The visage, framed by unruly hair, features bulgy orbs and a wide mouth. It portrays the frogman!

"Ready? Watch this!" says Petrica, releasing the pages. The pages, fanning out from his thumb, demonstrate the evolution of the frogman's countenance. They reveal that the frogman has, by degrees, reduced the protrusion of his eyes. His mouth has shrunk as well.

The youngsters guffaw.

"So, this is what the frogman is up to," says Crina. "Haven't I said he was into a sort of scheme? He is mending his looks on the sly. The vials are potions he uses."

"He hasn't had much success, has he?" says Anton.

"No, not much," they howl with laughter.

"He oughtn't be too discouraged," says Petrica. "His bizarre features are fine with me."

"Fine? Are you serious?" says Anton.

"Trica always has a tender spot for the frogman."

Petrica grins.

"I've had a glimpse," says Anton, "of an appealing sketch."

He filches the stack from Petrica.

"Give it back to me! I found it!" shrieks Petrica, attempting to reclaim the papers. Anton holds the item out of Petrica's reach.

"Calm down, you two. Mind you don't rip the sheets. The frogman will be furious."

Anton locates the drawing he wants. It depicts a frog and a caped personage. The frog proffers its hand to be shaken. The dignitary has a long nose, analogous to that of the Count. His gesture radiates unbridled mirth. The next page portrays a frog immersed in a beaker of solution, bubbles emerging from his mouth. The next few leaves sketch the frog mutating into a human being.

"The frogman was a frog," cries Anton.

"Evidently so," says Crina. "I bet he's a man who got turned into a frog and is trying to change back."

"'Long Nose' is Count Dracula," surmises Petrica.

"Terrific deduction, Trica," says Crina. "He wears the smile the Count flashes at us. The frogman is quite an artist."

Anton, whose interest in the drawing pad has waned, shoves it back to Petrica and says, "This is not the room."

"What are you on about?" asks Crina.

"There is no window."

Crina and Petrica scan around.

Crina retrieves the candle from the table. Anton and Petrica explore with her. In a grate, an iron cauldron hangs above ashes.

"I maintain that it is," says Crina. "The steep tunnel, a bend, and then a level distance all argue that we're underneath the chamber across from mine."

"Then why the window in the painting?" inquires Anton.

Crina ponders for a while and says, "Remember the tale of the greedy king who has amassed a trove of treasure from his subjects and rivals? He is so selfish and miserly that he won't share the hoard, not even with his closest and dearest. He hides the riches inside a statue in the palace garden. Nevertheless, covertly he longs to flaunt how immense a fortune he has accumulated.

Without exception, he invites visitors to the palace to revere the statue even though neither its aesthetics nor artistry warrants such veneration."

"Are you saying the painter wanted people to know the existence of this room?" says Anton.

"Not the artist. Probably whoever was in authority. He wanted it to be a secret but not forgotten."

"Pathetic bastard."

"You're calling Count Dracula a bastard, Anton?" says Petrica.

"No, Trica," cuts in Crina. "The Count couldn't have built this castle. According to a record in the library, it was built in—the exact year has eluded me, but it was in the 1300s, over four centuries ago."

"Whether this is the mysterious room in the artwork is unimportant. It isn't what we are after."

Crina and Petrica concur.

46

Dracula stirs from his troubled dreams. The children must be having their morsels. He should get dressed.

He gets up and realizes he has regained a modest amount of energy.

Neculai, who is close by, hastens to his aid. "My lord, owing to your swoon, I let you rest. Is there anything I can do for you?"

"I'm ready to join the young ones. They must be expecting me."

"But Count, you mustn't exert yourself. The youngsters can divert themselves. You've fainted onto the floor. Crina laid your head on her thigh and fanned you. The boys ran for me. To be healthy is essential. Visit your lovers. Seek new ones if it pleases you."

"No, it doesn't please me. Haven't you listened to anything I said? I abhor my mistresses and any substitutes." He signals to Neculai with his hand to say nothing. "One more word from you on sucking blood from my wards, and I'll smack you so hard that you won't recover from it. Now, don't stand there like a log. Where is my broth? Let the children have their refreshments. I'll join them by and by."

The bowl of chicken broth wobbles in Dracula's shaky hand. He drinks the broth and eats a slice of oat bread. Without imbibing blood, his muscles have slackened and his flesh has chilled.

Neculai dresses him without censure. *It must have sunk into his thick skull that it is pointless to nag. Forgoing merriment isn't going to happen.*

Dracula has on knee breeches and a tight-fitting jerkin with sapphire buttons. The same gems adorn the buckles of his pumps. Over the jerkin floats his cape.

The trio joyfully sprints up to him in the courtyard. They miss him. Dracula is so touched that he kisses each child. Petrica loops his arms around his neck, greedy for a hug. He envelops Petrica. Barring his mistresses, he has not cuddled anyone since leaving the human world. *Has his life been secluded and solitary to such an extent?*

The warmth passing from the boy into himself evokes physical contacts and emotions that have been dismissed for ages. These rejuvenated sensations make him giddy. He lets it be, savoring the feeling. The consequences will take care of themselves.

He says, "Our stage glistens in the moonshine. Let us luxuriate in its glamor."

He swings Petrica in an ellipse. Petrica twitters delightedly.

Next, he bows to Crina and requests a dance.

Crina blushes and allows the Count to lead her.

Dracula twirls Crina up and down the courtyard. Crina's ivory pannier skirt oscillates, flaunting her silk mules. The moment the dancers are about to stomp on the creeping thyme in the cobbles, Dracula skillfully steers Crina away.

The dancers whirl round and round. Crina resembles a cloud, and Dracula, a dark-glinting thunderbolt hurtling through. The cape slashes the air, eclipsing a portion of the skirt. In a trice, the skirt reestablishes itself, puffy and whole.

Whether it is the result of the lack of nourishment or excess exercise, an onslaught of hunger grips Dracula. His nostrils tingle at a metallic scent. He inhales. There is no ambiguity in what the stench is. He stiffens, throwing Crina off balance. Crina staggers. Dracula relinquishes his hold on her.

Bolting across the courtyard is a headless chicken with gore on her feathers. Dracula's limbs go limp. He can taste blood on his palate. He flies at the chicken, seizing it by the wings. The fowl spasms but wilts as Dracula sucks at her wound. How palatable, how heavenly! In a trance, he drains the bird.

He licks the dregs off his lips. The children tremble and cling together. He has forgotten about them. They must have witnessed the incident.

Petrica's posture suddenly relaxes. "It is a trick, isn't it, Count?" he remarks and slips out of Crina's clasp.

"No, it isn't a trick," shrills Anton, snatching Petrica's wrist to prevent him from rushing to Dracula. "A headless chicken did totter forward: it scampered over my instep. And the Count—" The grotesque act overpowers Anton. Crina and Petrica whimper. Anton joins in.

Dracula is mortified. The hot intake coursing through his veins causes his brain to buzz. He reels as if intoxicated. He longs to shrink into himself. Instead, his pride sends him into a rage.

"Why are you moping about?" Seizing Crina's hand, he commands, "Let's conclude our dance."

Crina recoils.

Dracula tugs her from her mates. As Crina battles to free herself, Anton charges at Dracula. Dracula releases the girl to fend off Anton. He slaps his attacker with his cape. Anton tumbles, cutting his cheek, which the easy living has nurtured into a ripe peach. Dracula's flesh prickles. To appease his appetite, Dracula pins the boy down with his knees and blows him a breath. His quarry capitulates, lapsing into pliancy. Dracula digs his fangs into the boy's neck.

He shakes off Crina, who is straddling his back and yanking his hair. His next victim is Petrica. The petrified child mounts no resistance.

The nourishment in his veins revives the Count. Crina retreats to the foot of the bench, where she defies him with boldness. "Don't you dare touch me," her demeanor shouts.

Dracula steadies himself. On the ground lie the ashen corpses. Minutes ago, the departed were full of life; now, they are dead. Their inert eyes stare, reluctant to forsake humanity.

He stumbles to the bench and flops down on it. Face buried in his palms, violent tremors convulse him. Crina squeezes into a ball several feet away. Chin on her bent knees, she rocks with vacant rhythm.

Neculai materializes from behind the boxwoods, where he has been hiding. He decapitated the chicken and sent forth the remains. There was no alternative, Dracula being seriously ill. The brats didn't do themselves any favors. They raided his sanctuary and ransacked the laboratory, pawing through his papers and leaving them in disarray. The volume of Alchemy had clearly been handled. They invaded his privacy. He was furious at them. Maniacally so.

His fury has facilitated the execution of his stratagem. Dracula's health is of paramount importance. Neculai would have done what he has done—regardless. To atone for his sin, he will bury the boys properly. He shall hammer stakes into their hearts to guard them from joining the ranks of the undead. They have served the Count well and should rest in peace.

He tosses Petrica onto his shoulder and assesses the situation. Crina sways like an automaton. Dracula weeps on. The two have forgotten about each other and the world in general.

Anton's heavier corpse is harder to heave, necessitating a few tries to succeed. With a load on each shoulder, Neculai lumbers toward the gate to the lawn and graveyard. He unbolts the gate and shuffles through without relocking it. Crina is not in an adventurous frame of mind at the moment. In the improbable event that she wanders into the graveyard, no harm will be done since Dracula's tomb is well concealed.

Crina believes if she focuses on the cobbles, congruity will prevail. Neculai's maneuvers and the creak of the gate fail to weaken her concentration.

The courtyard lies dormant. Crina's intellect reasserts itself. She frees herself from her stupor. Where her companions lay is empty. They don't need to be there. The cadavers are as vivid to her as if they were present.

The Count trembles with his noiseless sobs. This silent suffering maddens Crina. She unfurls herself and storms toward Dracula, raining blows upon him. Astonished, Dracula flinches and then endures the pounding.

With her anger spent, Crina slumps next to Dracula, leaning into him. She yearns to snuggle up to the Count. She wants to forgive him. She wants to forget. Affection, she craves. "Why did you do it?" she murmurs—more a comment than a question.

In a trance, Dracula casts Crina aside and absconds into the murk. A mist enfolds him. He, too, wants to forget. Out of the opaque mist flees a bat. Higher and higher, the bat ascends, abandoning the moonlit stage and the lone remaining actor.

Part III

A Love Story

47

The bat lands on the mausoleum. He kept an assignation with a mistress. His vigor deters him from retiring into the vault. He swings under the eaves. Images of Violetta linger in his mind. The she-devil was especially cunning during their tryst. Contrary to tensing up at his whispers as she always did, she managed to be as pliant as ever. She engaged in her pretenses, and he shammed along. He nibbled her earlobe and squeezed her breasts greedily. She maintained her masquerade. Her neck was velvety smooth and without a vein. He detached himself from her and protruded his fangs. He pecked her neck. No reaction. Second peck, still no reaction. Third peck, and her neck arched. At the fourth peck, she moaned, and at the fifth, surrendered. A jugular popped out, robust and irresistible. The fangs drove into it.

A sound interrupts Dracula's thoughts. He fixes his attention on the source: a woman tiptoeing out of the chapel. Her back faces Dracula. The white bow tied at her waist stands out in the murky predawn. The metal clangs faintly as she slides the latch into its groove; she is trying not to wake up the denizens. But who is there to be disturbed? She steps onto the gravel path. The graveyard and a lawn constitute the grounds; tangled nettles and brambles screen most of the headstones. The woman's strides herald firmness and resolution.

Dracula sees that she is actually in her teens. This accords with the bow and the freshness she carries about her. At the water pump, the girl fills the pitcher sitting beneath its mouth. Behind the pump, clotheslines—lacking laundry at this moment—are strung.

Dracula flies at a height behind the girl so as not to alarm her.

The miss walks toward the gate, switching the loaded vessel from hand to hand. Down the path, she gazes upward.

Ah, the belfry, that is what she is admiring.

The base of the belfry is a pyramid with the upper one-third sliced off; red tiles array its slanted faces. The spire is as refined. Nature has blanched its charcoal tiles into a cool gray. The bell chamber between the base and the spire is built of aged oak. In it rests an iron bell.

The belfry commands esteem. The miss has taste.

The budding creepers on the chapel exterior enter her vision. She sighs and moves her gaze to the heap of clippings below. She must be the creator of the heap, thinks Dracula. The travail occurred recently. Shearing, removing the stems, and scraping the remnants off the depressions must have been a project. And now, shoots have sprouted.

The girl presses on and pushes open the gate to the enclosed court. She suppresses the vibration to stifle the rattling. Her attempt at noise control is futile. The hinges weep for lubrication. Even that may be ineffectual; the gate is as ancient as the estate itself. Who is around to be annoyed by the squeak anyway? Why is she so cautious? Maybe she loathes harsh sounds.

Dracula flies over the fence as the girl advances into the courtyard, an area he has neglected.

The sapling has evolved into a hawthorn with branches tipping into wide arcs. As usual, the fountain is not in operation, but it has been scrubbed clean along with the statue—a warhorse on its hind legs—in its center. The basin is clear of debris, and the statue is rid of moss. The girl must have done the tidying. It would surprise Dracula if Neculai handled such domesticity.

The girl waters poppies bordering the exterior of the hexagonal apse. The flowers are in bloom, and there are also buds. Above them, decorative windows exhibit their grace. With each window, overlaying arches encase stained glass. The mullions divide the lower glass into three lights, while a tracery of rosebuds adorns the upper section.

The rusty-red, emerald, and gold glass shards, paired with the yellow poppies and the white of the girl's bow, form a flawless palette.

Dracula wishes to tarry awhile, but the rousing morn cautions him. The mild beams on his skin, though not as deadly as the scorching rays, will age him by several years. This is not a serious concern the way he looks, but he despises the idea of it and hates the potential damage it may cause. With reluctance, he retreats to his tomb.

He plops onto the sofa, too restless to change out of his suit. His cape is dumped on the wing chair. He is not conscious of his deeds, his mind bursting with the girl. Is she through with the watering? Will she potter about? Apparently, she has undertaken a great deal of upkeep in the courtyard. Who is she? She must be about eighteen. Why has Neculai omitted mentioning her?

He regrets having raced back to the tomb. The fret escalates to the point that he jumps up. He manages not to whiz back out; he has more sense than that. Back down on the sofa, he sinks.

Why is he so besotted? What fuels the magnetism? He can't say that it is her beauty: he only glimpsed her profile. Not her voluptuousness either. The girl is thin. Even when she fills out, voluptuousness won't be a word attached to her. It doesn't suit her. What is it, then?

48

He waits for Crina in the graveyard. The mist covering the crag is too thin to obscure the scenery, but it instills a soothing coolness. Dracula summoned Countess Constantin in her dream earlier.

Among his mistresses, Countess Constantin is the kindest, always putting his urges and comfort above all else. He had neglected her, coveting a bit of naughtiness from the other mistresses. He decided to pay her a visit. Her body, which he enfolded, was eager and lithe. He felt just as ardent. He also felt safe: Countess Constantin would never harm him. Be that as it may, he was merely buying time with her.

Crina is his devotion.

Regrettably, the girl is nowhere in the vicinity. Dracula plunges into a frenzy. He flies to the courtyard, longing for her to be there. She is not. He loops around the crag to quell his nerves.

The succeeding mornings are disappointing as well. The defeats, instead of discouraging him, foster his obstinacy to locate the girl. Come what may, he will track her down. He could ask Neculai about her whereabouts. Neculai must be acquainted with the residents of the castle. But Dracula is averse to involving Neculai. It is Dracula's private affair: he shall handle it himself. He could catch her in her dreams but refuses to resort to that. He wants to partner with her in life, not in dreams.

His tenacity is rewarded on his fourth effort. Visibility is clear for miles. He believes events will proceed as anticipated.

And here she is, on the bench facing the fountain. Dracula's countenance enlivens, a representation of which appears on the navigating bat. Dracula is approaching the girl from behind, which works well for him. He is reluctant to show himself as a bat.

Dracula swoops behind the protruding apse to undergo his transformation. He smooths his hair, adjusts his cravat, and discards his cape by the poppies. His velvet coat is unbuttoned to boast an olive vest. His shoes are also olive, with ornamented buttons of diamonds. White hose flaunt his calves. A dashing devil he is.

He rounds the apse. Crina sits at an angle to him. He coughs. The girl turns toward him. For a moment, her expression is blank, then shock replaces it. Dracula stiffens. The girl controls herself.

"Pardon my intrusion, madam," Dracula says, bowing. "I haven't given you a fright, have I?"

The girl shakes her head. "Not a soul has ever appeared at this hour before. I was taken by surprise," she explains.

"What pleasant weather," Dracula comments. Gesturing toward the bench, he inquires, "May I join you?"

The girl nods.

"I'm Count Dracula," says Dracula.

The girl suppresses her confusion and says, "I'm Crina," without offering her hand to be kissed or declaring it an honor to meet the Count.

Catching the name, Dracula's throat constricts. A recollection wrestles to burst out but is swiftly pushed back into its slot.

An awkwardness hovers. Dracula sits alongside Crina. Beyond the fountain is a strip of space enclosed by edifices at odd angles. Haws bedeck the hawthorn in a corner.

The girl speaks to him, "I'm glad of your company. I'm usually alone."

Dracula twists his body to appraise Crina. She is pretty, awfully so. Her complexion is devoid of blemishes. Her cheeks are dimpled. The boyish characteristic about her is wonderfully alluring. It's evident in her gaits, which he caught a few days earlier, as well as in her frank and amiable countenance. Even the wavy bangs suggest a degree of boyishness. All this augments her charm without undermining her femininity. The girl is on the verge of blooming into a woman. A captivating enchantress she will mature into.

Crina withdraws her regard, disrupting his musing. He ought to muster a reply.

"The pleasure is mine," he says and falls silent. How idiotic! What's wrong with him? Is that the entirety of what he can say? As his eagerness mounts, his wits grow duller. Even the marble warhorse on the fountain loses patience. With its mane blown in the wind and forelegs kicking, it snorts at him to get on. Assuredly, his fancy has invented these theatrics, but the very fabrication of them proclaims the depth of his frustration. As he is thwarted by his ineptness, a nerve on his cheek pulses. The parapet has deflected a shaft of dawn light onto his cheekbone. He winces and is on his feet.

His animation bewilders the girl.

He bows and says, almost in a stutter, "I must take my leave, ma'am. May I call on you soon … does tomorrow suit?"

There is a short irresolution before the granting of a nod.

Dracula is outraged at himself. To avert embarrassment, he must equip himself with adequate topics of conversation. About what does he talk to his mistresses? They don't talk, do they? Their actions are their language, voicing their longings and thoughts. Crina and his mistresses are of different natures; he must avoid associating one with the other. Crina overflows with health and life and is totally uncorrupted.

They could prattle about her poppy garden and daily employment. But are not these themes too mundane? He would love to recount his flights—the freedom gifted by the vast sky, with the wind and mist brushing his body. Hindrance is nonexistent for miles. He can glide on and be himself. He can dive and soar. Stars coat him silver and wink at him—she will rejoice in the scene; girls are partial to this sort of spectacle.

How is he to describe these experiences without exposing himself? That he flies. As a bat. Under no circumstances will he reveal this aspect of himself to her. He longs for her to deem him human.

49

The sudden advent of Dracula has jolted and unsettled Crina. How many years has it been? Seven? She identified him in a trice. Immaculately attired. Fetching. As striking as ever. The Count has not aged a day.

How the boys died still angers her and still saddens her. She blocks out the atrocity, preventing it from muddling her judgment. To be distressed by it is nonsensical. She has accepted the incident as a thing of the past.

The tragedy had swathed her in grief. She missed Anton. She missed Petrica. She also missed the Count. They had worshipped him. As the months progressed, the pain lessened, and as the years progressed, the memories faded, though not forgotten.

Now, he is back.

He supposed her a stranger. His irises flickered at her name. It likely signified nothing. At any rate, it is reasonable that the Count didn't recognize her. She is a head taller than the girl he deserted in the courtyard. The girl with whom he danced has blossomed.

The Count acted shy, unsure of himself, which was at variance with her remembrances of him. Where is the character who commanded, teased, and galvanized them?

They had never gathered with him in daylight as she did this morning. He had always championed the night. Has his preference changed? She doubts that. His escaping from the morning rays serves as a sound basis for her suspicion. He is as peculiar as he has always been.

To allay her edginess, Crina distracts herself with activities.

The poppy bed is overcrowded. The plants rise high. Bees hum and flit from flower to flower. Crina roots out the weaker stalks to create healthy spacing between the plants. She clips the blooms, which she deposits in a pewter pail. The far boundary of the cemetery is her next destination.

She passes the mausoleum; its ancient, battered façade has acquired an ash gray. The keystone of the central arch is a skull. Moss has equipped a socket with a green eye. Its sibling is a dismal hole, echoing the gaping mouth underneath. Set within the arch is a mammoth portal. Instinct warns Crina to shy away from the sepulcher, to avoid the wraiths inside. Neculai, by contrast, reveres it as a shrine. He maintains the surrounding terrain diligently so that the stately monument stays clear of invading shrubs and thorns.

As always, the eye spies on Crina, and the mouth beckons her. Crina scampers away.

She stops at two well-tended graves. The tomb inscriptions bear the names of Anton and Petrica and their dates of birth and death. No funerary art is chiseled.

Neculai has erected the slabs. Crina tends to them, scrubbing away the algae and lichens on the slabs and removing the encroaching weeds.

She swaps the wilted plants in the vases with the blossoming poppies. Should she report Dracula's return? She dismisses the idea lest the communication rattle her deceased friends.

For lunch, she eats vegetable barley soup in the kitchen. Neculai is elsewhere. He may be in bed or in his laboratory; there is no way to tell. They eat supper together—a habit formed since the death of Anton and Petrica. It was a display of sympathy from Neculai, Crina speculates, but has ripened into a practice they are both unwilling to give up.

With the meal finished, she takes the ledger and sheets of paper from a drawer in the cabinet, along with a quill and an inkstand from a shelf. The amounts spent on the butchers, fishmongers, bakers, and grocers have been recorded on the sheets. So are the charges from the milliners, clothiers, and wine merchants. Expenditures need to be registered and balanced. Neculai has taught her arithmetic and deputized her to manage the budgeting.

Today she is unable to concentrate, having erred in a calculation. Why does Dracula have to spring up suddenly? Her life is flourishing. She is her own mistress. True, only the keep is unlocked. She has options where to loiter, nevertheless. Neculai has opened the chapel for her to pray. The court and the back lawn are at her disposal. And she and Neculai make excursions to town.

The first outing had been a wonder. She had been cooped up in the fortress since her arrival. Neculai reversed the route they had clattered over with Anton and Petrica. Her mood soared. It was great fun to thunder down the road. She had forgotten how steep it was and how the gradient lasted for such a distance.

They disembarked at Council Square in Braşov. Neculai lent her his arm. She was delighted. Such gallantry was novel to her.

She peeked at Neculai. His diligence was rewarded. He no longer resembled a frog. Normalcy had been restored. His hair was as fiery as ever. Waves cascaded in layers from his crown down. It was thrilling to be escorted by a handsome gentleman.

Produce, livestock, and wares for sale overflowed the square. Vendors and buyers alike arrived from the abutting villages. Multitudes came from the local community. Unused to crowds, they overwhelmed her. Discerning her discomfort, Neculai pulled her to him and shielded her from a throng bustling through.

The throng having passed, he released her, and they sauntered on. Crina understood that Neculai would have behaved as chivalrously to any girl. Even so, she was enthralled.

One alley meandered into another. The boom of the square diminished into a hum. They stopped at an establishment with a saffron façade.

A lady, in a lace mantua and shaded by a lace parasol, was perusing the window displays. The gentleman accompanying her frowned and tried to ease her away. The lady, defying her spouse, held her ground.

Neculai and Crina continued into the clothier's, leaving the couple to their discord.

A man abandoned his seat at the sewing table. Thin hair covered his skull. His smile flattened his sagging jowls.

"Good day, Lungu," Neculai said.

"Good day, prince. It's a privilege to have you. What do you require, sir? A vest? A greatcoat? A suit? Lungu is always at your service."

"Nothing for me," replied Neculai. "This young lady, on the other hand, requires new gowns."

Lungu, the tailor, peered at Crina over the rim of his oval spectacles. Crina reddened. She was sensible of the too-short frock she wore. She had outgrown her wardrobe overnight.

After winking at her, Lungu said to both her and Neculai, "We have just the things—of the latest mode—for such a lovely young lady. I vow the miss will look magnificent in them. If the miss will permit my wife to measure her, we'll discuss the material subsequently."

The wife halted sewing. A cap screened her hair. Crina imagined the hair to be snowy, in line with the deep wrinkles. The junior seamstresses, at the table, also wore caps to deter hair from shedding onto the fabrics. Their focus was on their stitching since they had already weighed up the patrons. Chins down, they toiled on.

Without exchanging pleasantries, the tailor's wife led Crina into an alcove, where she drew a curtain to isolate them inside. Sunlight flooding the shop illuminated the interior. Lungu's wife helped Crina strip down to her chemise. Then she removed the measuring tape from around her neck to conduct her business. Strenuous tasks were obviously mapped out for the woman, both at the shop and residence. This was enough to turn anyone aloof and gaunt.

Lungu's endeavors to commit Neculai to leather gloves wafted into the alcove. Crina envisioned Neculai assessing a collection of hand-stitched gloves, with the enthusiastic storekeeper beside him.

With her measurements in hand, Crina browsed the garment templates. They reflected the current fashion; the designs were sumptuous. The dresses were low-cut, with curvaceous bodices and skirts split to disclose the petticoat beneath. Crina favored a less elaborate pattern. Even so, there were copious amounts of trimmings: the sleeves were tiered with flounces.

"Should the same pattern be employed for both gowns?" asked Lungu.

Crina replied in the affirmative, "With different fabrics, they will appear distinct, won't they?"

"They will, ma'am. We have an assortment of fabrics."

From a shelf, Lungu dislodged a bolt and laid it on the counter between himself and Crina. The floral print in magenta and bronze was gorgeous. He draped an unfurled length over his torso and said, "The silk is of the finest weave—luxurious to the touch, and it shows off the contour of the body, as you can see."

For everyday wear, she selected a tan cotton cloth. It was sufficiently soft. The dress was meant for tending to chores.

It was a fruitful outing. In addition to the habiliments ordered, she had purchased a straw hat beautified with chiffon flowers and, from the shoemaker, satin mules. They also bought a bag of barley, a sack of millet, bell peppers, cabbage, herbs, a jar of honey, and smoked ham.

There have been subsequent jaunts to the markets. They explored the vegetable and food stalls, both eager to test out their culinary skills.

Dracula is sure to throw her life into disorder, if he hasn't already done so. Should she steer clear of him? But she has promised to see him tomorrow. What if she breaches her promise? Will he search for her? If he finds her, what then? Deep down, it is clear to her that she will honor her word for tomorrow. Did she not hesitate but relent to Dracula's entreaty? She had then resolved to accede to his request.

The gaieties she and Dracula enjoyed long ago were most memorable. He was authoritative but could jest without constraint. The Count was intrigue incarnate. It was impossible to foretell his next action. Being kept in wonderment was exhilarating.

But he executed that wicked deed; Anton and Petrica are dead.

He will not repeat the atrocity on her. Her gut says so. Nevertheless, she foresees perils. As to what kind, she can't say.

Restlessness impels her to straighten up, bashing her knees against the table. Ink spills from the inkstand, soaking into the tabletop and staining it. She must bolt out of the keep and into the yard.

Light fills the courtyard. She inhales and exhales. The intimacy of the environs calms her. She finds enough to praise. The chapel glistens. It must have been a job to construct the exterior. Assembling the round pebbles and arranging them aesthetically must have been taxing.

She wanders into the nave and down to the south transept. In the recess spirals a stairway which Crina climbs. She ascends to the base of the belfry. A sturdy rope snakes down from the wheel overhead. Attached to the wheel is an iron bell.

Crina is not there to toll the bell but to reach her special hideaway. Above, a large aperture in the ceiling allows the ringer to manipulate the bell rope. Built into this ceiling is a trapdoor. With a hooked pole, Crina swings it open. A rope ladder rolls down. Crina scales the rungs. After she steps off, the ladder sways before subsiding into place.

The bell, attached to a sturdy headstock, is free of nests of any kind. So are the masses of joists and mechanisms supporting the headstock and its motion. They were far from being so. Dust, cobwebs, windblown debris, rodents, and birds had overtaken the bell chamber. Crina washed and tidied the place.

The courtyard below is sectioned into shadows and lights. The bench she frequents has its back to her. The warhorse on the fountain faces her.

She ambles to the opposite side and lowers herself onto the floor so that her skirt sprawls out over the pitched wall below. The probability of her falling off is virtually zero: she adopts this posture regularly. The absence of a balustrade was unnerving at first, but she has quelled the disquietude. Since then, it has worked out perfectly: no balusters exist to partition her view and cage her in. The monumental pillars at the four corners have always furnished reassurance.

A bird has fluttered in previously. At arm's length from her, it hopped nonchalantly and then performed a comical move. It tilted its beak upward in the manner of a man thumbing his nose! Crina chuckled at the furry ball's audacity. Her chuckle kindled in the bird a sense of danger. Without delay, it catapulted away. The bird's plumage exhibited a tint of brown, and the bill was slender and sharp. It belonged to the host of birds about.

She has not had guests in her retreat since. Here she can unravel problems or fritter away the hours without disruption.

The vicinity is precious to her.

Her vegetable garden is below. She peers at the carrot tops. Neculai primed the plot with her, removing the sod, pebbles, and rocks. They plowed the soil together. The patch bathes in the sunshine and drains well. Neculai has granted her charge of the cultivation—a duty she handles without difficulty owing to her prior practice at the orphanage.

Wildflowers and flowering weeds overrun the lawn. Two droll-looking apple trees lean into each other to conspire. Beyond the lawn lies the graveyard. A footpath separates the two. Where the graveyard begins, the maze of brambles starts. The southern corner of the graveyard entombs Anton and Petrica.

The ground is semicircular. The chapel is located vertically in its middle. What she beholds is the southwest half. The peak of the mausoleum protrudes above the nave in the distance. That is her view of the northwest section. The skull is out of sight—which she prefers, as spying on her is blocked.

She visualizes the linens drying on the laundry lines. She has washed and hung them. A breeze would have carried the flapping of the linens over the roof, but there is no breeze—and no billowing. Nature is in recess.

She is grateful for the life that has been allotted to her. She has lived in luxury. If she had been less fortunate, where would she be? She would have had to work for her keep, perhaps as a scullery maid with the prospect of becoming a cook or as a seamstress at Lungu's. As it is, she is spared from earning a livelihood.

There are drawbacks. She is almost always by herself. Besides Neculai, Mitu is her only contact. Mitu performs his rounds periodically, replenishing the firewood and taking care of the lawn. Scything the grass, he pauses at intervals to wipe away his perspiration or scratch his gray beard. Mitu is never a mate. The disparity in their age aside, Mitu shies away from chatter. He responds chiefly in grunts.

She is unversed in the ways of the world. She desires to discover and be acquainted with peers. Will Dracula facilitate the fulfillment of these missing aspects?

She can't depend on Dracula. The Count may be adroit in the social code. Yet will he be willing to take her into society? Does the Count engage in social events? Where has he been since he forsook her? She is ignorant of his life and concerns. His unsavory trait she has witnessed. She shudders at the memory of it.

50

Crina has been allowed to prepare dinner. She washes and chops the vegetables and often takes charge of the cooking as well. She particularly welcomes Neculai's entrance into the kitchen this evening. She sets aside the whisk she has been using to beat the cornmeal.

"Excuse my tardiness, Crina," Neculai apologizes. "I was out fetching an ingredient for my latest experiment and got tied up. Freshening up has further delayed me."

Neculai is radiant. Crina suspects she isn't the sole bearer of tidings. Unsure of how to unburden herself, she says, "We will have a game pie with cornmeal and cheese—if that's agreeable with you."

Neculai has baked the pie. He has honed his culinary skills, and his pies are delicious. The width of the table separating them promotes conversation. The length of it would have forced them to raise their voices, which would resonate in the hollow space. In any case, the head of the table is reserved for Dracula. Transgression of this bound is inconceivable.

After Dracula deserted her, she was sick for a fortnight, delirious for days. Her constitution gradually revived, and her mind was fortified. Eventually, she resolved to forget about the Count.

Flashes of the man had cropped up uninvited in her head. They came and went—these flashes. She supposed them to be a premonition of his return. She waited but was proven wrong.

Her dreams of him had been sporadic. His breeziness in the dreams gladdened her. Contrarily, his coldness and rejection pained her.

She has refrained from inquiring about Dracula. It is best to ignore the topic. What is there to ask, anyway? Neculai has not volunteered any information either. She trusts the two are in contact.

How should she broach the fact that she has spent a few minutes with the Count?

Neculai halts eating, prompting her to copy him.

With glee, he says, "I've got news."

So, he does have something to share.

"You'd never guess whom I bumped into in the village!"

"I wouldn't," Crina replies with grace. "But I'm dying to be enlightened."

"I was at the druggist's to purchase medicinal powder. A customer was in the store. From his attire, I took him for a merchant. The smell of grains on his clothing supported my conjecture. His drawl enlivened me, not because his speech validated my guess. He was in the grain trade. To fulfill his schedule, he had to push on with his merchandise, despite his fever. He relied on the druggist to provide relief. His Suceava accent was music to my ears!"

Neculai's diligence in tracking down his beloved has been unproductive. He has come across merchants from Moldavia. The merchants were unacquainted with Camelia or the Crişans.

His fortune seems to have taken a turn for the better.

"Were you able to learn anything useful from him?" Crina asks, anxious for Neculai.

"Not exactly," says Neculai. "Though disappointing, it's fitting. The Crişans are not eminent nobility. Merchant Moraru said he hadn't met the lady or heard of her. But he promised to inquire for me. On his next trip to Braşov, he'll update me."

"Fabulous. I have faith he'll furnish you with a promising missive."

There was a brief lull in the chat.

Then Crina says, "I also have news to relate."

Apprehension seizes Neculai.

"Count Dracula approached me earlier."

"What?" exclaims Neculai.

"I was lounging in the courtyard. He showed up without warning."

"I understand how you must have felt. What o'clock was it? Was it light out?"

"Seven or thereabouts. The courtyard was on the verge of livening up."

"What was he thinking—endangering himself?!" Neculai cries.

"We were in the shade—untouched by the sun."

"How long were you together? What did he want?"

"We weren't together long—about fifteen minutes, I guess. As for what the Count wanted, I can't say. He did not remember me, which could have to do with my having grown. He introduced himself and asked to be allowed to join me. It so disconcerted me that I knew not what to do or think. He asked for my name and received it without any reaction. We avoided eye contact. All of a sudden, he recoiled as though struck by lightning. He has requested a rendezvous tomorrow."

"And you have consented?"

Crina nods.

What he has heard troubles Neculai extremely. Life has been harmonious for him and Crina, and for Dracula, too. Crina's getting together with the Count poses a threat. He is powerless to eliminate it. Nobody can oppose Dracula. It is a consolation that their dealings occur in real life, not in Crina's dreams.

"Believe me, Crina, it is rather a bad idea for you and the Count to associate."

"If you are uneasy that he may harm me, pray don't. I'm sanguine he won't."

The girl has determination but is untried. What does Dracula want from her? Will he be able to find out without bringing up the past? They have shunned any discussion of Anton and Petrica. Dracula must have inferred that Neculai was the architect of the scheme instigating the demise of the boys. What he did has both saved Dracula and brought Dracula shame. He is ashamed of it himself. The episode should be buried.

When the girl was afflicted by Dracula's brutal act, he fed her gruel and sponged her forehead. During her infirmity, he nursed her by the bedside. She was nurtured back to health and became attached to him. Out of guilt, he let her bond with him and grew to value her company. By degrees, he opened up to her, recounting his childhood, his life as a lord's son, Camelia, and even his laboratory endeavors. Crina told him about her life in the orphanage and how she never knew her parents. They reciprocate support and confidence. Crina is strong-willed and self-sufficient; her attachment to him is nonintrusive.

He aims to insulate Crina from hurts, just as he does Dracula.

He must be vigilant and keep an eye on the duo.

He says, "You should do as you please. I suggest an early appointment. Remember how the Count prizes the night."

51

Dracula is anxious to be with Crina. He rushes his tryst with Countess Ciorbă. Back at the tomb, he tends to his toilet, scenting behind the ears with perfumed water and fastidiously arranging his hair. The suit, tailored for the occasion, is laid out for him.

Preened, he strides out of the crypt, which strikes him as odd. Flying is his normal way. He accelerates into a sprint, with thoughts of Crina spurring him on.

Crina is already in the courtyard. She looks in his direction. She has taken a bite of an apple. A streak of juice dampens her lower lip. His heartbeats escalate, and he hurries toward her.

Crina swallows the morsels of fruit. The contractions of her throat muscles rivet Dracula. Crina places the half-eaten apple among the others on a handkerchief on her lap. One of the apples has a deep depression where the stem rests.

Dracula bows and says, "Apologies for interrupting your breakfast. I didn't expect you to be here so early, madam. I thought I would wait for you. How wrong I was. Pray don't let me interrupt you; continue enjoying your apple."

Crina nibbles on her apple while offering another to Dracula.

Dracula declines her offer. Crina finishes eating. Scanning the courtyard, Dracula says, "Madam, are you not afraid of the dark?"

"No, not really. You have to get accustomed to it, and you always do. I'm familiar with the objects in this courtyard and can distinguish them well enough. No threats lurk nearby."

Dracula grins and says, "I'm glad to hear that. Threats or not, they won't be able to hide from my vision. For instance, the hawthorn bears madam's name. I can see it from here."

Crina stares at Dracula in astonishment.

"Shall we examine the carving?"

With Crina's nod of assent, Dracula rises and extends his arm to Crina, which she accepts, having removed the handkerchief of fruit from her lap. They stroll toward the hawthorn.

Wrens burst into song from the branches. As Dracula and Crina approach, the birds flutter away as if escaping from grave peril. Their frantic flapping underscores their terror.

"We've agitated the poor wrens," remarks Crina.

Dracula sneers at the scattered birds.

On the hawthorn, the split bark exposes the cambium layer beneath. There it is: her name presented as fissures in the bark.

"How could I have missed it? I pass by the tree daily but overlooked it."

"Perhaps it's a recent creation. It's beautiful, isn't it?"

The composition of the carvings is splendid.

"I'm grateful for your sharp eyesight."

Dracula bows. Crina inspects the artwork. Then they saunter on.

With Crina hanging on to his arm, Dracula's chest swells with pride. The girl has twined and pinned up her bangs. Her dress is brocaded in the prettiest and most feminine floral design. Along with the bell-sleeves, it is especially charming. Is she thus arrayed for his benefit?

His eyes linger on her. The tip of her lovely nose, sloping upward, invites kisses. He shall plant many on it. Her curled-up lashes are equally appealing. And then there are those slightly parted lips.

The girl wears no jewelry except for dangling earrings. The simplicity suits her.

They complete their round. The surrounding gray has whitened.

"I don't want to detain you any longer, madam. Do you plan to enjoy the morning out here, or shall I accompany you back to your residence?"

"The weather is perfect for idling outdoors. Thank you, Count, for the pleasant stroll."

"I'm delighted to be of service. Will madam be here tomorrow?"

Crina responds with a smile.

With a bow, Dracula departs and retraces his steps.

Once he passes the gate, Dracula whistles. The whistling trills on until he disappears into the vault.

"How did it go with the Count?" asks Neculai. He has wanted to inquire much sooner. To avoid appearing anxious, he postponed the question.

Earlier, while preparing the meal, Crina was preoccupied with her plants.

"The eggplants have traces of worms. The infestation is on the leaves, not the fruits. I've found no worms despite my best efforts," she said.

"Let me handle it. There may be tiny beetles that cleverly spring away when you approach."

"Worms are most active after dusk. These beetles are likely the same. Let's investigate together then."

"Alright, if you say so. You're the gardener."

"I gained this knowledge at the orphanage."

Eventually, Neculai asks about her meeting with Dracula.

"It went well," replies Crina. "I was out before the rooster crowed. The Count and I chatted for a bit." Neculai remains silent. Crina continues, "He informed me of my name engraved on the hawthorn."

Neculai frowns.

"Yes, it's most remarkable. Delicate calligraphy is displayed on the trunk. I always have faith in nature as an artist, but I am astounded by its elegant carving of my name."

Neculai scoffs. Clearly, Dracula is the artist who crafted the inscription. It worries him that Dracula has gone to such lengths to captivate Crina. A relationship between Dracula and Crina foretells destruction. Intimacy between them should be prevented. He intends to keep them safe, even from one another.

Crina also harbors suspicions about the artist. She says, "You believe the Count is responsible, don't you? I suspect that too. He devised numerous tricks for Trica, Anton, and me. He called them illusions. I figure this is also a deception but find the calligraphy intact. Can an illusion last that long?"

"I'm ignorant of illusions. Dracula is ingenious. He has the means to create the artwork. There is undoubtedly a specific purpose behind his actions, though."

"What could that purpose be?"

"To enchant you."

"To enchant me?"

"Listen, it would be best for you to distance yourself from the Count. Involvement between the two of you won't yield positive outcomes. It may lead to dire consequences. The tragic fate of Anton and Petrica serves as proof of the danger. If I am correct, the Count is quite infatuated with you. He will pursue you. It's up to you to end the courtship. I implore you to consider my advice."

"It's none of your business with whom I should or shouldn't associate." Anger seeps into Crina's tone. "Things aren't as serious as you seem to think. The Count and I have had brief chats. He might have planned to amuse me. But it hardly implies he's besotted with me. To astonish is in his nature. He revels in his tricks and skills. What he did to Trica and Anton was abominable. But he'll never harm me. I don't understand why he and I shouldn't meet." Crina chokes up. "It's hard to be alone all the time. I miss greeting new faces and having friends, apart from you, to spend time with. Couldn't you appreciate that?"

"I'm sorry I've upset you, which is not my intention. Both you and the Count are important to me. I don't want either of you to get hurt. Let's drop the subject for now. Shall we? Dusk is steadily approaching. Let's rescue your eggplants."

Crina's mood lifts.

52

Dracula and Crina promenade the courtyard. No words are exchanged between them. The absence of conversation persists after they reseat themselves on the bench. Eventually, Dracula says, "Madam is comfortable with silence."

"I'm used to it. A chunk of the day, I am by myself. It's near dinner that Neculai joins me." At the mention of Neculai, Crina gauges Dracula's reaction. Not gaining any, she continues, "We cook and eat together. Afterward, I resume being solitary."

"A mentor once stated how magnificent the silence within us was. He alleged that it was capable of enveloping our senses and emotions. With practice, he said, we could control this sheathing. And by varying the cadence of the silence, we transformed our essence. Phenomenal concepts, wouldn't you say?"

"I'm too callow to decipher these extraordinary beliefs, sir."

"Not merely you, dear. I am a great deal older than you, and I've barely been able to unravel his sentiments."

"Actually, I prefer a modicum of noise. Such as the cooing of the songbirds, the caw of the crows, and the chirp of the insects among the grass. They bespeak life. In the winter, under thick quilts, the howls of the gale entrance me."

Dracula beams at the guileless girl.

Crina resumes, "I'd like to travel. I'm grateful to you, Count, for providing me with such an abode. But I fantasize about what's out there."

"Don't you get out at all?"

"Yes, with Neculai. To the village and occasionally to Brașov. It would be nice to undertake longer distances."

"Ah," says Dracula. He sympathizes with the girl. Blooming and vivacious, she ought to explore and experiment. It would give him boundless satisfaction to be her partner on her quests. If he were to gratify Crina's aspirations, he must detach himself from the dominion of the night and rejoin the practical world of humans. The degree of sacrifice entailed is so substantial that he must ponder long and intensely.

The interactions with Crina are pleasurable to Dracula. It is difficult to separate from the girl. He lingers beyond the onslaught of the sun. For nobody else would he have imperiled himself.

Crina shows him the vegetables she has cultivated. Her zest for the stringy beans is rather endearing. Together, they harvest a container.

On all fours, he tends Crina's poppies. This gesture amuses him and the girl, who rewards him with the prettiest chuckles. Unaccustomed to gardening, he is clumsy at it. The girl teases his clumsiness and advises him, "Pull the weed by its stem near the dirt." She also teaches him to use a hoe. He weeds while Crina trims the poppies. He leads her outside via the round tower and assists her down the winding stairs. The agile Crina can manage by herself but allows him the courtesy. The brow of the crag yields a sweeping view below. The road weaves through the scrubland, buffered by hills and crags. Crina shows no interest. He recalls the excursions she has taken with Neculai. She is acquainted with the panorama.

The girl possesses an appetite for substantial expeditions.

Dracula contemplates how to address this situation. To escort her on her adventures is what he thirsts for, yet his nocturnal life prevents such fulfillment. He is reluctant to consign her to the dream sphere, which will alter the nature of their relationship. He values Crina's authenticity and vivacity. They shall remain in their separate domains. He must rely on the girl's imagination, as there is a wealth of information to share.

The weather is sultry. Crina, at her usual spot, fans herself.

Luminous, Crina is the sun Dracula covets.

A scent tickles his nose. He sneezes and notices the apple cores on a handkerchief placed between him and Crina.

"Forgive me, Count," says Crina, sniffing the air. "The scent has grown pungent. It's inconsiderate of me not to have heeded it. The apples taste scrumptious in this heat, though."

Crina wraps the cores up with the handkerchief. Her fingers are nimble: the nails are petite, with a healthy gloss.

Crina lowers the bundle by her feet, turning away from Dracula. He addresses her gently, "Has madam perused materials on deserts?"

"Deserts?" Crina inquires verbally and through her expression.

"Deserts are regions with scant precipitation, mostly barren or sparsely vegetated. The sandy deserts are mesmerizing, breathtaking. Observe the dunes—one side shaded, the other soaking in fierce sun. Smoky gray meets sizzling gold; cool meets hot. The ridges are sharp, evoking the sensation of a fine cut on flesh." Dracula rasps an *Ouch* and then smooths his tone back into silkiness. "The dunes undulate. Rain trickles down. The drops dimple the sand."

Crina envisions the sand—hot and cold, dimpled from rain. The "ouch"—brisk and husky—which Dracula perfectly intoned also stirs something in her, as seen in the heaving of her bosom. It is evident that she embraces both the exquisite and sensual aspects of the scenes Dracula portrays.

"As stunning and breathtaking are the seas of ice, constantly shifting with the ocean currents," continues Dracula. "The floes shift and wail. Shift and wail. An explosion resounds as a section of a glacier severs and crashes into the water. Debris sprays. Not all the icebergs calved are pure white. Many bear streaks of ice-blue, turquoise, and indigo. When they are pure white, the seascape dazzles. The warm climate nibbles at the formations. The sun strokes where the water laps."

Dracula grants Crina a pause. She has stopped fanning herself, thoughts elsewhere. Her breathing is pronounced and her cheeks flush. Dracula allows a suitable interval to pass. He surveys the courtyard. Where the diffused light is intercepted, shadows lie.

"Don't neglect the beauty around us, which deserves our devotion but receives none. Note the umbra over there," he says, gesturing, "where a plant begs to be praised. We ought to oblige, for it is no less exquisite than the dunes and the ice, no less seductive as well."

"I'm familiar with the shrub. Its tear-shaped, purple foliage erupts into bright red in autumn."

"Right," agrees Dracula. "Take pleasure in it now."

As he speaks, the moon emerges from seclusion to grace the shrub with its beam. In the moonlight, the purple tears flare up.

Crina utters a cry, so divine is the spectacle.

"The leaves ache for love. Now that the moon has liberated them, they yearn aloud. Aren't they intoxicating? You mustn't underestimate the darkness that envelops most of the shrub. The contrast between the sublime blackness and the splash of shimmer brings out the essence of the teardrops. The shrub is a shy maiden in retreat, gathering courage to unveil what her heart craves …"

Tiny beads of sweat moisten Crina's temples. Slowly, she transfers her scrutiny from the shrub onto Dracula. Their gazes meet. Her eyes blaze.

Dracula loses control of himself. He presses Crina to his chest. Crina's heart throbs, its drumming in tandem with his own.

Crina submits briefly, then struggles to break free. Dracula tightens his clasp. She shoves Dracula hard. Dracula releases her.

Crina stands and flees toward the keep. Dracula rises as well, starts to follow her, then refrains. It is best that he abandon his pursuit. His passion has confounded Crina. He must not discomfit her further.

How could he have controlled his passion? He has fallen for the girl. He refuses to curb his fervor. It is obvious that Crina is unready for him. They belong to conflicting worlds. If she were more experienced, their love might flourish. As it is, the constraints of their different worlds may frustrate her. He aspires to indulge her and finds himself in a quandary.

53

Crina locks herself in her boudoir. She plops into the armchair, perspiring and panting loudly. She should change out of her sweaty raiment but remains where she is.

Has the Count wooed her? Implausible! Even if he doesn't recognize her as his ward, he is aware that she is a member of the manor, a dependent. Her station is inferior to his. Not that she's ashamed of her class. But a count is a count; a penniless orphan is a penniless orphan. Marriage between them is improbable. Dracula wouldn't have courted her. Then, what was the import of his embrace, wherein their hearts thumped in unison?

She misses having someone to confide in besides Neculai. Neculai has been her mentor and the facilitator of her accomplishments. By virtue of her education, she can comport herself in a fetching manner and read Latin. Neculai has been supportive and patient—in general, that is.

The issue at hand is rather personal. Neculai has cautioned her about the Count, and she has refused to listen. His caution might be justifiable. However, has she inflated the Count's intentions?

The dunes, the floes, and the words with the inflection Dracula employed fascinate her. They are his devices of cajolery.

A warmth shoots through her; she gasps.

To the casement, she dashes. No breeze lends rescue. The glare of the sky blinds her briefly and informs her of the fleeting morning. She knows what to do. After tidying up her hair and donning a dainty cotton frock, she seeks support from Neculai down the corridor.

"Neculai, would you care to share a simple meal with me?"

Grunts sound behind the closed door.

"I wish to consult you."

Crina's concern trickles into Neculai's sleeping consciousness, stirring alarm. Crina seldom fusses. Hitherto, she has sought succor twice. He has pulled down the trapdoor in the belfry for her, because the rusty hinges were stuck. To prevent potential damage, he has secured a dangling limb of the hawthorn. He hopes Dracula is not the cause of this appeal. "I'll be with you in a minute," he calls out.

Crina carves lamb sausages into slices. They can end the meal with a piece of the walnut cake she has baked.

Once she decides to consult Neculai, agitation abates. Her merry disposition exerts itself. Whether Dracula has seduced her no longer overwhelms her. She will forbid him from repeating it. His caressing, suggestive words she can handle. What he has described is exotic. The scenes enthrall her. She is hungry to see them with her own eyes and render them with words of her choice.

Neculai arrives. The table has been set. Slices of sausages and cheese are arranged appetizingly alongside plump figs. On the cutting board lies a loaf of bread. Crina has a talent for such creativity. Basic dishes become alluring under her resourceful touch. Her ebullient reception allays Neculai's apprehension; she is not afflicted.

They settle down to their food.

"There's something you propose to discuss?"

 Crina nods.

"I'm listening."

"I think the Count tried to woo me."

Neculai gags and coughs.

"Don't be so worked up over it," says Crina amiably. "He enfolded me in his arms, but I wrestled free. No harm was done, I assure you."

The cough rages on.

"Should I fetch you some water?"

"I'm fine—" attempts Neculai. "A swallow went awry. Give me a minute."

Neculai's coughing subsides.

"He has acted inappropriately," says Neculai, whose complexion has regained its normal color. "Did he frighten you? This is why I beseeched you not to have anything to do with him."

"Above all, I was confused. I debated with myself the meaning of his behavior. Had I inflated his purpose? I vacillated over the answer and got myself woolly-headed. My decision to confer with you has relieved me. There's little to be nervous about. The gulf between our classes is so enormous; he couldn't have implied anything."

It suits Neculai to have Crina reason in this line. He is disinclined to confess to her the realm in which Dracula dwells. In fact, Dracula is far beyond convention to be bothered with classes. Neculai says, "You see, the Count is a great man but tends to get carried away. To him, nothing is amiss with that—to be carried away. I beg to differ. Letting loose of oneself is permissible to a limited extent. It is wrong of him—emphatically so—to have lost control and imposed on you. I dare say he's made an ass of himself. My advice holds: you'd best avoid him."

"It hasn't come to that."

"Hasn't it, now? Don't tell me you're already attached to the Count."

"Oh, no," protests Crina. "The time I spent with him was brief. And, in general, I've already told you how we spent it. Trica, Anton, and I—we idolized him once. He erased all that.

"I'm an adult now. My opinion of him has changed. He's been to places I've not dreamed of. It is entrancing to hear about them and be enlightened about their magnificence. The Count has been kind and proper. It would be a shame to sever our tie.

"I can protect myself. He won't overstep the bounds again."

"Let's hear how you ensure that."

"Tell him plainly: I won't tolerate it."

The life of a recluse has engendered Crina's naïveté, Neculai reflects. She is too impressionable to resist Dracula's powerful nature. Her firmness on rendezvousing with him betrays how deeply Dracula has swayed her. Things have gotten serious.

He coaxes, "Could you use a breather from him?" Perceiving Crina's reluctance, he adds, "It'll enable you to recompose."

Crina acquiesces. She says gaily, "Shall we rummage the shops tomorrow?"

"Let's do that."

"The ribbon on my straw hat has had a rip for ages. I shall replace it." She then envisions herself browsing through an assortment of ribbons.

Neculai agonizes over Dracula. If Dracula is serious about Crina, to maintain a relationship, he will have to drag himself back to the human world. Dracula may just do that if he wants Crina badly enough. The impact will be detrimental to Dracula and ultimately to Crina as well. Their union spells disaster.

In the tomb, Dracula is dressed and seated.

Neculai loiters.

At last, Dracula bellows.

"What do you want?"

"Will you require my service tonight, my lord?"

"Don't you see that I'm clothed?"

Neculai shrugs off the snub and says, "May I have your ear before you go out, my lord?"

"Who says I'll go out?"

"No?" moans Neculai.

"Speak your mind and be gone."

Neculai swallows and says, "I've been apprised of what transpired between you and Crina."

"She's told you?" Dracula says.

Dracula's irritation provokes Neculai's instinct to defend Crina. "Not the details, of course—discreet as she is."

An awkward pause ensues.

Neculai ventures, "Are your actions wise, my lord?"

"Who are you to—" Neculai's earnest demeanor checks Dracula. Neculai has been a loyal servant and a confidant of sorts, always solicitous about Dracula's welfare. Moderating his temper, Dracula says, "But how can I curb my passion?"

"Your intimacy with Crina foreshadows trouble. Passion is well and fine—but passion fades. Practicality will gain control. What then?"

"Passion is well and fine," Dracula echoes with a snort.

"There may come a stretch during which you rejoice in being together," Neculai says evenly. "But Crina is not easily contented. The fortress will evolve into a trap for her. The worlds you're in preclude a successful relationship."

"Don't you think I comprehend that? I've debated over it. Love rules, as it always does. It's futile to claim back a heart that has been given away. You deem me impulsive. Let me clarify this: I'm not, though I obey my impulses. I debate and analyze. It happens that my impulses usually take control."

"Are you saying you will court Crina?"

"I cherish her. Passion rarely befalls me. When it does, it's potent. During my life, the number of occasions I've succumbed to love doesn't even rival the number of digits on my hand. Since it's here, I am determined to honor it. I'll not force myself on her if that's what worries you. I've nothing else to say to you."

Their conversation has confirmed Neculai's hunches: Dracula is besotted with Crina and will not concede.

54

The clock ticks one-forty. The constant checks on the time have not sped it up.

An assignation is apt.

Dracula ushers in the dream world.

Activities abound.

Dreamers immerse themselves in their dreams. Exhilarated and eager. Dreamers fight against their dreams. With passion. With tenacity. With a sinking heart. Nevertheless, the majority of the dreamers abdicate their ascendancy and go wherever their dreams lead.

Dracula blinks.

A belle traipses over an expanse that resembles a field but is not one. It lacks contour and lies barren.

The road she travels on is rolling and sinuous, with no discernible end. The paved surface is rough. The breadth is wide enough for a mule cart. Not that any mule cart has trundled past. Nor has a man or an animal passed by. Defying the spasms in her calves—caused by her wanderings—she hastens up the incline. At the crest, dismay constricts her throat.

Emptiness stretches.

Despair devours the wretch. Her sagging posture and tired visage divulge: *Am I ever able to find my way?*

Dracula pities her.

He beckons, "Sweet lady …"

At the gentle murmur, her ears perk up. The propinquity of Dracula, rather felt than seen, assuages her melancholy.

Dracula enfolds her in his cape.

The landscape loops, bundling them up.

Next, she is in her boudoir with Dracula lilting into her ear.

The rendezvous has been rewarding. He has pacified the belle, who resembles Crina. Crina might be as plagued and lost as she. At their age, they are vulnerable to bewilderment. The woman's anguish has found its way into her dream.

To quell Crina's misgivings, he must avow his love to her. She ought to be confident of his devotion. It is the least he can do. He will be patient and not pressure her.

He dons a new suit. Normally, he favors black or some shade of it. Today, there shall be a shift to celebrate the changes that are to come.

His suit is elegantly cut. The regal blueness is thrown into relief by the gilt trim on the cuffs. A white cravat rounds off the palette. For shoes, he has chosen a brocade pair.

He whistles to himself. The birds have been seducing their mates with their songs. In answer to Dracula's whistles, they suspend their chorus and shrink into their nests.

In Dracula's hand is a sheaf of sprouting shoots. The stems comprise tiers of leaf buds on the verge of bursting into vigor. The dazzling buds had enticed Dracula. Believing Crina would adore them, he picked a handful for her.

His keen hearing captures the sound of Crina's footsteps. *Here she is!* The next instant, resentment supplants his rapture. There is an accompanying tread: that of Neculai.

The duo will be visible in a twinkling.

Dracula vanishes around the apse.

Why is Neculai up? Where are they headed?

Ambling forward, Crina smiles brilliantly at Neculai, who blushes. Her words have evoked the blush. The sudden arrival of Neculai has disturbed Dracula, causing him to miss Crina's raillery.

He notices Neculai's restored countenance. Flaming curls frame the sweatband of a felt tricorne. Sensual lips hover above a firm chin. He has beheld the transformation but has not acknowledged them, not even to himself.

Jealousy floods Dracula; his hand tightens on the sprouts.

He wills himself to remain still. If Crina and Neculai turn their heads his way, his concealment will be exposed.

They walk past, engrossed in their gossip. The crisis is over.

They are on their way out.

He could follow them. But for what purpose?

He lowers himself onto the bench where he has pined for Crina. As he sits, he remembers the stems in his hand. The crushed plants sadden him. He tosses them aside and broods.

He has overreacted. There might be mutual affection between Crina and Neculai; theirs is a platonic association. Despite their intimate conduct, they aren't lovers.

There is no denying that they are comfortable with each other (a bond he must prepare to rival), and there is always a danger of putting young people in close proximity. Again, he is fretting needlessly. The depth of his love for Crina will prevail; he reassures himself. Deep down he is skeptical.

The waits for her over the next two days demoralize him. Apprehensions besiege him. Is she recuperating from the excursion, or is she lying sick and not being nursed? Worse yet, is she evading him?

If Crina fails to show, he shall search for her. He shuns such action but may have to resort to it. Uninformed of where she is located, he has to call on each chamber in the fortification. The prospect gets ghastlier and ghastlier. However, he must do whatever is necessary.

On the third day, emptiness greets him afresh in the courtyard. He persuades himself that it is still early. Drastic measures should be deferred.

On the bench, three apples lie. He is euphoric. Crina should be nearby.

He sits down. A bee buzzes around his head. He wards it off with his gloves. Once the waves of the gloves subside, it drones back with renewed verve. Since the bee rejects mercy, it can't blame him for being ruthless. He blows out a breath. The vapor freezes the bee. It topples onto the cobblestones, where it wriggles until life is spent.

Dracula regards the miniature carcass with a feeling of triumph, absurd as it may be. As he is thus engaged, footfalls resonate—two sets of them, navigating the chapel path.

Crina is once again with Neculai!

Dracula fumes. He has to decamp. Confronting Crina alongside Neculai, under the current circumstances, is repugnant to him.

The usual nook will betray him if Crina and Neculai approach the bench. They will detect him if they glance toward the apse. He had better steal into the arcade leading to the transept. There, the murk will swallow him. Damn the bee, which has distracted him and nearly thrust him into pure mortification.

He snatches up the apples.

The gate whines. Crina and Neculai trot through. The lantern in Crina's hand reveals an apothecary box slung over Neculai's shoulder.

"Thank you for treating the eggplants," announces Crina. "I'm famished, aren't you?"

"Why don't we fix breakfast?"

"Let's—a sumptuous affair it shall be!"

"Fine."

The pair marches toward the keep in amity.

"I hope it will work. The—"

Crina cuts herself off.

"I've plucked some apples," she says, "and have completely forgotten about them. They are on the bench. I'll fetch them."

"I'll accompany you."

The pair reverses course.

Dracula hides deeper within the arcade.

"Where have the apples gone?"

"Could an animal have stolen them?"

"That can't be. Even the handkerchief that held them has vanished."

She crouches down and, with the aid of the lantern light, combs underneath the bench for the missing fruit. Her brows furrow. Neculai looks over the area.

Crina's knitted brows, though giving Dracula no pleasure, denote a sort of victory for him. Purloining the apples was an impulse. Impulses, conscious or not, have reasoning behind them. She, who has driven him to despondency and anxiety and cast him in ridiculous plights, deserves to be punished.

Reducing himself to an apple-pilferer is preposterous. *Oh, blast!*

Crina observes the courtyard. No one is in sight. Smoothing her frown, she says blithely, "Never mind. Let it be among the mysteries in life we can't solve. Shall we repair to our sumptuous meal?"

The two accelerate off.

Dracula eases out of the shade.

"What were you saying before you cut yourself off?" asks Neculai.

"Oh, that. I was musing aloud. Holes are still forming on the leaves of the eggplants. I hope the increased dosage we've administered will stop the infestation."

"We'll apply the solution again this evening. We may have to wait until we're back to learn the outcome, though."

"We will be gone for a while. During our absence, the beetles will damage the plants if the solution is ineffective."

"We will be gone for a while" reverberates in Dracula's ears. He storms out into the open.

Crina and Neculai pivot to the commotion. A figure thunders toward them, a bundle in his hand. Crina eyes the bundle. Her eyebrows arch and then relax: her hunch that the Count has taken the apples is confirmed.

"What was it you said, ma'am?" Dracula demands of Crina as he looms over them.

Crina is perplexed.

"You said, 'We will be gone for a while.' Explain yourself immediately."

"My lord," says Neculai, screening Crina with his body. "We've arranged a trip. I intend to notify you when I dress you."

Dracula grimaces.

"My lord may remember Camelia, my ladylove," continues Neculai. "All along, my desire has been to be united with her. I am ready to fulfill it."

"And I'll go with him," cuts in Crina. "We shall start tomorrow. Our destination is Suceava."

"I've arranged a chap—" says Neculai.

"I bid you a pleasant trip, ma'am," says Dracula, disregarding Neculai and bowing stiffly to Crina.

As he bows, he notices the bundle in his hand. Crina's earlier expression upon seeing the handkerchief of apples flashes in his mind. He feels extremely foolish and embarrassed. His only recourse is to flee.

As the gate squeaks from his push, the whispers of Crina and Neculai flow into his ears. To deter eavesdropping, they have delayed chatting until they are in the keep. It is a wasted ploy since Dracula hears their conversation as if he were with them.

"The Count has your apples, doesn't he?"

Dracula imagines Crina nodding.

"He must have wanted to guard them for me and, somehow, forgotten about them."

He appreciates her kindness—trying to excuse his bizarre behavior.

Dracula moves on.

At the water pump, he drops the bundle onto an upside-down bucket. The handkerchief spreads open. The apples tip over. One rolls off the bucket onto the ground. The absurdity of the whole affair—the stealing, hiding, and pretending to be a human—hits him. He scorns himself.

He is thoroughly defeated. And he knows it.

55

They traverse the moat, the spirit of adventure firmly gripping Crina. It has always been within her. As it surges to its peak, she feels giddy with excitement. Braşov, the city of her birth and subsequent abandonment, sprawls behind them. She has renounced Braşov as her home; it now merely provides occasional interludes from her daily routine.

She has never ventured this far out.

Definitely a milestone in her life.

She offers a silent blessing to the bulwarked city.

An impregnable wall encircles its twin. The double barriers ring the metropolis. Beyond the battlements, the Black Church looms above the rooftops, its bell tower visible for miles around. Among the buildings in the western part of the city nestles the orphanage. She often reflects on the schoolmistress and the waifs who once resided there. Yet she has never felt the urge to visit them. They would query her about Anton and Petrica. How could she answer them? The inability to rejoin deters her.

The city recedes until it is altogether obscured by the curve of the road. Vast forests stretch out before them. Familiar trees take on an exotic air. The beeches, conifers, alders, and oaks command her admiration. She revels in the sight of woodpeckers and nuthatches adroitly climbing their trunks. If warblers and other songbirds inhabit the branches, the thick canopy has enshrouded them, and the clamor of wheels against the uneven lane has drowned their melodies. Whether birdsongs fill the air or not, sunbeams sieve through the dense foliage.

Eventually, the allure of the countryside ebbs. Drowsiness creeps over her, only to be interrupted by her nagging conscience. How could she have allowed herself to doze off? It's inexcusable! Her awareness is suddenly sharpened.

They have halted at a modest farmstead. What details has she missed during her slumber? Grimy and fatigued, Neculai assists her in disembarking. She feels a pang of guilt and vows to remain vigilant on the road from this point forward.

A sow reclines on her side next to a trough, her offspring busily suckling at her teats. Gigantic, pink ears mark the young pigs. Among them, the tiniest piglet fights his way back into position. The sow lets out a squeal as Neculai and Crina approach, setting off a chorus of quacking and rasping from the nearby ducks.

From the farmhouse, a sheepdog darts out, a collie with sable and ivory fur. The dog growls at the intruders before being reprimanded by its master, who follows close behind.

"She won't bite," the farmer says gruffly. To Neculai, he adds, "What can I do for you, sir?"

The dog sniffs Crina curiously.

"Come here, Lass," bids the farmer.

Crina looks at the farmer, only to realize that the directive was intended for the collie. Noting her mistake, Neculai winks at her. He proceeds to arrange their accommodations.

The aroma of dill, parsley, and lard whets her appetite, causing her stomach to emit an audible growl. Without delay, Crina indulges in the hearty stew prepared by the farmer's wife. Meanwhile, Neculai munches on the succulent chunks of pork and potatoes.

The farmer's wife refills their emptied bowls with hot stew. She is muscular and tall, just as tall as Neculai and at least an inch taller than her husband. The skin exposed beyond her clothing is parched—no doubt from farm chores, Crina surmises.

Rugs are heaped up by the fireplace to serve as a makeshift bed for Neculai.

A snug nest is made available to Crina. It had belonged to the daughter before her marriage. The sun-bleached curtains suit the cozy ambiance of the room. On the table, a candle illuminates the treasures on a tray: a thimble, scissors, and a pincushion with needles and pins protruding from it; an assortment of threads; scraps of fabric; and a mended sock.

The mattress is of inferior quality compared to what Crina is accustomed to, but the sheets and blankets are freshly cleaned. The farmer's wife has ensured that.

Crina blows out the candle. Something bumps against the door. A shape skulks through—the collie.

Moments later, movement stirs in the passage: deliberate, steady. It dies at Crina's threshold. The firm ultimatum of the farmer's wife wafts in: "Out of there, you."

Advance or retreat? The shape debates its next move.

"It's fine if she wants to visit."

"Are you positive, miss?"

"I am," says Crina with emphasis.

Paws scrabble toward the recumbent Crina.

Morning thrives. The collie is nowhere to be found.

A pitcher and a washbowl with a towel draped from its side are placed on the table next to the sewing tray. The farmer's wife must have provided the articles.

Crina yawns away her lethargy.

New expeditions await. Crina snaps into readiness as the thought crosses her mind. She vaults off the pallet. In a few swift hops, she reaches the table. While washing up, she takes heed not to splash water on the table.

In the kitchen, Neculai has made himself comfortable. It is as if he has not moved since dinner. He sips from a steaming mug, the aroma promising a robust brew. Mush smeared the plate by his forearm, and breadcrumbs clung to its rim.

Neculai pats the seat beside him, inviting Crina to sit down.

"Help yourself to the mămăligă and bread," her hostess offers from the hearth. "These buns are crusting on top. They're almost done baking. Feel free to have them if you'd like."

The mămăligă is delectable, and the tea is earthy.

Their hostess brings over the hot buns.

"Did the dog cause any inconvenience, miss?" she inquires.

"No, not at all. I welcomed her company."

"The dog slept in your bed?"

"Yes," affirms Crina. "She curled up next to me on the fur coverlet. Where is Lass?"

"She's gone with my old man to the field."

Crina feels a twinge of disappointment—she won't have the chance to bid farewell to Lass.

"Lass was Anca's dog. They were inseparable. Anca's departure deeply affected her. Over time, she shifted her loyalty to my husband. She still misses Anca. That's likely why she paid you a visit."

"Your daughter doesn't want Lass with her?"

"No, she does. However, with the addition of Anca, there are four adults, five minors, and any number of animals at the Plugarus'. They're hard-pressed for space. Without an option, Anca deserted Lass. It broke her heart."

They sip their tea.

"Where will your next stop be?" the farmer's wife asks Neculai.

"Bacău. We'll have to take a recess in between. Although it's out of our way, Bacău offers accessible roads to Suceava." Neculai sets down his cup and exhales. "A strenuous journey is imminent."

Bacău is larger than the towns in which they have sojourned since the start of their trip. They lodge in an inn by the Bistrița River.

It is lovely to be lulled by the river's murmur throughout the night. When she wakes, Crina jogs to the window to determine its whereabouts. There it is, beyond the shrubs. The river is unappealing by itself. The hearths along the opposite bank and the pines behind them are picturesque. Their reflection quivers as the water flows southward.

She retraces the words and phrases Count Dracula has used but is unable to emulate them. It must be the setting itself; she is not particularly fond of rivers. Beyond the quivering likeness that hints at urgency, the scene leaves her uninspired.

Outdoor ruckus has supplanted the river's lullaby.

She is well rested and fit to go.

They depart with fresh horses from the inn. Their geldings, sheltered in the stable, will be ready to serve them on the journey home.

56

Crina's attempts to stay alert have failed. Neculai has rejected her proposals to sit on the driver's box with him. She should have tried other ways to stay awake. Without her, Neculai would have ridden on horseback to gain speed. All the more reason for her to lend him support.

Pulling into Suceava, her self-reproach diminishes. Being in town, the likelihood of her nodding off is slim. The crimson horizon, the lazy puffs of clouds with a pink tint overhead, and the fields of maize delight her. She is prepared for what lies ahead.

Their carriage rattles along.

The fields morph into a rippling meadow.

Neculai slows to a moderate pace as traffic has increased. A curricle directly precedes them, and riders travel out of town on the opposite side.

Residences and churches on verdant slopes replace the farmsteads and grazing cattle. She might be partial, but the churches are inferior to her beloved castle chapel in beauty.

Trees provide shade along the road and near the homes.

A lassie skips in a yard on a slope, her skirt bobbing about. A woman summons her from the dwelling. She skips on until a firmer instruction persuades her to comply and prance indoors.

Crina slides to the opposite window.

Two gentlemen trek up a winding trail. Both are animated. The gentleman wearing a hat points with his cane. His companion gesticulates in reply. Ruins crown the hilltop. Whatever the construction was, it must have been substantial. Crumbled bastions, a charred tower, and unidentifiable segments survive.

Neculai must have heard her changing position and guessed what she was musing on. He yells from the box seat, "These are the remains of the Suceava Citadel. It was set aflame in 1675 and ravaged by an earthquake in 1684."

Buildings mushroom as the road winds on. They pull into a by-street and up to an inn.

An eleven- or twelve-year-old, with sleeves rolled up, scuffs along. He has come from the stable behind the inn. In the main, his attire is clean. Cleanliness does not apply to his boots on which mud cakes. The muck appears to be as old as his years. His jacket below the waistline is damp. The residual water on his hands reveals how the blotch came to be: he wiped his hands on his jacket. The crunching of wheels must have disrupted his task, prompting him to use his garment as a cloth.

The boy tends to the carriage. The reception of the newcomers falls to a hunchback, who trudges out of the inn.

The hunchback ushers Crina and Neculai inside with due civilities.

Crina hears the boy guiding the coach away, presumably to the stable yard, where he will unhitch the bays. She expects him to walk the horses gently to cool them down, then unbridle them, offer them a light drink, and groom and feed them. She and Neculai always follow the procedure after an outing.

Several parties have gathered in the public room beyond the vestibule. The boisterous chatter among the men abates as those in position assess the arrivals. Crina is thankful that she has lowered her veil.

Crina and Neculai ensconce themselves in a suite.

A knock follows the departure of the hunchback. At the sight of Crina, a stout adolescent opens his mouth wide. He stands at the threshold, looking like an imbecile, the heavy luggage weighing him down.

Crina invites the porter in.

He lowers the trunk without releasing his gaze. Crina's blush leads him to recognize his rudeness. Consequently, he flushes to the root of his hair. On his way out, he surrenders to the temptation to sneak another look.

Crina listens to the boy's footsteps fading away.

Then Neculai asks for permission to enter and says, "We'll wash up and have supper, if you agree?"

Crina consents, pained by how exhausted poor Neculai must be.

She soaks the towel in the wash basin. Footsteps resume in the corridor. They slow down outside her room but quickly speed up again and then suspend at Neculai's. A loud rap sounds, followed by Neculai's response, the adolescent's lurch forward, and then a muffled thud—all resonating in sequence.

Neculai must have received his luggage.

Crina envisions the boy's freckled cheeks and double chin. He possesses an amiable countenance, decidedly so. She doubts he grins as broadly at Neculai and chuckles at the thought.

Boots pound the floor for the third time and stop at her door. A thrill of delight runs through her. She freezes, a damp towel in her hand.

The pounding resumes and gradually subsides.

She smiles at her own foolishness.

The anticipation must be unnerving for Neculai. He intended to await news from the merchant whom he encountered at the druggist's but reconsidered and hastened to Suceava. Who can blame him? He and Camelia have been apart for so long. Soon, they will reunite! What if Camelia no longer resides in Suceava? She prays that won't be the case.

What is delaying Neculai? Has he not finished grooming?

Snores rumble through the connecting door. She opens it. Neculai, in his travel attire, is fast asleep. His boots remain on his feet.

Hunger grips her. The hunchback has mentioned that if she needs anything, she should simply pull the bell cord. This she now puts into action.

A lass answers the ring. In a way, Crina has hoped it would be the porter. After a quick appraisal, the lass performs a bob. Crina ventures, "Could you please bring me a tray?"

The hint of unease in Crina's demeanor has an effect. The lass dimples up. Her attitude seems to convey, "The lady isn't as superior as her clothing suggests."

"My friend is asleep. He will want his supper. Will he be able to request his meal later?"

"The kitchen staff retires at nine. A cold meal is always available. Just tug the bell rope."

57

Crina stretches, catlike, under the sheet. Brightness envelops her.

She listens but hears no movement. Perhaps Neculai has not yet risen?

She springs out of bed and, at the connecting door, asks, "Are you up, Neculai?" All is quiet. She says, "I'm coming in."

The bed is empty. Only the furniture and the baggage greet her. Has Neculai gone exploring without her? Anxiety tugs at her. No, no, he would not have done that. If he has, it is her fault for sleeping so soundly. She can't be angry with him; he must be anxious to reunite with Camelia.

Neculai returns without Camelia and is reticent during breakfast. He eats his mush languidly. Crina lets him be, trusting that he will shake off the trance.

The porridge, bread, and slices of browning pears totally engage an eater seated diagonally from them. Crina suspects the absorption owes less to the taste of food and more to his being in a hurry. Her unpalatable serving lends weight to her suspicion.

The eater by the window, in contrast, is in no rush. He sits straight in Crina's line of vision, as Neculai has turned sideways. The man twists the tip of his mustache, mesmerized by the stable yard outside.

The hostler, the boy with the mud-caked boots, is bridling a cob. It is not the hostler or the cob but the wheelbarrows that have engrossed the mustached gentleman. Crina identifies no intrigues in the wheelbarrows. What could the man be attracted to?

The scraping of chair legs halts her musing.

The diner who was absorbed in his food stands up. A servant is collecting the silver coins scattered beside the pewter mug and plate on the table. It is the maid who had answered her bell pull.

Earlier, the maid attended to Neculai with due deference but behaved jauntily toward her. Her former awkwardness in dealing with the maid must have been the origin of the familiarity.

Suddenly, it occurs to Crina that Neculai has spoken.

"Sorry, what did you say?"

Neculai, who has swiveled back to talk to Crina, says, "I've chatted with the proprietor of the inn. He hasn't heard of Camelia or any Crişans."

"I'm sorry—"

"Our best bet is to visit the Crişans' old home. The current residents may have information about them."

They are on their way. Crina sits on the box seat next to Neculai.

On the main road, they pick up where they left off the prior evening. They pass through areas comparable to what they have already experienced. What is noteworthy is the heavy traffic, particularly that destined for the town square in the opposite direction.

Casks weigh down one cart, and bulging sacks burden another. On a pushcart, water sloshes from the pails, and as it bounces by, the fetor of fish assails their nostrils. The fishmonger pushing the cart lumbers on, unfazed by the smell.

Neculai urges their horses away from the foul odor. The sudden acceleration generates a gust of wind, blowing the hat off the operator of a passing wagon. The woman perching next to the wagoner achieves an acrobatic stunt, leaping up and retrieving the hat from midair with an outstretched hand.

At the back of the wagon, identical pixies scrutinize Crina. She wonders if she is seeing double. Of course, she isn't. Squatting there are a boy and a girl: identical twins. The boy is hatless; the girl wears a bonnet knotted underneath her chin. Each has frizzy hair, coils of which have evaded the girl's cap. They stick their tongues out at Crina. She crosses her eyes and sticks her tongue back at them, sending the twins into fits of laughter.

Crina giggles to herself and exclaims, "Hurrah, fairs!" However, Neculai's distracted demeanor dampens her glee. How could she have forgotten that he has urgent concerns?

Although abstracted, Neculai has heard her and says, "We could visit it later on." He then returns to his pensive state.

58

Six miles from the inn, stone blocks soar. On each block, columns extend at intervals from the apex of the frontage to the eaves, forming a lofty arcade. Far below this colonnade stands the portal. Windows are sparse. The blocks are ancient. The timber buildings in the vicinity are of similar antiquity. They tend to be ornate, with exquisitely carved balconies and exterior staircases.

Neculai halts the rig at an iron gate, which is unlatched. Neculai and Crina let themselves in.

An oak tree fashions an awning over half of the courtyard. A branch threatens to puncture the roof of the house. The tune of a flute drifts from within. The musician disregards Neculai's knocks and plays on. At Neculai's fourth rap, the flute music ceases. Someone shambles forward.

The man in the entryway is a vision of hostility. In his fist, he clenches a lacquered flute with silver keys.

"Sorry to intrude," says Neculai. "I'm Neculai Costin Anghel of Moldavia."

The man blinks and mutters, "Prince Neculai?" Neculai nods. The man's lower jaw drops in disbelief. He recovers swiftly. "I beg your pardon, prince. You've been away for over a decade. My astonishment is too immense for me to compose myself. Claudiu Bălan at your service," he says and bows.

"Do I know you, my good sir?"

"I was a vassal of Lord Costin. Perhaps you remember me in your father's household. Pray, come in."

Bălan backs away to let Neculai and Crina into the vestibule.

"May I present Mistress Crina Roşu—Count Dracula's ward?"

Bălan bows as Crina bobs. He conducts them into the drawing room and excuses himself.

With Neculai anxious to find Camelia, Crina has assumed he would resolve the suspense straight away. Now she understands why Neculai has allowed Bălan to get away: he is immersed in the setting.

The arched window is three times as wide as those on its flanks. The curtains are tied up to the side. The permeating brilliance cheers up the worn furniture.

Crina and Neculai sit abreast in armchairs. Between them, on a side table, hyacinths release their fragrance. An identical setup is arranged across from them, excluding the vase of flowers. The mulberry-hued upholstery complements the gold fleur-de-lis wallpaper; both have lost their splendor.

"This drawing room has not been refurbished," Neculai says, digesting the items as he names them. "Here are the same curtains, chandelier, and wallpaper." Emotion tinges his voice. "I proposed to Camelia in this room."

It is Crina's turn to survey the furnishings, sensible of their significance to Neculai. She hopes Neculai will learn where Camelia is.

Bălan returns and positions himself opposite Neculai. The flute is absent from his hand. "Refreshments will be ready momentarily. It's a great pleasure to have you, prince, in my abode," he addresses Neculai. To Crina, he adds, "And, naturally, my lady too."

A scar runs from the right earlobe to Bălan's nose. Instead of being disturbing, the scar grants dignity to the man, complementing the powdered peruke. Like the drawing room, its fittings, and the manor as a whole, the master of the property carries a faded aura. And like the resplendent sunrays that vitalize the surroundings, the scar ennobles his visage.

"I'm trying to locate the Crişans who used to live here."

"Ah, the Crişans. This was their dwelling a decade ago. We all followed your father into exile, and Baron Crişan died soon after. My wife and I moved in here when the banishment ended."

"Was his daughter exiled too?"

"His daughter?"

"Camelia."

"You're right. There was a daughter—now I remember."

"She was his only child—"

Neculai is interrupted by a thump against the drawing room door, which is being pushed open by the back of a woman. The lady is laden with a tray. Once inside, she maneuvers her elbow to suppress a slam. It is obvious she has abundant practice with this act. Ash-gray hair caps her head. A ribbon, blue as the hyacinths, binds the coiffure and accentuates the green in her worsted kirtle. She deposits the tray on the table next to Bălan, who introduces her as his wife.

The food and drink sampled, Neculai launches his question.

"You said the Crişans had been exiled to the Holy Russian Empire with my lord father. What has befallen Camelia Crişan, Baron Crişan's child?"

"To secure the future of his child, the ailing baron married her off to a wealthy Russian merchant," answers Bălan. Neculai pales. The tidings are reasonable, yet difficult for him to hear. He shifts from the edge of the chair and collapses onto the seat. Oblivious to the impacts of his words, Bălan continues. "As far as I know, she's still there."

"No, you're wrong, husband," says Bălan's wife.

The correction catches the group's attention.

"Do tell, madam, if you are acquainted with her whereabouts—I'd be eternally grateful to you."

"Yes, prince, she's here—"

"Here—in Suceava?"

Bălan's wife nods.

"And her husband is with her?"

"No, she is widowed."

"Poor soul," says Bălan.

Neculai perks up and leans forward.

Bălan's wife says, "I've not actually met her. The information is obtained from hearsay. Lucia who does our laundry and tidying boasted about how lucky a fellow servant was. The servant earned a generous wage for tasks she herself performed, as well as lodging. I discarded her insinuation, which was designed to shame me into increasing her pay. Grasping that I wasn't to be tricked by her ploy, she changed her tune. You see, Lucia is the type of girl who can never keep quiet. She said with gusto, 'That servant is employed by a successful merchant—a widow.' This caught my interest. Female merchants are rare. A flourishing trader is peerless. 'What sort of trade is she in?' I asked. Coin dealing was mentioned. I inquired about the widow's name. Lucia had no idea but said with amusement that the lady was the daughter of this manor's previous owner."

"Do you have her address?"

"No, but her business is in the square."

"Excellent! You should be able to connect with her there," says Bălan.

"According to Lucia's associate, she's a formidable individual. That is inevitable if she's as estimable as Lucia has described her," remarks Bălan's wife.

Neculai finds it unbelievable that Camelia could be formidable.

59

They express gratitude to the Bălans and depart. An east wind blows; rain may fall. The road is emptier than it has been since most participants are already at the square. Fortunately, this is the case; otherwise, the pandemonium would be tenfold.

Traffic is thrown into chaos. A cow has wandered off and led the herd along with her. The cattle, blocking the road, oblige riders and drivers to rein in their mounts and conveyances. Neighs burst forth, nostrils flare, and hooves clop. Wheels screech. People swear. The fracas and cacophony drive the herd into a tight knot, bringing the traffic to a standstill.

Neculai tenses up. Crina aches for a way to soothe his nerves.

It takes the cattleman half an hour to get his drove under control. An extra quarter passes before movement can resume.

To get around the congestion ahead, Neculai barrels down the wrong side of the road, barely squeezing back in when carriages and wagons approach. At one point, as they stray, a coach comes off a by-street. Neculai maneuvers his horses to dodge the onslaught, and the coachman halts his hackney in the nick of time. An accident is averted by a hair.

The near collision dampens the ferocity of Neculai's emotions and curtails his recklessness. Crina's pallid complexion elicits ample apologies from him. They adopt a normal speed from then on. Neculai asks if Crina needs to freshen up at the inn. Divining his anxiety, Crina requests that Neculai drive on to the square.

Activities are underway. A crowd floods the fair. People drift about, clustering at the stalls or loitering in groups. Chatter, haggling, moos, clucks, and bleats are raucous and constant.

"We'd better park and cross the length of the square on foot," says Neculai. "This is the closest we can get."

They press on.

Rain starts to pelt down. Peddlers and purchasers alike tilt their faces to the rain. A downpour intensifies. Plops fill the marketplace. The mass scurries for shelter. Those who have shielded themselves under the stalls are dismayed to find rainwater cascading off the canvases onto their garments. Even those who have equipped themselves with oilskin cloaks are discouraged.

Neculai tugs Crina along.

The downpour stops. Its termination is as unpredictable as its inception. Sighs of relief are audible. The crowd pours from their havens, wet but in fine spirits. The din of the market soars.

Neculai and Crina are at the well, out of breath from racing down the square. Another ten yards will deliver them to their destination.

A cattle cart is tethered to the well, and the ox has excreted. Ignoring the stench of the dung, they tidy themselves. Neculai shakes raindrops off his fiery orange hair while Crina pats hers with a handkerchief. They mop themselves dry as best they can. The indigo of Neculai's cloak hides most of the wetness left by the rain. Crina's shawl has shrouded her body, but her toes in the embroidered shoes are drenched.

The buildings bordering the square are three to four stories high; they share a wall between them. Camelia's business occupies the ground floor of a three-story structure. The building on its left is taller and serves as a tavern. A flag with the coat of arms of Suceava flies on a pole angled on the façade. Boisterous prattle and clanks of pewterware reverberate within. The right-side neighbor of Camelia's establishment ends the row. The marble portico, boasting grand columns, proclaims it to be the residence of a prominent townsman.

Neculai hesitates in front of Petrov's Rare Coins, palms sweaty.

He acts, feeling both relieved and discouraged to find a clerk serving behind the counter. Has he lost his nerve? He never thought he'd feel intimidated by Camelia's presence.

The furnishings include a sofa with three seats; a commode and a chair; a divan by the hearth; and a counter with stools along its side. These pieces are crafted out of walnut in elegant lines. A woven rug of pale blue is thrown among them to accentuate their refinement.

The dealer is tending to patrons—a lady in a silk ensemble and her escort in a stylish suit. The lady rests on a stool. The gentleman, having pushed his stool away, stands. The entry of Neculai and Crina has interrupted their discussion. The dealer signals his welcome while the escort assesses the newcomers. The lady refuses to be distracted, pinning her interest to a tray.

The transaction proceeds, the tone softened, for the sake of privacy as well as civility.

They hear the dealer saying in prim accents, "These staters are best displayed in pairs with the obverse alongside the reverse …"

Not in the mood to hear the rest, Neculai diverts his attention to the commode, which is a masterpiece. The carving and ormolu gilding are flawless. Atop it reposes a glass box, exhibiting the coins encased within.

"I didn't realize coins were minted in so many designs," Crina murmurs. "Note the wig and jewelry—such detailed engraving. It must be a portrayal of a king. This man clutching a staff must be a shepherd."

Neculai disagrees, saying, "His robe characterizes that of a monk. I believe he is a saint."

Crina is abashed.

A genteel tongue, in accordance with the comportment and attire, says at the counter, "It's a precious piece. I'm much obliged to you, Mr. Albu." In the hand of the lady is a miniature ruby velvet box.

"Happy to be of service, ma'am," Mr. Albu, the dealer, replies. "I'll dispatch a message if coins appealing to you fall into our possession."

The satisfied patrons exit the shop.

To his neglected customers, Mr. Albu begs pardon and asks how he could assist them.

"We wish to speak to Mrs. Petrov."

"May I ask who is inquiring? And for what purpose?"

"Prince Neculai, an old devoted friend of Mrs. Petrov, and Miss Roşu, my companion, are here to call on her," says Neculai. He has nearly overcome his cowardice and is ready to greet Camelia.

"Mrs. Petrov returned from an out-of-town obligation yesterday, and earlier she had an appointment with a client. Needless to say, she's fully employed. If you'd make yourselves comfortable," he gestures to the sofa, "I'll inquire if she's available."

Mr. Albu shuffles to an office behind the counter and taps.

"Yes—come in," comes the response, laced with a touch of brusqueness. The voice differs from what Neculai recalls, but he wouldn't place much stock in a mere few words.

Quickened steps and the rustling of a skirt commence in the office.

Neculai detaches himself from the sofa. He holds his breath. A woman bursts out of the office. Neculai is transfixed. The lady is at least twice as wide as his memory of Camelia. The Camelia in his mind is a beauty with a slim waist, yet the person advancing toward him is noticeably fuller. The somber costume she wears is at variance with the style and color Camelia used to wear.

The shock reflected in Neculai's countenance momentarily halts the lady. She composes herself before ambling forward—not bouncing with excitement as she has been—and, at a suitable distance, curtsies to the prince.

Neculai stares at the respectful woman, passive and mute. Crina is horrified. Should she rouse him? Is it the right thing to do?

The curtsy transports Neculai back to the moment of Camelia's presentation twelve years prior. She bent her knees to him as gracefully as this woman does now; her head was bowed, her lashes were thick, and the half-lowered eyelids were bewitching. He fell in love right then and there—he couldn't help it—and the same woman is bending in front of him.

"It's been ages," the prince says with feeling.

As he guides his ladylove up with his hand, their eyes meet. Reminiscences surge within them, threatening to overwhelm them if not for the entrance of a man with a beard, a mustache, and a wig of curls.

Camelia disengages herself.

"I beg your pardon for intruding," the man says, sensing the charged atmosphere.

"Not in the slightest, Mr. Marin," Camelia replies. "This is Prince Neculai, a beloved friend who hasn't been in contact for ages. His visit is a joyful surprise."

Mr. Marin bows.

It is then that Camelia notices Crina. Dubious about the appropriate protocol to adopt, Crina has remained seated on the sofa. Rescued by Camelia's smile, she rises from the seat.

"Apologies, ladies, for having neglected the introductions," Neculai interjects. The introductions are conducted, and salutations are exchanged among the party.

"Prince Neculai, I regret that I'm unable to attend to you. Mr. Marin and I have pressing matters to address. If it suits you, you and Miss Roşu could retire to the parlor above, and I'll join you shortly."

Neculai looks to Crina, who nods her agreement.

"As Mihai is on an errand, Mr. Albu will have the honor of showing you to the parlor."

Camelia motions to the dealer—who has discreetly observed the proceedings from behind the counter and adroitly resumed arranging the coins in a tray—to carry out her instructions.

285

60

Camelia's parlor, painted beige, is imbued with charm. The carpet is garnet. A gilded mirror hangs above a marble fireplace. A bouquet of lilies graces a Chinese porcelain vase, and a crystal chandelier casts rainbows.

Neculai pulls away from the window to lounge on the lime chair across from Crina.

A servant has brought wine and fruit, both untouched.

Crina places the book she has been skimming on her lap. It had lain on the sofa, a ribbon marking a page. Etchings of ancient coins punctuate the Latin words on the pages. The title *Roman Coinage*, printed in Latin, reinforces the book's purpose.

Neculai is as stationary as he was at the window. He seldom fidgets but sinks into meditation. Crina is judicious enough not to disturb him.

The servant resurfaces. "Mrs. Petrov sends her apology," she says. "She is delayed by her work but expects to join you shortly."

Neculai straightens his posture and says, "Inform your mistress that we shall be here."

The servant curtsies and withdraws.

Neculai lets out a huge sigh. "Pardon me. That does me good," he declares. "Would you care for some wine?"

Crina declines but is elated that dear Neculai has rallied.

Neculai serves himself and takes a slow sip. Sinking back into the chair, the glass stem cradled in his fingers, he says, "You must excuse my recent behavior. I ought to have been prepared. It's stupid—and unfair—of me to expect Camelia to remain unaltered." He is referring to Camelia's size, Crina deduces. "Her figure was divine—any man would have affirmed that," continues Neculai. The nostalgia pleases him. "She had barely passed childhood then. Transitions in life are inevitable."

"Were you disconcerted?" Crina asks solicitously.

Neculai twirls the wine in the glass. He replies, "I was. Exceedingly. But then I recalled my frog face. I reiterated to myself the ridicule and snickering I'd endured and how I swore never to judge anything by its cover. It's right to live by what I've sworn to." He appeals to Crina, "You do agree, don't you?" He chortles and announces, "She'll always be my bright-eyed mink."

"She must be successful," says Crina, alluding to the surroundings.

Neculai concurs. "The trappings in this parlor adhere to the taste of the Camelia I betrothed. The style here differs from that of the shop's décor."

"The furniture in the shop is nonetheless refined."

"The pieces suit the clientele more than the proprietor of the enterprise, I submit."

At this point sashays in the proprietor whom they have been discussing.

She has changed into a satin mantua. The cut is in the latest mode. Flounces and ruffles are absent. The gown's simple style and exquisite cut sculpt her figure into a harmonious shape that tapers to a waist just beneath her bosom.

She advances, at ease with her large physique. Her form reciprocates and serves her well. The sways of her hips ripple the gown. A painted mole now adorns her cheekbone. It is incredible how well the minute ornament brings out her flawless complexion. Above the square neckline, the tops of her breasts are visible.

Neculai, who has risen from his seat, strides toward his sweetheart, his gaze fixed on the sparkling diamond pendant nestled in her cleavage. He regards Camelia with an inquiring look.

The twinkle in Camelia's eyes confirms his suspicion—it was a gift from him. She has kept it.

Neculai lifts Camelia's hand and kisses it passionately.

Camelia disengages her hand, her delight evident. The withdrawal is intended for Crina's sake.

Neculai ushers Camelia to sit next to Crina before taking a seat himself.

Crina's cheeks flush. To alleviate her embarrassment, Camelia asks, "What is your impression, Miss Roşu?"

Crina is momentarily baffled but quickly grasps Camelia's intent. "Call me Crina—I prefer it," she responds earnestly. "I've browsed the pages. They encompass a chronicle of Roman coins and the mintages of the emperors. It's the kind of reading that demands focus—but it can be thoroughly enthralling."

"It's not a subject that appeals to a wide audience, especially young ladies. You're an exception, Miss—I mean, Crina—if the topic captivates you."

Neculai interjects, addressing Camelia, "And your thoughts?"

"Are you referring to coinage? Or my profession?"

Neculai offers a nonchalant shrug.

"At first, I found it to be a rather dry field. I must have been Crina's age. Mr. Petrov, my husband, sought assistance with Latin translations. He wasn't as proficient in the language as the profession required. By chance, I was fluent in it and was recruited to help. I translated documents and inscriptions on coins. I was provided with coinage literature to read and wanted to be spared of the responsibility. Gradually, the stress dissipated. The knowledge I acquired drew me into the field. Coins embody history," she tosses a glance at Crina, "as well as culture. I felt proud of myself. Mr. Petrov shared the same sentiment. Believing me a natural, he discussed executed and pending transactions with me, as well as the buyers and sellers. With his praise and reassurance, I delved deeper—researching the coins, updating his catalog, and managing his records. This was behind-the-scenes work; Mr. Petrov would never have considered my direct involvement in the deals. His passing changed the circumstances."

"And you reestablished yourself in Suceava?"

"You do know me well, prince," Camelia replies sweetly. "I missed Suceava. Because of Mr. Petrov, I had no choice but to reside in Tomsk. His death was sudden. He had enjoyed good health and showed no signs of any clogged arteries. You can understand how shocked and saddened I was. He cherished his business. Fortunately, by the time of his passing, I had gained enough expertise in the profession to continue."

"It must have been challenging," Crina expresses her admiration. "I can't imagine starting a business on my own."

"Well, I didn't build the establishment from scratch. Petrov's Rare Coin has always been respected by its peers. However, you're right: I was on my own. I operated on a small scale, renting a place in an alley behind the square. The traders gradually adjusted to trading with me in lieu of my husband. The resistance was fierce at first, but I prevailed. Their having learned of me from Mr. Petrov benefited me. My fluency in Latin, Romanian, Russian, and French has been an asset as well."

Neculai values the heroine Camelia has matured into. Crina desires to emulate Camelia.

The pleasure of being admired tints Camelia's cheeks pink. She says, "Enough of talking about myself. Tell me about yourselves, my prince." She turns to Crina to add, "And Miss Roșu."

Neculai embarks on his tales as a frog. He boasts of his jumps, which sealed the five-foot mark—a leap nearly twenty of his lengths. A feat! Naturally, his popularity among the female frogs is mentioned: he was tiny, with lips shaped into a perpetual grin. He was endowed with orange toes, a white belly, and a lime back. Few frogs compared to him in vocalization, for his songs projected for miles.

He croaks and leans to murmur into Camelia's ear. Giggles bubble up from Camelia's throat.

Crina can fathom why years ago Neculai went mad for the girl. Camelia must have been just as dazzling then as she is today. As the owner of a business, she exudes poise and finesse, and as the lady of the house, she radiates glamour.

The conversation grows serious as they relate their lives.

"We're recluses, free of the constraints of society," says Neculai.

"It would be delightful to be introduced to unfamiliar locales and activities, though," Crina remarks. Her audience listens. "Don't misunderstand me—I am grateful to the Count for what he has lavished me with. He adopted me and made me a lady. I'm well-fed, well-clothed, and well-educated. I'm also grateful for Neculai's tutelage and support." Neculai acknowledges her gratitude with a nod. "For all that, my world is limited."

"Doesn't Count Dracula have plans to present you? Perhaps at a ball in the manor? You're at the proper age to have a ball of your own, aren't you?"

"No, I'm nineteen. Too ancient to be presented. At any rate, I don't care for a ball of my own. To be conversant with the ways of the world and journey abroad are my ambitions. Maybe even roam the globe. To meet people is a start. The Count won't be of use. He may not interact with the public himself."

"Not in the usual sense," explains Neculai. In defense of his patron, he adds, "Though he's well-connected after a fashion."

Camelia says, "Are you saying that the Count stealing the dreams and hearts of countesses and princesses is a reality, my prince?"

"Stealing dreams?" says a mystified Crina.

"You haven't heard? Anecdotes of Count Dracula using dreams as an instrument to woo maidens and married women have been circulating for ages. He steals each and every one of their hearts. None of the maidens or women have corroborated the stories, nor have they denied them. The tales, as tales do, grow ever bolder from narrator to narrator. They are now quite fanciful. You both are associated with the Count. Could you elucidate whether they're fables or truths?"

"Sorry, being ignorant of this matter, I'm incapable of enlightening you, Mrs. Petrov. The Count and I lost contact several years ago. We reconnected only recently." Crina suspects that the provocative tales are without exaggeration. Has the Count not beguiled her with his words? This she keeps to herself. She feels bashful to harbor these reminiscences, let alone having to express them.

Crina defers to Neculai, who says, "I'd rather not analyze it. Such an exercise would mean invading the Count's privacy. It's insignificant how authentic the stories are. Let's admit that my benefactor is resourceful, capable of achieving what most of us can't."

"I'm in accord with Neculai. The Count is gifted. I've seen him in nonhuman forms."

"Have you really?" exclaims Camelia. "What forms are these?"

"A bat and a lizard."

"How extraordinary! Tell us everything!"

"Well, there isn't much to tell. We were playing hide-and-seek—I was a child at the time. He always assumed one of the two guises … He said it was an illusion."

"No doubt," says Camelia. "Like a conjuror's trick."

"But the transformations were extremely real. If he can enter into dreams, is it not too far-fetched for him to engineer such metamorphoses? A statement he has made might lend credence to my conjecture."

"What was it he said?" probes Camelia, leaning into Crina.

"Let me recollect the particulars. I'll recite to you verbatim his words," replies Crina. Organizing her memory, she says, "The Count said, 'It's an illusion—which is also a truth.'"

"It's an illusion, which is also a truth," murmurs Camelia. Then she says, "Did he say truth? Could it have been reality?"

"No, he said truth. I was foolish and too absorbed in the games to be bothered with what he had said. I suppose his aim was to convey this: it was an illusion as well as a reality."

"Then why use the word truth?"

Neculai, who has been observing the exchange, chimes in: "Reality doesn't always align with established facts—that was what he maintained, I'm convinced of it."

"I concur. He was a lizard and a bat. These illusions were indisputable facts," remarks Crina.

"How fascinating. He must be quite a character. But don't forget what he said. He had placed illusion ahead of truth. Hence, illusion should carry more weight. Was his metamorphosis an illusion or a truth?"

"I'd say select one, to avoid going in circles," suggests Neculai.

"I think it was both—as the Count had asserted," says Crina.

Camelia is about to comment but, considering Neculai's assessment, refrains. She agrees with Crina. Illusion can be truth; truth can be illusion. That is that. They are the faces of the same coin; they are of the same entity.

61

To tour the river valley is what has been arranged. Neculai cuts a dash in his riding coat, breeches, and tall boots. He and Camelia have proposed a gallop over the meadows in the valley. Crina refuses the ride but not the outing. Her excuse is that she has not been taught to ride. Her actual intention is to give the lovers space. She has been in the way and is eager to rectify it, even if it is for a brief spell.

They are off to collect Camelia.

Camelia's property lacks a stable. She believes it is wiser to hire a carriage than to own one. On top of having to house it along with the horses, she would have to hire a driver and a groom if she kept a carriage.

Neculai hears prancing. The quick footfalls are too sprightly to be Camelia's. The youngster saluting him in the vestibule confirms his suspicion. He must be the footman of the house. Camelia has said, besides herself, her household includes a cook, a footman, and two maids. In addition to overseeing the kitchen, the cook also manages the other servants' schedules. The apartments on the upper floors serve as Camelia's domicile, while the attic serves as living quarters for the servants.

"You must be Mihai. Could you announce that Prince Neculai has arrived?"

"Would you be so kind as to wait here, sir?" says the youth and hastens away. Swiftly, he is at the upper landing. There, he slows down and disappears into the recesses.

Mihai resurfaces with Camelia, a picnic hamper strapped to his shoulders. Camelia beams down at Neculai. She wears a riding habit: a mauve waist-length jacket paired with an ankle-length skirt. Her feet are secured in ankle-high boots. She has abandoned the puffy coiffure and braided her hair. On her crown is a hat, purple as the boots and embellished with white plumes. Mihai descends behind Camelia.

"Mihai will act as the groom. He'll direct you through the back streets. The river valley is about fifteen miles to the southeast. The coach road imposes extra miles. The back streets will benefit us."

"As you command, ma'am," says Neculai, pressing Camelia against himself.

Out on the street, Camelia climbs into the carriage to join Crina. Mihai vaults onto the front to squat at Neculai's feet.

Painted flowers or geometric designs decorate the passing façades. Camelia points out an ecclesiastical complex off the road. "That's the august metropolitan cathedral, notable for its interior and exterior frescoes. Aren't the mosaic roofs gorgeous?" She also gestures toward a cemetery within the city limits, where her ancestors are interred. One day, she says, she will be buried there too.

The artisan alleys animate Crina. There, saddles spill from a store onto shelves placed along the street. They display a variety of browns: fawn, tan, chestnut, and umber. A few parade intricate carvings. The saddler is sanding a saddle. Around the corner, a shoemaker advertises his trade with a gigantic sign of a buckled shoe. He and his apprentice are occupied. He stitches a leather upper while the apprentice hammers in a heel. There are also the potter's, chandler's, carpenter's, and bookseller's stores. Taverns mix in among them.

They rumble out of the urban community to tilled lands. Their destination is a farm, where lush slopes undulate. The barn, with its back to the dwelling, is attached to a paddock. Within a fence of stumps and rails, horses graze. A hen clucks to her chicks.

Once they stop the carriage, Mihai hustles to let the ladies alight. A girl of eight or nine rushes up to appraise the arrivals. In her wake toddles a baby, whose sex—owing to the neutral visage as well as the loose smock and delicate locks that could belong to either sex—is undefined but rapidly revealed. Beholding Camelia, the girl pivots and nearly bumps into the infant. "Get out of the way, Ileana!" she hoots and flies off, hollering, "Papa, Mrs. Petrov is here. A gentleman and a lady are with her."

Her shrieks travel with her to the hammering at the back. The pounding ceases. The girl, whose name happens to be Maria, tramps back, her papa by her side. Frustrated with her inability to tail her sister, baby Ileana screws up her face and wails. Maria heaves her up and coos at her.

"Your timing is perfect, Mrs. Petrov," says Maria's father, removing his hat. "Fluier has eaten and been exercised. I'll have Ion fetch him for you."

"Marvelous, Mircea. Would you harness a horse for Prince Neculai as well?"

Mircea bows to Neculai. "What about the young lady? A pony will suit her."

Camelia looks at Crina.

"Thank you, but no. You should proceed without me," says Crina.

"Ion can walk you along the fence if you prefer that," proposes Mircea.

Crina rejects the suggestion.

"Are you sure now?" asks Neculai. "It could be fun taking a turn on a pony."

"I have my sketchbook with me. The place is quaint. There's plenty to sketch."

Mihai is to mind their vehicle. Mircea shepherds the party, excluding Mihai, through the gate into the paddock. Maria lugs Ileana along. Despite her load, she is sparkling with energy. They tread toward the barn, passing horses drinking from a trough.

A dripping muck rake and the puddles indicate that cleaning has been performed recently. Nevertheless, a trace of manure lingers. Several of the boxes are empty; the horses must have been let out. Ion, who has his father's stubby build, is strewing shavings and straw in a box. His motions are as energetic as Maria's.

"Son, harness Fluier for Mrs. Petrov," instructs Mircea and steers the team to a lean, fine-boned Friesian.

"Isn't she a beauty?" praises Mircea.

The Friesian extends her head out of the stall and sidles toward her master.

"She's intelligent, well-bred," says Mircea, rubbing the neck of the horse. "And as swift as any of the stallions in the barn." The Friesian nickers at the caresses. "She's groomed and fed."

Mircea makes room for Neculai. "Greet Prince Neculai, Curaj."

Neculai eases in and entices, "A gallop will be jolly, won't it?" The horse rounds her nostrils.

Fluier and Curaj are saddled. The riders straddle them and canter away.

Crina carries her sketchbook to an elm near the garden in the backyard.

The corn has been harvested from the cornstalks. Carrots, purple cabbage, and chard are thriving. Next in line is a row of potato plants. The missus, stooped, is digging out the tubers.

A yowl fills the air. Both Crina and the missus locate its source. By the barn, Ileana, on her rump, bawls. Her tubby legs sprawl from under her smock, sooty soles for all to see. Inches away, a hen puffs up her cinnamon plumage and cackles. Maria stops her swing on a low tree branch, drops onto the turf, and sprints toward Ileana. The missus halts her chores. Mother and child gather around Ileana.

The mother cuddles her baby and shoos the hen away. The baby sticks out her chubby fingers. The mother kisses them. Ileana winds her sobs down to a snivel. Her mother sets her down to scold Maria. Maria springs into action. She defends herself with rapid words while her hands mime grabbing. Ileana eyes her sister, all innocence. Their mother issues an order. Crina speculates on what she says, "Baby grabs things, assuredly. But it's your responsibility to shield her from harm while Mama cultivates the legumes and crops and attends to household duties."

What is it like to be reprimanded by one's mother? Cook's reproaches are in the distant past. She can't say how much she was affected by them. In any event, Cook is not her mother. Does scolding from one's mother hurt more? She will never know. Neculai is her family. The Count, who may revert to seclusion, is unreliable. Now she may lose Neculai.

A tune rescues her from choking up. The approaching Mihai discontinues his song and rolls down his sleeves. "The horses are fed and rubbed down. The hooves picked out. If you have no requests, miss, may I dally on the grass a bit?"

"Please, do. It's peaceful here even though the canopy of leaves above renders the spot fairly chilly."

Neculai and Camelia have ascended to a plateau. The farm is situated some distance below them. They spot Crina's carmine dress. Further away reclines a figure whom they assume to be Mihai.

The exercise has invigorated them.

"Should we tie up the horses and take a stroll?"

"Splendid idea. We may encounter native highland flora."

Neculai dismounts Curaj and helps Camelia, who has shifted sideways on her saddle. He places his hands on Camelia's waist to lift her off but underestimates her weight. Camelia remains on her saddle. He repeats his attempt and, with aid from Camelia, succeeds. They stand, bodies touching. She gazes up at him; his arms around her waist. They chuckle.

"I'm sorry," he says.

"*I* am sorry," she says. "My days of being light as a feather are behind me."

"You're as stunning as ever."

He bends down to kiss her softly. He sucks at her lips, which respond eagerly. His desire intensifies, and he is happy his ardor is reciprocated. They lock in passion and rejoice in their intimacy.

After the horses are tethered, Neculai offers Camelia his arm, and the two wander off.

The wind gusts and then abates.

Pine seeds whirl overhead.

"I'll have to appraise some rare coins with a merchant in an adjacent county. He's passing through the region. I am unable to delay the session. Will you be willing to extend your stay until at least my return?"

"No, I won't be able to." The words sting Camelia. Pressing Camelia tighter, Neculai explains, "I want to notify Count Dracula that I'm quitting the stewardship. The sooner I conclude that, the quicker I'll be back with you."

"Will you really do that?"

"Of course, darling. I've been wanting to be with you since your debut. I'm ecstatic that my wish is finally going to be realized." This avowal gladdens his beloved. "I'm indebted to the Count. No question about that. His potion enables me to restore my appearance and form."

"Your gratitude toward the Count is evident. He must be aware of it."

"The Count and I haven't signed any contracts. I'm not bound. However, I'll do right by him. He has disclosed alternative realities to me. Whether I can ever access these realities is immaterial. My view has been broadened. Count Dracula is a man of unrivaled abilities."

"Pray tell me all you know about him someday."

They walk on.

"Will Crina be lonesome with you gone?"

"I intend to invite her along. You don't object to that, do you, darling?"

A moment elapses.

"No, I don't. I'm fond of the girl. But will the Count allow it? She's his ward."

"He has to. Crina will welcome my invitation. I'll do my utmost to persuade her. You see, regrettably, Count Dracula has formed an attachment to Crina."

One of Camelia's brows dances up.

"The attachment is detrimental to both of them. It'll confine Crina and make her resentful."

"Yes, she absorbed the stories of my trips. Her enthusiasm for novelty is pronounced. Does Count Dracula bring her out into society at all?"

"If he does, it would exact sacrifices from him that may destroy him." Camelia's brow rises again. Neculai adds, "I'll elaborate on it later. Trust me, sweetheart: it'll be for the best if Crina leaves the castle with me. The odds are she will. I've corresponded with my father since restoring my facial features. With the approval of the hospodar and the Ottoman Empire, he has reclaimed his lands and title. We can reside on his estate in Suceava. You'll have a conveyance at your disposal. Crina can be our charge until her marriage."

"Are we going to live together?" probes Camelia, dimpling up.

"I've asked for your hand once. I'll do it again. And will do it properly. For now, I crave a kiss. May I, darling?"

The kiss is granted.

The gust holds its breath.

The couple entwines in the middle of the vast plain. He encircles her waist; she clings to his neck. Their bodies press together, his tall boots enwrapped in the folds of her skirt.

The gust blows out its breath. Hearty whiffs sway the foliage, the grass, and the plumes on Camelia's hat. Fluier farts; Curaj copies.

With felicity in their hearts, the couple saunters back to the horses, still in a close embrace.

The topic of Crina comes up again.

"We've chatted about rare coins, and Crina seems to be intrigued by them. I am in search of an assistant. She might fit. She was reading the tome I own on Roman coinage. I presume she can read Latin."

"She's proficient in it. I tutored her, and she improved with the help of books. The same goes for arithmetic—I taught her the basics, and she furthered her education on her own. She manages the ledger at the castle."

"Terrific. She can manage my ledgers and apprentice in the coin trade, as I did. If she's as shrewd as you've described, I'd suggest she learn Greek to complement the languages I'm skilled in."

"What a wonderful arrangement! This puts me at ease—I'm grateful to you, my love. She is intelligent and reliable, I assure you."

"Will you break the news to her, then?"

Neculai pauses, then says, "It might be better if you deliver the invitation. It shows you approve of the plan."

In the parlor, Camelia voices the suggestion. She and Crina are alone.

"The prince and I had a conversation. The prince plans to resign from his service with Count Dracula."

Crina straightens up. She senses that a development has occurred and a decision has been made by Neculai and Camelia. Their behaviors have not been different. But the glances exchanged between them are telling. She has prepared herself for the announcement. That they are engaged. That Neculai is leaving her behind. Camelia being the bearer of the news startles her. She mustn't cry; she cautions herself.

"He will relocate here and would love to have you move with him. Would that be suitable for you?"

The invitation touches her. Tears well up.

Camelia cradles her. "There, there," Camelia soothes.

"I'm grateful to you and the prince," says Crina between sobs. "Neculai has been like a brother to me, my only family. I was worried sick that our tie would come to an end. And now, my fears are dispelled." She laughs and weeps simultaneously.

62

Once Dracula sheds his cape, the lid of his coffin slides open and his protégé requests admission. A solemn face looks down. It is the expression his protégé wears for him. But what expression should Neculai have worn? It should not have been the playful mien Neculai shows Crina. Dracula himself has never given Neculai a reason for such behavior. The travelers are back. Dracula can't say he is glad, despite how much he has missed Crina.

Sorrow looms.

In their absence, he loitered in the courtyard, yearning for Crina. It was silly of him. He recalled their intimacy and how she had kindled a sweet happiness within him. He conjured up images of her that beckoned his soul. She bit an apple. Her bust heaved in her excitement. Her body pressed to him as they embraced. Why didn't he kiss her? Then he could relive it.

No matter how much he pines away, their union will not materialize. The eagerness with which she went away with Neculai supports this foreboding. Her attachment to him is weak. An impassioned Crina would never have separated herself from him. His ardor is not reciprocated.

Neculai descends into his tomb.

Dracula continues to remove his garments.

"Your Lordship has been out," says Neculai, slipping Dracula into his lounging robe. "We have just returned from our expedition. I'm glad to report that it was fruitful."

"I can tell—you reek of the wilderness and dust."

Neculai sniffs at his clothes and says, "I've cleaned up and changed. Perhaps it's my hair that betrays me." He sweeps the locks from his temples and chuckles.

"Did you enjoy your trip?" inquires Dracula.

Neculai's surprise is obvious.

Has he been so aloof that his protégé is startled by his asking such a trivial question?

"Thank you. We thoroughly enjoyed ourselves. Crina relished all our activities. Most of all, I have good tidings. I've found Camelia, the love of my life."

Sadness weighs upon Dracula.

Neculai seeks approval: "I've promised to settle in Suceava. Unfortunately, it necessitates the termination of my service at the fortress. I sincerely thank Your Lordship. I'm forever indebted to you, my lord, for enabling me to regain my princely status and providing me shelter."

Neculai bows deeply.

Dracula waves his hand. "All I did was provide the potion. The achievement is entirely yours. When will you start?"

"I'll start when someone is appointed as my successor. I have a fellow herb enthusiast in mind. Our shared hobby has brought us together. He is familiar with the estate, having stocked our firewood and tended to the grounds. Being discreet and having minimal ties, he is ideal for the position."

Dracula dismissively waves his hand again. "Use your discretion. I am tired and will rest."

"I have one more matter to discuss, my lord."

Dracula loathes hearing it but gathers he might as well get it over with.

Neculai swallows and says, "Crina will join me."

Crina will join me. How final! Shouldn't Neculai at least request permission? Dracula's pallid complexion darkens. Neculai's mask of firmness deceives nobody. Dread—of causing pain and of having to fight his way—oozes out of him. Dracula stifles his displeasure. What is the use of getting angry? Has he not anticipated this? The thread of hope he retains has not disillusioned him. Why fume at the inevitable?

Dracula's manner softens.

Neculai is mollified.

"She wishes to thank you in person."

"That's unnecessary," Dracula says and banishes Neculai.

Dracula mopes.

He seeks to numb his flesh in the icy tomb.

His protégé and ward are determined to desert him. They are preparing for their journey. The wretchedness he experiences in losing Neculai confuses him. Does it stem from the man's loyalty? After all, Neculai *is* leaving him—how loyal can such an action be? To hell with the fool. He might as well dispose of him. This line of reasoning does not improve his mood. He grieves almost as much for Neculai's impending departure as for Crina's. Could it be right?

He is shattered by Crina's parting but must bow to the unavoidable. Crina desires variety and adventures. Who can blame her, at her stage of life? Here lies his problem: the young and unsophisticated incline to be unstable and unreliable.

That said, anything beats excess certainty in people. Their certitude disgusts him. Introspection could help them realize that their arrogance entraps themselves and others. Their blind trust in themselves worsens with age.

Dracula sighs.

"So, he prefers to skip my farewell to him?" says Crina, aggrieved.

"I believe he doubts what to say to you."

"I wish to thank him for his benevolence. Maybe he is right, and it is best to depart without seeing him."

They are having breakfast together, a rare occasion. Serving Count Dracula and experimenting with his herbs and concoctions usually tire Neculai out and keep him in bed. By eating with her, he has preserved the schedule on the road.

Neculai says, "I was so exhausted that after reporting to the Count, I went straight to sleep. I'm glad I'm up early. Loads have to be organized and handled. I have to sort through my papers and discard those that are dispensable. We can't cart the lot with us. The carriage forbids it."

"We are going to have the carriage?"

"No. I will procure one. First, I must ride to Braşov and discuss the arrangements with Mitu."

"Will Mr. Mitu accept the position?"

"He will. He's abreast of the responsibilities involved and has stated his partiality for the place."

"Won't he miss his relatives, and won't they miss him? They'll be unable to call on him—the Count will prohibit that."

"He has no family."

"I'm aware he is a widower and has no offspring. I'm referring to a nephew or a niece or something similar."

"He does have a nephew from his wife's side, but they haven't maintained contact. He'll have to undertake the duties of a steward. There are enough tasks to engross him. He can cultivate the garden—expand it, even. Obviously, he has to attend to the Count. He is resourceful and an exemplary listener. He and the Count shall get along."

Neculai goes about his business. Crina dawdles in the scullery. The stillness of the keep contrasts with the clamor of Suceava. She will be abandoning the sanctuary that has sheltered her for over seven years and can't envision returning after she leaves. She can endure traveling the vast distance, but the Count will shun a casual visit. He has rejected a farewell from her. Why must he be so eccentric?

The Count is mesmerizing, both in deportment and intellect. His magnetism, baritone, and mysterious aura appeal to her. Is she infatuated with the Count? Yes, a little.

Yet it is an inadequate reason for her to stay with the Count. Her ambition is to broaden her horizons and, in the future, have a family with a spouse who adores her, whom she loves, and children to whom they both devote themselves. Life with Count Dracula will be thrilling. He will dote on her. On the other hand, his intensity may consume her, and she is incapable of reciprocating his passion with equal strength. The Count's refusal to receive her is appropriate. She will use the remaining period to cherish this home and adjust her vision toward the future.

63

The land of dreams is nothing but an extension of the domain we are in. We do not realize this fact; to us, dreams are images and emotions that stir in our sleep. Although this belief is valid, there are more facets to dreams.

Man begets them. The kingdom of dreams has existed alongside mankind. Layer upon layer accumulates. If you burrow into the trove, you will meet our forefather. Behold the nimrod on the boulder, his naked torso taut. A swine runs below him. The hunter, with his spear poised above his head, flies high. As he falls, he brings the spear down and plunges it into the swine. The spear perforates the quarry's hide. Terror and pain fuel the ferocity of the animal. She snarls and shakes the hunter off her back. The hunter scrambles to his feet where he is flung, as furious as the swine. He is bent on capturing the animal. As the swine charges toward him, he leaps for a bough and swings onto the swine. Riding backward on the animal, he thrusts the spear deep into her. With the kill in hand, he bellows out his joy. As his jubilation mounts, he breaks from the dream.

Dreams record man's history, fantasy, and secrets.

Wherever humanity exists, secrets flourish.

Witness Monsieur M tiptoeing into the corridor. The household is at rest. He is barefoot and meagerly clad. The chill nibbles at his soles. It is rash of him to venture out without his slippers or a wrap over his thin nightshirt. A little suffering is the price he has to pay, he surmises.

He steals along. His bedchamber and the servants' quarters are in opposite wings of the manor. Hence, he has to traverse its length. The trek leaves him out of breath. The flight of stairs ahead of him is far from inspiring. *Is it worth all the exertion? It is. Definitely, it is.* Whenever he chances upon the temptress— Maddie, isn't it? Or is it Addie?—she is dressed. It will be wonderful to savor her otherwise. He has covered more than half of the trip; it would be a shame to lose heart now.

He stretches to invigorate himself. His bones crack. The sound is so alarmingly loud that his valet may pop up from nowhere to offer support. Luckily, the valet never materializes. Monsieur M releases a sigh and heads down the stairs.

A lamp casts an ash-yellow tint in the vestibule.

Monsieur M enters the passage behind the stairs. Just as he is dismayed by having to grope his way, the moon emerges, lighting up the corridor. Vases are arrayed on both sides of the narrow space. The tall floor vases are empty, whereas their shorter counterparts on tables overflow with flowers. *Do we need so many vases? It's quite absurd.* He could easily have collided with them without the moonlight. As he praises the moon, the fickle thing fades away. Monsieur M huddles into a compact mass and plows onward.

The servants' accommodations are nowhere close. The passageway is interminable. The muscles at the base of his neck ache from tension. Should he quit?

A whisper flits over to rescue him from his dilemma: "You are tardy, Monsieur. I've been expecting you for hours."

"Is that you, Maddie?"

"The name is Frédérique," says a sugary tone with a hint of displeasure.

How could he have been so off with her name? Never mind. She is going to be his.

He strokes his crown, deprived of a wig. It is a pity not to be presentable. The scant hair he has left will have to suffice.

"Come on, then. What's the dawdling for?"

He fancies catching a glint of flesh (an elbow, a hip?).

With an agility he never imagined possessing, he dives for paradise.

A flash. He is transported into an orderly study.

Dwarfing him is his austere father. He, a miniature version of himself, hangs his head. The only positive aspect in this scene is that he has a shock of hair. He curls into a heap.

"Come on, boy. Straighten yourself. Out with it: who were you spying on outside the servants' chambers?"

Monsieur M bites his lower lip.

"Out with it!" His father barks.

He casts a glance at his father. That is enough. He flies from the study and bumps into a vase. A loud crash ensues. Bits and pieces of porcelain fly high and low.

Monsieur M dissolves out of the clutches of his dream. The fright of dual punishments knots his stomach.

You don't have to delve into the layers to be exposed to secrets of this kind. For they occur in the past, the present, and the future.

Secrets are private. You want to hide them, often even from yourself.

Whether by design or not, you let them out in your dreams. Don't panic. They have been woven into the fabric of the layers. No one is the wiser.

Dracula seldom dreams. As a component of the dreamscape, there is no reason to. But he did dream.

***

The sky was overcast. The poor visibility did not impede Dracula's flight. He smirked at the mating stag beetles on the dead wood. The earth had lost its lushness. He used to link autumns with forlornness. The melancholy association had vanished. The waning of the vegetation now imparted beauty and changes to come. Winter would rage. Snow would blanket the earth.

A bleat drifted forth with the crackling of twigs. A fluffy animal scurried through the woods. Distress and despair mingled in its dash. The sheep let out a *baa* and darted into the wind. It must have wandered off among the locusts and poplars, and an abortive attempt to find its way home had led to a complete loss of direction. Hysteria struck. The village was a mile away. If the wind had been kinder, it would have channeled his wails to the herd and, in turn, the calls of the herd back to him.

The sheep scuttled out of sight. His bleats lingered.

***

As Dracula awakens, the phantoms of Neculai and Crina rush through his mind. They vacate the premises today.

Is the dream a presage: the sheep Crina? Is she going to be lost in the outside world? Will Neculai and his betrothed be like the flock—unable to succor her?

No, the sheep is himself. His liaisons always ensnare him. Yielding his heart always leads him astray. This tendency is bound to endure as day usurps night and night usurps day. It is in his nature to be smitten with the uninitiated. Foolish, you may say. At his age, ridiculous. Many would concur.

He is heartened, though, at how well he has been handling Crina's desertion. Being jilted used to put him in acute pain. He became restless. His hurt oppressed him. Pride dueled with passion. He wound up humiliating himself and escalating his misery. He clung to the unrequited love, unable to free himself from it. He was pathetic.

Centuries later, he has matured to a certain extent. It doesn't mean that he is immune from suffering. It is harrowing to lose Crina. He revives his spirits by thinking that she may return after having braved the outer domains. He is clearly deceiving himself. Why would she come back? Once they're gone, they're gone. Regardless, a shred of hope stubbornly persists.

Neculai has paid his respects, practically in tears. It was touching, really. Dracula is conscious of his own loss. Losing Neculai forces him to appreciate Neculai more deeply.

Neculai has clasped Dracula's hand in both of his. For a second, Dracula feared his protégé was about to kneel down and kiss it. The apprehension passed. But the warmth of the grip settled in his chest.

Dracula wished Neculai success.

"Thank you, Count," Neculai said. "It will be ludicrous for me to proffer you, who are at the zenith, the same." Neculai tightened his grasp. "I'll perform my duty for the last time, my lord."

"Let us bid farewell," Dracula replied. "You ought to be vigorous for your journey."

His eyes moistening, Neculai left the crypt.

64

He is determined to watch Crina depart from the fortress. He decides, among numerous ensembles, on a suit with embroidered buttons. The coat hangs to the middle of his thighs. The breeches fasten at the outer knee. A sage-green ribbon bundles his hair. A cape of the same hue, thrown over his shoulders, lends the final touch.

Dracula navigates the sky, streaked with orange clouds. The keep is subdued. The courtyard is just as quiet. The birdsongs are over. Neculai and Crina have fled. He flies with terrifying swiftness. Even though he plans to conceal himself, he has dressed to perfection for Crina. Adorning his appearance has delayed him. If Crina is already inside the carriage, he would never forgive himself.

Fortunately, Providence is on his side.

At the bottom of the crag idles a landau. The windows are gold-rimmed. A gold stripe spans the width of each side. Portmanteaux and boxes are tied to the back rack.

Neculai is harnessing the horses while Crina waits by the vehicle, contemplating the castle in the distance. She wears the dress with the bow at the back, the same one she had worn when he first saw her. Dracula groans. He is unable to deduce Crina's mood, but he assumes she must be sad.

Crina suddenly squints upward. Dracula steals behind the clouds. If she sees a bat, she will infer who it is. This he wants to avoid.

Crina embarks. Neculai folds up the steps.

Dracula sneaks out from behind the clouds.

Crina withdraws into the interior.

Dracula's grief intensifies. He can do nothing and will do nothing.

Neculai nods at the bat and salutes from the coach box.

Dracula trails the landau until it dips into a valley.

Author's Note

Although Dracula is a prince, he is widely known as Count Dracula. For this reason, he is referred to as "Count" throughout the story.

Thank you!

Thank you for choosing *Enter the Dreams of Man*!

Your comments mean a lot to us.

If you enjoy the book, we'd be grateful if you could leave a review on Amazon and/or Goodreads. Your feedback helps us improve and helps other readers discover the story.

About the Author

Kitkoon Chan was born and raised in Hong Kong and earned a master's degree in mathematics from the University of Maine. She lived in Hawaii, Maine, Massachusetts, and California before retiring from the software industry to Washington. A lifelong lover of classical literature, she brings her passion for storytelling to life in her debut novel, *Enter the Dreams of Man*.